An Alcott Family Christmas

written and illustrated by

Alexandra Wallner

Holiday House/New York

Library of Congress Cataloging-in-Publication Data
Wallner, Alexandra.
An Alcott family Christmas/written and illustrated by Alexandra
Wallner. — 1st ed.
p.   cm.
Summary: Louisa May Alcott and her family not only give away their
much anticipated Christmas dinner, but they also celebrate the
holiday by sharing in many other ways.
ISBN 0-8234-1265-2 (hardcover: alk. paper)
1. Alcott, Louisa May, 1832–1888 — Juvenile fiction. [1. Alcott,
Louisa May, 1832–1888 — Fiction. 2. Christmas — Fiction. 3. Family
life — Fiction. 4. Sharing — Fiction.] I. Title.
PZ7.W15938A   1996   96–11652   CIP   AC
[E]—dc20

For Judi Beach ~ who
teaches me the love of words.
A.W.

$\mathcal{I}$t was early morning on Christmas Day. A delicious baking smell drifted through the house. Louisa was still in bed. She sniffed the air.

"Marmee's plummy cake," she thought. "Christmas wouldn't be Christmas without it."

Louisa heard the sound of clinking china as her sisters poured water into big bowls to wash their faces.

May, her youngest sister, burst into the room.

"Get up, Louisa. How can you sleep so late on Christmas morning?" she said, gently shaking her.

"Louisa probably stayed up late, writing," teased Anna, the eldest.

"Leave Louisa alone," said Lizzie, who was a little older than May. "If it weren't for Louisa's play, we'd have nothing for Marmee and Pa today."

The sisters sat down on Louisa's bed.

"I wish we could give Marmee a new shawl," said Anna.

"And a book for Pa," said May.

They all sighed. There was very little money this winter in the "Alcotts' Sinking Fund." Pa did not get the teaching job he wanted. He had given some lectures, but that hadn't paid much. What money there was came from Marmee. She sewed pillowcases and sheets for wealthy people in town.

"Someday I shall make pots of money from writing my stories, and I shall share it with all my family," declared Louisa.

"I believe you shall," said Anna, putting her arm around her younger sister. "But someday seems a long way off."

"Oh, come on, all of you!" said Lizzie. "Today is Christmas and it shall be the only Christmas this year. It would be a shame to waste it."

"You are right, as always," laughed Louisa. She gave Lizzie a hug.

The sisters jumped up and held hands. They danced in a circle and sang "Deck the Halls."

Downstairs, Pa was building a fire from the extra wood he had chopped yesterday.

In the kitchen, Marmee had many things to do. She was preparing a Christmas feast. It would be different from the apples, potatoes, and bread they ate for dinner every day. She had saved a little extra money from her sewing and bought a plump goose.

The girls came into the kitchen to help Marmee. They bustled about, making crusty rolls, stuffing, cranberry sauce, and baked apples with cinnamon butter. Wonderful smells filled the kitchen, causing everyone's stomach to growl.

"Before we eat dinner," said Marmee, "we must have our Christmas play."

"Oh, Marmee," groaned May. "Can't we have dinner first?"

"Actors perform better on an empty stomach," said Marmee.

"The thought of dinner will sharpen your acting skills," said Pa.

The curved doorway between the living room and dining room framed a perfect stage. Louisa had made a curtain out of two old patched quilts, which she hung from a rod. She'd made costumes from clothes that relatives had donated to the family.

Louisa had named the play "Pirate's Pleasure." It was about a pirate who traveled to tropical islands in search of adventure. Louisa played the part of the pirate. While on his travels, he saved a pretty girl (May) from evil pirates (Anna and Lizzie).

When the play was over, Marmee and Pa clapped until their hands were tired.

"Now it's time for dinner," Marmee announced. It was the girls' turn to clap.

May and Lizzie set the table with Marmee's best china and linen. They had been presents from Marmee's family, since she had not always been poor.

Pa put some extra wood on the fire. Anna and Louisa carried in the food, all but the goose. Marmee wanted to do that. And what a beautiful goose it was, lying on the platter ringed by cinnamon apples.

The Alcotts sat down and started passing the food. Just then someone knocked on the door.

"Now, who could that be?" said Pa, getting up.

It was Mr. Johnson, a neighbor from down the road.

"Merry Christmas," said Pa. "Come in, come in. Join our Christmas cheer."

"Thank you kindly," said Mr. Johnson, twisting his cap in both hands. "But it's Mrs. Alcott I've come for. My wife and the baby are feeling poorly again, and Mrs. Alcott knew what to do for them the last time."

Marmee got up when she heard this. "Go into the kitchen for a moment, Mr. Johnson. Anna will fix you a cup of hot tea," she said.

After the kitchen door closed behind them, Marmee looked at Pa for a moment and a smile passed between them. Pa nodded.

Marmee folded her arms across her chest and looked thoughtful, little lines appearing on her forehead.

The girls groaned inside. They knew what was coming.

"Now, girls . . ." Marmee began.

It was going to be bad.

"The Johnsons are very poor. They have very little food at home."

"We are poor, too," thought Louisa, but she said nothing.

"We can give them our dinner. That would be keeping the true spirit of Christmas in our hearts." She looked at the girls. One by one they nodded, even Anna who had come from the kitchen.

Slowly, Louisa and her sisters packed their Christmas dinner in baskets while Marmee put on her cloak and bonnet.

"Thank you kindly," said Mr. Johnson. "The Alcotts are a fine family, always sharing with those less fortunate."

Louisa blushed at the unkind thoughts she had had. The truth was she felt the same as Marmee.

She watched as Marmee and Mr. Johnson walked down the snowy path. The gate swung shut behind them.

"Someday I will make so much money with my writing that we will always have a fine Christmas dinner," Louisa thought. "And there will be enough to give to the poor people, too."

Pa put another log on the fire. He sat in his favorite wingback chair, staring at the flames as they spit and sizzled.

"Come, Sisters, we have work to do," said Anna.

They went into the kitchen. For the second time that day, they looked at one another and burst out laughing. Lizzie began to sing "The Holly and the Ivy" and the others joined in.

They made their usual dinner of apples, potatoes, and bread, putting it in the warming oven until Marmee came home.

It was twilight. The girls had lit the house with softly glowing candles. They heard Marmee come through the door. She put out her arms as they rushed toward her.

"How are Mrs. Johnson and the baby?" asked Lizzie.

"They are feeling much better," said Marmee. "Our good food made them stronger. Mrs. Johnson wanted me to thank you for giving up your dinner. I want to thank you, too. I know it wasn't easy. You all did a kind thing today."

May looked down at her shoes. "I didn't feel kind, Marmee. I was sorry we couldn't have our dinner."

"But the point is, May dear, that you *did* give it away. It was good of you."

"I feel sad that we have no presents to give one another," Louisa said.

"But we *do* have presents," said Marmee. She pulled out a small coin purse from the pocket of her skirt.

"A nickel for each of you," she said.

"Now I can buy some colored pencils," cried May, jumping up and down.

"More paper for writing," exclaimed Louisa.

"A ribbon for my hair," Anna said.

"I will save mine," said Lizzie.

Then Louisa said sadly, "We have nothing for you and Pa."

"Nothing!" Marmee said. "You gave Pa and me a wonderful time with your play. You gave us your love and talent. And we have each other. No coin can buy that."

They sat down at the dinner table again.

"This is the best Christmas ever," said Lizzie.

They all laughed because Lizzie said that every year.

Later, the family sang songs and read the Christmas cards they had given one another. Pa read aloud a poem he had written for the whole family.

After everyone had gone to bed, one candle still burned in the attic window. Louisa sat at her desk in the cap and shawl she wore when she was writing. As always, she wrote notes on everything that had happened that day.

"I will write a book about my family," thought Louisa.

She was planning the story in her head as she got sleepy. She knew that someday her pen would make her rich and famous. She blew out the candle and went to bed.

Author's Note

Louisa May Alcott was born on November 29, 1832, in Germantown, Pennsylvania.

During her life, Louisa worked hard at many things. Like her mother, she earned money by sewing sheets and pillowcases for wealthy people. She also worked as a teacher, a paid companion, and a nurse. During the Civil War, she nursed sick soldiers in a Washington, D. C. hospital for a few weeks until she became sick herself. She was given a drug called calomel, which contains mercury and is known today to be dangerous. She was ill her whole life as a result of the poisonous mercury.

Louisa also worked on behalf of women's suffrage, a struggle to win voting rights for women. She contributed many articles to *The Woman's Journal*, a women's rights newspaper.

She worked hardest at her writing. She used the notes in her journal to write about familiar people and events. She wrote hundreds of stories, articles, and books. Her most famous book is *Little Women*, which was based on her family. When Louisa was a famous author and was earning plenty of money, she shared it with her family just as she had said she would.

Louisa died on March 6, 1888.

Louisa May Alcott's Best-Known Books

Little Women 1868–1869	*Rose in Bloom* 1876
An Old-Fashioned Girl 1870	*Under the Lilacs* 1876
Little Men 1871	*Jack and Jill* 1880
Eight Cousins 1875	*Jo's Boys* 1886

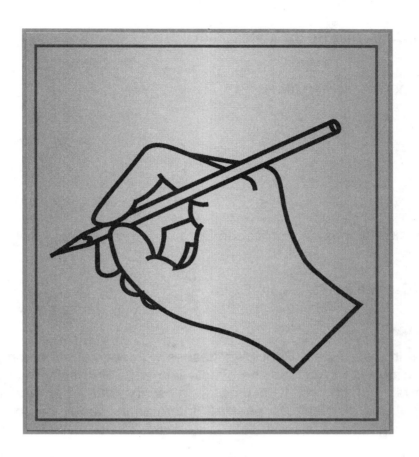

How To Pass The California Real Estate Exam

5th Edition

Walt Huber
Glendale College

Joseph F. Ribertelli
Special Review Editor

Joseph F. Ribertelli has been a licensed broker with his own real estate office since 1975. He taught at the well-known Lumbleau Real Estate Schools for ten years before starting his own real estate school. He is presently an adjunct professor at Glendale Community College, specializing in Real Estate Principles and License Prep. He has helped virtually tens of thousands of students pass the California Real Estate Exam over the past four decades. He is one of the most experienced, sought-after, and beloved educators in the real estate field.

How To Pass The California Real Estate Exam

Copyright© 2002
EDUCATIONAL TEXTBOOK COMPANY
P.O. BOX 3597
COVINA, CA 91722
626-339-7733
626-332-4744 (Fax)
www.etcbooks.com

Library of Congress Cataloging in Publication Data

Walt Huber
How To Pass The California Real Estate Exam

Summary:

Covers all material in Real Estate Principles classes with special stress on California real estate laws. It is written in very clear and simple language and easy-to-read format with photographs, charts, and graphs. It includes a glossary and index and is suitable for consumers, students, and teachers seeking information about personal real estate transactions.

1. Real estate 2. Real estate business—California 3. Real estate property—California

HD 266   C21-1824   333.33
ISBN: 0-916-77217-9

How To Pass The California Real Estate Exam

EXAMINATION—SUBJECT AREAS	SALESPERSON EXAM	BROKER EXAM
1. Real Property and Laws Relating to Ownership - Ownership of property - Encumbrances - Public power over property	**11%**	**9%**
2. Tax Implications of Real Estate Ownership - Knowledge of current tax laws affecting real estate ownership	**8%**	**8%**
3. Valuation/Appraisal of Real Property - Methods of appraising and valuing property - Factors which may influence value estimate	**15%**	**15%**
4. Financing Real Estate - Sources of financing - Common clauses in mortgage instruments - Types of loans	**17%**	**16%**
5. Transfer of Property - Titles - Escrow - Reports	**10%**	**9%**
6. Real Estate Practice - Listing of real property - Sales contracts - Marketing	**22%**	**21%**
7. Broker's Responsibility for Agency Management - State real estate laws and regulations - Laws relating to fair practices - Knowledge of trends and developments - Knowledge of commonly used real estate forms and math calculations	**17%**	**22%**

Dept. of Real Estate
% of Exam Questions
Testing Emphasis

For more information:

www.dre.ca.gov
(Department of Real Estate Home Page)

www.dre.ca.gov/salesqs.htm
(Salesperson Examination Content and Test Questions)

ACKNOWLEDGMENTS

Dr. Robert Bower
Fullerton College

Ed Culbertson
Mira Costa College

John Culver
Chabot College

Andrew Q. Do, PhD.
Professor of Finance
San Diego State University

Ed Estes
Palomar College

Paul R. Guess
Mt. San Jacinto College

Steve Herndon
Santa Rosa Junior College

Lowell Knapp
Cuyamaca College

Charles Leonhardt
Feather River College

Arlette Lyons
Mt. San Antonio College

Ron Maricich
Los Angeles Harbor College

Patricia Moore
Los Medanos College

R. S. Morgan
Compton College

Evan Morris
North Valley Occupational Center

Harvey Rafel
Merced College

Robert Sachaff
Antelope Valley College

John W. Shaw
Lassen College

Robin Sherman
Cabrillo College

James L. Short
San Diego State University

Robert J. Topping
Sacramento City College

Charles C. Vanzee
Mt. San Jacinto College

Glenn Vice
Mt. San Antonio College

John Warren
Cypress College

Reginald Woolfolk
West Valley Occupational Center

Alex Yguado
Los Angeles Mission College

Preface

Congratulations! By choosing this fifth edition of *How to Pass the California Real Estate Exam* by Walt Huber, you have taken the most important step towards passing the salesperson's or broker's exam on the first try.

Experience has taught us that students are more successful at passing the state exam by following our unique study guide format. We even incorporate easy-access page **Tabs** to take you directly to any of the following sections:

> **Sections 1-7 (pp. 1-115): Real Estate Basics** - Review of the most significant real estate fundamentals.
> **Section 8 (pp. 121-194): Math** - Manageable math segments including simple equations.
> **Sections 9-10 (pp. 195-240): Terms and Web Sites** - Essential definitions of key terms plus web sites.
> **Section 11 (pp. 241-437): Exams** - Five separate 150-question mock exams simulating the state exam experience, plus 100 of the most crucial **Appraisal** questions.

This book is designed to maximize the learning experience. By eliminating wasted time and energy, each student is better able to personalize the book to his or her needs. Need to review **Basics**? Thumb through the first chapter, reviewing highlighted essential information. Need to practice **Math** equations? Open to that section using the easy access tabs. Confident with your level of expertise? Go right to the first **Exam** and test yourself. Not sure of your appraisal skills? Skim through the ultimate **100 Appraisal** questions (or just the answers). Walking out the door to take the test? Glance over key definitions and **Terms**.

SUGGESTED STUDY TECHNIQUE

Step 1: Complete Your Course of Study

This book is designed to test the knowledge you have already acquired through completion of a Principles of Real Estate course. A thorough and up-to-date text, *California Real Estate Principles*, also published by Educational Textbook Company, is recommended for this course of study. *Principles* covers, in considerable detail, 95% of the topics you will find in these sample tests and on the state exam itself. A thorough understanding of the materials in *Principles* makes passing the real estate exam a near certainty.

Step 2: Review the Math Section

The math section in this book deals with the type of problems known to be on the state license exam. Review this section carefully before you attempt any of the sample exams.

The primary purpose of this math section is to develop, in more detail, the principles explained in the math chapter in *California Real Estate Principles*. A secondary purpose is to familiarize the student with a broader range of math problems, including some problems of greater complexity than those found in *Principles*. Upon completion of the exercises contained in this math section, the student should be well prepared to answer any math question found on the state exam, as well as handle with confidence the many math problems that come up in the day-to-day practice of real estate.

Just a word on pocket calculators - If a calculator is not already an important part of your personal and business life, it soon will be. To the practicing real estate agent, the pocket calculator has become an invaluable tool. Calculators that range in price from $10 to $75 enable today's agents to quickly and accurately solve mathematical problems ranging in difficulty from the simple to the complex. Commission, interest, amortization, proration, and depreciation problems are easily handled if the agent: 1) knows the appropriate formulas and 2) understands how to operate the pocket calculator.

To the license applicant, the pocket calculator is a terrific aid because California allows its use during license examinations. Questions that used to consume valuable time and bewilder license applicants should now represent the easy part of the examination.

Step 3: Take the Sample Exams In Order of Difficulty

Each exam is rated according to difficulty. The difficulty scale is 1 to 5, with 5 being the most difficult. You should not decide you are ready to pass the state license exam until you can comfortably pass a sample exam with a difficulty factor of 4, preferably 5.

Begin by taking a sample examination with a difficulty factor of 1. If you pass it comfortably, graduate to an exam with a difficulty factor of 2, and so on. In the final week to ten days preceding your license exam, you should spend **95% of your study time reviewing the sample examinations**, with particular emphasis on those with difficulty factors of 4 and 5.

SUCCESSFUL EXAMINATION TECHNIQUES

By using this book, you are practicing one of the keys to successfully taking and passing an examination: **preparedness**. However, once the time arrives to take the test, you can improve your chances of success even more by using a few simple techniques.

Be relaxed. Get a good night's sleep before the day of the exam. Arrive at the test site early so you are not rushed. Wear comfortable clothing and bring a sweater if there is a chance the exam site will be chilly.

Be confident. You've prepared for this test, and you can and will pass. Do not become discouraged if you cannot answer some of the questions; you don't need a perfect score.

Follow directions. Read the test directions carefully and be sure you understand them. If you have questions, ask the test moderator. When filling out your answer sheet, be sure to give all the information requested, and RECORD YOUR ANSWERS IN THE PROPER LOCATION.

Read the questions first. You should read each question thoroughly before you look at the possible answers. You may wish to cover the answers with your hand or a piece of paper while you read the question. If you jump ahead to answers, you may miss a key word or phrase in the question. For example, many questions ask you to choose the answer that is NOT a true statement. Be on the lookout for key words that can change the meaning of the question, such as NOT, EXCEPT, BUT, etc.

Skip the tough questions. As you work your way through the exam, temporarily ignore those questions that are very difficult or that you simply find impossible to answer. Don't waste time on the hard questions until you have answered all of the easy ones. Then you can go back and work on the more difficult questions if you have the time. (**When you skip a question, remember to skip a space on your answer sheet, too.**)

Eliminate wrong answers. If you know that a particular answer is wrong, cross it out in your question book. You run less of a risk of making a careless error if you work "backwards" in this fashion, eliminating all the wrong answers in order to find the right one. Also, if you skip a question and come back to it later, you will need to spend less time on it the second time around if you have already eliminated some of the wrong answers by crossing them out.

If you don't know, guess. There is no penalty for a wrong answer. If you find that you simply don't know the answer to a question, you have at least a 25% chance of getting it right just by guessing (as opposed to no chance at all if you don't). You can improve your odds even more if you have eliminated one or more of the answers. For example, if you know that answers (a) and (b) are incorrect, but you don't know whether (c) or (d) is correct, your chances of guessing correctly are 50-50.

Budget your time. There are always a few people who finish the exam in half the allotted time. Nine times out of ten, these people are not "geniuses"; they have simply given up. Don't rush to be the first one finished with your exam. In fact, we recommend that you use all the time available to you. If you have answered all the easy questions, work on the hard ones. If you have answered all the hard ones too, guess at the impossible ones. Finally, double check your answers and your answer sheet to make sure everything is correct and in the right place.

Answer every question. If it comes down to the wire and you still have not answered all the questions, guess at the remaining ones. Remember, it is better to guess than to leave an answer blank.

EXAM TIME IS EXTREMELY LIMITED

The salesperson's exam is 195 minutes (3¼ hours), and the Broker's exam is 300 minutes (two, 2½-hour sessions). In other words, **you have 78 seconds to answer each question** on the salesperson's exam and **90 seconds to answer each question** on the broker's exam.

Our best advice is to think of the license exam as "a race against time."

Pedal to the metal. Answer the shortest, easiest questions first. If you're fairly certain you know the answer to the question, answer it. This is the most efficient use of your time. If you waste time agonizing over questions you do not know, YOU WILL NOT FINISH THE EXAM.

Maintain the speed limit! Answer the questions that you can narrow down to two possibilities and math calculations that you can solve in less than two minutes. (If you have to spend more than two minutes, leave it blank and move on.)

Hit and run (Guess!) Save at least ten minutes to go back over the questions you did not answer. Go back and work on questions or calculations you didn't answer the first two go-rounds. Keep your eye on the clock here, and don't lose track of time.

A blank answer is a wrong answer! (If you're just guessing, you may as well pick answer "c." It will save you from agonizing, and you've got a one-out-of-four chance of getting it right.)

DEPARTMENT OF REAL ESTATE OFFICES

MAIN OFFICE

Sacramento
2201 Broadway
Sacramento, CA 95818-2500
(916-227-0931)

 **www.dre.ca.gov**

DISTRICT OFFICES

Los Angeles
320 W. 4th Street, Suite 350
Los Angeles, CA 90013-1105
(213-897-3399)

Oakland
1515 Clay Street, Suite 702
Oakland, CA 94612-1402
(510-622-2552)

San Diego
1350 Front Street, Suite 3064
San Diego, CA 92101-3687
(619-525-4192)

Fresno
2550 Mariposa Mall, Rm. 3070
Fresno, CA 93721-2273
(559-445-5009)

**All offices open
8-5 weekdays**

Table of Contents

Section 1
Real and Personal Property

I. Real and Personal Property

The two types of property are real property (**immovable**) and personal property (**movable**), formerly called "chattel real." Title to real property is passed with a "deed," whereas title to personal property is passed with a "bill of sale."

OWNERSHIP IS A BUNDLE OF RIGHTS

Property refers to "all the rights" or interests one has in the "thing" owned, rather than the thing itself. These rights are referred to as a "Bundle of Rights," and include the rights of:

1. **Possession** - the right to occupy, rent, or keep others out.
2. **Enjoyment** - the right to "peace and quiet" without interference from others.
3. **Control** - the right to physically change or keep the property the way you like it.
4. **Disposition** - the right to transfer all or part of your property to others as you see fit.

Ownership is the "interest and rights" (Bundle of Rights) that a person has in the object owned.

Section 1 - Real and Personal Property

A. REAL PROPERTY

The definition of real property includes:

1. Land;
2. Anything permanently attached or affixed to the land;
3. Anything incidental or appurtenant to the land; and
4. That which is immovable by law.

1. Land

LAND OWNERSHIP - *commonly thought of as owning the surface of the earth, but ownership also gives us rights to the space that is above our land and extends below our feet to the center of the earth.*

AIR SPACE - *the right to the use of the air space above the surface of the earth. It is real property.*

Inside a condominium, one only owns the air space (area within the finished walls). The owner also owns a fractional share of the entire project (common area).

MINERAL RIGHTS - *such as gold, silver, and borax, are solids that are part of the real property, but can be removed.*

RIPARIAN RIGHT - *the right of a landowner to use the water on, under, and adjacent to his or her land, provided that its use does not infringe on the rights of any neighboring landowners.*

A Riparian right allows for the reasonable use of river water. "Potable water" refers to water suitable for drinking.

APPROPRIATION OF WATER - *the taking of water flowing on the public domain from its natural course.*

2. Attached to the Land ("Improvements")

IMPROVEMENTS - *Anything attached to the land, such as buildings, fences, walls, built-in appliances, walks, and shrubs, which become real property when they are permanently incorporated or integrated in, or affixed or attached to, the land.*

3. Incidental or Appurtenant to the Land

APPURTENANT - *means ownership "runs with the land"; it transfers automatically without the need of a separate conveyance.*

MUTUAL WATER COMPANY - *organized by water users in a given district to supply ample water at a reasonable rate.* It is usually a corporation wherein the owner of each parcel of land is given a share of stock. The stock is appurtenant to the land; that is, each share of stock is attached to the land and cannot be sold separately.

Stock in a mutual water company is appurtenant; it transfers with the property.

4. Immovable by Law

That which by law is considered immovable is real property. Under California law, trees are a part of the land, and therefore sold with the land, unless a contract for sale is made before the land is sold.

B. PERSONAL PROPERTY

PERSONAL PROPERTY - *any property that is movable and cannot be properly classified under the definition of real property.* Items such as clothes, furniture, and automobiles are tangible, but easily movable. Mineral, oil, and gas, **when extracted**, are also considered personal property.

EMBLEMENTS - *planted growing crops that are cultivated annually by a tenant farmer on leased land.* These crops belong to the tenant even after the expiration of the lease.

C. FIXTURES

FIXTURES - *items of personal property that are attached to, or incorporated into, the land in such a manner as to become real property.*

The courts use these five tests to determine if an item is a fixture:

> M **1. Method of attachment**
> A **2. Adaptability**
> R **3. Relationship of the parties**
> I **4. Intention**
> A **5. Agreement** (Think of "M.A.R.I.A.")

1. Method of Attachment

If an item can be removed by simply being unplugged, it is probably personal property. On the other hand, if it is attached by cement, plaster, screws, nails, or plumbing, it is probably real property.

Cost, size, and time installed are NOT tests in determining what is real property.

2. Adaptability

The adaptability of personal property refers to ordinary use in connection with the land. If property is well adapted for the land or building, it is probably a fixture.

3. Relationship of the Parties

The relationship usually involves disputes between seller and buyer or landlord and tenant. If a fixture is not mentioned in a contract and is affixed to the property, most courts will give the seller the benefit of the doubt. Any questionable fixtures should be mentioned in the purchase agreement (deposit receipt).

4. Intention

If you plan to remove an item of personal property, you may not permanently attach it to the land.

The intention of the person attaching the personal property to the land is the most important test in a court of law.

5. Agreement

Any item can be deemed real or personal property if it is so stated in a contract.

It is advisable to secure in writing any personal property that you want to remain as personal property.

D. TRADE FIXTURES (Always Personal Property)

TRADE FIXTURES - personal property used in the normal course of business, such as shelving or refrigeration units. A tenant may remove any trade fixture he or she installed, provided the real property is left in the same condition as he or she found it.

II. Estate Ownership

A. ESTATES

ESTATE - an interest, share, right, or equity in real estate that varies from the minimal right of a renter to the maximum right of a full owner.

Estates are either freehold or less-than-freehold, depending upon the degree of ownership and the duration of interest. Freehold estates are real property, and less-than-freehold estates are personal property.

B. FREEHOLD ESTATES (Real Property)

The two types of freehold estates are: 1) fee simple estates and 2) life estates. **These freehold estates are the greatest degree of ownership you can have under the law.** Freehold estates receive title.

1. Estates in Fee (Fee Simple or Fee)

Fee or fee simple is the most interest (greatest) one can hold; it is of "indefinite duration," freely transferable, and "inheritable" (referred to as an estate of inheritance). This can be referred to as fee simple, fee ownership, or fee.

FEE or FEE SIMPLE - means an owner has transferred all rights of a property to a new owner for an indefinite duration of time (perpetual). All transfers are assumed to be fee or fee simple unless the grant part of the deed limits, by the use of conditions, the property's use.

a. Conditions that Restrict a Fee Estate (Fee Simple Defeasible Estate)

FEE SIMPLE DEFEASIBLE - an estate subject to the occurance of a "condition subsequent" whereby the estate may be terminated.

Breaking any condition of the transfer may be grounds for terminating or revoking the property transfer. The transfer can be undone ("defeased") and would revert to the grantor or the grantor's heirs. There are two categories of conditions: 1) condition precedent and 2) condition subsequent.

4

A fee simple defeasible estate with a condition (precedent or subsequent) hanging over it has less value than a fee simple estate.

> **CONDITION PRECEDENT** - *an event that must happen before the property can be transferred.*

> **CONDITION SUBSEQUENT** - *an event that happens after (in the future) the property is transferred that causes the property to revert (go back) to the grantor.*

I will give you this property "upon the condition that title will be forfeited and revert back to me if alcoholic beverages are ever consumed on the premises." (This is fee simple defeasible.)

2. Life Estate (Indefinite Period)

> **LIFE ESTATE** - *an ownership interest in real property that exists only for the life of any designated person or persons (grantee).*

> A life estate can be created by either a will or a deed. A person holding a life estate is free to lease the property to someone else, but this lease is also subject to the lifetime limitation. If the designated person dies, the estate ends and all rights, including any tenant rights, revert back to the original owner.

A person holding a life estate CANNOT grant more rights than he or she holds.

> **ESTATE IN REVERSION** - *the party (grantor) granting a life estate is said to hold an estate in reversion. The property returns (reverts back) to the grantor when the life estate holder dies.*

> **ESTATE IN REMAINDER** - *if an owner granting a life estate names another person to receive title, then upon the death of the current life estate holder, that other person claims an estate in remainder.*

The holder of an estate in remainder or estate in reversion has NO right to the use and enjoyment of the property until the current life tenant dies.

C. LESS-THAN-FREEHOLD ESTATES

LESS-THAN-FREEHOLD ESTATES - *personal rights to the use of real property for a period of time*. They are more commonly referred to as "leases" or "rental agreements," which give a tenant various rights to use real property for a specified period.

The lease or rental agreement is personal property because there is NO ownership in the property. The tenant has only the right of possession.

> **1. ESTATE FOR YEARS** - *a lease for a fixed period of time, agreed to in advance*. The lessee and lessor agree, prior to signing the lease, when it will expire (anywhere from a few days up to 99 years). No notice to terminate is necessary.

> **2. ESTATE FROM PERIOD-TO-PERIOD** - *a **renewable** agreement to rent or lease a property for a period of time, where the rental or lease amount is fixed at an agreed to sum per week, month, or year*. A notice to terminate must be given.

3. ESTATE AT WILL - *a rental agreement that can be terminated by either party at any time. By California law, there must be at least **30 days notice**.*

4. ESTATE AT SUFFERANCE - *occurs when the person renting or leasing a particular property remains after the expiration of the stated term.*

Other terms that relate to less-than-free-hold estates are:

1. LANDLORD - *the owner of the property being rented or leased (**Lessor**).*

2. TENANT - *the person or persons renting or leasing the property (**Lessee**).*

3. LEASE - *a contract for a set time, typically one year or longer.*

4. RENTAL AGREEMENT - *usually made on a monthly basis and renewable at the end of each period (week-to-week, month-to-month, or any period up to one year).*

5. LEASEHOLD - *an exclusive right to occupy and use the property on a temporary basis.*

6. REVERSIONARY INTEREST - *means the landlord can regain possession at the end of the leasehold period.*

7. LICENSE - *permission to use a property. A license can be revoked at any time.*

D. MINIMUM REQUIREMENTS OF A LEASE (or Rental Agreement)

A lease requires no particular language and can be either a written or an oral agreement, but must, at a minimum, include these four items:

L **1. Length of time or duration of lease**
A **2. Amount of rent**
N **3. Names of parties**
D **4. Description of property**   (Think of "L.A.N.D.")

E. RIGHTS AND OBLIGATIONS OF THE PARTIES

In addition to the minimum requirements, a number of contractual factors between a landlord and tenant should be considered before entering into a lease.

1. Duration of Lease

A lease for more than one year must be in writing and signed by the lessor; but if the lessee does NOT sign, moves in and pays rent, he or she is bound to the terms of the lease.

2. Amount of Rent

RENT - *the amount of money paid for the use of a property.* The actual amount of rent to be paid is called contract rent.

CONTRACT RENT - *the payment designated in a lease contract, at the time the lease is signed, for the use of the property.*

ECONOMIC RENT - the amount of rent a property might be expected to yield if it were available for lease in the current market. The economic rent and contract rent of a given property might differ if the lessor is receiving more or less rent than the property should reasonably yield.

3. Security Deposits

SECURITY DEPOSIT - provides the landlord with funds to pay for damages or unpaid rent when the tenant vacates. The deposit, minus itemized damages or required cleaning, must be refunded within **twenty-one days** of the tenant vacating the premises.

STATEMENT OF PROPERTY CONDITION - a report filled out by the landlord, in the presence of the tenant, that states the condition of the premises on moving in and moving out.

The maximum rental agreement deposit for a residential property (in addition to first month's rent) is 2 months rent for an unfurnished property and 3 months for a furnished property.

4. Assignment and Subleasing Provisions

The tenant, without a clause to the contrary, may assign or sublease the property.

ASSIGNMENT - a transfer of the entire lease.

SUBLEASE - a transfer of less than the entire time or space of the lease. For example, if there is a two-year lease, then an assignment could be for those two years, or a sublease could be for one year of the two-year lease.

A sublease transfers "possession," but not "ownership" of real property.

SANDWICH LEASE - a leasehold interest in a property that lies between the primary (ownership) interest and the possessory (tenancy) interest. The holder of a sandwich lease is both a tenant and landlord to the same property.

If the old tenant (assignor) signs a new valid lease with an assignee, the assignee is a tenant.

5. Liabilities for Injuries and Repairs

Generally, when the entire premises are leased, the landlord is not liable for injuries to the tenant or any guests that results from a defective condition on the premises. In apartments or situations where the tenant does not lease the entire property, the liability for injury in the common areas belongs to the landlord.

Possessory rights belong to the lessee, while reversionary rights belong to the lessor.

III. Termination of a Lease (or Rental Agreement)

A lease (estate for years) ends at the expiration of the term and without notice. Rental agreements (period-to-period) terminate by a written notice that must be at least one rental period in length. For example, if a tenancy is on a two-week basis and the rent is paid for that period, then two weeks' notice is required.

A. TERMINATION: EXPIRATION OF THE TERM

A lease ends without notice at the expiration of the term. Rental agreements can be terminated by either party with a 30-day written notice, unless a longer period is agreed to by both parties.

B. TERMINATION: LACK OF QUIET POSSESSION

A tenant is entitled to the quiet possession and enjoyment of the premises. The landlord has the responsibility to maintain reasonable quiet on the premises for his or her tenants, and must not harass them unduly. Failure on either count can give a tenant grounds for terminating a lease.

C. TERMINATION: REPAIRS FOR HABITABILITY

The landlord of a rented home has the implied responsibility to keep the premises maintained in a condition that meets at least bare living requirements. A tenant must give notice of any necessary repairs to the landlord. If the landlord, after a reasonable amount of time, has failed to make the necessary repairs, the tenant has two methods of recourse:

1. Spend no more than 1 month's rent on repairs (max. twice in a 12 consecutive month period).
2. Abandon the premises, which terminates the lease or rental agreement.

D. TERMINATION: EVICTION OR OPERATION OF LAW

EVICTION - *the legal process of removing a tenant because there is a breach of the lease or rental agreement.*

RETALIATORY EVICTION - *the illegal process whereby a landlord evicts a tenant in response to a complaint lodged by the tenant.*

It is unlawful for the landlord to lock out tenants, take the tenant's property, remove doors, shut off utilities, or trespass.

The landlord must protect the health and safety of tenants, obey fair housing laws and give 24 hours' notice before entering a rental.

When the tenant refuses to give up possession but does not pay the rent, the landlord normally serves a "three-day notice" and, if necessary, files an "unlawful detainer" action.

THREE-DAY NOTICE TO PAY - *a legal document that informs the tenant that he or she has* **three business days** *(no holidays or weekends) to pay all past-due rent or vacate the property.*

THREE-DAY NOTICE TO QUIT - *states that the tenant has breached the lease or rental agreement and has three business days to surrender (quit) the premises or face an unlawful detainer court action.* It is referred to as an **eviction notice**.

UNLAWFUL DETAINER - *a document filed with the court that asserts the charges against the tenant. After it is served, the tenant has five days to surrender possession or answer the complaint.*

An unlawful detainer action is used by the offended lessor (landlord) to gain possession.

If the tenant loses or does not answer the unlawful detainer complaint, a judge may issue a writ of possession.

WRIT OF POSSESSION - *a court order directing the sheriff to remove the tenant from the premises within five days.*

E. TERMINATION: SURRENDER

SURRENDER - *the giving up of a lease or other estate, thus terminating any further obligations.* Leases may be surrendered either by mutual agreement of the parties or through operation of law.

If a tenant abandons a property without cause, he or she has, by "operation of law," surrendered the property back to the landlord.

If a tenant's rent is 14 days' delinquent and the landlord has reasonable cause to believe that the lessee has abandoned the premises, the lessor may bring action to reclaim the property.

F. TERMINATION: BREACH OF CONDITIONS

The violation of any conditions of the lease is a breach of contract and may terminate the agreement. Both the lessee and lessor have the responsibility of being informed of all contractual conditions and understand that violation of the conditions may cause termination.

G. TERMINATION: DESTRUCTION OF THE PREMISES

If a structure is destroyed, there is usually a clause in the contract that automatically terminates the lease. If the damage is light, the tenant may stay while the landlord makes repairs. The lessee has the right to vacate the lease if the property is condemned.

Selling an apartment is "subject to the rights of tenants in possession." It does NOT terminate leases.

IV. Special Purpose Leases

SALE-LEASEBACK - *occurs when an owner sells his or her property to another party and leases it back for a stated period of time; the original owner becomes the lessee, and the buyer the lessor.*

LEASE-PURCHASE OPTION - *exists only when a tenant leases a property with the option to purchase it at some future date.*

GROUND LEASE - *for the exclusive use and possession of a specific parcel of land.*

GRADUATED LEASE - *provides for a varying rental rate. It is often based upon future determination, such as periodic appraisals. Also called a "stair-step" lease.*

GROSS LEASE (Income Property) - *the lessee pays only a rental fee for the use of the property.*

NET LEASE (Income Property) - *the lessee pays the property taxes, insurance, and other operating costs in addition to rental payments.*

The lessor benefits from a net lease because it generates a fixed income.

PERCENTAGE LEASE (Retail Sales Property) - *a commercial (retail sales) lease in which the lessee pays, or may pay, a certain percentage of the gross sales to the lessor.*

Percentage lease payments are based upon gross income receipts.

V. Forms of Ownership

A. TITLE

TITLE - *the evidence that one has the right to possess a parcel of real property.*

VESTING - *the placing of a person's (or persons') name on the deed and the description of the method by which that person will hold title.* There are six distinct methods of holding title:

1. Severalty (Separate Ownership)

SEVERALTY - *the sole and separate ownership of property by one individual or by a corporation.*

CORPORATION - *a body of persons treated by law as a single "legal person," having a personality and existence distinct from that of its shareholders. A corporation can go on forever; it does not die.*

2. Tenancy in Common

TENANCY IN COMMON - *When two or more people concurrently own property (without survivorship rights or community property rights).*

If there is no other agreement, they will each share an equal interest in the property. All tenants in common have "unity of possession," which means they each have the right to occupy the property. Tenancy in common gives all owners a share of the income and expenses of the property. Each owner may sell or transfer his or her interest separately from the others.

PARTITION ACTION - *the courts have the responsibility of selling the property.*

3. Joint Tenancy

JOINT TENANCY - *occurs when two or more people own a property together with the rights of survivorship.* If one of the joint tenancy owners should die, his or her interest is then split evenly with the surviving owners. Joint tenancy can never be willed.

When a joint tenancy is established, there are four unities ("**T-Tip**") involved:

T   **1. Title** - All owners are granted title by the same instrument.
T   **2. Time** - All owners obtain title at the same time.
I   **3. Interest** - All owners share an equal interest.
P   **4. Possession** - All owners have an equal right to possess the property.

To create joint tenancy, there must be intention by the owners. The deed must be in writing and contain the phrase: "as joint tenants" or "in joint tenancy." If it does not "state" that it is a joint tenancy, joint tenancy does not exist.

4. Tenancy in Partnership

TENANCY IN PARTNERSHIP - *refers to two or more people who are co-owners in a business.*

GENERAL PARTNERSHIP - *the partners share all profits and losses and share management responsibilities.* All partners must agree to a sale or transfer of real property. Each has a right to possess the partnership property. If a partner should die, his or her interest passes to any heirs who then have a right in the partnership, but not in any particular property.

LIMITED PARTNERSHIP - *is one consisting of one or more general partners and limited partners.* A limited partner's losses are limited to the amount of his or her investment. A limited partner does not share management responsibilities.

5. Community Property

COMMUNITY PROPERTY - *refers to all the property acquired by a husband and wife during their marriage, when not acquired as the separate property of either spouse.*

California is a community property state, which means that any property acquired during a marriage is shared equally. Both husband and wife must sign all transfer documents to convey community real property. If only one spouse signs a transfer document, the "injured" spouse could void the sale within a one-year period. The right to manage the community property is shared by both the husband and wife.

Each can will his or her respective half to whomever they wish. If there is no will, the half belonging to the deceased would go to the surviving spouse. If willed to an heir, the heir and the remaining spouse would then be tenants in common.

6. Community Property With Right of Survivorship

The California legislature enacted legislation which allows married couples in California to hold title to real and personal property as "community property with right of survivorship." The goal of the legislation was to establish the right of survivorship benefit while maintaining the favorable tax status of community property under federal tax law. The survivorship benefit allows title to pass to the surviving spouse at the death of one spouse. Since the property is held as community property, the surviving spouse also gets the benefit of a stepped up basis for 100% of the property upon the death of a spouse. The surviving spouse may use an affidavit of death of spouse to satisfy title company underwriting requirements to convey or encumber title. Probate proceedings are not necessary to transfer title to the surviving spouse.

VI. Encumbrances (Money and Non-Money)

ENCUMBRANCE - *a right or interest in real property other than an owner or tenancy interest.* It is a burden to the property that limits its use.

The two main types of encumbrances are: (1) liens and (2) items that affect the physical condition or use of the property.

All liens are encumbrances, but NOT all encumbrances are liens.

VII. Liens (Money Encumbrances)

LIEN - *a document that uses a property to secure the payment of a debt or the discharge of an obligation.* It is money owed for one reason or another on a property.

Liens include trust deeds or mortgages, tax liens, special assessments, mechanic's liens, judgments, attachments and bankruptcies. Liens are either voluntary or involuntary, and specific or general.

BLANKET ENCUMBRANCE - *a voluntary lien (money owed) placed over more than one parcel.* A release clause releases portions of the property.

A. VOLUNTARY AND INVOLUNTARY LIENS

VOLUNTARY LIENS - *are money debts that an owner agrees to pay.* A lien is created when the buyer takes out a loan to finance the purchase of real estate. He or she voluntarily agrees to pay for the money borrowed.

INVOLUNTARY LIENS - *money obligations that create a burden on a property by government taxes or legal action because of unpaid bills.* Both involuntary liens and voluntary liens must be paid or assumed in full before the owner can sell or refinance the property.

B. SPECIFIC AND GENERAL LIENS

SPECIFIC LIENS - *liens against just one property.* Property taxes assessed against real property automatically become a specific lien on **only** that property on **July 1st** of each year.

GENERAL LIENS - *liens on all the properties of the owner, not just one.* Federal or state income taxes and judgment liens can become a general lien on all real property.

C. TRUST DEED (Security Device – Voluntary and Specific)

TRUST DEED - *a written instrument that makes real property collateral for a loan.* The evidence of debt is created by the promissory note that accompanies the trust deed. The trust deed pledges (hypothecates) the property as collateral, or security, for the note.

D. MORTGAGE (Security Device – Voluntary and Specific)

MORTGAGE - *a lien (rarely used in California) that secures real property for the payment of a promissory note (debt).*

E. MECHANIC'S LIENS (Involuntary and Specific)

MECHANIC'S LIENS - *liens that may be filed against a property by a person who was not paid after furnishing labor or materials for construction work on that property.*

Architects, plumbing supply companies, and truck drivers can file mechanic's liens if unpaid. Mechanic's liens are involuntary and specific.

The form used to enforce a mechanic's lien action must be recorded to be effective. **A mechanic's lien is a lien against the property itself**. The property cannot be transferred until the obligation is paid and the title cleared.

1. Preliminary Notice

PRELIMINARY NOTICE - *a written notice that should be given before filing a mechanic's lien and within 20 days of supplying labor or services.* This notice must be given, either by mail or in person, to the owner, general contractor, and the lender.

2. Determining the Start Time for Mechanic's Liens

An important determination, when considering a mechanic's lien, is the **date that work started**, known as the "scheme of improvement."

Mechanic's liens, once recorded, have priority "over all other liens" except 1) taxes, 2) special assessments, and 3) trust deeds.

3. Notice of Completion and Notice of Cessation (Limits Time to File)

A "Notice of Completion" should be recorded by the contractor within 10 days of completion. Work is considered complete if there is a cessation of labor 30 days after a "Notice of Cessation" is filed.

All of the following may affect the filing date of a mechanic's lien: notice of non-responsibility, notice of cessation, and notice of completion.

4. Filing Time (Limited)

A mechanic's lien may be filed any time after the preliminary notice and until 30 days after completion if you are a supplier or subcontractor, and 60 days after completion if you are the general contractor. If there is no notice of completion recorded for the project, all parties have 90 days after completion to file.

COMPLETION BOND - required by lender to ensure that an insurance company will complete the job if the contractor cannot.

5. Notice of Non-Responsibility (Must be Recorded and Posted)

NOTICE OF NON-RESPONSIBILITY - *posted (within 10 days of discovery) on the property stating that the owner is not responsible for the work being done.* This action releases an owner from any liability caused by the unauthorized activity and prevents suppliers from filing a valid mechanic's lien.

F. TAX LIENS (Specific or General Liens)

If any government tax is not paid it may become a lien, through law or a court action, on real property. If the lien is not settled, the property can be sold to pay back-taxes. Tax liens are either: (1) specific liens or (2) general liens. Property taxes and mechanic's liens are specific liens, whereas income taxes and judgments are general liens.

G. SPECIAL ASSESSMENTS

SPECIAL ASSESSMENTS - *local improvements paid for by the property owners in a given district.*

Improvements such as streets, sewers, street lighting, and irrigation projects are generally paid for by the property owners who have benefited from the work. If these assessments are not paid, they become a lien against the property.

H. JUDGMENTS (Involuntary and General Liens)

JUDGMENT - *a court decision determining the rights of the parties involved and the amount of compensation. A judgment can be appealed.*

ABSTRACT OF JUDGMENT - *or formal filing of the judgment, must be recorded for a judgment to become a lien.*

The judgment then becomes a lien upon all non-exempt property of the debtor. It also becomes a lien on all future property he or she later acquires until the lien is paid.

A judgment is a general and involuntary lien against all real property in the county in which the judgment is recorded. It is good for 10 years.

1. Small Claims Court

Anyone can take someone else to small claims court regarding civil cases for a $6 filing fee plus the fee for serving the subpoena. Neither party is allowed to be represented in the courtroom by legal counsel. The current maximum amount of a judgment is $5,000. For a plaintiff, the judge's decision in a small claims action is final. The defendant, though, has the right of appeal.

I. TERMINATION OF JUDGMENT LIEN

SATISFACTION OF JUDGMENT - *compensation made by the payment of money or the return of property.* It clears the lien from the record.

J. ATTACHMENT (Court-Seized Property)

ATTACHMENT (LIEN) - *a process of the law that creates a lien. It gives custody of real or personal property to the courts to assure payment of a pending lawsuit in that county.*

An attachment creates a specific and involuntary lien on one property which is good for 3 years.

PLAINTIFF - *the person filing a court action to obtain an attachment lien.*

DEFENDANT - *the person who is being sued.*

K. LIS PENDENS (Lawsuit Pending)

LIS PENDENS - *the recording of a notice that a lawsuit is pending concerning a particular property.* It places a cloud on the title, and remains on the public record until judgment is rendered or suit is dismissed.

A lis pendens may affect title to real property based on the lawsuit outcome.

L. SHERIFF'S SALE (Court Ordered to Sell - Execution)

SHERIFF'S SALE - *the forced sale of a debtor's property to satisfy a judgment under a writ of execution.*

WRIT OF EXECUTION - *court order requiring the sale of certain property to satisfy a judgment.* The writ of execution extends the lien against the real property for one year.

14

M. INJUNCTION

INJUNCTION - *a court order to stop doing something.*

VIII. Items That Affect Physical Use (Non-Money Encumbrances)

ITEMS THAT AFFECT PHYSICAL USE - *are non-money encumbrances that affect the physical use of real property.* They include easements, building restrictions, zoning and encroachments, which are conditions that limit physical use of the property.

A. EASEMENTS (The Right to Use Another's Land)

EASEMENT - *the right to enter, use, and exit another person's land for a certain purpose.* Included in this definition is the right to profit from the easement, such as the right to take minerals, oil, and gas. Easements are of two types: (1) easements appurtenant and (2) easements in gross.

An easement is the right to use another's land. It is a right, but NOT an estate.

INGRESS - *The right to enter land.*

EGRESS - *The right to exit land.*

1. Easement Appurtenant (Runs with the Land)

EASEMENT APPURTENANT - *an easement "created for and beneficial to" the owner of neighboring or attached lands.* The easement appurtenant becomes part of the land and cannot be transferred separately from the land.

DOMINANT TENEMENT - *the land that obtains the benefits of an easement.*

SERVIENT TENEMENT - *the land that gives the easement for the benefit of another.*

The owner of the servient tenement CANNOT terminate the easement; it must "serve" the dominant tenement. The dominant tenement and the servient tenement do NOT need to physically abut (touch) each other.

2. Easement in Gross (Does not Benefit Adjoining Landowner)

EASEMENT IN GROSS - *an easement created for the benefit of others who do not own adjoining or attached lands.*

An example of an easement in gross would be a utility company obtaining the right to run natural gas lines across your land.

UNLOCATED EASEMENT - *a right granted by an owner to cross his land and not limit how or where a person would have to cross.*

3. Creation of an Easement

Easements are created in three basic ways:

a. Expressed in Writing, as in Deed or Contract

If a property is transferred as part of the deed, an easement appurtenant to the land would be included in the grant. The same thing is accomplished by transferring a property, but reserving an easement over the land.

b. Creation by Implication of Law (Implied Easement)

If an easement is implied in a transfer, or if it is necessary for use of the land, then the easement is said to be implied by law.

EASEMENT BY NECESSITY (Landlocked) - an easement granted by a court if it is absolutely necessary for access.

c. Easement by Prescription (Long Use)

Possession for **5 continuous years** can create a prescription, as long as there is:

1. Open and notorious use.
2. Uninterrupted use for 5 years.
3. Hostile use (without permission of the owner).
4. Under a claim of right.

4. Transfer of an Easement

Easements are transferred automatically if they are easements appurtenant. Easements in gross can be transferred only by an express agreement, provided the easement is not made to a specific individual.

5. Termination of an Easement

Easements may be terminated in several ways:

a. Express Release

Only the servient tenement can benefit.

b. Merger of Dominant and Servient Tenements

An easement terminates when the dominant and servient tenements merge into a common, or single, ownership.

c. Excessive Use

Increases the burden on the servient tenement; easement may be forfeited through a court injunction.

d. Abandonment and Non-Use

Abandonment easements may be lost through court action. An easement gained through prescription may be extinguished if non-use exists for a period of five continuous years.

Non-use can only terminate an easement created by prescription.

e. Destruction of Servient Tenement

When a servient tenement property is taken through eminent domain, the dominant tenement easement is terminated.

6. Building Restrictions (CC&Rs) and Zoning

There are three types of private building restrictions: **Covenants, Conditions** and **Restrictions**. They are usually included in the deed at the time the property is subdivided, or may be created by a written contract. Their main purpose is to keep use of the land uniform throughout certain tracts of land.

PRIVATE DEED RESTRICTIONS *- limit the use or occupancy of the land.* A typical restriction would be to limit the types of buildings on a given piece of land to single family residences.

COVENANT *- an agreement or promise to do or not to do a certain act.* For example, a covenant not to sell alcoholic beverages on the property.

CONDITION *- a future and uncertain event which must happen to create an obligation or which extinguishes an existent obligation.* The penalty for not following the set conditions is the reversion of the property to the grantor.

PUBLIC RESTRICTIONS (Zoning) *- limits made by governmental agencies; usually cities and counties in the form of zoning.*

Public restrictions promote health, safety, morals, and general welfare of the public. This is the use of "police power."

ZONING *- the restriction on the use of private property by the local government agency.* Zoning dictates how the property can be used, the setbacks required, and the height limit on any structures.

PRIVATE RESTRICTIONS *- placed on the property by the grantor or developer. If there are two restrictions, the most restrictive of the two will take precedence.*

RACE RESTRICTIONS (Illegal) *- restricting the right of an individual to sell, rent, lease, use a property because of race or membership in a certain ethnic group.*

7. Encroachments (3 Years to Act)

ENCROACHMENT *- the wrongful, unauthorized placement of improvements or permanent fixtures on property by a non-owner of that property.* You must pursue the right to have an encroachment removed within 3 years or lose your right.

If your neighbor builds a driveway over your land, it is considered "trespass."

IX. Homesteading Your Residence

HOMESTEAD *- a special provision of the California law that allows homeowners to protect their homes from forced sale to satisfy their debts, within certain limits.* A homestead consists of the house and adjoining dwellings in which the owner resides.

A. DECLARATION OF HOMESTEAD

DECLARATION OF HOMESTEAD - *the form that, after being acknowledged and recorded, protects a residence from judgments that become liens.* It does not protect that person against trust deeds, mechanic's liens, or prior-to-filing liens.

B. TERMINATION OF HOMESTEAD

DECLARATION OF ABANDONMENT - *terminates a homestead. It must be acknowledged and recorded by the involved parties.* A sale or other conveyance of the property also terminates the homestead, but the removal of the dwelling does not.

X. Doctrine of Police Power

The state and local governments have the responsibility (under the doctrine of police power) to enact and enforce legislative acts to protect the general public. This public protection in the real estate area prevents fraud, misrepresentation, and deceit.

A. POLICE POWER

POLICE POWER - *the power to make rulings to control the "use and taking of private property" for the protection of the public's health, safety and welfare.* Police power allows the state, county, or city to protect its citizens by controlling how land is being used.

XI. The Basic Subdivision Laws

SUBDIVISION - *a parcel of land divided into five or more parcels with the intent to sell, lease, or finance them now or in the future.* It can also be some form of common or mutual ownership rights in one parcel. A **condominium** is sometimes referred to as a "one lot subdivision." Two basic laws control subdivisions in California.

A. SUBDIVISION MAP ACT (Enforced by Local City or County)

SUBDIVISION MAP ACT - *provides an outline of the methods for the subdivision filing procedure with the city or county and assures that subdividers comply with a city's or county's master plan.* This permits the city or county to enact subdivision ordinances. The two objectives are:

    1. To coordinate subdivision plans including lot design, street patterns, and sewers.
    2. To ensure that parts of the subdivision area will be dedicated to the city or county.

The Subdivision Map Act gives "cities and counties" control over the physical design of a subdivision.

B. SUBDIVIDED LANDS LAW (State Law Enforced by the DRE)

SUBDIVIDED LANDS LAW (Public Report) - *protects the purchasers of property in new subdivisions from fraud, misrepresentation, or deceit in the marketing of subdivided lots, parcels, condominiums, or other undivided property interests in the state of California.*

No subdivision unit can be offered for sale in California until the commissioner has issued a final subdivision public report. The report is not issued until the commissioner is satisfied that the subdivider has met all the statutory requirements.

The Subdivided Lands Law (public report) requirements apply when a parcel is divided into 5 or more lots (units).

XII. Final Public Report (Consumer Information)

PUBLIC REPORT - *a formal disclosure report of the important facts regarding a subdivision.* A public report may be obtained by anyone.

DESIST AND REFRAIN ORDER - *an order issued by the Real Estate Commissioner to stop sales for violations.*

FINAL PUBLIC REPORT - *"Real Estate Commissioner's Final Subdivision Public Report" is the official report that must be given to the buyer.* The buyer must sign a receipt stating that the report has been received. There is a five-year time limit on the report and it can be updated and renewed.

A. PUBLIC REPORT RECEIPTS

PUBLIC REPORT RECEIPT - *receipt stating that the buyer has received a copy of any public report and has had the opportunity to read it. The report must be kept on file for* **three years** *by the owner, his or her agent, or the subdivider.*

B. MATERIAL CHANGES (Notify Commissioner)

Any material change in the subdivision or its handling, after the filing is made or the public report is issued, must be reported to the Commissioner of Real Estate.

Change in price is NOT a material fact.

XIII. Subdivision Defined by Law

In general, the Subdivided Lands Law applies to five or more units, while the Subdivision Map Act applies to two or more units. They both, however, cover two or more units where cooperative ownership apartments or condominiums are concerned.

A. LAND PROJECTS (State Law)

LAND PROJECT - *a remote subdivision of* **50 or more vacant lots** *in a rural area (having less than 1,500 registered voters within two miles).*

By law, any contract to buy or lease in a land project may be rescinded, without cause, through written notice before midnight on the **fourteenth day** after the contract is signed.

XIV. Common Interest Development (CID)

COMMON INTEREST DEVELOPMENT (CID) - *a project where there are common areas used by all and separate interests for the use of individual living units. It is managed by a nonprofit association.*

COMMON AREA - *that part of a lot or unit in a subdivision that is shared equally by all owners (undivided interest).*

UNDIVIDED INTEREST - *the right of any owner to use any part of the project.*

C. CONDOMINIUM (Most Common Type)

CONDOMINIUM - *the ownership of the land, buildings, and sidewalks in common with other owners and the individual ownership of specific air spaces.* Condominiums may be used for residential, industrial, or commercial purposes.

A condominium owner gets a deed (fee interest) to a unit and a separate tax bill.

With the sale of a condominium, the seller must provide the buyer with a copy of the:

1. **CC&Rs** (covenants, conditions, restrictions);
2. **by-laws** (governing rules of the association); and
3. **financial statement** (the condo's most recent).

XV. Zoning (Use)

ZONING LAWS - *regulate the use of property by prescribing what uses that land can be put to, and by establishing uniformity throughout the community.*

If zoning conflicts with deed restrictions, the most restrictive controls.

Zoning laws use the "police power" granted to every county and city to regulate the use, planning, and setbacks of land. They can change an area from commercial to residential or change a residential area from R-4 to R-1. This is called **down zoning**.

Owners, subdividers and government agencies can petition for zone changes.

SPOT ZONING - *a small area that is zoned differently from the surrounding area.*

NONCONFORMING USE - *a property that is not used according to the current zoning.* An example would be an apartment with one parking space per unit where zoning changes require two parking spaces per unit.

VARIANCE - *an exception to the existing zoning regulations in cases of special need for circumstances that might create serious hardship for property owners.* Zoning restrictions such as setbacks may be removed by petitioning or by a variance.

GRANDFATHER CLAUSE - *allows an owner to continue using his or her property in a way prohibited by the new zoning.*

CONDITIONAL USE PERMIT - *an exception to the current zoning for the public welfare or benefit. Variances, on the other hand, are based on hardship.*

XVI. Housing and Building Laws

Regulatory authority of the housing and construction industry is accomplished by the state contractor's license laws, the local building codes, and the State Housing Law.

A. STATE HOUSING LAW (Health and Safety Code)

California has adopted a State Housing Law that sets the minimum construction and occupancy requirements for all apartments, hotels, and other dwellings. Any city or county may impose more stringent requirements.

B. LOCAL BUILDING CODES

BUILDING CODE - *the basic minimum construction standard for a structure.* This code includes regulation of all the basic methods, materials, and components of a structure, from the foundation to the plumbing and electrical system. **BUILDING PERMIT** - *an approved building application that includes plans, specifications, and a plot plan.* No construction or alteration can be started until the building permit has been issued.

MANUFACTURED HOUSING - *a transportable structure in one (or more) eight-foot (or more) wide by 40-foot (or more) long sections that will cover 320 or more square feet that meet HUD Code standards.* If sold in California, it must meet the California Department of Housing standards.

If there is a building code conflict, the highest construction standard controls.

C. CONTRACTOR'S STATE LICENSE LAW

Contractors are licensed by the Contractor's State License Board, whose main purpose is to protect the public against incompetent building contractors and subcontractors.

XVII. Eminent Domain (Involuntary/Voluntary Conversion, Condemnation)

INVOLUNTARY CONVERSION - *the legal conversion of real property to personal property (money) without the voluntary act of the owner.* This occurs when property is taken by eminent domain (condemnation).

EMINENT DOMAIN - *the right of the government to take private property from a landowner (with the fair market value paid as compensation to that owner) for the "public good."* The use of the right of eminent domain is often referred to as "condemnation."

SEVERANCE DAMAGE - *the compensation paid an owner for "devalued remaining property" as the result of an eminent domain action.* In some instances, the property owner will feel that the property is so devalued that he or she will file an inverse condemnation action.

INVERSE CONDEMNATION - *an action where the property owner files suit to force the government to take all of the property, not just a part.*

Section 2
Tax Implications

DRE Testing Emphasis:
Salesperson 8%
Broker 8%

I. Property Taxes

REAL PROPERTY TAXES - *taxes determined according to the value of the real property, and paid semi-annually.* These taxes are called ad valorem taxes.

AD VALOREM TAX - *a tax that is charged in proportion to the value of the property.*

Property taxes are based on a person's ability to pay. In the case of real estate, the higher the value of the property, the higher the property taxes.

Real property is assessed each time it is transferred (sold) at 1% of its selling price (or market value, if it is higher).

COUNTY ASSESSOR - *the county officer who has the responsibility of determining the assessed valuation of land, improvements, and personal property used in business.*

In general, all real property and tangible personal property are subject to property tax assessment in California. Intangible personal property, such as shares of stock, promissory notes, and personal effects of individuals, are not taxed.

County Assessor assesses; County Tax Collector collects; County Board of Supervisors sets tax rate.

COUNTY TAX COLLECTOR - *the county officer who collects the real property taxes.*

A. PROPERTY TAX TIME TABLE

The city or county fiscal year starts on July 1 and ends on June 30. Assessable property is evaluated by the assessor on January 1st for the upcoming year in the name of the property's legal owner on that date.

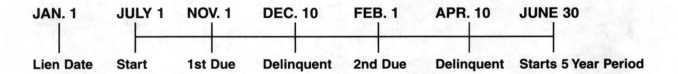

JAN. 1	JULY 1	NOV. 1	DEC. 10	FEB. 1	APR. 10	JUNE 30
Lien Date	Start	1st Due	Delinquent	2nd Due	Delinquent	Starts 5 Year Period

Fiscal Year: July 1 through June 30 by the government.

January 1: Tax becomes lien-date (preceding the fiscal year).

Important tax dates can be remembered "No Darn Fooling Around" as follows:

N	**November 1** (first installment)
D	**December 10** (first installment is delinquent)
F	**February 1** (second installment)
A	**April 10** (second installment is delinquent)

The second installment would be due February 1 and delinquent on April 10.

B. PROPERTY TAXES BECOME A SPECIFIC LIEN

Property taxes for the following fiscal year become a lien against the real property on January 1 of the current year.

C. HOMEOWNER'S PROPERTY TAX EXEMPTION

HOMEOWNER'S PROPERTY TAX EXEMPTION - *a deduction, on the property tax bill, of the first $7,000 of assessed value of an owner-occupied property.*

California has NO special exemption for low-income families.

Any California resident who served in the military during a time of war is entitled to a $4,000 property tax exemption against the assessed value of the property.

Property of non-profit organizations used for religious, charitable, medical, or educational purposes is tax exempt.

D. PROPERTY TAX APPEALS

The "Assessment Appeal Board" is where a property owner may file an appeal to object to a property tax assessment that was set too high.

E. DELINQUENT TAX SALE (Book Sale)

Each year, on or before June 8, the county tax collector publishes a list of tax delinquent properties. This is his or her "notice of intent to sell" all such properties on which the property taxes have not been paid for one year. Strictly speaking, this is not a true sale, but is a formality, called a Book Sale.

BOOK SALE - *starts a five-year redemption period. If the property is not redeemed within five years, it will be deeded over to the state.*

If taxes are NOT paid on or before June 30, the property is sold to the state. This sale starts the running of the redemption period, which is five years.

F. SECOND SALE (After Five Years)

After five years, if the property has not been redeemed, the delinquent property is deeded to the state. This is the official sale, and the former owner may now only redeem the property if the state has not sold the property at public auction.

Although property taxes are NOT paid, a owner can remain in possession and could redeem for 5 years.

G. SALE TO THE PUBLIC

The county tax collector will sell the state-owned properties to other taxing agencies or to the highest bidder at a public tax auction. The minimum bid is established by the tax collector and approved by the county board of supervisors. All such sales are for cash at the time of the sale. The purchaser then receives a tax deed. Most title insurance companies will insure the tax deed sale after one year has elapsed. But, if any difficulties are encountered, the buyer may clear title through a "quiet title" court action.

II. Special Assessment Tax (Specific Improvements)

Special assessments finance only off-site improvements, NOT purchase of land.

STREET IMPROVEMENT ACT OF 1911 - *finances street and highway improvements through an assessment to property owners based upon the frontage they enjoy facing the improved street. Also* called the **Bond Act of 1911**, it allows property owners, through the issuance of municipal bonds, up to 30 years to pay off their portion of the improvement assessment.

If you purchase a lot for $40,000 and assume a $1,200 assessment bond, your cost basis for income tax purposes would be $41,200.

MELLO-ROOS LIENS - *municipal bonds issued to fund streets, sewers, and other infrastructure needs before a housing development is built.* The developer is usually responsible for making payments on the bond until the home is sold; then the homeowner is responsible for payment.

III. Documentary Transfer Tax

DOCUMENTARY TRANSFER TAX - a tax that is applied to the consideration paid or money borrowed when transferring property, except for any loan(s) that stays with the property (new money only).

This tax rate is: **55 cents for each $500 of consideration** or any fraction thereof.

If a house were sold for $150,000 and a buyer assumed the old loan of $25,000, the documentary transfer tax would be $137.50.

$$\frac{\$125,000}{\$500} \times \$.55 = \$137.50$$

IV. Federal and State Income Taxes

The annual Federal Income Tax Form 1040 and the State Income Tax Form 540 are bookkeeping or accounting summaries of the prior year's financial facts.

Tax shelters are a way to reduce income taxes.

V. Taxes on Personal Residence

Homeowners can annually deduct these three items from their income taxes based on their personal residence:

1. Mortgage Interest on Loan (Trust Deeds)
2. Property Taxes
3. Prepayment Penalties

Interest, property taxes, and prepayment penalties paid on your personal residence can be deducted from your income taxes.

A. SALE OF YOUR RESIDENCE

When selling a personal residence, the seller can deduct up to $250,000 ($500,000 if married) of any financial gain (profit) for each spouse. This can be used every two years.

You can deduct a loss on sale of a personal residence if you have turned it into income producing property by renting it.

VI. Taxes for Income Producing Properties

Prepaid rent money collected by a landlords is taxable income when received.

When a tenant pays the last month's rent on a five-year lease, it is taxed when received, not in five years' time.

Investors of income producing properties can annually deduct these items from their income taxes:

1. Mortgage Interest on Loans (no maximum)
2. Property Taxes
3. Prepayment Penalties
4. Operating Expenses
5. Depreciation of Improvements

Owners CANNOT deduct losses due to vacancies.

A. DEPRECIATION OF INCOME PRODUCING PROPERTY ("Book" Depreciation)

DEPRECIATION FOR TAX PURPOSES - *a yearly tax deduction for wear, tear, and obsolescence on investment property that is deducted from the taxpayer's income on his or her income tax form.* This deduction applies only to investment property or property used in a business, not on a taxpayer's personal residence.

Only the buildings and other improvements can be depreciated, NOT the land.

One can only depreciate property that is improved. Since land cannot be depreciated, only the improvements can be depreciated. Currently, the straight-line method is the accepted way to depreciate buildings and other improvements for tax purposes.

Residential (home or apartment) – Minimum of 27½ years to depreciate.

Commercial improvements – Minimum of 39 years to depreciate.

Example: If you own a cabin that you rent to vacationers and the cabin cost $100,000 and the land value is $25,000, this leaves improvements of $75,000. Divide this $75,000 by 30 years, giving you a depreciation of $2,500 for each year of the 30 years. If we had used a 27½ year formula, the yearly depreciation amount would be slightly higher.

VII. Sale of Real Property

A. FEDERAL INCOME TAX RATES

PROGRESSIVE TAXES - *taxes where the rates (percentage paid) increase as the amount to be taxed increases.* Income tax rates are progressive.

MARGINAL TAX RATE - *the rate that the next dollar earned puts you into.*

REGRESSIVE TAXES - *use the same rate no matter how much is spent or earned.* Sale tax is an example of a regressive tax.

Income tax rates are progressive. Sale taxes are regressive.

B. ACCOUNTING FOR THE SALE OF REAL ESTATE

The method of determining a profit or loss on the sale of real property is spelled out by the Internal Revenue Service. Steps 1 and 2 must be completed before determining the profit or loss on a sale (Step 3).

BASICS

"Adjusted cost basis" is the base cost, plus capital improvements (that stay with the property), minus depreciation and sale expenses. A broker's commission is an expense of the sale.

(1) Cost Basis (Purchase price)	$500,000
+ Improvements	**+ 200,000**
	$700,000
- Depreciation (tax records)	**- 30,200**
= Adjusted Cost Basis	$669,800
(2) Sale price	$1,000,000
- Sale Expenses	**- 32,500**
= Adjusted Sale Price	$967,500
(3) Adjusted Sale Price	$967,500
- Adjusted Cost Basis	**- 669,800**
= Capital Gain	$297,700

VIII. Installment Sales and Exchanges

In addition to depreciation, two major tax benefits of owning income producing property are installment sales and 1031 tax-deferred exchanges.

A. INSTALLMENT SALES OF REAL ESTATE

INSTALLMENT SALE - *the sale of real estate in which the payments for the property extend over more than* **one calendar year**. This method is usually used when selling large tracts of land held for a period of time, or large buildings owned by one individual.

Installment sales are used because a gain is only taxed in the year that it is received. Spreading the gain over several years may drop you into a lower tax bracket (marginal tax rate).

B. EXCHANGES TAX-DEFERRED (Federal and State) (Section 1031 I.R.S. Code)

In an exchange, the adjusted cost basis of the old property becomes the basis of the new property.

EXCHANGE - *a transfer of real estate in which one party trades property for another's property.* The property must be of "like kind" in nature or character, not in use, quality, or grade. The exchange may be a straight trade (tax-free) or one party may receive cash in addition to the property (partially tax-free).

BOOT - *any net cash or net mortgage relief that a participant in an exchange might receive in addition to the actual property.* All boot is taxable to the extent of the gain in this partially tax-free exchange.

Boot is debt relief from a loan in a 1031 tax-deferred exchange.

Exchanges are popular among apartment owners and commercial property investors. This is because these owners are usually in high-income tax brackets, and exchanging enables them to move up to a more valuable property without paying taxes on the gain.

C. ADVANTAGES OF "SALE - LEASEBACK"
(Buyer Gets to Depreciate New Building Cost)

If the owner of a business sells her building for cash and then leases it back, the seller has become a lessee and the buyer the lessor.

The advantage to the seller: all lease payments can be deducted from income taxes, and he or she has received cash for his or her building. The advantage to the buyer: he can use the purchase price as the new basis for depreciation and establish a new depreciation schedule.

The seller, now the renter, deducts 100% of future rents paid. The buyer can depreciate new cost basis of improvement.

IX. Other Taxes Paid by Brokers

A. BUSINESS LICENSE TAXES (City Income Taxes)

BUSINESS LICENSE TAX - *A tax levied by the city against real estate brokerage firms, which is based upon the gross receipts.*

The "local building inspector" (city or county) usually enforces the State Housing Law.

Section 3
Appraisal

DRE Testing Emphasis:
Salesperson 15%
Broker 15%

I. Appraisal

APPRAISAL is an **opinion** as to the value of a particular property **at a given date**.

The appraiser estimates a property's value based on an analysis of the facts as of a "given date."

MARKET PRICE (Selling Price) - *the total price, including down payment and financing, that a property actually brought when sold.* Market price is what it sold for, whereas market value is what it should have sold for in a competitive market.

MARKET VALUE - *the price that a willing buyer will pay and a willing seller will accept, both being fully informed and with the sale property exposed for a reasonable period.*

Appraisers want truly "open market" results, NOT prudent values or prudent prices.

A. VALUE

VALUE - *a relationship between the thing desired and a potential purchaser.* The four essential elements of value are: (Remember: "**D.U.S.T.**")

D **1. Demand** - the desire, need, and ability to purchase
U **2. Utility** - usefulness; ability to instill a desire for possession
S **3. Scarcity** - in short supply, usually more expensive
T **4. Transferability** - can change ownership, as with a deed

Cost (or Price) is NOT one of the four essential elements of value.

II. The Appraisal Process

APPRAISAL PROCESS - *an orderly program by which the problem is defined and the work is planned; the data is gathered, analyzed, and correlated to estimate the value.*

The appraisal process consists of four logical steps.

Defining the "appraisal problem" is the first step in the appraisal process.

A. DEFINING AND CLARIFYING THE PROBLEM

The first objective of an appraisal is to determine the highest and best use.

HIGHEST AND BEST USE - *the use that will produce the maximum amount of profit or net return.* Appraisers do a **site analysis** to determine highest and best use.

B. GATHERING THE DATA

1. General Data (Includes Region, City (or County), and Neighborhood Data)

a. Residential Neighborhood

RESIDENTIAL NEIGHBORHOOD - *normally a limited area where the homes are physically similar and where the occupants have a common degree of social and economic background.*

2. Specific Data (Property Itself)

The most important economic characteristic is "area preference" (location).

a. Location

SITE - *a particular parcel within a neighborhood.*

b. Physical Aspects of a Lot

There are four major physical aspects of an actual site.

1. Size and Shape of Lot

In general, the more land or frontage on the street, the higher the value of the land.

DEPTH TABLE - *a percentage table that illustrates how the highest value is located in the front part of a lot.* Since the front portion of the lot has the most value, the more frontage there is, the better.

FRONT FOOTAGE - *the width of the property in the front, along the street.*

"Plottage" (Assemblage) brings under single ownership two or more contiguous lots, previously owned separately.

2. Lot Design Layouts

There are several ways to lay out lots in a parcel of land being subdivided. Zoning regulations usually state the minimum amount of square feet a lot can have, but a developer can get better prices if he or she divides the land wisely.

3. Slope, Drainage, and Soil

The slope of a lot will lower its value if it will be costly to improve. A lot that is higher or lower in relation to the street level may be costly to improve because of possible slope and drainage problems.

4. View, Exposure to Sun, and Weather (Orientation)

In a new tract of homes, the lots with the best views usually sell first, and apartments with views rent for more.

ORIENTATION - *planning the most advantageous place on a parcel of land for an improvement to be located.* The exposure of a house to the sun and weather elements may influence a person's decision to buy a house.

AMENITIES - *those improvements or views that increase the desirability or enjoyment rather than the necessities of the residents.* For example, a view of the ocean, mountains, or city lights at night increase the value of a home.

The south and west sides of streets are preferred by merchants because pedestrians seek the shady side, and displayed merchandise is NOT subject to damage by the afternoon sun. The northeast corner is the least desirable.

III. Improvements

HOUSE STRUCTURE TERMS

OPEN SHEATHING - *boards nailed to rafters as foundation for the roof covering. Open sheathing is used with wood shingles.*

BUILDING PAPER - *heavy waterproof paper used between sheathing and roof covering or siding.*

FLASHING - *sheet metal used to protect against water seepage.*

RAFTERS - *sloping members of a roof used to support the roof boards and shingles (maximum 24" apart).*

EAVE - *protruding under part of roof overhanging exterior walls.*

CLOSED SHEATHING - *boards nailed to studding as foundation for exterior siding. "Closed" means butted together.*

CRIPPLE - *stud above or below a window opening or above a doorway.*

SILL - *bottom portion lining doorway or window.*

MUD SILL - *treated lumber (or redwood) bolted to the foundation.*

CRAWL SPACE - *unexcavated area under the house (Min. 18").*

FOUNDATION - *concrete base of house.*

FOOTING - *expanded portion of concrete foundation.*

ANCHOR BOLT - *large bolt used for fastening mud sill to foundation. Bolt is anchored into concrete foundation.*

SOLE PLATE - *support on which the studs rest.*

HEADER - *the beam over a doorway or window.*

FIRE STOP - *blocking used to restrict flames from spreading to attic. May be placed horizontally or diagonally.*

STUDS - *vertical 2" x 4" framework in the walls spaced 16" on center.*

BRACING - *board running diagonally across the wall framing to prevent sway.*

JOISTS - *structural parts supporting floor or ceiling loads. A beam which supports them would be called a girder.*

RIDGE BOARD - *highest point of construction in a frame building.*

MORE CONSTRUCTION TERMS

ACRE - *has 43,560 sq.ft. or (4,840 sq. yards).*

BACKFILL - *the replacement of excavated earth against a structure (wall).*

Backfill is used to fill in excavations or to brace around foundations.

BEARING WALL - *a strong wall supporting any vertical load in addition to its own weight, usually a roof or floor above.*

BOARDFOOT - *a unit quantity for lumber equal to the volume of a board 12 x 12 x 1 inches (144 sq. inches).*

BTU (BRITISH THERMAL UNIT) - *a unit of measurement used to calculate heat; the quantity of heat required to raise one pound of water one degree Fahrenheit.*

CAPITAL ASSETS - *expenditures of a permanent nature that increase property values. Examples: buildings and street improvements.*

CASH FLOW - *in investment property, the actual cash the investor will receive after deduction of operating expenses and debt servicing (loan payment) from his or her gross income.*

CONDUIT - *a flexible metal pipe used to protect the electrical wiring inside.*

DRY WALL - *plaster walls that are installed in dry sheets.*

EER (ENERGY EFFICIENCY RATIO) - *a measure of energy efficiency; the higher the EER, the higher the efficiency.*

ELEVATION SHEET - *A rendering which shows the front and side views of a building; it shows the exterior views.*

Elevation sheets are drawings of the front and side views of the house when it is finished.

FOUNDATION PLAN - *plan that shows footing, piers, and sub-flooring.*

H_2O PRESSURE - testing water pressure by turning on all faucets and flushing all toilets.

HOSKOLD TABLES - concept of a "sinking fund" as a compound interest-bearing account, into which the portion of the investment returned each year is reinvested immediately.

INWOOD TABLES - concept of using present value of income in a perpetuity table to help appraisers determine the present value of a future income stream.

KIOSK - an information booth.

LOCAL BUILDING INSPECTOR - person who enforces construction standards (building code).

OVER-IMPROVEMENT - an expenditure to a property that doesn't improve its value.

PERCOLATION TEST - a test to determine how well water is absorbed by the soil.

PLOT MAP - the directional orientation of buildings on a lot.

POTABLE WATER - drinkable water.

PROPERTY RESIDUAL, BUILDING RESIDUAL, AND LAND RESIDUAL - all are methods of working backwards to find the unknown variable when appraising property.

R-VALUE - a measure used to calculate the heat resistance of insulation (the higher the better). Insulation is considered adequate if the temperature on the inside of an exterior wall is the same as the temperature on an interior wall.

> If the inside of an exterior wall is the same temperature as the other interior walls, the wall insulation is adequate.

REHABILITATION - the restoration of a property to a satisfactory condition without changing the interior or exterior design.

SOIL PIPE - a pipe used to carry waste and sewage from a property.

STRUCTURAL PEST CONTROL REPORT - a copy of the structural pest control report, if requested, must be given to the buyer as soon as practicable.

TOXIC WASTE REPORT - a report evaluating how harmful the dangerous material is on a property.

TURNKEY PROJECT - built, equipped, or installed complete and ready to occupy.

UNEARNED INCREMENT - an increase in value of real estate due to no effort on the part of the owner; often caused by population increase.

WAINSCOTING - the wood lining of the lower portion of an interior wall with the upper portion wallpapered or covered with another material different from the lower portion.

IV. Basic Appraisal Principles

There are several "principles of appraisal." These principles are valid economic concepts that are applied to the appraisal of real estate.

A. PRINCIPLE OF SUPPLY AND DEMAND

PRINCIPLE OF SUPPLY AND DEMAND - states that as the supply of land decreases, the value of land increases, because more people are competing for the desirable land.

B. PRINCIPLE OF CHANGE

PRINCIPLE OF CHANGE - states that real property is constantly changing. Value is influenced by changes in such things as: population size, shopping centers, schools and colleges, freeways, economic and social trends.

TREND - a series of changes brought about by a chain of events (causes and effects).

"Change" is evidenced by the fact that neighborhoods tend to pass through the three stages of the real estate "life cycle" (or age cycle).

1. Development (Integration)

This is the stage when the land is subdivided into lots, the streets are paved, and street lights are installed.

2. Maturity (Equilibrium)

Most of the residents are long-time homeowners and the community has a solid, well-established look.

3. Old Age (Disintegration)

In this stage, the buildings show some wear and tear, and the oldest buildings are starting to deteriorate.

C. PRINCIPLE OF CONFORMITY

PRINCIPLE OF CONFORMITY - states that the maximum value is obtained when a reasonable degree of building similarity is maintained in the neighborhood.

So if all the homes in an area are similar (not identical), the maximum value of real property is created. The principle of conformity is one of the primary reasons for zoning regulations. They protect the neighborhood from other non-conforming uses and from infiltration of incompatible structures.

D. PRINCIPLE OF CONTRIBUTION

PRINCIPLE OF CONTRIBUTION - states that the value of a particular component is measured in terms of its contribution to the value of the whole property.

Consequently, cost does not necessarily equal value. It either adds more or less to the value of real property. The principle of contribution is also referred to as increasing up to a point and then decreasing ("diminishing returns set in").

An appraiser would apply the "principle of contribution" to determine if adding a swimming pool to a 30-unit apartment building would be economically justified.

E. PRINCIPLE OF SUBSTITUTION

PRINCIPLE OF SUBSTITUTION - *states that a buyer will not pay more for a particular property if it costs less to buy a similar property of equal utility and desirability.* When appraisers use the principle of substitution, they compare properties to adjust for differences.

F. PRINCIPLE OF REGRESSION

PRINCIPLE OF REGRESSION - *states that between properties in the same neighborhood, the value of the best property will be adversely affected by the value of the other properties.* For example, if a house that would easily be worth $290,000 in a neighborhood of similar homes was to be built in a neighborhood of $135,000 homes, it would not sell for $290,000.

G. PRINCIPLE OF PROGRESSION

PRINCIPLE OF PROGRESSION - *states that the value of a lesser residence is increased in value by its location in a neighborhood of better homes.*

V. Market Data Method (Comparative Approach)

MARKET DATA METHOD - *simply takes the current selling prices of similar properties and adjusts those prices for any differences.*

The market data method approach uses the principle of substitution; a person will NOT pay more for a property if he or she can buy something similar for less.

A. HOW TO ADJUST FOR A COMPARABLE SALE (Comps)

Adjustments should be made to the selling price of the comparable house for any differences between the properties. **The usual adjustments are made for differences in location, age, lot size, building size, condition of the property, and any time difference between the sales. Subtract or add from or to the selling price of the comparable property to adjust for differences.** The term ***"COMPS"*** *is used to mean comparable properties.*

The market data method is the most common approach for houses and condominiums. It is also the best method for appraising lots, unimproved property, and obtaining rental rates.

B. ADVANTAGES OF THE MARKET DATA METHOD

This method is excellent for appraising single family homes. This method is used mostly for houses or condos, which makes it the most relevant to homeowners, salespeople, or investors.

The unit of comparison in the market data approach for a house would be the "entire property."

C. DISADVANTAGES OF THE MARKET DATA METHOD

This method requires many recent comparable sales of similar properties and is **least reliable when there are rapid economic changes.**

VI. Cost Approach (Replacement Cost Method)

COST APPROACH - *the process of calculating the cost of the land and buildings (as if they were new today) and then subtracting the accrued depreciation to arrive at the current value of the property.*

To use the cost approach, the appraiser must be able to determine the new construction cost of replacing the building today, using current construction methods. Depreciation is estimated by the appraiser and is then subtracted from the estimated cost of the new building. The value of the lot and depreciated building is then added to find the market value. The cost approach is most useful when appraising 1) new buildings and 2) special purpose or unique structures. Estimating depreciation is critical in this approach. As a building gets older, the depreciation becomes more difficult to estimate, eventually making the cost approach impractical. Since newer structures have little depreciation, the cost approach is the most suitable.

Value of the land plus (+) new cost of buildings today minus (-) depreciation equals (=) current market value of the property.

A. COSTS ARE BOTH DIRECT AND INDIRECT

Any method used for estimating cost requires the calculation of direct (hard) or indirect (soft) costs.

DIRECT COSTS - *expenditures for labor and materials used in the construction of the improvement(s).* A contractor's overhead and profit are generally treated as direct costs.

INDIRECT COSTS - *are expenditures other than material and labor costs.*

B. STEPS IN THE COST APPROACH

1. Step 1: Appraise the Land (Lot) Separately

Estimate the value of the land. The cost approach requires the appraiser to identify land values separately by the use of the market data approach.

2. Step 2: Estimate Replacement Cost

Estimate the replacement cost of the building as if it were new.

"Replacement cost" is the present cost to build a building having the same amount of utility.

REPLACEMENT COST - *the cost of building a similar (having equivalent utility) new structure today using modern construction methods.*

REPRODUCTION *or* **REPLICATION COST** - *the cost of reproducing a structure (usually destroyed) at current prices using similar (older) style, materials, and methods used in the original structure.*

a. Three Replacement Methods

COMPARATIVE-UNIT METHOD - *used to derive a cost estimate in terms of dollars per square foot or per cubic foot, based on known costs of similar structures and adjusted for time and physical differences.* The comparative-unit method represents a relatively uncomplicated, practical approach to a cost estimate and is widely used.

Although there are several ways to determine replacement cost, the simplest way is to measure the outside of the building to determine **SQUARE FOOTAGE**. After you determine the square footage, multiply it by the current cost of construction, per square foot, to get the value (as if it was new) of the building. To determine **square feet**, use the formula: **LENGTH x WIDTH**.

The cubic foot method is used to appraise warehouses because pallets can be stacked up high.

To determine **cubic feet**, use the formula: **LENGTH x WIDTH x HEIGHT**.

UNIT-IN-PLACE METHOD - *employs unit costs for the various building components such as foundations, floors, walls, windows, and roofs as installed and uses square foot, linear foot, or other appropriate units of measurement to estimate each component part.* These estimates include labor and overhead. To use this method, the appraiser must have specialized construction knowledge.

QUANTITY SURVEY METHOD - *involves detailed estimates of the quantities of raw materials used, such as brick, lumber, cement, the price of such materials, and the labor costs.* It is the most comprehensive and accurate method of cost estimating, but too complicated to fully explain here.

3. *Step 3: Estimate and Deduct Depreciation*

DEPRECIATION - *a reduction in the value of a property due to any cause.* The difference between replacement cost of a property and its market value is depreciation.

Depreciation is a loss in value from any cause. Depreciation is either curable (profitable to repair) or incurable (unprofitable to repair).

ACCRUED DEPRECIATION (Has Occurred) - *the loss in value of improvements from any cause at the date of the appraisal.*

STRAIGHT-LINE METHOD (Age Life) - *assumes the value declines in equal amounts of depreciation each year, until it reaches zero.* When using the age life method, an appraiser will use an age other than the actual age of the building. This is known as the effective age.

EFFECTIVE AGE - *determined by the condition of the building rather than the age. If a building has been maintained, its effective age may be less than the actual age; if there has been inadequate maintenance, it may be greater.*

ECONOMIC LIFE - *the estimated number of years of anticipated usefulness of the improvements.*

The economic life of an improvement is usually "shorter" than its estimated physical life.

ACCRUAL FOR DEPRECIATION - *the concept of estimating the amount of depreciation there will be in the future.* The three types of depreciation are: 1) physical, 2) functional, and 3) economic.

a. Physical Deterioration (Curable or Incurable)

PHYSICAL DETERIORATION - *the loss in value due to wear and tear.* As a building gets older, its age will start to show visibly.

CURABLE DEPRECIATION - *repairs that add more to a building's value than they cost.*

INCURABLE DEPRECIATION - *refers to repairs that would be so expensive they are not economically feasible.*

Examples of physical deterioration (curable or incurable) are:

1. All forms of wear and tear.
2. Damage from dryrot and termites.
3. Negligent care (deferred maintenance).
4. Depreciation that has already occurred.

Obsolescence is NOT wear or tear or a method of calculating depreciation, but is a term meaning a "major cause" of depreciation.

b. Functional Obsolescence (Curable or Incurable)

FUNCTIONAL OBSOLESCENCE - *the loss in value due to outmoded style or non-usable space.*

Types of functional obsolescence (curable or incurable) are:

1. Out-dated kitchen.
2. Antique fixtures.
3. Four bedroom, one bath home.
4. One-car garage.
5. Massive cornices.

The cost approach would be the least useful for appraising older structures with many functional deficiencies.

c. Economic Obsolescence

ECONOMIC OBSOLESCENCE (Social Obsolescence) - *the loss in value due to factors that are external to the property itself and not within the control of the owner.* It is always incurable.

Types of economic obsolescence (incurable) are:

1. Over supply of similar or competitive units.
2. Beyond the confines of the property.
3. Aircraft noise.
4. Adverse zoning and legislative acts.
5. Economic recession.
6. Departure of major industries from the area.
7. Rental increases (tenants in area are prospering).

An example of "economic obsolescence" is seen when a city increases the amount of land needed for a front yard set back.

4. Step 4: Value of the Property

The last step in the cost approach is to add the depreciated value of any improvements to the value of the land. This figure is the market value of the property using the cost approach.

C. ADVANTAGES OF THE COST APPROACH

The main advantages of the cost approach is that it can be used on: 1) newly constructed buildings, 2) unique structures, and 3) public buildings.

"Cost equals value" when improvements are new and are the highest and best use.

D. DISADVANTAGES OF THE COST APPROACH

The cost approach is limited (least reliable) for an older property. Older properties are harder to appraise because depreciation is difficult to estimate.

VII. Capitalization Approach (Income Approach)

INCOME APPROACH - *the process of changing the net income projection from a property into its market value.* Another word for this process is "capitalization."

The actual process of capitalization is simple. Divide a capitalization rate into the net income; the answer you obtain is the value of the property.

$$\frac{\text{NET INCOME}}{\text{CAPITALIZATION RATE}} = \text{VALUE OF PROPERTY}$$

Determining the appropriate capitalization rate is the most difficult step in the capitalization approach.

Rent producing (income) properties such as apartments, offices, warehouses, and manufacturing concerns should be appraised by the income approach.

The basis for the income approach is to determine the quality, quantity, and durability of the property's net income (future income).

A. STEPS IN THE INCOME APPROACH

There are five basic steps to establish value using the income approach:

Rental income schedules for various units are best established by the market approach.

1. Step 1: Calculate the Annual Effective Gross Income

EFFECTIVE GROSS INCOME - the gross income **minus any vacancies or rental losses**.

ANNUAL GROSS RENTAL INCOME - will be the annual rent that a owner receives if he or she charges the going rental rates with no vacancies.

VACANCY FACTOR - the loss in rents due to any cause. This is commonly expressed as a percentage.

Subtract deductions from the gross rental income for vacancies or any rental losses to arrive at the "effective gross income."

2. Step 2: Complete an Operating Expense Statement

The seven basic operating expense categories for this type of statement are listed below:

a. Property taxes
b. Insurance and licenses
c. Manager fees
d. Utilities
e. Maintenance and repairs
f. Services (i.e., gardener)
g. Replacement reserves

Management fees and replacement reserves must always be included in the basic operating expenses.

Never, never deduct "mortgage payments of principal or interest" from the operating expense statement. They are part of an investor's analysis, NOT an appraisal.

REPLACEMENT RESERVE - consists of funds set aside for the purpose of replacing items in the future.

VARIABLE COSTS - are operating expenses that can vary (utilities and repairs).

FIXED COSTS - remain constant; such as property taxes and fire insurance.

3. Step 3: Deduct the Related Operating Expenses

To determine net income, simply deduct the related operating expenses (Step 2) from the annual effective gross income (Step 1).

4. Step 4: Divide Net Income by the Appropriate Capitalization Rate

Rule: Always convert a monthly or quarterly net income into an annual net income before dividing by the capitalization rate. The capitalization rate is composed of a return to the investor "on" (depreciation) his or her original investment and "of" the amount to replace the building later.

The capitalization rate is the percentage rate that an investor expects to earn "on" a real estate investment.

The capitalization rate represents the integration of the 1) rate on income, expressed as interest, and the 2) rate of recapture, expressed as depreciation.

The higher the cap rate, the lower the value; the lower the cap rate, the higher the value.

5. Step 5: Result of Dividing Net Income by Capitalization Rate

This is the easiest and final step in the income approach. It is simply the result of dividing net income by the capitalization rate.

Net Income divided by Capitalization Rate = Market Value.

The appraised value increases when the capitalization rate is decreased.

B. GROSS INCOME MULTIPLIER (Rule of Thumb)

GROSS INCOME MULTIPLIER (GIM) *- a multiplication rule of thumb used to convert the rental value into market value.* If we use a gross income multiplier of 15 times the yearly rent of $12,000, the property is worth approximately $180,000 (15 x $12,000).

A quick way to convert gross income into the approximate value is to use the gross income multiplier. To determine an appropriate gross multiplier, divide the selling price of a similar property by its yearly income.

GROSS RENT *- is the money received from a property before any expenses are deducted.* To use an annual **gross rent multiplier**, simply determine the total annual rents and multiply this times the annual gross rent multiplier. Remember: this is an approximation device and should be used only as a quick estimate—not in place of an actual appraisal.

The "gross rent multiplier" is based on monthly rent and is used for residential properties. The "gross income multiplier" is based on annual rents and is used for commercial properties.

C. ADVANTAGE OF THE INCOME APPROACH

The advantage of the income approach method is that no other method focuses solely on determining the present value of the future income stream from the subject property. "If the

purpose of the property is to generate income; use the income approach." The **"present worth of future benefits"** is what the income approach is all about. It is most often used for multi-family residential income property but could be used on any type of property that generates income.

D. DISADVANTAGE OF THE INCOME APPROACH

The disadvantage of the income approach is that it may be difficult to determine the proper capitalization rate.

VIII. Correlation of Value (Bracketing)

The last and most important part of the appraisal process is the correlation (sometimes referred to as reconciliation) of the three approaches to value.

CORRELATION - *the process of selecting the most appropriate approach for the particular appraisal job and giving it the most consideration in pinpointing the final value.* Although all three methods are used in appraisal, one is usually most appropriate for a specific appraisal problem.

In general, the "market comparison approach" is best for single-family homes or lots; the "cost approach" is best for new, unique, or unusual structures; and the "income approach" is best for properties that can be used to generate income.

IX. Final Estimate of Value (Appraisal Report)

APPRAISAL REPORT - *the documentation of the appraiser's findings.* It can be a prepared fill-in form.

There are two main types of written appraisal reports:

1. Short form (a form with checks and explanations)
2. Narrative report (most complete and extensive)

A narrative report is thought of as the most comprehensive and complete appraisal report.

A. COST OF AN APPRAISAL

Appraisal costs can vary from relatively small amounts to thousands of dollars. The cost of an appraisal may be affected by its purpose, the qualifications of the appraiser, and how detailed the appraisal. The appraisal fee and an outline of what is to be accomplished in the appraisal should be set in advance. It is unethical to set an appraisal fee as a percentage of the determined value.

A lender must provide a notice to a loan applicant stating that the applicant is entitled to a copy of the appraisal report if the applicant requests and pays for the report.

X. Fee Appraisers

All appraisers are required to be licensed or certified for all federally related loan transactions.

All state licensed and certified appraisers are required to follow the Uniform Standards of Professional Appraisal Practice (USPAP).

While the Standards permit an appraiser to appraise a property in which he or she has an interest as long as that fact is disclosed to the lender/client in writing, it would be unusual for it to be accepted by any lender/client.

FEE APPRAISER - *an independent, self-employed appraiser; he or she appraises for a fee or charge*. In California a license or certification is required to appraise real estate as a profession.

Appraisers and real estate agents are concerned with the marketability of real property.

Section 4
Financing

DRE Testing Emphasis:
Salesperson 17%
Broker 16%

I. Leverage

LEVERAGE - *the practice of purchasing real estate using a small amount of your own money and a larger proportion of borrowed funds.* The more money borrowed to buy a property, the greater the leverage.

To utilize the "principle of leverage," an investor would use the maximum amount of borrowed money.

A. HYPOTHECATION

HYPOTHECATE - *to pledge a thing as security for a loan without the necessity of giving up possession.*

Although one can hypothecate, or "put up," stocks as security for a bank loan, most real property buyers hypothecate their property as security for a real estate loan. In neither case does the person surrender the use or possession of the property.

II. The Promissory Note

PROMISSORY NOTE - *the basic instrument used to evidence the obligation or debt.* It is an unconditional promise, in writing, by one person to another, promising to pay on demand, or over a fixed determinable time, a certain sum of money.

Borrowers hypothecate real property as security for payment of the promissory note. The trust deed or mortgage is used with the promissory note to hypothecate the property as security for the note.

PRINCIPAL - *the dollar amount of the loan. Commonly we call it the amount of money remaining to be paid off on a promissory note (the loan balance).*

INTEREST - *the rent charged for the use of money.*

Interest on most real estate loans is "simple interest." Simple interest is interest paid only on the principal amount owed.

A. STRAIGHT NOTE (Interest Only)

STRAIGHT NOTE - *a promissory note in which a borrower repays the principal in one lump sum, at maturity, while interest is paid in installments or at maturity.*

B. INSTALLMENT NOTE WITH BALLOON PAYMENT

INSTALLMENT NOTE WITH BALLOON PAYMENT (Partially Amortized Note) - *a promissory note with periodic payments of principal and interest and a large payment at the end (maturity date or due date).*

C. FULLY AMORTIZED INSTALLMENT NOTE

FULLY AMORTIZED INSTALLMENT NOTE - *a promissory note where both the principal and interest are paid in equal installments until the debt is paid in full.*

EQUAL MONTHLY PAYMENTS - *the monthly payment amount, including principal and interest, is constant, but as the loan is paid off, the amount of the payment attributed to interest decreases and the amount attributed to principal increases.*

III. Negotiable Instruments

Negotiable instruments are easily transferable from one person to another. Promissory notes are negotiable. The most common example is a personal check.

NEGOTIABLE INSTRUMENT - *any financial document (promissory note, check, or other) that can be passed easily from one person to another, if it meets certain legal requirements.*

HOLDER IN DUE COURSE - *one who has taken a negotiable instrument from another, in good faith, without knowledge of defect.*

IV. Important Clauses in Financial Instruments

ACCELERATION CLAUSE - *upon the occurrence of a specific event, the lender has the right to demand immediate payment of the entire note.* The main purpose of an acceleration clause is to make the entire balance of the loan due and payable at once.

ALIENATION CLAUSE - *a form of the acceleration clause stating that the entire loan becomes due and payable when the property is sold, assigned, transferred, or otherwise alienated.*

LATE PAYMENT - *a payment, unless otherwise stated, more than ten days past due.*

In order to assume an existing loan, the promissory note CANNOT include an alienation clause.

ASSUMPTION - *When a buyer assumes a loan on a property that is already encumbered, and he or she accepts responsibility with the lender's consent, for the full payment of the loan.* The name on the loan is changed to that of the buyer.

A seller is protected from liability for payments on an existing loan when the buyer "assumes" the trust deed (and note liability).

SUBORDINATION CLAUSE - *part of a trust deed or mortgage that allows for a future change in the priority of financial liens.*

A subordination clause gives the borrower (buyer) the ability to obtain additional loans on the property that have a higher priority.

PREPAYMENT PENALTY - *a charge to the borrower for paying off all or part of a loan balance before the due date.*

Most financial institutions use a prepayment penalty clause on fixed rate loans, but they are rarely employed with the adjustable rate loans.

A prepayment penalty is only enforceable during the first five years of a (1-to-4 unit) home loan.

IMPOUND ACCOUNTS (RESERVES) - *are moneys collected in advance from borrowers to assure the payment of recurring costs, such as property taxes and fire insurance.*

ASSIGNMENT OF RENTS CLAUSE - *allows a lender, upon default of the borrower, to collect rents and apply them to delinquent payments.*

V. Interest and Types of Loans

A. INTEREST (Simple Interest)

INTEREST - *the charge for borrowing money.* In real estate we use simple interest. Interest can be thought of as a rental charge for the use of money.

NOMINAL INTEREST RATE - *the rate stated in the note.*

EFFECTIVE INTEREST RATE - *the rate the lender receives (including interest, points, and loan fees).*

The formula for calculating interest is: I = P x R x T (Interest = Principal x Rate x Time)

B. FIXED INTEREST RATES (Fixed Rate)

FIXED INTEREST RATE LOAN - *a loan where the payments are the same each month for the life of the loan.* The equal monthly payment includes both the principal and the interest. A loan with this kind of fixed rate of interest is said to be a "fully amortized fixed-rate loan."

C. AMORTIZATION PAYMENTS

AMORTIZATION - *the repaying of a loan (principal and interest), in regular payments, over the term of the loan.* This repayment is usually in monthly payments but can be paid quarterly or semi-annually.

NEGATIVE AMORTIZATION - *when the interest rate charges are higher than the monthly payment.* Negative amortization means that the loan payment does not cover the interest charges, and the amount of unpaid interest is added to the unpaid loan balance.

Lenders determine monthly payments by using amortization tables.

D. ADJUSTED RATE MORTGAGES (ARMs)

ADJUSTED RATE MORTGAGE "ARM" (or Trust Deed) - *a loan in which the interest rate fluctuates periodically, based on a specific index, which makes the payment amount also change.* An ARM allows the interest rate to fluctuate (go up or down) depending on money market conditions.

INDEX - *is the starting interest rate used as the indicator from which changes can be calculated.*

ADJUSTABLE INTERVAL - *the frequency with which interest rates are reset. This period can be monthly, quarterly, every six months, or even once a year.*

CAP - *a percentage rate ceiling or restriction on the 1) periodic (adjustable interval); and 2) lifetime change in interest rates or payments.*

MARGIN - *the spread between the index rate and the initial contract rate from which the lender will make a profit and cover its costs.*

E. SOME SPECIAL PURPOSE TYPES OF LOANS

GRADUATED PAYMENT MORTGAGE (Trust Deed) - *a type of fixed interest rate loan in which the monthly payments start out lower and then gradually increase (for example, after five years it levels off for the remainder of the loan payment).*

BIWEEKLY MORTGAGE (Trust Deed) - *a fixed interest rate loan in which the payments are made every two weeks, but each payment is one-half the amount of a regular monthly payment.*

15-YEAR FIXED AND ADJUSTABLE RATE LOANS - *gaining in popularity because, for a slight increase in the monthly payment, the loan can be paid off in only 15 years.*

REVERSE ANNUITY LOANS - *loans where the lender pays the borrower a fixed monthly payment based on the value of the property.* The loan is not repaid until the last owner dies, at which time it is paid back through probate.

BLANKET ENCUMBRANCE - *one loan using two or more pieces of real property as security.*

VI. Points, Loan Fees, and Usury

POINT - *a fee (origination fee) of 1% of the amount borrowed, charged by the lender.* Most financial institutions charge the borrower points when he or she obtains a new loan.

Points and percentage are the same thing; in other words, 2 points is 2%, 3 points is 3%.

> *A point is one percent of the loan amount. Five points on a $300,000 loan is $15,000. It is also called an "origination fee."*

LOAN FEE - *the fee charged by the lender in order to apply for a loan.*

USURY - *charging more than the legally allowed percentage of interest on private loans.*

VII. Security Devices (Financial Instruments)

SECURITY DEVICES (Financial Instruments) - *written documents that pledge real property as security for a promissory note.*

> *The three financial instruments (security devices to collateralize real property) used in California are: mortgages, trust deeds, and land contracts.*

A. MORTGAGES

MORTGAGE CONTRACT - *a financial instrument, in the form of a lien, that secures a property for payment of a promissory note.*

If the mortgagor defaults in his or her payments, a foreclosure action may be started. After the foreclosure sale, the borrower has one year to redeem (buy back) the property, pay all the accumulated charges, or pay the mortgagee rent.

MORTGAGOR - *the buyer/owner who is borrowing.*

MORTGAGEE - *the lender.*

1. Power of Sale Clause

POWER OF SALE CLAUSE - *allows the mortgagee to sell the property without a court proceeding (much like a trustee's sale) if the mortgagor is in default.* If there is no power of sale clause, court (judicial) action is required for a foreclosure.

2. Remedy for Default

In a mortgage, the only remedy of the mortgagee (lender) is judicial (court) foreclosure, unless the mortgage contains a power of sale clause. Although the actual mortgage foreclosure takes a short period of time, the redemption period is very long (1 year). In a deed of trust, the entire process, including any redemption or sale, requires a short period of time (4 months).

REDEMPTION PERIOD - *the legally acceptable time period for buying back one's property after a judicial sale (one year).*

During the one-year redemption period, the right of possession remains with the mortgagor (borrower).

B. TRUST DEEDS

Trust deeds are personal property. A trust deed needs a note for security, but a note does not need a trust deed. A trust deed is not a negotiable instrument; the note is negotiable. If the conditions of a note and the trust deed are in conflict, the note prevails.

TRUST DEED *- security device that makes the real property collateral for the promissory note.* In California the trust deed, sometimes called a deed of trust, is the usual financing instrument.

1. Parties to a Trust Deed

A trust deed must have three parties: **trustor**, **trustee**, and **beneficiary**. The trust deed and note form the lien, which conveys the "bare naked title" of the property to the trustee.

TRUSTOR *- the party that is borrowing the money.* This is usually the buyer, but may also be the owner if the property is being refinanced.

The trustor signs the promissory note and trust deed, as he or she owes the debt.

BENEFICIARY *- the lender who is lending money for the purchase of real property.* The beneficiary holds the trust note and the trust deed.

TRUSTEE *- the third, disinterested party that holds **bare naked title** to the property, but only in so far as the trustee may have to sell the property for the beneficiary, should the trustor default.* This is normally a title insurance company.

EQUITABLE TITLE *- held by a trustor while he or she is repaying a trust deed and note.* It is true ownership in that the trustor may enjoy all customary rights of title and possession.

LEGAL TITLE (Bare Naked Legal Title) *- held by a trustee until the terms of a trust deed and note have been fulfilled.*

In a trust deed, the "power of sale clause" is given from the trustor to the trustee.

FULL RECONVEYANCE *- provides proof that a promissory note and the accompanying trust deed have been paid in full.* A full reconveyance must be recorded on the county records to give public notice that it has been paid.

VIII. Default and Foreclosure of a Trust Deed

A. DEFAULT OF A TRUST DEED

The lender has the legal right to receive the trust deed payment on time. By law the lender can start default action after the 10- to 15-day grace period.

GRACE PERIOD *- a set number of days in which a lender will allow a payment to be late without any penalty.*

If a note and deed of trust is "silent" on the grace period, the law states it must be more than 10 days.

When the trustee is notified by the lender (beneficiary) of the trustor's nonpayment, the trustee records a "notice of default." Within 10 days after the recording, the borrower (trustor) and all people who have filed a "request for notice," such as junior lienholders, will receive (by certified or registered mail) notification from the trustee of the default. In addition, the notice of default must be published in a newspaper of general circulation once a week for three weeks.

B. TRUSTOR'S RIGHT OF REINSTATEMENT

During the three-month reinstatement period after the notice of default is filed, the trustor may reinstate the loan.

REINSTATEMENT PERIOD *- the time within which the trustor may pay all past due payments.*

1. Reinstatement Period (Three Months)

If the trustor does not pay the past due payments, taxes, interest, and other charges within the three-month reinstatement period, the reinstatement rights are lost. This reinstatement period runs until five days before the date of sale.

2. Notice of Sale (21 Days)

NOTICE OF SALE *- a recorded notice by the trustee stating the time, place, property description, and type of sale.*

The notice must be published in a newspaper of general circulation once a week, not more than seven days apart, during the 21-day publishing period. A copy of the notice must also be posted on the property and in a public place, such as the city hall. Most title insurance companies also post a copy if they are acting as trustee.

3. The Trustee's Sale (Foreclosure Sale)

A trustee's sale is only for the real property backing up the trust deed.

The trustee's sale is held **out of court** at the time and place stated in the notice of sale. All bids must be in the form of cash or cashier's checks. The first deed holder may bid up to the total amount of the debt without cash. Any money more than the amount owed is reimbursed to the trustor. The new owner is entitled to immediate possession.

4. Judicial Court Foreclosure for a Trust Deed (Rare)

In rare cases, a beneficiary (lender) in California may want to foreclose by court action instead of the simpler trustee's sale. The reason would be to obtain a deficiency judgment if it was not a purchase money trust deed.

5. Deed in Lieu of Foreclosure

DEED IN LIEU OF FORECLOSURE *- is a deed given by an owner (borrower) to a lender to prevent the lender from bringing foreclosure proceedings.* It is up to the lender to accept or reject such an offer.

C. LIENS NOT ELIMINATED BY FORECLOSURE SALE

Most junior liens are eliminated by a foreclosure sale. The following liens are not eliminated:

1. Federal tax liens;
2. State, county, and city taxes or assessments; and
3. Mechanic's liens for work begun before the trust deed was recorded.

D. PURCHASE MONEY TRUST DEED OR MORTGAGE

PURCHASE MONEY INSTRUMENT - *a trust deed or mortgage obtained during the purchase of a home (1-to-4-units, owner-occupied).* It is called a purchase money instrument only when it is obtained at the time of purchase, not on a refinanced loan.

DEFICIENCY JUDGMENT - *the deficient difference between the money that a property brings at a court foreclosure sale and the amount owed on the property.* This does not apply to a purchase money loan.

IX. Second Trust Deeds (Junior TDs)

When a buyer does not have enough cash to cover the gap between the sales price and the loan amount, another loan, or "second" trust deed, is sometimes obtained (often from the seller).

A. JUNIOR LIENS

JUNIOR LIEN - *any loan on real property obtained after the first trust deed and secured by a second, third, or subsequent trust deed.* The most senior lien, on the other hand, is the first trust deed.

When a buyer wants to make a smaller cash down payment, or an owner wants to convert equity into cash, the best source for a junior loan is a private lender.

B. HOMEOWNER EQUITY LOANS

EQUITY - *the fair market value of a property, minus the amount of money owed to lenders and all other lienholders.*

HOMEOWNER EQUITY LOANS - *loans based on the homeowner's increase in equity caused by inflation, rising property values, or the reduction by payments of the existing loan balance.*

Second trust deed notes have a stated interest rate, so they are sold at a discount (reduction in value).

C. HOLDER OF A SECOND TRUST DEED (Lender)

The holder of a second trust deed or any junior trust deed has the same rights as does the holder of the first deed of trust. He or she is entitled to his or her payment each month, as is the first trust deed holder. If the trustor defaults on the second, the second trust deed holder, just like the first trust deed holder, can start default action.

D. REQUEST FOR NOTICE

REQUEST FOR NOTICE - *a recorded document notifying junior lienholders that a "notice of default" is recorded on a particular property.*

X. Land Contract
(Conditional Installment Sales Contract)

Trust deeds, mortgages, and land contracts are all methods of financing: they are financing instruments referred to as "security devices."

LAND CONTRACT - *an instrument of finance in which the seller retains legal ownership of the property until the buyer has made the last payment.* It is usually called a land contract in California, but may also be referred to as a "contract of sale," "agreement of sale," "conditional sales contract," or an "installment sales contract."

An installment sales contract (land contract) can be for both real and personal property. Mortgages and trust deeds are only for real property.

VENDOR - *an owner selling under a land contract.*

VENDEE - *a buyer using a land contract.*

With a conditional sales contract, the seller (vendor) gives the buyer (vendee) "equitable title" and possession but keeps "legal title." The vendor is the lender and the vendee is the borrower.

A vendor can sell his or her store (real property) and store fixtures (personal property), by use of a land contract, to a vendee. A land contract is a common way to sell a business.

If a buyer (vendee) defaults on a recorded land contract, the seller (vendor) should file a "quiet title action" to remove the "cloud on title."

XI. Truth in Lending Act
(Regulation "Z" and Other Acts)

The purpose of the Federal Truth in Lending Act is for the lender to disclose the cost of credit terms to the borrower.

This disclosure must be presented to the borrower within three business days of receiving the borrower's loan application.

"Regulation Z" applies to dwellings with only one-to-four residential units. Agricultural loans are exempt from the truth in lending law, as are business and commercial loans.

A. TRUTH IN LENDING

The Truth in Lending Act, known as Regulation Z, was enacted to protect the consumer by requiring that the lender (creditor) tell the borrower how much he or she is paying for credit.

Regulation Z also states that the lender (creditor) must express all related financing costs as a percentage, known as the annual percentage rate (APR).

Regulation Z requires a creditor to make the following important financial disclosures:

1. *Annual Percentage Rate (APR*)*
2. *Finance charges*
3. *Amount financed**
4. *Total number of payments*
5. *Total sales price (credit sales)*

*The two most important items according to Regulation Z are the APR and the amount financed.

1. Annual Percentage Rate (APR)

APR is the "cost of credit" expressed in percentage terms: It is a percentage rate, NOT an interest rate. If the APR appears in an advertisement, NO other disclosure of terms need be stated because it includes all credit costs.

ANNUAL PERCENTAGE RATE (APR) - *represents the relationship between the total of the finance charges (interest rate, points, and the loan fee) and the total amount financed, expressed as a percentage.* It must be computed to the nearest one-quarter of one percent and must be printed on the loan form more conspicuously than the rest of the printed material.

The APR includes all "finance charges," including assumption charges, but it does NOT include 1) cost of a credit report and 2) appraisal fees, which are exempt.

2. Advertising Terms May Require Additional Disclosures

Anyone placing an advertisement for consumer credit must comply with the advertising requirements of the Truth in Lending Act. If any credit terms are mentioned, the advertising must disclose the specifics of all credit terms. Disclosures must be made "clearly and conspicuously." If only the annual percentage (APR) rate is disclosed, additional disclosures are not required.

B. RIGHT TO CANCEL (Federal Notice of Right to Cancel)

Loans subsequent (future loans) have a 3-day right of rescission by the borrower.

A first trust deed loan to finance the purchase of the borrower's home carries no right of rescission.

RIGHT TO CANCEL - *the federal law that gives a borrower the right to rescind (cancel) any loan transaction only if it is a business loan or a second trust deed, secured by the borrower's home.* The borrower has until midnight of the third business day following the signing to cancel.

The borrower has the right to rescind when a loan is secured by a second trust deed on an owner-occupied single family residence already owned by the borrower.

C. EQUAL CREDIT OPPORTUNITY ACT

EQUAL CREDIT OPPORTUNITY ACT - *a federal law prohibiting those who lend money from discriminating against borrowers based on their race, sex, color, religion, national origin, age, or marital status.*

XII. Our Ever Changing Economy (Economic Cycles)

Inflation (when prices appreciate) protects both the lender and trustor. There is more equity protecting the lender if there is a default. General level of prices: When prices decrease, the value of money increases and when prices increase, the value of money decreases.

INFLATION - *the result of too much money chasing too few goods.*

Equity interests are an excellent way for an investor to hedge against inflation.

DEFLATION - *when prices of real estate, goods, and services go down.*

BUYER'S MARKET - *when the prices of real estate are down, terms are easy and there is usually a great deal of real estate listed for sale or rent.*

In a seller's market, prices rise due to a shortage of properties available.

SELLER'S MARKET - *the prices of real estate are up and there is less real estate listed for sale or rent.* This is due to increased demand and lagging supplies.

Changes in consumerism, land use, and the real estate industry all affect real estate in future years.

A. THE FEDERAL RESERVE BANKING SYSTEM ("FED")

FEDERAL RESERVE BANKING SYSTEM (The "Fed") - *the nation's central banking authority.*

FEDERAL RESERVE BOARD - *a committee, appointed by the President but politically independent, that regulates the amount and flow of loan money available to banks.*

The board has indirect, but far reaching influence, over all lending institutions and the economy as a whole. The Federal Reserve's monetary policies influence the supply of money by:

1. buying and selling government T-bonds and T-securities,
2. raising and lowering the reserve requirement,
3. raising and lowering the discount rate to member banks, and
4. establishing or setting margin requirements (percentage loaned on stocks and bonds).

B. GROSS DOMESTIC PRODUCT

GROSS DOMESTIC PRODUCT (GDP) - *the total value of all goods and services produced by an economy during a specific period of time.* It serves as a kind of monetary barometer that shows us the rate and areas of greatest growth.

C. CHANGING INTEREST RATES (Affect Real Estate)

REFINANCING - *the process of obtaining a new loan to pay off the old loan.*

XIII. Shopping for a Loan

For the average person, borrowing the money necessary to buy a house is the largest financial obligation he or she is likely to assume in his or her lifetime. Shopping around for a loan from several different loan sources is an excellent idea.

The three areas of demand for borrowing money are: construction funds, financing a purchase, and refinancing.

A. LOAN TO VALUE (Percent of Appraised Value Lender Will Loan)

LOAN TO VALUE - *the percentage of appraised value the lender will loan the borrower to purchase the property.* It is abbreviated as "L-T-V" or "L to V." The lower the L to V, the higher the down payment has to be. The lower the L to V, the more equity is required.

Most lenders commonly request an 80 percent L-T-V ratio, but this varies depending on many factors. The lower the L-T-V, the greater the down payment (more equity funds are required).

B. ESTIMATE OF SETTLEMENT COSTS (RESPA)

The primary purpose of RESPA is to require lenders to make special disclosures, without cost to the borrower, for loans involving the sale or transfer of 1-4 residential dwellings.

The lender must give the applicant the HUD booklet that explains closing costs and has until three business days after receipt of a loan application to provide a good faith estimate of the actual settlement costs to the borrower.

C. THE LOAN APPLICATION

The lender needs a loan application from the borrower so that the borrower's financial condition can be analyzed.

D. EQUITY (Market Value Less Debt)

EQUITY - *your worth; it is the amount that is left after subtracting all that you owe (debt) from what you own (assets).*

The equity (worth) you have in a home is its market value minus what you owe on it.

E. LIQUIDITY (Convert Assets into Cash)

LIQUIDITY - *the ability of a borrower to quickly convert assets into cash.*

BASICS

F. OPPORTUNITY COST (Cost of Non-Liquidity)

OPPORTUNITY COST - *lost profit that a person could have made if he or she had the cash available to invest now.* It is the cost of non-liquidity. If you own a home, the lost return on that equity is referred to as opportunity cost.

XIV. Institutional Lenders

INSTITUTIONAL LENDERS - *very large corporations that lend the money of their depositors to finance real estate transactions.*

Institutional lenders are big lenders who pool funds so they can lend to individual borrowers. They include: insurance companies, savings banks, banks, and mutual saving banks.

A. FEDERAL DEPOSIT INSURANCE CORPORATION (FDIC)

FEDERAL DEPOSIT INSURANCE CORPORATION (FDIC) - *a government corporation that, for a fee, insures each account of a depositor up to $100,000.*

B. SAVINGS BANKS (Greatest Source of Money for Home Loans)

Savings banks make more real estate loans than any other financial institution. They primarily make loans on single family homes or condos that are owner-occupied. They will also make loans on apartment buildings and manufactured homes.

Savings banks have the highest percentage of funds invested in real estate loans.

C. BANKS

Banks are general purpose lenders, which means they lend money for anything from real estate to sailboats. All national banks are required to be members of the Federal Reserve System, while a state bank may be a member by choice. Any commercial bank may lend money on real property if it is a first loan on that property. In general, there are four types of real estate financing:

1. **First Trust Deed Loans** - The bank finances long-term loans for existing land and the buildings.

2. **Construction Loans (or "Interim Loans")** - Money is provided for the construction of a building, to be repaid when the construction is complete.

A construction loan (or interim loan) is a short-term loan.

3. **Take-Out Loans (Replace Interim Loans)** - Money arranged by the owner, builder, or developer for the buyer. The construction loan made for the construction of the improvements is usually paid in full from the proceeds of this more permanent loan.

When computing the unspecified maturity date on a construction loan, the repayment date is computed from the date of the note.

4. **Home Improvement Loans** - This loan is for repairing and modernizing existing buildings.

D. LIFE INSURANCE COMPANIES

A primary source for a very large loan would be a life insurance company.

These companies supply most of the loan funds for properties where a great deal of capital is required (such as high-rise office buildings, shopping centers, industrial properties, and hotels).

Life insurance companies seldom make construction loans.

Life insurance companies also invest large amounts of money in trust deeds that are either insured by the FHA or guaranteed by the VA. Mortgage companies make such loans for insurance companies. Quite often these mortgage companies, in return for a servicing fee, collect the loan payments for the insurance company.

XV. Noninstitutional Lenders

Noninstitutional lenders are smaller lenders, which include: private lenders, mortgage companies, investment trusts, pension plans, and credit unions.

NONINSTITUTIONAL LENDERS - *individuals and organizations that lend on a private or individual basis.* Unlike institutional lenders, they are not governed by the Federal Reserve System.

CONVENTIONAL LOANS - *loans that are not insured or guaranteed by the U.S. government.*

A. PRIVATE INDIVIDUALS

Any real estate loan by an individual is considered a private individual loan. Most individuals who lend money on real estate are sellers who take back a second trust deed as part of the real estate transaction.

Many second loans on real estate, called junior loans (second trust deeds), are obtained from private investors.

B. CREDIT UNIONS

CREDIT UNION - *a co-operative association organized to promote thrift among its members and provide them with a source of credit.*

C. REAL ESTATE INVESTMENT TRUST (REIT)

REAL ESTATE INVESTMENT TRUST (REIT) - *a type of company that sells securities specializing in real estate ventures.* A REIT requires a minimum of 100 investors.

Real estate investment trusts are of two types: (1) equity trust and (2) mortgage trust.

EQUITY TRUST - *an investment in real estate itself or several real estate projects.*

MORTGAGE TRUST - *a company that invests in mortgages and other types of real estate loans or obligations.*

BASICS

D. PENSION PLANS

PENSION PLAN - *an investment organization that obtains funds from people before they retire and invests this money for their clients' retirement.*

E. MORTGAGE BANKERS (COMPANIES) - Secondary Mortgage Market

The secondary mortgage market is a resale market place where smaller lenders sell their loans to larger lenders.

MORTGAGE BANK - *a company whose principal business is the originating, financing, closing, selling, and servicing of loans secured by real property, for institutional lenders, on a contractual basis.*

Mortgage companies like to make loans that can be sold easily on the secondary mortgage market.

WAREHOUSING - *the action of a mortgage banker collecting loans prior to sale.*

F. PRIVATE MORTGAGE INSURANCE (PMI)

PRIVATE MORTGAGE INSURANCE - *a guarantee to lenders that the upper portion of a conventional loan will be repaid if a borrower defaults and a deficiency occurs at the foreclosure sale.*

XVI. Government-Backed Loans

FHA insurance (part of Housing and Urban Development - HUD) and VA guarantees are federal programs. They approve loans made by private lenders, but lend no actual money. The CAL-VET program makes direct loans to qualified California borrowers.

Unlike conventional lenders, the FHA does NOT make loans, but insures them.

A. FHA (A Division of HUD)

The FHA has three main programs that affect California homeowners and buyers: 1) Title I home improvement loans, 2) Title II (Section 203b) purchase and construction loans, and 3) Title III, the Federal National Mortgage Association (Fannie Mae), buys and sells loans.

1. FHA Title I: Home Improvement Loans

The FHA **insures** lending institutions against loss on loans made to finance improvements to existing structures.

2. FHA Title II: Home Purchase or Building Loans

Section 203b program - Insures home loans (1-to-4 units) for anyone who is financially qualified. An FHA loan is based on the selling price when it is lower than the appraisal.

The FHA does not lend the money; it only insures the approved lender against foreclosure loss. The FHA collects a fee for this insurance called the mortgage insurance premium.

MORTGAGE INSURANCE PREMIUM (MIP) - *the protection for the lender that insures the loss if there is a foreclosure*. It is an up-front fee (paid by the borrower) in cash, or through insurance as part of the loan.

When assisting a homebuyer in obtaining an FHA loan, a broker would most likely contact an institutional lender.

3. Federal National Mortgage Association (FNMA)

Commonly referred to as "Fannie Mae." See section titled "Secondary Mortgage (Trust Deed) Market."

B. VETERANS ADMINISTRATION

1. VA Loans (Guaranteed Loans)

The Congress of the United States has passed legislation to assist veterans in obtaining housing. A **VA LOAN** *is not a loan, but rather a guarantee to an approved institutional lender.*

2. Certificate of Reasonable Value (CRV)

CERTIFICATE OF REASONABLE VALUE - *an appraisal of the property to be purchased by the veteran.* The property is appraised by an independent fee appraiser who is appointed by the Veterans Administration.

The amount of down payment required for a VA loan is determined by the CRV.

3. VA Loan Provisions

VA loans require NO down payment, but may require the veteran to pay an origination fee of up to 3% of the loan amount. In addition, the seller may have to pay discount points.

C. CALIFORNIA DEPARTMENT OF VETERANS AFFAIRS (CAL-VET)

1. Cal-Vet (Land Contract; Direct Loans)

Land contracts (real property purchase contracts) are used, and legal title is held, by the California Department of Veterans Affairs until the loan is paid in full.

CAL-VET LOAN PROGRAM - *administered by the California Department of Veterans Affairs.*

Cal-Vet has NO points; NO one pays for points.

D. CALIFORNIA HOUSING FINANCE AGENCY (CHFA)

CALIFORNIA HOUSING FINANCE AGENCY (CHFA) - *a state agency that sells bonds so that it can provide funds for low-income family housing on project or individual home basis.* It is self-supporting and has political support across party lines.

XVII. Lending Corporations and the Secondary Market

A. SECONDARY MORTGAGE (TRUST DEED) MARKET

Lenders in the secondary mortgage market are concerned with the "liquidity and marketability" of loans.

THE SECONDARY MORTGAGE (TRUST DEED) MARKET - *provides an opportunity for financial institutions to buy from, and sell first mortgages (trust deeds) to, other financial institutions.* The secondary mortgage market enables lenders to keep an adequate supply of money for new loans.

The secondary mortgage market is the market where lenders buy and sell mortgages. The secondary mortgage market is the transfer of mortgages among mortgagees.

1. Federal National Mortgage Association (Fannie Mae)

The Federal National Mortgage Association (FNMA), which is commonly referred to as Fannie Mae, dominates the secondary mortgage market. It sells securities over the stock exchange to get money so that it can buy and sell conventional loans, besides government backed notes. The FNMA is not a demand source to borrow money.

2. Government National Mortgage Association (Ginnie Mae)

The Government National Mortgage Association (GNMA) is a government corporation referred to as Ginnie Mae. It sells secondary mortgages to the public and provides the federal government with cash. These trust deeds are grouped together in pools, and shares are sold on the stock market exchange. All shares are federally guaranteed, making this one of the safest investments available.

The FNMA was created to increase the amount of funds available to finance housing.

3. Federal Home Loan Mortgage Corporation (Freddie Mac)

The Federal Home Loan Mortgage Corporation (FHLMC), commonly known as Freddie Mac, is a government corporation that issues preferred stock to the public. It is supervised by the Federal Home Loan Bank Board. It helps savings banks maintain a stable and adequate money supply by purchasing their home loan mortgages and repackaging them for sale to investors. The savings banks use the money obtained to make new loans available for home buyers.

Conventional loans have lower "loan-to-value" ratios, which offer greater protection for the lender. Compared to FHA loans, conventional loans are riskier. The higher the risk, the higher the interest rates.

XVIII. Real Estate Broker as Mortgage Loan Broker

The broker or salesperson, as part of most real estate transactions, may help the buyer fill out a loan application for a financial institution or arrange financing for the buyer. The "Mortgage Loan Broker Law" (sections 10240-10248 of Article 7) of the Business and Professions Code requires loan brokers to give a Mortgage Loan Disclosure Statement to all borrowers before they become obligated for the loan.

Besides providing the borrower with the disclosure statement, the broker is prohibited from doing certain things, and is restricted as to the amount of commission that he or she may charge the borrower. Anyone negotiating real estate loans must be a real estate licensee. If you make collections on real estate loans and you make more than ten a year or collect more than $40,000, you must also be a licensed real estate broker.

A. MORTGAGE LOAN DISCLOSURE STATEMENT

A real estate licensee negotiating a loan for a prospective borrower must present to that person a completed loan disclosure statement. This statement must be given to the borrower prior to his or her signing the loan documents. It is usually referred to as the Mortgage Loan Disclosure Statement.

MORTGAGE LOAN DISCLOSURE STATEMENT - a form that completely and clearly states all the information and charges connected with a particular loan. It must be kept on file for four years.

B. BUSINESS AND PROFESSIONS CODE

1. Article 7 - Commissions and Other Requirements

On loans of $30,000 and over for first trust deeds, and $20,000 and over for junior deeds of trust, the broker may charge as much as the borrower will agree to pay.

Brokers negotiating trust deed loans are subject to certain limitations regarding commissions and expenses and must meet other requirements set out by the real estate commissioner. Legislation also requires that brokers provide both the borrower and the lender, on property for first trust deed loans under $30,000 and seconds under $20,000, with copies of the appraisal report. Anyone performing these services, whether soliciting borrowers or lenders in home loans secured by real property, must have a real estate license. This restriction applies even if no advance fee is paid.

Loans on owner-occupied homes negotiated by brokers for a term of six years or less may not have a balloon payment. If non-owner occupied, loans are exempt from balloon payments when the term is less than three years. Neither of these restrictions apply to transactions where the seller extends credit to the buyer. When such transactions have balloon payments, the seller is obligated to notify the buyer 60 to 150 days before the payment is due. Also, the broker is obligated to inform the buyer regarding the likelihood of obtaining new financing.

2. Article 5 - Broker Restrictions

The licensee is prohibited from pooling funds. A broker may not accept funds except for a specifically identified loan transaction.

Before accepting a lender's money, the broker must:

1. *Own the loan or have an unconditional written contract to purchase a specific note.*
2. *Have the authorization from a prospective borrower to negotiate a secured loan.*

3. Article 6 - Real Property Securities Dealer

DRE broker's license and endorsement are required, as well as a $100 fee plus a $10,000 surety bond. A DRE permit is required to sell specific security.

No real estate investment-type security shall be sold to the public without first obtaining a permit from the commissioner.

COMMISSIONER'S PERMIT - *the approval of the proposed real property security and plan of distribution.* The duration of the permit is one year, and the permit may not be used in advertising unless it is used in its entirety.

REAL PROPERTY SECURITIES DEALER (RPSD) - *any person acting as principal or agent who engages in the business of selling real property securities (such as promissory notes or sales contracts).* He or she must be a real estate broker.

Section 5
Transfer of Property

DRE Testing Emphasis:
Salesperson 10%
Broker 9%

I. Escrows in General

An escrow is the processing of the paperwork and money involved in a sale or other real estate transaction. The purpose of an escrow is to meet the terms of the contract.

ESCROW - *created when a new written agreement instructs a neutral third party to hold funds and only proceed when all the agreed to conditions have been performed.*

The Escrow Act is found in the Financial Code.

A. REQUIREMENTS FOR A VALID ESCROW

The three requirements for a valid escrow are:

1. Signed escrow instructions, forming a binding contract between two or more parties, usually a buyer and seller.
2. A neutral party, which is the escrow company, acting as a dual agent of the buyer and seller.
3. Conditional delivery of funds and documents when all the conditions in the escrow are met.

When escrow closes, dual agency (representing both parties, usually buyers and sellers, at once) changes to separate agency (handling each party's separate paperwork requirements).

B. ESCROW OFFICER

An escrow holder can be: 1) a corporation, 2) an attorney, or 3) a real estate broker, who also acts as a real estate agent in the transaction.

NEUTRAL DEPOSITORY - *an escrow business conducted by a licensed escrow holder.*

ESCROW OFFICER, HOLDER, OR AGENT - *though not licensed by the state, is an employee of a licensed escrow company that acts as the agent.*

An independent escrow corporation must be licensed by the Department of Corporations to handle escrows. Corporations that are exempt from the escrow law but can handle escrows include: banks, savings banks, and title insurance companies, because they are under the supervision of their respective authorizing agencies.

There are two other types of escrow holders. They are attorneys who perform escrow duties as a part of their practice and **brokers who handle their own escrows** (must be an agent in the transaction).

C. REAL ESTATE BROKERS CAN CONDUCT ESCROWS

A broker can handle escrows, for a fee, only if the broker is acting as a real estate agent in that transaction.

This right is personal to the broker and the broker shall not delegate any duties other than escrow duties normally performed under the direct supervision of the broker.

All written escrow instructions executed by a buyer or seller must contain a statement, in not less than 10-point type, that includes the licensee's name and the fact that he or she is licensed by the Department of Real Estate.

II. How Escrows Work

Escrow amendments must be signed by the parties to change the escrow.

A. WHO SELECTS THE ESCROW COMPANY?

Selection of an escrow company and an escrow officer are part of the negotiation between buyer and seller. Like any other item in a real estate transaction, it is part of the negotiated agreement. When the escrow company is named in the listing agreement, the real estate listing agent cannot change the escrow company without the consent of the seller or the seller's agent. It is imperative that the salesperson disclose, in writing, any interest that salesperson or his or her broker share with the selected escrow company.

A real estate licensee is prohibited by law from receiving any "kickback" for solicitation of escrow business.

B. ESCROW RULES

Once the escrow instructions have been drawn from the original contract (deposit receipt) and signed by each party, neither party may change the escrow instructions without the knowledge and consent of the other.

The escrow is complete when: 1) all conditions of the escrow have been met, 2) all conditions of the parties have been met, and 3) the parties have received an accounting of the procedure. If both parties mutually agree to change the instructions, the change can be put into effect at any time. If the parties cannot agree to terms, an escrow company will settle a dispute by bringing an **interpleader action** (court action) to determine where the money or consideration goes.

The seller CANNOT rescind an escrow without the consent of the buyer.

C. ESCROW INSTRUCTIONS

A conflict between escrow instructions and the deposit receipt contract will be controlled by the escrow instructions.

ESCROW INSTRUCTIONS - *formal instructions drawn from the information contained in the original agreement, usually the signed deposit receipt.* When these instructions are drawn and signed, they become an enforceable contract binding on all parties.

D. FINANCING IS AN IMPORTANT ASPECT OF THE ESCROW

Most escrows for the sale of a home include obtaining a new loan and the payoff or assumption of an old loan.

PAYOFF DEMAND STATEMENT - *a formal demand statement from the lender that details the amounts owed, as calculated by the lender, for the purpose of paying off the loan in full.* The failure to obtain a payoff statement in a timely manner could hold up the escrow. A payoff demand statement is different from a beneficiary's (lender's) statement.

BENEFICIARY'S (LENDER'S) STATEMENT - *a demand statement by a lender, under a deed of trust, that provides information, such as the unpaid balance, monthly payment, and interest rate, necessary if the loan is to be assumed.*

E . CLOSING IS THE DATE OF RECORDATION

Closing, in a broad sense, is the process of signing, transfer of documents, and distribution of funds. When time is NOT specified, the escrow will close by mutual consent or within a reasonable period.

CLOSING DATE - *the date that the documents are recorded.*

Escrow usually approximates the closing date, but the actual date is when all the conditions of the escrow have been completed, the buyer's remaining money (cashier's check) is received, and all the documents are recorded.

III. Proration

Property taxes, interest, fire insurance, and rents are prorated, but NOT title insurance fees and non-recurring fees.

PRORATION - *the process of proportionately dividing expenses or income to the precise date that escrow closes.* It enables the buyer and seller to pay or receive their proportionate share of expenses or income.

A. 30 DAYS IS THE BASE FOR PRORATION

All escrow companies use 30 days as a base month, which results in a 360-day year, called an escrow (or bank) year.

Property tax prorations are based on the amount of tax the seller is paying. Escrow uses the old assessed valuation when prorating.

The seller is credited for any property taxes paid in advance, and the buyer is debited.

Taxes are prorated either from July 1, which marks the beginning of the county fiscal year, or January 1, the middle of the fiscal year.

The two rules of proration: (1) date escrow closes and (2) date item is paid.

IV. Termites and Other Problems

A. STRUCTURAL PEST CONTROL CERTIFICATION REPORT (Report and Clearance)

A Structural Pest Control Report is usually a condition of the escrow.

STRUCTURAL PEST CONTROL CERTIFICATION REPORT - *a written report, given by a licensed pest control company, identifying any wood destroying pests or conditions likely to cause pest infestation.* The report states the condition and correction cost of any pest, dry rot, excessive moisture, earth-wood contacts, or fungus damage in accessible areas of a structure.

Escrow accepts and holds the pest control report and awaits further instructions from both parties. If there is infestation damage (required work), it is usually paid for by the seller. If there is only non-infestation (recommended work), the extent of repairs is up to the parties.

FHA and VA termite certificates and repairs are paid for by the seller. The seller is allowed to include a clause stating what the maximum cost of repairs will be as a condition of the sale.

California law requires that the seller must receive a copy of the pest control certificate before the close of escrow.

The best time for a seller to have a termite report issued is before putting the home on the market.

B. BROKER MAINTAINS PEST CONTROL DOCUMENTATION

The Civil Code requires that the broker shall deliver a copy of the Structural Pest Control Certification Report, and any Notice of Work Completed, to the buyer, if such a report is a condition of the deposit receipt or is a requirement imposed as a condition of financing.

V. Fire Insurance

A. FIRE INSURANCE... A MUST!

A lending institution will require coverage for the amount of its loan. However, it is in the owner's best interest to carry sufficient fire insurance to replace the structure if it is totally destroyed. It is only necessary to insure the current replacement value of the dwelling, since the land itself cannot be destroyed by fire.

CALIFORNIA STANDARD FORM FIRE INSURANCE POLICY - *insures the dwelling against (1) fire and (2) lightning.*

EXTENDED COVERAGE ENDORSEMENT - *insures against the additional perils of wind storm, explosion, hail, aircraft, smoke, riot, and vehicles not attributed to a strike or civil commotion.*

B. FIRE INSURANCE PRORATION

When purchasing property, you as a buyer may assume the existing fire insurance policy or obtain a new policy. If the old policy is canceled, the seller is charged a higher rate; it is said to be "short-rated." If the old policy is assumed, an endorsement designating you as the new owner is forwarded to you and the premium amount will be prorated in escrow.

VI. Title Insurance

A. CHAIN OF TITLE (Recorded Public History)

A title insurance company is primarily concerned with a search of the public records, which includes: the Federal Lands Office, the County Clerk's Office, the County Recorder's Office, and other sources. This search establishes what is called the "chain of title."

CHAIN OF TITLE - *recorded public history of conveyances and encumbrances affecting title as far back as records are available. This is used to determine how title came to be vested in current owner.* These public records include files at the county recorder's office, various tax agencies, federal court clerk, and the secretary of state.

Abstract of title - a written summary of a property's documents that evidence title.

TITLE PLANT - *all such information about people and their real property stored in computers.*

B. TITLE INSURANCE (Four Functions)

TITLE INSURANCE - *insures a lender (and property owner for an additional fee) against losses that result from imperfections in title.* Title insurance companies examine the records documenting chain of title, review any risks that might not be found in the public records, seek legal interpretation, help the seller correct any defects, and insure marketable title to the property. Title insurance is paid only once, unlike auto or fire insurance, which must be paid annually.

C. PRELIMINARY TITLE REPORT (Ordered First)

The first event to occur in a title search is the ordering of the preliminary title report by the escrow officer (after the buyer or borrower completes the statement of information).

PRELIMINARY TITLE REPORT - *a report showing the condition of title before a sale or loan transaction.* After completion of the transaction, a title insurance policy is issued.

A "preliminary title report" gives the current status of items (from the county records) that affect the property's title.

VII. Types of Title Insurance Policies

All title insurance policies in California cover policyholders as of the date of the policy.

A. CALIFORNIA LAND TITLE ASSOCIATION (CLTA) - (Standard Coverage Policy)

The California Land Title Association (CLTA) policy is the "standard" title insurance policy.

It may be issued to insure a lender only, or an owner only, or it may insure both the lender and the owner (a joint-protection standard coverage policy). This standard policy insures the lender only unless the owner requests and pays for owner coverage.

The CLTA policy protects against: 1) lack of capacity of a party in the chain of title, 2) deeds not properly delivered and 3) forgery.

It is very important to note those items not included in the standard CLTA policy, which are included in the ALTA policy. These items are:

1. Easements and liens that are not shown by the public record.
2. Rights or claims of persons in physical possession of the land.
3. Unrecorded claims not shown by the public record that could be ascertained by physical inspection or correct survey.
4. Mining claims, reservations in patents, water rights, and government actions, such as zoning ordinances.

Standard Title Insurance (CLTA) does NOT insure against undisclosed liens placed on a property by a grantor (although it is warranted in a grant title).

B. AMERICAN LAND TITLE ASSOCIATION (ALTA)
(Extended Coverage Policy - Survey Included)

Most lenders require more protection than provided for by the standard coverage (CLTA) policy; they require the extended coverage (ALTA) policy.

AMERICAN LAND TITLE ASSOCIATION POLICY (ALTA) - *an extended coverage policy that insures against many exclusions of the standard coverage (CLTA) policy.*

The ALTA policy (which includes a competent survey or physical inspection) is usually required by California lenders and by out-of-state lenders who are not able to make personal physical inspections of property.

An extended ALTA title insurance policy is a lender's policy. It protects only the lender. If an owner wants this kind of protection, he or she should request the extended ALTA Owner's Policy.

C. ALTA-R (One-to-Four Residential Units)

ALTA-R POLICY - *recommended by title companies for one-to-four owner-occupied residential dwellings.* It doesn't include a survey because the property lines are already established by a recorded subdivision map.

D. WHO PAYS TITLE INSURANCE FEES?

Title insurance fees are a part of the escrow closing costs. Because there is no law determining who must pay, it should be stated in the deposit receipt to prevent any misunderstanding. This, however, covers only the standard CLTA policy. The additional cost of the ALTA extended policy is usually charged to the party purchasing the property (the buyer).

E. TITLE INSURANCE DISCLOSURE

In any escrow transaction for the purchase or exchange of real property in which a title insurance policy will not be issued to the buyer (or exchanger), the buyer (or exchanger) must sign and acknowledge a disclosure statement stating that it may be advisable to obtain title insurance.

VIII. Real Estate Settlement Procedures Act (RESPA)

RESPA provides borrowers the opportunity to shop for settlement services. The law covers first loans on one-to-four-unit residential dwellings.

REAL ESTATE SETTLEMENT PROCEDURES ACT (RESPA) - *a law for the sale or transfer of one-to-four residential units requiring: 1) specific procedures, and 2) forms for settlements (closing costs) involving most home loans from financial institutions with federally insured deposits, including FHA and VA loans.*

The settlement statement must be delivered on or before the date of settlement, at NO charge. The buyer can request it one business day before closing.

There are penalties for "kickbacks" and unearned fees. The seller may request a specific title insurer, but only the buyer can require a specific insurance company.

IX. Acquisitions and Transfers

A. TRANSFERS

The seven basic ways to transfer real property are:

1. Deed
2. Will
3. Probate
4. Intestate succession (no will)
5. Accession
6. Occupancy
7. Dedication

1. Transfer by Deed

The deed is NOT the title, but is "evidence" of the title.

The most common method of acquiring title to a property is by deed transfer.

CONVEYANCE - *the document used to effect the transfer of title to property from one person to another.* This is usually accomplished by a simple written document known as a deed.

DEED - *a written instrument that conveys and evidences title.*

GRANTOR - *the person who grants property or property rights (seller).*

GRANTEE - *the person to whom the grant is made (buyer).* A grantee cannot be a fictitious person (example: Batman or Catwoman). It can be a person with a fictitious name (example: Microsoft, Inc.).

All deeds must have a "granting" type clause (action clause). The grantor is the person transferring real property. Both grant deeds and quitclaim deeds are signed only by the grantor. The deed is said to be "executed" when signed by the grantor.

There are two basic types of deeds: (1) grant deed and (2) quitclaim deed. All other deeds are versions of these two deeds.

GRANT DEED - *a document that transfers title, with the key word being "grant."*

The granting (or warranty) aspect of the deed is a promise that:

a. The owner (grantor) has not conveyed title to the property to any other person (grantee).
b. The property is free of any encumbrances (liens or other restrictions) other than those already disclosed to the grantee.
c. The grant deed also transfers any after-acquired title, meaning that rights obtained after the sale has been completed are also conveyed.

IMPLIED WARRANTIES - *are not expressed in writing, but imply that: 1) the owner has not conveyed title to another; and 2) the property is free of any encumbrances.*

Grant deeds contain "implied warranties" even if they are NOT expressed in writing.

It should be noted that the grant deed does not necessarily give one all the rights to a property. Easements, rights of way, mineral rights, building restrictions, and other types of restrictions may still restrict the use of the property.

QUITCLAIM DEED - *a deed that conveys only the present rights or interest that a person may have in a property.*

Quitclaim deeds make NO "covenants" (promises); they guarantee nothing, and only convey all rights the grantor may have.

A quitclaim deed can give absolute ownership or only such title as one may hold. If there is no ownership interest, then nothing can be acquired. Note that there are no warranties; just the clause, "I quitclaim." This deed is used primarily to clear a cloud on title from the records.

CLOUD ON TITLE - *a claim, encumbrance, or condition that impairs the title to real property until disproved or eliminated, as, for example, through a quitclaim deed or a quiet title legal action.*

If a buyer purchases a property on an installment plan and abandons that property after a few payments, then there will likely be a "cloud on the title," if the contract was recorded.

A **VALID DEED** has all the following essential elements:

    a. It must be in writing.
    b. The parties (grantee and grantor) must be properly named and have legal capacity.
    c. The property must be adequately described (need not be legal description).
    d. There must be a granting clause (action clause).
    e. It must be signed by the granting party (grantor).

A valid deed passes title when the deed is recorded (which is a form of delivery), thereby giving constructive notice.

A deed does not take effect until it is delivered and accepted. In order for title to be transferred, the grantor must sign the deed and deliver it with the intention of passing title immediately.

Some subtypes of grant or quitclaim deeds used in California are:

GIFT DEED - *Granted as a gift of love and affection. No other consideration is necessary, but is void if given to defraud creditors.*

TAX DEED - *Given if property is sold as payment of past-due property taxes.*

ADMINISTRATOR'S DEED OR EXECUTOR'S DEED - *Given to the purchaser of the deceased person's real property.*

SHERIFF'S DEED - *Granted to the purchaser at a court-ordered sale.*

TRUSTEE'S DEED - *Given to the purchaser of property at a trust deed foreclosure sale.*

GUARDIAN'S DEED - *Used by a guardian to transfer the real property of minors or incompetents.*

LAND PATENT - *Used by the government to grant public land to an individual.*

a. Delivery of a Deed

Delivery and acceptance of the deed is presumed with recording.

The following are the three basic methods of delivery:

1. **Manual Delivery** - direct transfer of the deed from the grantor to the grantee.
2. **Delivery Through Recording** - putting the title of record in the grantee's name at the county recorder's office. The grantee must have agreed to the recording.
3. **Conditional Delivery** - requires that a specific event take place before title can be passed and MUST be handled by a third disinterested party. The deed is then delivered manually.

A deed delivered "by grantor to grantee" with a condition involved is a manual delivery, NOT a conditional delivery.

2. Transfer By Will (Testate)

WILL - *a document, created by a person, stating how that person's property is to be conveyed or distributed upon his or her death.* It also leaves instructions as to the disposition of the body upon death.

DYING TESTATE - *means having made and left a valid will.*

The two types of wills that can legally dispose of real and personal property are witnessed (typed) and holographic (handwritten).

WITNESSED WILL - *a typed document usually prepared by an attorney, dated, and signed by the property owners, and declared to be a will by at least two witnesses.*

HOLOGRAPHIC WILL - *entirely handwritten by the owner, dated, and signed.* Since it is in the owner's own handwriting, no other formalities and no witnesses are required unless the will is signed with an "X," in which case it must be witnessed.

CODICIL - *a change in a will before the maker's death.*

3. Transfer by Probate (Superior Court Approval)

PROBATE - *a Superior Court procedure to determine a will's validity and any creditors' claims and to establish the identity of the beneficiaries.*

After a person dies, an **administrator (male)** or **administratrix (female)** is appointed by the court to temporarily take possession of the property until probate is finalized. If the will has appointed a particular custodian, then that person is known as an **executor (male)** or an **executrix (female)**.

A probate court must approve the sale of real property for a commission.

4. Transfer by Intestate Succession (No Will)

INTESTATE SUCCESSION - *the procedure used for transferring the deceased's property to his or her heirs if there is no will.* With intestate succession, the law provides for the disposition of the property.

Separate property: If the decedent leaves a spouse and one child, property is divided equally, 50-50. If there is a surviving spouse and two or more children, 1/3 to spouse and 2/3 to children. If NO surviving spouse, property is divided equally among the children.

ESCHEAT - *the term used if there is no will and there are no heirs; the property reverts to the state of California.* This is not automatic; it must be initiated through legal proceedings.

Individuals do NOT acquire property by escheat; if there are no heirs, it goes only to the state.

5. Transfer by Accession (Natural Causes)

ACCESSION - *occurs when an owner acquires title to additional land by natural causes; that is, additions to the property by improvements or natural growth.*

ACCRETION - *the addition to land from natural causes, such as earthquakes, volcanoes, or the action of moving water.* For example, a river over time may slowly deposit soil on one of its banks.

ALLUVIUM - *deposits of earth made through the natural action of water that become the real property of the landowner who holds title to the river bank.*

AVULSION - *the sudden, violent tearing away of land.* Title to that land is lost by the property owner.

ENCROACHMENT - *placement of improvements and permanent fixtures on property that do not legally belong to the person who placed them.*

Permanent fixtures attached to the land or buildings by residential tenants must be left with the building. Any improvements that are mistakenly placed on the property must also remain.

6. Transfer By Occupancy

Ownership of real property, or the use of real property, can be gained through three types of occupancy: abandonment, adverse possession, and prescription (by use).

a. Abandonment

ABANDONMENT - *the process of acquiring property that someone has left.*

One cannot acquire title to abandoned real property without court action, but a landlord can acquire possession of a property that is left (abandoned) by a tenant simply by gaining full control of the property.

b. Adverse Possession

ADVERSE POSSESSION - *acquiring title to another's property through continuous and notorious occupancy for five years, under a claim of title.* It is the legal way to acquire title without a deed. Title may be obtained through adverse possession only as long as certain conditions are met:

1. **Open and notorious occupancy** -The adverse possessor must live on, or openly use, the property in such a way that the titled owners might easily detect his or her presence.

2. **Hostile and adverse** - The adverse possessor must possess the property hostile to the legal owner, without his or her permission or any rental payment (consideration).

3. **Uninterrupted use for five years** - The adverse possessor must use the property continuously for at least five consecutive years.

4. **Claim of title** - The adverse possessor must have some reasonable claim of right or color of title (perhaps a defective written instrument) as a basis for his or her assertion. For example, a person could claim that his uncle gave the property to him before he died, but the deed is missing.

5. **Property taxes** - The adverse possessor must have paid all taxes levied and assessed on the property for five consecutive years.

A "quiet title" action is brought in court to prove that all five requirements have been fulfilled. Adverse possession is not possible against public or government lands, but only against privately owned lands.

c. Easement by Prescription

PRESCRIPTION - *an easement, or the right to use another's land, which can be obtained through five years of continuous use.*

Its requirements are similar to those of adverse possession, the differences being: **(1)** By prescription, only the use of the property has been obtained; **(2)** By prescription, taxes are still paid by the property owner. There are no property taxes and no confrontation.

Prescription is the "use" of a property, NOT the transfer of the title.

7. Transfer by Dedication

DEDICATION - *the gift (appropriation) of land, by its owner, for some public use.* To be fully dedicated, the land must be accepted for such use by authorized public officials. Dedication may be either (1) voluntary or (2) mandated by statute.

X. Recording and Acknowledgment

A. RECORDING

RECORDING - *the legal process of making an instrument an official part of the records of a county, after it has been acknowledged.*

Instruments that affect real property are legal documents, such as deeds, mortgages, trust deeds, leases, and contracts of sale. Recording gives constructive notice of the existence and content of these instruments.

CONSTRUCTIVE NOTICE - *any recorded notice that can be obtained from the county recorder's office.* Any document recorded with the county recorder is assumed to be "public knowledge."

ACTUAL NOTICE - *knowing, or one's responsibility for knowing, that a transaction has taken place.*

If you have found, for example, that someone other than the owner is living in a house you are buying, you should have been aware of the possible existence of a signed lease. This is actual notice, whereas public records are representative of constructive notice. The act of taking possession (holding an unrecorded deed) gives actual notice.

The recording process is a privilege rather than a legal requirement. Some documents have to be recorded to be valid. These include **mechanic's liens** and **declarations of homestead**. You may record an acknowledged instrument at any time. However, failure to utilize the privilege of recording at the earliest possible date can result in a question of legal or rightful title. **If the same property is sold to more than one party, the individual who has recorded first will usually be recognized as the rightful owner.** Therefore, time of recording is very important to a bona-fide purchaser who is protected only if he or she records first.

If there are NO prior arrangements (such as a subordination clause), the deed having priority is the one recorded first.

In order to establish priority, the documents affecting real property must be recorded by the county recorder in the county where the property is located. If the property is located in two counties, it should be recorded in both counties.

B. PRIORITY OF RECORDING

Under the recording system in California, "the first in time is the first in right." If an owner sells his or her house twice, the first deed recorded is the valid deed. This person must not have knowledge of the rights of the other party. This is the reward granted in California for recording any real estate transaction. However, there are four exceptions to the rule that protects a person from later recordings. They are:

1. Government liens, property taxes, and special assessments.
2. Actual or constructive notice of another person's prior rights.
3. Mechanic's liens.
4. Agreements to the contrary.

C. ACKNOWLEDGMENT (or Notary)

All documents must be acknowledged before they are recorded by the county recorder. This acknowledgment must be performed in the presence or a witness, usually a notary public, authorized by law to witness acknowledgments.

ACKNOWLEDGMENT - refers to a signed statement by the named person that he or she has signed that document of his or her own free will; in other words, that person "acknowledges" his or her signature.

A deed does NOT have to be acknowledged to be valid, but must be acknowledged to be recorded.

NOTARY PUBLIC - a person who is authorized by the Secretary of State to witness the acknowledgment of documents.

VERIFICATION - an oath or affirmation made before a notary public that the content of an instrument is true.

Section 6
Contracts

DRE Testing Emphasis:
Salesperson 22%
Broker 21%

I. Contracts in General

CONTRACT - *an agreement to perform or not to perform a certain act or service.*

Every contract consists of a promise or a set of promises that are enforceable by law. These promises may be created in two ways, either in an expressed manner or in an implied manner.

EXPRESS CONTRACT - *an agreement that is made either orally or in writing.* Listings, deposit receipts, and leases are all expressed contracts.

IMPLIED CONTRACT - *created when an agreement is made by acts and conduct (implication) rather than by words.* Implied contracts are not used in the practice of real estate.

Contracts are express (words), or implied (actions). Implied contracts are NOT used in real estate.

BILATERAL CONTRACT - *a promise made by one party in exchange for the promise of another party.* It is a promise for a promise.

UNILATERAL CONTRACT - *only one party makes a promise for an act of another.* It is a promise for an act. If someone acts upon an offer, the one making the offer is obligated to complete his or her promise.

A contract can be either bilateral (two promises) or unilateral (one promise).

A. CLASSIFICATION OF CONTRACTS

Contracts may be classified in any of these four ways:

1. **Valid** - A fully operative contract that is binding and enforceable in a court of law. Performance is expected or legal action can be filed.

2. **Voidable** - A contract that can be affirmed or rejected at the option of a party. Victim can rescind, cancel, or annul. A voidable contract remains binding until it is rescinded.

3. **Void** - A contract which has no legal effect. It does not exist. It lacks one of the essential elements of a contract. A contract for an illegal purpose is void.

4. **Unenforceable** - A valid contract that for some reason cannot be enforced in court (proved or sued upon). For example, a law that has been changed can make a performance illegal.

B. LIFE OF A CONTRACT

A contract has three basic phases.

1. Phase 1 - Negotiation

During the negotiation period, the buyer and seller discuss the possibility of a contract. If there is mutual interest between the parties, then an offer, or perhaps several offers, can be made. The offer becomes a contract when accepted, provided that all the other elements necessary for the creation of a contract are present.

TO EXECUTE A CONTRACT - *to sign a contract.*

2. Phase 2 - Performance

EXECUTORY CONTRACT - *a legal agreement, the provisions of which have yet to be completely fulfilled.*

An exclusive listing just signed by an owner is an example of an express, bilateral, executory contract.

A deposit receipt is executory until payment is made and title is transferred, then it becomes executed.

3. Phase 3 - Completion

EXECUTED CONTRACT - *a contract that has either been discharged or performed.*

EXECUTION OF A CONTRACT - *the act of performing or carrying out the contract.*

A contract to be performed is called "executory"; a completely performed contract has been "executed." The contract lives on until legal right to bring legal action has expired. This is called the "statute of limitations."

II. Elements of a Contract

Money, writing, and performance are **not** essential elements of a valid contract.

There are four elements of any contract: 1) Capacity, 2) Mutual Consent, 3) Legality, and 4) Consideration. If it involves real estate, there is a fifth element (Proper Writing).

A. CAPACITY

For a contract to be valid, there must be two or more parties who have the legal capacity to contract. Everyone, except for the following, is capable of contracting: 1) minors, 2) incompetents, and 3) convicts.

1. Minor - *a person under the age of eighteen.*

EMANCIPATED MINOR - one who has the contractual rights of an adult. A minor can become emancipated through marriage, by joining the armed forces, or be declared self-supporting by the courts.

2. Incompetent - *a person who is judged to be of unsound mind.*

Both minors and incompetents may acquire real property by gift or inheritance.

3. Convicts - *persons who have lost their civil rights during imprisonment.*

They may acquire property by gift, inheritance, or will, but can convey property only if the action is ratified by the California Adult Authority.

B. MUTUAL CONSENT

MUTUAL CONSENT - an offer of one party and acceptance by the other party.

This is the second major requirement of a valid contract. The consent must be genuine and free from fraud or mistake, and there must be a true intention to be obligated or it may be voidable by one or both of the parties.

Death does NOT cancel most contracts; they are binding on the estate, except a listing agreement, which is an employment (personal service) contract.

1. The Offer

OFFER - expresses a person's willingness to enter into a contract.

A buyer can withdraw his or her offer at any time prior to receiving communication in writing—personally or by registered mail—of its acceptance and receive a refund of the money deposited.

OFFEROR - the person (buyer) who has made the offer.

OFFEREE - the person (seller) to whom the offer has been made. The offer made by the offeror must be communicated to the offeree. Every offer must have contractual intent.

CONTRACTUAL INTENT - *exists when a party communicates an offer to another with the intention of forming a binding contract.* In real estate, a condition must often be met before a contract becomes binding. If the condition is not satisfied, there is no contractual intent and no binding agreement.

ILLUSORY CONTRACT - *one in which the terms are so uncertain as to impose no obligation.*

An "illusory contract" appears to be a contract, but it is unenforceable because it is NOT definite and certain.

DEFINITE AND CERTAIN - *means that the precise acts to be performed must be clearly stated.*

2. Acceptance

ACCEPTANCE - *the consent to the terms by the offeree.* Acceptance of an offer must be in the manner specified in the offer, but if no particular manner of acceptance is specified, then acceptance may be made by any reasonable or usual mode.

Silence cannot be interpreted as an acceptance of an offer. There must be a **communicated acceptance** of an offer in writing personally, or by registered mail. The acceptance must be absolute and unqualified, because if it modifies the terms of the offer, it becomes a counter offer.

If an offer is accepted by the offeree and communicated to the offeror, it is a legally binding contract. Should the buyer now die, there is still a legally binding contract.

COUNTER OFFER - *the rejection of an original offer and the proposal of a new offer with different terms.* Once there is a counter offer, the previous offer is automatically rejected.

3. Termination of an Offer

There are six ways an offer can be terminated:

a. **Lapse of Time** - If the offeree fails to accept the offer within a prescribed period, the offer is terminated.
b. **Revocation of Offer** - An offer can be withdrawn any time before the other party has communicated his or her acceptance.
c. **Failure of Offeree to Fulfill a Condition** - A specified condition must be accepted in a prescribed manner or the offer is terminated.
d. **Rejection** - If the offer is rejected, it is terminated.
e. **Death or Insanity of the Offeror or Offeree** - The death of the offeror or offeree constitutes a revocation of the offer prior to acceptance—the offer died with the death of the offeror. It voids the offer.
f. **Illegality of Purpose** - If the conditions or the purpose of a contract are illegal, then the contract is terminated.

4. Genuine Consent (Contract is Void or Voidable by Victim)

The final requirement for mutual consent is that the offer and acceptance must be real or genuine. If not, the contract is void or voidable by the victim. Genuine consent does not exist if any of the following conditions are present:

a. **FRAUD** - *Occurs when a person misrepresents a material fact, knowing it is not true, or is carelessly indifferent to the truth of the stated facts.* The contract is void or voidable, depending on the degree of fraud.

b. **MISREPRESENTATION** - *Occurs when one makes false statements.*

c. **MISTAKE** - *Exists when both parties are mistaken as to the matter of the agreement, or where the subject matter of the contract ceases to exist (e.g., a building burned down).* A mistake makes a contract void or voidable.

d. **DURESS** - *The unlawful detention of a person and/or that person's property.*

e. **MENACE** - *A threat to commit duress, but it also can be a threat of unlawful violent injury to a person and/or his or her character as a party to the contract.*

f. **UNDUE INFLUENCE** - *Occurs when a person in a position of authority, such as a person in a confidential relationship, uses that authority to an unfair advantage.*

C. LEGALITY

A contract must be legal in its formation and operation. Both the consideration and its objective must also be lawful. The objective refers to what the contract requires the parties to do or not to do. If the contract consists of a single objective that is unlawful in whole or in part, then the contract is void. If there are several objectives, the contract is normally valid as to those parts that are lawful.

A contract that forces one to break the law is void.

D. CONSIDERATION (Anything of Value)

VALUABLE CONSIDERATION - *in a contract is anything of value given by one party to another party to make the agreement binding.* A valid contract must have sufficient consideration, which is the amount of consideration a judge would hold necessary to support a contract.

Payment of money is NOT needed as consideration. It can also be a benefit, like the performance of an act or the nonperformance (forbearance) of an act.

E. PROPER WRITING (Real Estate Contracts)

A listing agreement must be in writing to enforce the payment of a commission. Oral agreements between brokers to share commissions are binding.

Personal property contracts, such as rental agreements, for one year or less, need NOT be in writing. Any contract that can't be performed within a year from the date of signing must be in writing.

1. Parol Evidence Rule

PAROL EVIDENCE - *refers to prior oral or written agreements of the parties, or even oral agreements concurrent (contemporaneous) with a written contract.*

Real Estate
Exam

The parol evidence rule is a principal that a writing intended to be the final embodiment of the agreement cannot be modified by evidence that adds to, varies, or contradicts the agreement.

However, the courts will permit such outside evidence to be introduced only when the written contract is incomplete, ambiguous, or when it is necessary to show that the contract is not enforceable because of mistake or fraud.

III. Performance, Discharge, and Breach of Contract

Acts described in a contract must be performed in a TIMELY MANNER (within time limits described in the contract).

A. PERFORMANCE OF A CONTRACT

The successful completion of contractual duties occurs in most contracts. Sometimes with performance of a contract, one of the parties would prefer to drop out of the picture without terminating the contract. He or she may, under proper circumstances, accomplish this by assignment.

ASSIGNMENT - *the transfer of a person's right in a contract to another party.*

ASSIGNOR - *the party to the original contract who transfers his or her rights in the contract to another party.*

ASSIGNEE - *the party to whom the contract rights are transferred.*

Any contract, unless it calls for some personal service, can be assigned if the contract does not state otherwise. For example, listings are not assignable because they are personal service contracts. If the assignee does not perform, the assignor remains liable (secondary liability) for the contract.

In some cases, the original contracting party may want to drop out of the contract completely. This can be done by novation.

NOVATION - *the substitution or exchange (by mutual agreement of the parties) of a new obligation or contract for an existing one with intent to cancel the old contract.* Since it is a new contract, it requires consideration and the other essentials of a valid contract.

Novation replaces the old contract with a new contract.

By statute, if no time is specified for the performance of an act, a reasonable time is allowed.

B. DISCHARGE OF A CONTRACT

The discharge of a contract occurs when the contract has been terminated.

Contracts can be discharged in many ways, from the extreme of full performance (which is the usual pattern) to breach of contract (nonperformance).

1. Full Performance

The contract is completed according to the terms specified in the original agreement.

2. Substantial Performance

Sometimes one party attempts to discharge a contract when the contract has almost, but not entirely, been completed. In certain cases the courts will accept this as a discharge of the contract. Otherwise there are usually slight monetary charges for damages.

3. Partial Performance

If both parties agree to the value of the work partially completed, the contract is discharged. This agreement should be in writing. However if a dispute arises, the courts will determine the obligations of the defaulting party.

4. Impossibility of Performance

A party may be released from a contract if uncontrollable circumstances have rendered performance impossible, for one reason or another.

5. Agreement Between the Parties

If a contract is not completed, the usual way to discharge the contract is by mutual agreement (agree to disagree). A mutual agreement not to complete the contract is also a contract.

6. Operation of Law (According to Statutes)

Whenever a contract, or parts of a contract, become illegal, the contract is discharged by operation of law.

7. Acceptance of a Breach

Contesting the contract sometimes only creates more problems, such as expensive interruption of work in progress and postponement of other contracts.

BREACH - the failure to perform a contract, in part or in whole, without legal excuse.

8. Breach (Nonperformance)

This is the nonperformance by one of the contracting parties.

The most common breaches, from the agent's point of view, are: (1) the buyers who decide NOT to buy after signing the deposit receipt or (2) the seller who decides NOT to sell after signing the listing and/or deposit receipt.

9. Statute of Limitations (For Breach of Contract)

The statute of limitations establishes the time limit for suing a party in a civil action. If the civil action has not been started within that given time, no legal recourse will be possible.

C. REMEDIES FOR BREACH OF A CONTRACT

A breach of contract occurs when one party fails to perform his or her contractual obligations. By law, the party who has been wronged has only four choices: 1) acceptance of breach; 2) unilateral rescission; 3) action for dollar damages; and 4) specific performance.

1. **ACCEPTANCE OF BREACH** - *the wronged party does not pursue legal action.*

2. **UNILATERAL RESCISSION** - *the wronged party (1) discloses the wrong and (2) restores everything of value to the offended party.* The legal grounds for a rescission are: fraud, mistake, duress, menace, undue influence, and faulty consideration.

3. **ACTION FOR DOLLAR DAMAGES** - *occurs when a court suit for a breach requests payment of a fixed amount of money as compensation.*

LIQUIDATED DAMAGES AGREEMENT - *sets, in advance, a specified amount of money as a penalty if there is a breach.* This clause is used because it is usually impractical or difficult to determine the actual damages caused by a breach.

The current award for liquidated damages on a deposit receipt form is a maximum of 3% (by law) of the home purchase price. Any deposit amount in excess of 3% must be refunded to the offeror. The damages are usually split 50%-50% between the seller and listing agent.

4. **SPECIFIC PERFORMANCE** - *means that the party causing the breach is forced to perform the terms of the contract by a court.*

IV. The Deposit Receipt

A. THE OFFER AND ACCEPTANCE (With Deposit)

A deposit of money or items of value must accompany a deposit receipt to be a valid offer. If a postdated check or promissory note is given as consideration for a deposit with an offer (deposit receipt), the agent must disclose this fact to the seller.

DEPOSIT RECEIPT - *an offer and deposit to purchase a specific property on certain terms and conditions.*

The Deposit Receipt is also called: "The Contract" or "Residential Purchase Agreement," but it is most commonly referred to as the "Deposit Receipt."

When acceptance is communicated, this becomes a binding contract on the buyer and seller. Acceptance is communicated in writing, in person, or by registered mail. In addition, the deposit receipt discloses (as in the listing agreement) the percentage of commission to be paid to the brokers involved.

An agent must always give a copy of a signed contract to the parties.

When using preprinted standard forms, (1) inserted typewritten parts have priority over preprinted parts; and (2) inserted handwritten parts have priority over inserted typewritten parts and preprinted parts. All corrections must be initialed by both parties.

B. THE DEPOSIT *(Consideration for Deposit Receipt)*

The deposit is collected as consideration from a prospective buyer on behalf of the seller for the deposit receipt contract. Suppose the seller accepts the offer on the CAR® Deposit Receipt form and the buyer later defaults on the transaction. If the liquidated damages clause is initialed by both the buyer and seller, the seller may retain the deposit (up to three percent of the sales price). This would then be split 50-50 between the seller and the listing broker, unless otherwise stated in the deposit receipt.

Deposits are always the property of the seller (after the removal of contingencies on the binding Deposit Receipt contract), never the broker.

ERRORS AND OMISSIONS INSURANCE - *the liability insurance that brokers and salespeople are required to carry in order to pay for any costly lawsuits.*

C. THE COUNTER OFFER *(Replaces Original Offer with Changes in Terms)*

A counter offer automatically rejects the original offer if terms of the new offer vary from the original. The different terms stated on the counter offer must be accepted by the other party.

Rather than preparing a whole new deposit receipt when presenting a counter offer, most sellers prefer to use a standard counter offer form.

In a counter offer, the offeree becomes the offeror.

D. COVENANTS *(A Promise in the Deposit Receipt)*

COVENANTS - *promises between the parties to a contract.* Covenants represent promises, obligations, and considerations exchanged to fulfill a contract.

If you break a contractual promise, the other party can sue for damages.

Failure to perform a stipulated covenant does not release either party from his or her responsibility. The contract is still in effect, although the offended party may sue for damages.

E. CONTINGENCIES, CONDITIONS, OR SUBJECT TO
(An "IF" Clause in the Deposit Receipt)

CONTINGENCIES, CONDITIONS, OR SUBJECT TO - *provisions by which all parties are released from any obligations of a contract if some stated condition fails to materialize.* For example, purchase offers may be made contingent upon the availability of financing, or subject to the successful sale of another property. If the contingency falls through, the contract is voidable by the buyer.

A contingency clause is an "if" situation, so it should be used sparingly. Example: Only if I qualify for the loan will I purchase the property. They are also referred to as conditions or "subject to" provisions.

V. Purchase Options

A. OPTIONS (A Unilateral Contract)

OPTION - *a right to purchase a property upon specified terms within a specific time period, which is granted in exchange for money.* An option is normally purchased to take a property off the open market. The prospective purchaser holds an exclusive right to buy during the option period.

An option contract CANNOT be revoked by optionor who could be forced to sell the property by specific performance.

OPTIONOR - *a property owner who gives an interested buyer an exclusive right to purchase a property.*

OPTIONEE - *a potential buyer who purchases an agreed-to amount of time to buy a specific property upon set terms.* The optionee does not have to go through with the purchase.

A salesperson who has a listing and an option to purchase a property at the same time must disclose: all offers, material information, and obtain consent of any anticipated profits from seller before exercising the option to purchase.

If the optionee decides to buy the property during his or her option period, the optionor must sell. In this case, the option will become a purchase contract, and both parties are bound by its terms.

An agent who exercises an option to buy his own listing has a conflict of interest. He or she must disclose the full amount of his or her commission and profit and obtain the seller's approval before buying the property.

Section 7
Broker's Responsibility

> **DRE Testing Emphasis:**
> Salesperson 17%
> Broker 22%

I. Agency Overview

A. AGENT, PRINCIPAL, AND THIRD PARTY

The relationship between a seller, a broker (and his or her salespeople), and a buyer is called "agency."

AGENCY - *the authority (or power) to act for or in place of another (a principal—person who hires), in a specified act for a stated period of time.*

AGENT - *one who acts for and with authority from another (the principal).*

PRINCIPAL (CLIENT) - *a person who hires or employs an agent to work for him or her. If the principal is a buyer, the agent represents the buyer.* On the other hand, if the principal is a seller, the agent represents the seller.

A salesperson employed by a "listing" broker is an agent of the owner/seller.

THIRD PARTY - *is the other person in a contractual negotiation, other than the principal and his or her agent.* If an agent works for the seller, the third party is the buyer, but if the agent works for the buyer, the third party is the seller.

ESTOPPEL - *a principal is estopped from denying that a person is his or her agent if the principal has misled another to his prejudice into believing that a person is the agent. For example, if you let a broker act as if he or she had your authority to sell your house, you cannot later say he or she did so without your consent.*

OSTENSIBLE AGENCY - *that authority which a third party reasonably believes an agent possesses because of acts or omissions of the principal.*

A broker providing services for both buyer and seller, unaware they both consider him to be their agent, has created an "ostensible agency."

RATIFICATION - *approval of a transaction which has already taken place.* For example, when you authorize a broker to have acted for you after he or she has already done so, the action is called ratification.

The agency of a real estate broker may be established by express agreement, implied agreement, ratification, or estoppel.

B. TRADITIONAL AGENCY RELATIONSHIP

Traditionally, the broker was called the agent, the owner/seller was called the principal, and the buyer was called the third party. Conventionally, the broker worked for the seller. This is still true in many other states. However, the broker can act as an agent for the buyer, the seller, or both.

C. RESPONSIBILITIES OF AGENCY

The California Civil Code boils the law of agency down to three basic rules applying to licensed brokers and licensed salespeople:

1. The agent must inform the principal of all facts pertaining to the handling of the principal's property. The agent must put client's interest above interest of self or others.
2. The agent may not gain any monetary interest in the property without the principal's prior consent.
3. An agent may not use the principal's property to his or her own advantage.

FIDUCIARY - *a person acting in a position of trust and confidence in a business relationship.*

FIDUCIARY RELATIONSHIP - *requires the highest good faith from the agent to his or her principal.*

The broker (agent) owes certain duties, rights, and responsibilities to both the principal and third party. The broker owes a fiduciary duty of (including, but not limited to) honesty, utmost care, integrity, accounting, disclosure, and loyalty to the principal. To a third party, an agent owes honesty and disclosure of material facts.

D. LISTING AND SELLING AGENTS

When a salesperson obtains a listing agreement to sell a particular property, he or she is referred to as the "listing salesperson." That salesperson's broker is referred to as the "listing broker." If a different brokerage company negotiates the sale, that agency is the "selling broker" and "selling salesperson." A broker or salesperson who both lists and sells the same property is referred to as the "listing and selling broker or salesperson."

In a real estate transaction, agents are identified as the "listing agent" or "selling agent."

II. Real Estate Agency Relationship Disclosure

A. AGENCY DISCLOSURE LAW

The Real Estate Agency Relationship Disclosure Form states that an agent must disclose an agency relationship as soon as practical. An agent can represent a seller, a buyer, or both.

The only requirement is that the listing broker must at least represent the seller (owner). This law applies to the sale of one-to-four unit residential property.

The seller's agent CANNOT keep silent about any material facts that affect the value of the property (for example, that the property is in an earthquake zone or backs up to a freeway or school).

It is LEGAL for an agent to work for both the buyer and seller ("dual agency") if the agent has the written acknowledgment and consent of all parties to the transaction.

B. SALESPEOPLE MAY BE INDEPENDENT CONTRACTORS OR EMPLOYEES

INDEPENDENT CONTRACTOR - sells results rather than time, and his or her physical conduct is not subject to the control of another.

EMPLOYEE - works under the direct control (designated hours and breaks) and supervision of the employer.

The Department of Real Estate considers a salesperson an employee of the broker for the administration of the real estate broker law, even if he or she is an independent contractor. This makes the broker responsible for the real estate activities of the salesperson.

III. Listings and the Multiple Listing Service (MLS)

A. LISTING AGREEMENTS

LISTING - a contract to employ a broker, legally referred to as an agent, to do certain things for the owner/seller. It is an employment contract for personal service.

A listing may be for any period of time. If NO beginning date is specified, the effective date is the date when the listing is signed.

Real estate law requires that "exclusive listings" have a definite, final termination date. If not, the agent may lose the commission and possibly his or her license.

All real estate listing agreements or contracts should be in writing, and must be in writing to assure collection of a commission. There are three basic types of listings used in California. They are:

1. Open Listing (Unilateral, Non-Exclusive Contract)

OPEN LISTING - *an authorization to sell a property. It may be given to several brokers or the property may be sold by the owner.*

Open listings are the simplest form of broker authorization. They can be given to several brokers concurrently, and no notice of sale is required to terminate the listing. If the owner sells the property, he or she is not required to pay a commission. Usually, no time limit is placed on an open listing.

NOT all listings are a promise for a promise (bilateral). The open listing is unilateral (only seller promises). Exclusive listings are bilateral.

2. Exclusive Agency Listing (No Commission If Owner Sells)

EXCLUSIVE AGENCY LISTING - *a listing where the listing broker is entitled to a commission if he or any cooperating broker sells the property.*

The owner still has the right to independently sell the property without paying a commission to the listing broker. The drawback with this type of listing is that the broker is, or could be, in competition with the owner for the sale.

An "exclusive agency listing" and "exclusive right to sell listing" both require a DEFINITE termination date.

3. Exclusive Right to Sell Listing (Commission if Sold Within the Listing Period)

EXCLUSIVE RIGHT TO SELL LISTING - *entitles the listing broker named in the agency contract to a commission even if the owner sells the property.*

To protect themselves, brokers must furnish the owner/seller with a list of persons to whom they have shown the property during the listing period. If the owner sells the property himself to someone on the list within the negotiated period, the broker will be entitled to a commission. This list is called a safety clause and must be furnished, in writing, either in person or by registered mail.

SAFETY CLAUSE - *a clause stating the negotiated period (any agreed to time period), after the termination of a listing, in which the listing broker may still be entitled to a commission.*

4. Net Listing (Must be Used with Other Listing—Seldom Used)

NET LISTING - *an authorization to sell that must be used with one of the other three listings. The broker's commission is any amount above the selling price set by the owner.*

This listing may take the form of an open listing, an exclusive agency listing, or an exclusive right to sell listing. With this type of listing, it is imperative for the broker to explain, in writing, the exact meaning of a net listing so that there is no confusion about any earned compensation.

B. MULTIPLE LISTING SERVICE (MLS) - (Subagents and Cooperating Brokers)

MULTIPLE LISTING SERVICE (MLS) - *an association of real estate agents that provides a pooling of listings, recent sales, and the sharing of commissions on a specified basis.*

MULTIPLE LISTING - *a listing, usually an exclusive right to sell, taken by a member of a multiple listing service, with the provision that all members of the multiple listing service have the opportunity to find an interested buyer.*

A "pocket listing" is the unethical practice of NOT giving a new listing to the MLS until the listing broker first tries to sell that listed property within the company.

SUBAGENT - *a licensed broker or salesperson upon whom the powers of an agent have been conferred, not by the principal, but by the agent with the principal's authorization.*

The agent can delegate purely mechanical acts such as typing to anyone, but a subagency can only be created with the principal's consent. The subagent has the same duties and responsibilities as the agent. All subagents derive their fiduciary obligation from the listing broker.

Subagents only have the powers that are given to them by the listing agent.

C. COOPERATING BROKERS

COOPERATING BROKER - *a non-listing broker (subagent) who also works to sell the listed property.* The cooperating broker performs the same acts as the agent to find a buyer. Cooperating brokers and salespeople are therefore subagents of the listing broker, but they can also represent the buyer if it is disclosed to all parties.

1. Selling in Other States

Since each state has its own licensing laws, how can a cooperating broker sell a property, for commission, in another state? The answer is simple. Find a licensed, cooperating broker in that state.

IV. Commissions

COMMISSION - *in real estate, a fee paid, usually as a percentage, to an agent as compensation for his or her services.*

COMMISSION SPLIT - *a previously agreed to split between a broker and his or her salesperson of a commission earned on a sale.* The listing agreement states that a commission is to be paid only when all the terms of the listing or other acceptable terms of the sale are met.

Commission rates are NEGOTIABLE; the listing must have this statement printed in a TEN POINT BOLD font.

If an offer meets the exact terms of the listing, the agent has earned the commission, even if the owner refuses to sell to the buyer.

PROCURING CAUSE - *defined as a series of unbroken events that lead to an acceptable agreement with the seller.*

A broker or his or her salesperson must be the procuring cause of a sale to earn a commission. If there are several brokers trying to sell the same property, the one who is the procuring cause of the sale is entitled to the selling broker's portion of the commission.

A listing of one-to-four residential units must contain the clause "the amount of or rate of commission is not fixed by law. They are set by each broker individually and may be negotiable between the buyer and seller."

V. Transfer Disclosure Statement

A. EASTON v. STRASSBURGER

The agent has a duty to inspect and disclose.

A 1984 California Court of Appeals decision in the case of *Easton v. Strassburger* greatly extended the liability of brokers engaged in real estate sales. Both the listing and selling agents must conduct a reasonable, competent, and diligent inspection of residential property. They must disclose, on the Transfer Disclosure Statement, any relevant facts that materially affect the value or desirability of the property.

B. TRANSFER DISCLOSURE STATEMENT

The law requires sellers of residential property of one-to-four units to provide prospective buyers with a Real Estate Transfer Disclosure Statement. This form provides an opportunity for the seller to completely disclose any problems of any kind that might adversely affect the value of the property. The obligation to prepare and deliver the Transfer Disclosure Statement to the prospective buyer is imposed upon the seller and the seller's broker.

Legally, the listing (selling) broker and the buyer's broker must conduct a reasonably competent, diligent, and visual inspection of accessible areas of the property and disclose to a prospective buyer all material facts affecting value and desirability.

The Transfer Disclosure Statement (or amended Disclosure Statement) must be given to the prospective buyer as soon as practicable before the offer (Deposit Receipt) is signed.

VI. Broker's Responsibilities

A. AGENT SUPERVISION

The broker must supervise his or her salespeople and any brokers working as salespeople for his or her agency.

Whenever a real estate salesperson enters the employ of a real estate broker or whenever the salesperson is terminated, the broker shall immediately notify the Department of Real Estate in writing.

B. WRITTEN BROKER-ASSOCIATE CONTRACTS

As required by the Real Estate Commissioner's Regulations, brokers must have a written contract with each licensed member of the sale's staff. It shall cover all material aspects of the relationship between the parties, including supervision of licensed activities, duties, and compensation. A copy of this contract must be retained by all parties for three years from the date of termination. These requirements become an integral part of a company's policy manual.

C. TRUST ACCOUNTS (Other People's Money)

COMMINGLING - the mixing together of the funds of a principal and a licensee. **Never mix other people's money with your private money**.

The opposite of commingling is "segregating" (keeping separate).

CONVERSION - the unlawful misappropriation and use of a client's funds by a licensee. This is a much more serious violation than commingling, and has heavy criminal penalties. **Never spend other people's money**.

A broker, when receiving a buyer's money deposit (and instructions), either 1) opens an escrow, 2) gives it to the principal, or 3) puts it in the broker's trust fund account.

If not instructed otherwise, the money must go into the broker's trust fund account no later than **three business days** following receipt of the funds by the broker. Placing a buyer's cash or check in the broker's personal account is a violation of the Commissioner's Regulations. By law, each entry in the broker's trust fund account (bank) must be identified.

D. TRANSACTION FILE (Keep for Three Years)

TRANSACTION FILE - a folder of all documents kept for three years by the broker for each real estate transaction in which the broker or his or her salespeople participated. The commissioner of real estate has the right to inspect this file.

The Real Estate Commissioner requires that all records of a broker or salesperson be kept for a minimum of three years, except the mortgage disclosure form, which is four years.

E. AGENTS WHO BUY AND SELL FOR THEIR OWN ACCOUNT

The Real Estate Commissioner created a regulation requiring disclosure of license status (buyer and seller) which has the full force and effect of law. The commissioner has strongly suggested that it would be in the licensee's best interest to disclose this fact, in writing, as soon as possible.

F. POWER OF ATTORNEY

POWER OF ATTORNEY - an acknowledged, written authorization of one person to act for another.

GENERAL POWER OF ATTORNEY - allows the person so authorized to perform any act the principal could perform.

ATTORNEY IN FACT - *under a general power of attorney, an agent who may have the power to transact all of a principal's business.*

The power of attorney must be recorded in the county where the property is located in order to be properly exercised.

SPECIAL POWER OF ATTORNEY - *allows the person so authorized to perform only a specific act (for example, sell your house).*

A real estate agent under a special power of attorney is an "attorney in fact" who is usually authorized to find a ready, willing, and able buyer.

G. TORTS BY AN AGENT (Broker/Salesperson)

TORT - *any civil injury or wrong committed upon a person or that person's property.*

Fraud, misrepresentation, negligence, and secret profit all stem from a breach of an agent's duty. In some cases they can even be considered criminal acts. The broker and his or her salespeople, as professionals, are expected to maintain a high standard of ethics. They are responsible for their own acts and representations, even when following the seller's directions.

H. MISREPRESENTATION OF A MATERIAL FACT

A misrepresentation by a broker or salesperson may be material or immaterial. When a broker misrepresents his or her authority to act as an agent for someone else, he or she may be liable to the person who relies on the misrepresentation.

"Puffing" is a statement that exaggerates a property's benefits. It is common practice, but an agent should never misrepresent a material fact.

A misrepresentation of a material fact can financially injure someone, and may be punishable under the Civil Code or the Commissioner's Regulations. There are three types of misrepresentations:

INNOCENT MISREPRESENTATIONS - *false statements that are not known to be false at the time they are made.* These statements do not usually warrant legal liability for the broker, but can cause a rescission of any contract. Everyone involved would then be reinstated to their original positions.

NEGLIGENT MISREPRESENTATIONS - *statements believed to be true but made without reasonable grounds and are, in fact, false.* This is breach of duty without fraudulent intent. The broker is liable for any negligent statements made to a buyer or seller. Such statements are, in effect, a form of deceit.

FRAUDULENT MISREPRESENTATIONS - *statements made at a time when the broker knows the statement to be false, or statements in which the broker does not disclose material facts.* This is actual fraud. Any contract made under the influence of fraudulent information may become void, and the person making the fraudulent statements may be liable for civil or even criminal fraud.

"Intentional deceptions" or the "concealment of material facts" are fraudulent misrepresentations.

I. SECRET PROFITS

An agent may not make any secret profit. This is a breach of the fiduciary relationship between the principal and the real estate agent. All legitimate financial offers must be presented to the seller. So, if a real estate agent is offered a secret profit, he or she has a duty to let the principal know of the bribe. In addition, the broker may not allow others (friends and relatives) to make a secret profit with his or her knowledge.

J. WARRANTY OF AUTHORITY

The broker, as an agent, warrants that he or she has the authority to represent another person. If there is a written listing between the seller and the broker, he or she has an expressed warranty of authority to offer the property for sale. A broker gives implied warranty of authority to act for a seller by the mere fact that he or she shows the seller's property.

EXPRESSED WARRANTY OF AUTHORITY - *a written listing between the seller and the broker giving the broker authority to offer the property for sale.*

IMPLIED WARRANTY OF AUTHORITY - *the mere act of showing a seller's property gives a broker an implied warranty of authority.*

When a broker represents a seller, he or she does not warrant that the seller has the capacity to sell. However, if the broker has knowledge that the seller could not contract, then the broker could be liable to the buyer.

K. A BROKERAGE MUST BE RUN LIKE A BUSINESS

A "company dollar" is the dollar (income and commissions) a broker receives after all commissions have been paid.

GROSS DOLLAR - *is all the income that is received by the office before commissions.* "**TOE**" is the acronym for Total Operating Expense.

- *T* **Total**
- *O* **Operating**
- *E* **Expense**

DESK COST - *the total operating expense divided by the number of salespeople.* The desk cost tells the broker the financial loss caused by an empty desk or an unproductive salesperson.

POLICY MANUAL - *a written collection of policies to be used in the operation of a real estate office—the written constitution of an office.*

VII. Terminating An Agency Relationship

A. REASONS FOR TERMINATION OF AGENCY

An agency relationship between a seller and a real estate broker can be terminated by operation of law or by the acts of either the broker or the seller.

1. **Expiration of the agency (listing) agreement.** The Exclusive Agency Listing Agreement and the Exclusive Authorization and Right to Sell Listing Agreement have a definite (automatic) termination date. An open listing can be terminated at any time.

2. **Destruction of the property.** If the property is destroyed or damaged by certain causes, such as earthquake or fire, the listing agreement is terminated.

3. **Death or incapacity of the broker or owner/seller.** If either the agent or owner/seller is not mentally or physically able to complete the agency relationship (personal service contract), it is terminated unless either party is a corporation (legal person).

4. **Agreement by both the broker and owner/seller.** If both parties to a contract want to end it, it may be terminated by mutual agreement.

5. **Renouncement of the listing agreement by the broker.** The broker can refuse to fulfill the listing agreement but may be subject to damages for breach of contract.

6. **Revocation of the listing agreement by the owner/seller.** The owner/seller can refuse to sell the listed property but may be liable for the commission if the broker has found a buyer who is ready, willing, and able to purchase the property.

B. LISTING AGREEMENT COPIES (Give Copy When Signed)

Always give the buyer and seller a copy of any agreement when signed.

A copy of the listing agreement or any other real estate agreement, including the agency relationship and the transfer disclosure statements, must be given to the signing party immediately after they are signed. This is a requirement of the Commissioner's Regulations, and a violation could result in license suspension or revocation.

VIII. Fair Housing Laws

California was among the first states with fair housing laws. Our first law was the Unruh Civil Rights Act (no discrimination in business), then the Rumford Act (no discrimination in housing), and later these were reinforced with the Federal Civil Rights Act of 1968.

A. STATE LAW - UNRUH CIVIL RIGHTS ACT

The Unruh Civil Rights Act was the first civil rights act in California; it prohibits "steering" and "block busting" as a real estate business practice.

B. STATE LAW - RUMFORD ACT (California Fair Employment and Housing Act)

The Rumford Act (NO discrimination in housing) established the Department of Fair Employment and Housing to investigate and take action against property owners, financial institutions, and real estate licensees who engage in discriminatory practices.

It clearly defines discrimination as the refusal to sell, rent, or lease housing accommodations, including misrepresentation as to availability, inferior terms, and cancellations, on the basis of race, color, religion, sex, family status, national origin, ancestry, or age. It also outlaws sale or rental advertisements containing discriminatory information.

C. STATE LAW - HOLDEN ACT (Housing Financial Discrimination Act)

The Housing Financial Discrimination Act of 1977 (Holden Act) prohibits discriminatory loan practices by financial institutions called "redlining."

REDLINING - *practices by financial institutions who deny loans or vary finance terms based on a given property's location, regardless of the borrower's credit worthiness.*

The Holden Act (NO redlining) covers 1-to-4 residential units (at least one owner-occupied). An owner seeking a home improvement loan need NOT occupy the property.

A grievance under the Holden Act is directed to the U. S. Department of Business, Transportation, and Housing. Lending institutions in violation of the Holden Act may be required to pay for damages, limited to $1,000 for each offense.

D. FEDERAL LAWS (Federal Civil Rights Act of 1968)

Federal law prohibits discrimination on the part of owners of property and their agents based on the U.S. Supreme Court Case Jones v. Mayer (1968) and the Thirteenth Amendment to the U.S. Constitution.

At the federal level, the Federal Civil Rights Act of 1968 reinforced the Unruh and Rumford Acts: 1) Any discrimination that the two acts did not prohibit was explicitly outlawed. THERE ARE NO EXCEPTIONS; 2) It makes it illegal for real estate licensees to engage in discriminatory practices regardless of any instructions the agent may have received from the seller or landlord. If asked to discriminate in the sale of a property, the salesperson must refuse to accept the listing; 3) It bars real estate boards or multiple listing services from discriminating by denying participation or restricting terms and conditions of membership; 4) It requires a fair housing poster to be displayed at all real estate offices and subdivision model homes. The poster must also be displayed at all financial institutions or by mortgage lenders who make loans to the general public.

1. Federal Civil Rights Act Expanded in 1988
(HUD Can Initiate Housing Discrimination Cases)

A 1988 federal law allows the U.S. Government to take court action if it believes discrimination exists in home sales or apartment rentals. Landlords are explicitly forbidden to discriminate against families with children under 18 years of age. The only exemptions from this would be in retirement communities where most of the residents are more than 55 years of age. This federal law also extends protections to handicapped home buyers or tenants. As of 1991, builders of all new apartment buildings are required to include ground floor rooms suitable for use by residents in wheelchairs.

The only time an agent can refuse to show a property to a buyer is when the owners have instructed the agent that they will be on their vacation and, during their absence, the broker has been instructed NOT to show the property to anyone.

IX. Department of Real Estate (DRE)

A person working for compensation (agent) must have a real estate license from the DRE.

CALIFORNIA DEPARTMENT OF REAL ESTATE - *the regulatory agency for real estate in California.*

The main purpose of this department is to protect the public by enactment and enforcement of laws relating to real estate and by establishing requirements for real estate salespersons' or brokers' licenses.

The Real Estate Commissioner, deputies, and clerks (as employees of the Department of Real Estate) are NOT allowed to have an interest in any real estate company or brokerage firm.

The California Department of Real Estate is governed by the Real Estate Commissioner. The Commissioner, who sets all the rules and regulations for the Department of Real Estate, receives his or her power from the state legislature. The legislature, in turn, used police power to create the position of Commissioner.

POLICE POWER - *the right to enact and enforce laws beneficial to the health, safety, morals, and general welfare of the public.*

A. REAL ESTATE COMMISSIONER (Appointed by the Governor)

REAL ESTATE COMMISSIONER - *the chief executive of the Department of Real Estate and chairperson of the State Real Estate Advisory Commission.*

The Commissioner cannot settle commission disputes, does NOT take the place of a court of law, and does NOT give legal advice.

The Real Estate Commissioner has the power to call formal hearings to discuss any issue concerning an applicant for a license, a current license holder, or a subdivider. The commissioner may subsequently suspend, revoke, or deny a license. He or she could also halt sales (desist and refrain order) in a subdivision.

A licensee can be disciplined by the Real Estate Commissioner, but the local District Attorney prosecutes for the Real Estate Commissioner.

The Real Estate Commissioner does NOT settle commission disputes; they are settled by arbitration or civil lawsuits in local courts.

BASICS

X. Real Estate License Requirements

Any person who is actively involved in a real estate transaction at the service of another, in the expectation of receiving a commission, must be licensed.

A. OBTAINING THE SALESPERSON'S LICENSE

The candidate for a real estate salesperson's license examination must:

1. be 18 years of age to apply for a license, although there is no age restriction for taking the exam;
2. provide Proof of Legal Presence in the United States;
3. if not a California resident, refer to "Out-of-State Applicants" on DRE Web site;
4. be honest and truthful;
5. complete a college-level Real Estate Principles course; and
6. pass the required examination.

B. SALESPERSON'S EXAMINATION

1. Conditional Salesperson's License (The 18-Month License)

To obtain a conditional salesperson's license (18-month), the applicant must 1) complete a college-level Real Estate Principles course; 2) pass the DRE salesperson's exam; and 3) pay the necessary fees.

CONDITIONAL SALESPERSON'S LICENSE - *the license of a person who has taken only the Real Estate Principles course.* This license expires 18 months after issuance unless the salesperson has submitted evidence to the DRE of the completion of two other college level (broker-required) real estate courses.

2. Four-Year Salesperson's License (Regular, Renewable License)

To obtain a regular four-year salesperson's license, the applicant must complete a college-level Real Estate Principles course and two other approved college level (broker-required) courses, pass the DRE salesperson's exam, and pay the necessary fees.

If an applicant has already completed a college-level Real Estate Principles course and at least two other (broker-required) approved courses, he or she can apply for the regular four-year salesperson's license.

3. Salesperson's Examination

To pass, an applicant must achieve a score of at least 70% in the three-hour fifteen minute salesperson's exam, which has 150 multiple choice questions. The use of silent, battery-operated, pocket-sized electronic calculators that are non-programmable and do not have a printout capability is permitted.

4. Notification of Examination Results

You will be notified of your examination results by email or postal mail after the examination. Those who pass will receive an application for a license. Those who do not receive a passing grade will automatically receive a reexamination form. There is no limitation to the number of reexaminations you may take during the two-year period following the date of the filing of the original application. If you wish to take additional examinations after the two-year period, you must complete a new application.

5. Electronic Fingerprint Requirement (Salesperson and Broker)

Upon completion of the real estate license exam, a copy of RE Form 237 (the Live Scan Service Request Form) will be mailed to all applicants.

Applicants for the salesperson's license must apply for a license within one year from exam date.

C. OBTAINING THE BROKER'S LICENSE (Renewable Four-Year License)

BROKER'S LICENSE - *required of any individual in order to operate a real estate office.*

1. Broker's Qualifying Experience

A candidate must be able to prove that he or she has experience in real estate before applying for a broker's license. Generally, two years of full-time work (104 forty-hour weeks) as a salesperson is required. This two-year requirement may be replaced by an equivalent amount of part-time salesperson work. Such experience must have been completed within the five years immediately preceding the date of application.

The broker's 200-question exam takes five hours to complete. The applicant must answer 75% of the questions correctly to pass.

2. Broker's Required Education (Eight Courses)

Applicants for the real estate broker's license examination must have successfully completed the eight statutory-required college-level courses. The required salesperson's courses can be found on the list of required broker's courses, but the number of required courses is different: three for the regular salesperson's license and eight for the broker's license.

D. RENEWAL OF LICENSE - EVERY FOUR YEARS (Salesperson and Broker)

Brokers' and salespersons' licenses can be renewed; a conditional (18-month) salesperson's license CANNOT.

E. CONTINUING EDUCATION REQUIREMENT (45 Hours Every Four Years)

The continuing education requirement (45 hours every 4 years for license renewal) is NOT the same as the required broker courses.

All real estate licensees are required to attend 45 clock hours of Commissioner-approved courses, seminars, or conferences during the four-year period preceding license renewal. Three of these hours must be in an Ethics course and three hours must be in Agency. On a salesperson's license first renewal, required courses include three hours **each** of Ethics, Agency, Trust Fund Handling, and Fair Housing. Thereafter, however, the 45-clock-hour requirement continues indefinitely with every renewal.

1. "Six-hour Continuing Education (C.E.) Survey" Course

The six-hour CE Survey course can replace the 12-hour combination of four separate 3-hour courses in Ethics, Agency, Trust Fund Handling, and Fair Housing, starting with your second license renewal. So if a licensee takes the six-hour CE Survey course, he or she still needs an additional 39 hours of CE to complete the 45 total hours required every four years at license renewal time.

F. OTHER REAL ESTATE-RELATED LICENSES

1. Prepaid Rental Listing Service License

PREPAID RENTAL LISTING SERVICE (PRLS) LICENSE - *required when running a business that supplies prospective tenants with listings of residential real property for rent or lease while collecting a fee for such service.* Negotiation of the rental of property is not a part of this activity. An individual may obtain, without examination, a two-year license to conduct PRLS activities.

2. Real Property Securities Dealer Endorsement

REAL PROPERTY SECURITIES DEALER (RPSD) - *any person acting as a principal or agent who engages in the business of selling real property securities (such as promissory notes or sales contracts).*

RPSDs also accept, or offer to accept, funds for reinvestment in real property securities or for placement in an account. Before a licensed real estate broker may act in the capacity of a RPSD, he or she must obtain an RPSD endorsement on his or her broker's license.

XI. Illegal Advertising

A . ILLEGAL ADVERTISING

1. Blind - *an advertisement that does not include the name and address of the person placing the ad, only a phone number or post office box address. Licensed brokers are generally prohibited by state license laws from using blind ads.*

2. Deceptive

3. Over-The-Phone Financing

"Call our toll free number for a loan" is an example of prohibited advertising because it implies that a borrower can obtain a loan over the phone without credit checks and other verifications.

4. Misleading Advertising

XII. Business Opportunity Brokerage

In a sale of a business (Business Opportunity), the real property is transferred by "deed" and the personal property is transferred by a "bill of sale." If money is owed on the business, the proper forms are filed with the Secretary of State's office.

A. BUSINESS OPPORTUNITY SALE

BUSINESS OPPORTUNITY - *is the sale or lease of a business, including the goodwill of an existing business.* It involves the sale of personal property and therefore must conform to the rules and laws that govern the transfer of chattels (personal property).

BUSINESS - *an establishment whose main purpose is the buying and reselling of goods, or the performance of services, with the intention of making a profit.*

The three documents in a personal property security transaction are: 1) a promissory note; 2) a security agreement; and 3) compliance with the UCC-1 financing statement.

B. BULK SALES (Transfer of Business Inventory: Notice to Creditors Required)

BULK TRANSFER - *any sale of a substantial part of the 1) inventory and items purchased for resale; 2) other supplies and equipment associated with a business.*

Division 6 of the Uniform Commercial Code (UCC) requires the purchaser (transferee) in a bulk transfer to give the seller's (transferor's) creditors fair warning that a sale of all or a major part of the inventory is about to take place.

1. Buyer (Transferee) Must Comply With The UCC

If a retail or wholesale merchant transfers a substantial part of his or her materials, supplies, merchandise, or inventory, the transferee involved in the transfer must give notice by:

    a. **Twelve business days** prior to the transfer, recorded notice with the County Recorder's Office.

    b. **Twelve business days** prior to the transfer, published notice in a newspaper of general circulation in the county or judicial district.

    c. **Twelve business days** prior to the transfer, delivered notice (by hand or registered mail) to the County Tax Collector.

C. CALIFORNIA SALES TAXES (Selling Retail)

SALES TAXES - *imposed on the sale of tangible personal property by retailers.*

A seller's permit from the State Board of Equalization is the permit that allows sellers to buy at wholesale without paying sales tax as long as they collect sales taxes from their customers and forward these taxes to the State Board of Equalization. Escrow cannot close without a **clearance receipt** from the State Board of Equalization showing there are no unpaid sales taxes by the seller.

XIII. Real Estate Law and Regulations

CALIFORNIA REAL ESTATE LAW - *the portion of the Business and Professions Code that refers to licensing and subdivisions.*

COMMISSIONER'S REGULATIONS - *rules that form part of the California Administrative Code established and enforced by the Commissioner of Real Estate.*

A. HEARINGS

One function of Real Estate Law is to hold a hearing when there is a question as to the rights of persons to obtain or keep their real estate licenses. All hearings must be conducted in accordance with legal regulations set forth in the Administrative Procedure Act. A decision is made by the hearing officer based upon his or her findings. The commissioner may reject or accept the proposed decision or reduce the proposed penalty, and then make his or her official decision. The respondent has the right of appeal to the courts.

B. LICENSES: REVOKE, RESTRICT, SUSPEND

The real estate commissioner can revoke, restrict or suspend the license of any real estate agent for misconduct.

The commissioner of real estate can 1) issue, 2) revoke, 3) restrict, or 4) suspend the license—courts cannot.

XIV. Common Real Estate Law Violations

All agents must adhere to the ethical and legal requirements of Section 10176 and Section 10177 of the Business and Professions Code, which include violations such as misrepresentation and failure to disclose hidden relationships.

SECTION 10176 OF THE BUSINESS AND PROFESSIONS CODE - *legal guideline for the licensee engaged in the practice and performance of any acts within the scope of the Real Estate Law.*

SECTION 10177 OF THE BUSINESS AND PROFESSIONS CODE - *applies to situations where the licensee involved was not necessarily acting as an agent or as a licensee.*

These regulations, which are known formally as the Regulations of the Real Estate Commissioner, have the force and effect of the law itself.

XV. Real Estate General Fund

All the money collected from license and exam fees goes into the Real Estate General Fund. Eighty percent is used for the operating expenses of the Department of Real Estate, eight percent is set aside for the Real Estate Education and Research Fund, and twelve percent to the Recovery Fund.

RECOVERY FUND - *established for the payment of damages and arbitration awards to people who have suffered financial loss due to the wrongful act of a licensee in a real estate transaction.*

To qualify for these funds, plaintiffs must first obtain a judgment in civil court (or through arbitration) against a licensee on the grounds of fraud, misrepresentation, deceit, or conversion of trust funds. If, after reasonable effort, the judgment remains uncollected, a claim may be filed with the Commissioner's office.

A license is suspended until the fund is reimbursed (plus interest). The total liability of the recovery fund in any one transaction is $20,000, and the total series of judgments against any individual licensee is limited to $100,000.

XVI. Trade and Professional Associations

TRADE OR PROFESSIONAL ASSOCIATION - *a voluntary, non-profit organization made up of independent firms in the same industry.* It is formed to promote progress, aid in solving the industry's problems, and enhance its service to the community.

A "Realtor®" is a member of a real estate trade association.

A. LOCAL REAL ESTATE BOARDS

LOCAL BOARD OF REALTORS® - *a voluntary organization of real estate licensees in a particular community.*

B. CALIFORNIA ASSOCIATION OF REALTORS® (CAR)

CALIFORNIA ASSOCIATION OF REALTORS® - *the state division of the National Association of Realtors®.*

www.car.org (California Association of Realtors®)

C. NATIONAL ASSOCIATION OF REALTORS® (NAR)

NATIONAL ASSOCIATION OF REALTORS® - *the national trade association for all the state associations and local boards of Realtors® in the United States.* NAR unifies the real estate industry at the national level. It encourages legislation favorable to the real estate industry and enforces professional conduct standards on behalf of its members across the nation.

www.realtor.com (National Association of Realtors® - NAR)

1. Trade Name

Use of the term "Realtor®" without proper group affiliation is grounds for revocation of your license.

2. Code of Ethics

It is the generally accepted code of ethics for real estate people, and every Realtor® swears to abide by it.

D. REALTIST DEFINED

The National Association of Real Estate Brokers, whose members are called "Realtists," is a national organization of brokers with a predominance of black members, but whose membership is by no means limited to black membership. The organization has local boards in the largest cities in most states.

 www.nareb.org/index.htm (National Association of Real Estate Brokers)

E. NATIONAL ASSOCIATION OF HISPANIC REAL ESTATE PROFESSIONALS (NAHREP)

The National Association of Hispanic Real Estate Professionals (NAHREP) is a national non-profit trade association made up primarily of Hispanic members. The mission statement of NAHREP is "to promote the general success of Hispanic Real Estate Professionals and to increase the percentage rate of home ownership amongst Hispanic-Americans."

 www.nahrep.org (National Association of Hispanic Real Estate Professionals)

F. NO AFFILIATION NECESSARY

A real estate licensee need not be a member of any trade or professional association. In this case, he or she is simply referred to as a salesperson or broker. There is no compulsion for any licensee of the department of Real Estate to join or affiliate with any local or state organization.

Methods of Land Description

COMMON ADDRESS - *the address used for mail delivery, or the address posted on the property.*

A common address does not give all the information needed to properly describe or locate a property. In California, every parcel of land must be properly described or identified. If the property is to be sold or financed, a recognized legal description is required.

A. METES AND BOUNDS (Surveyor's Maps)

METES AND BOUNDS - the method of identifying (describing) property in relationship to its boundaries, distances, and angles from a given starting point. **MONUMENT -** a fixed object and point set in the earth by surveyors to establish land locations.

B. SECTIONS AND TOWNSHIPS (U.S. Government Survey)

The United States Government Survey system was established to identify all public lands by the use of "base lines" and "meridians" starting from a precise surveying point.

1. California's Three Base Line and Meridian Line Intersections

a. Humboldt; b. Mount Diablo; c. San Bernardino

2. Base Lines and Meridian Lines

BASE LINE - a is horizontal line that runs east and west from any one of the three starting points in California.

TOWNSHIP OR TIER LINES - are lines running parallel to the base line. Each township line is up and down in six-mile increments. It is possible to move north or south a designated number of townships (a 6-mile increment equals one township) from the base line.

MERIDIAN LINES - vertical lines that run north and south from any one of the three starting points in California. Meridians are also marked off, but each 6-mile increment north or south on a meridian is called a township or tier.

RANGE LINES - are north and south lines (parallel to the principal meridian) in increments of six miles each (a 6-mile increment equals one range).

TIERS, RANGES AND TOWNSHIPS

				A	Tier 3 North
		6 Miles x 6 Miles			Tier 2 North
	BASE	LINE			Tier 1 North
San Bernardino					Tier 1 South

Range 1 West, Range 1 East, Range 2 East, Range 3 East, Range 4 East

3. Townships

TOWNSHIP - a 6-mile by 6-mile square of land where a tier intersects with a range. Thus, each township contains 36 square miles. Townships are the main divisions of land in the rectangular survey system. Each township is identified according to its distance from the principal meridian and base line intersection.

4. Sections (There are 36 sections in a township)

SECTION - a 1-mile square of land consisting of 640 acres. A section can be broken down into halves or quarters.

6	5	4	3	2	1
7	8	9	10	11	12
18	17	16	15	14	13
19	20	21	22	23	24
30	A	28	27	26	25
31	32	33	34	35	36

SECTION "A"

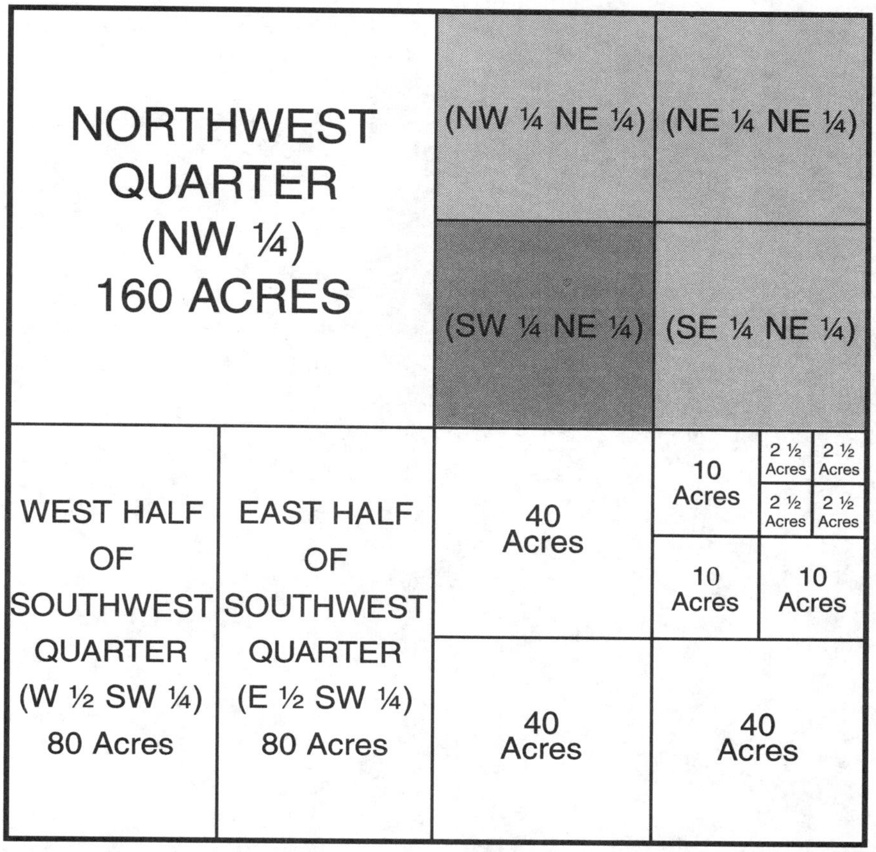

NORTHWEST QUARTER (NW ¼) 160 ACRES		(NW ¼ NE ¼)	(NE ¼ NE ¼)
		(SW ¼ NE ¼)	(SE ¼ NE ¼)
WEST HALF OF SOUTHWEST QUARTER (W ½ SW ¼) 80 Acres	EAST HALF OF SOUTHWEST QUARTER (E ½ SW ¼) 80 Acres	40 Acres	10 Acres / 2 ½ Acres / 2 ½ Acres / 2 ½ Acres / 2 ½ Acres / 10 Acres / 10 Acres
		40 Acres	40 Acres

C. LOTS, BLOCKS, AND TRACTS (RECORDED SUBDIVISIONS)

In California, subdivisions are granted by the Department of Real Estate. The subdivision map, however, is approved by the county or city in which the property is located. The approved subdivision map is recorded at the County Recorder's Office. Once it is recorded, all future transactions can be referenced to that map.

D. OTHER TERMS

PLAT MAP - another name for approved subdivision map.

ACRE - 43,560 square feet.

SQUARE ACRE - 208.71 square feet, but this number is generally rounded off to 209 feet square.

MILE - 5,280 feet long.

SQUARE MILE - contains 640 acres.

SECTIONS - are one square mile.

TOWNSHIP - six miles square (36 square miles).

COMMERCIAL ACRE - an acre minus any required public dedications.

ROD - 16.5 feet long (5.5 yards).

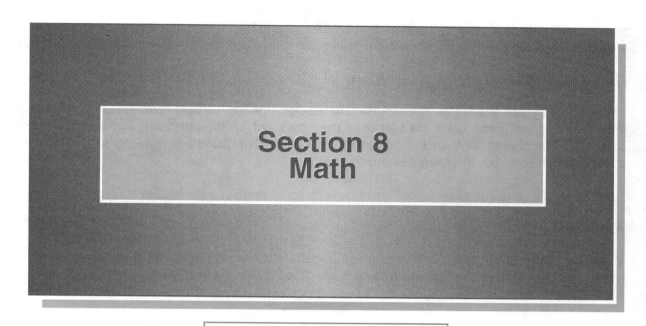

DRE Testing Emphasis:
Salesperson Approx. 10%
Broker Approx. 10%

I. Introduction

Math is a fundamental tool used by real estate licensees in all aspects of their profession. When you become a licensee, you will be using math to compute loan amounts, closing costs, commissions, and the square footage of property. Because math is such a vital part of the real estate profession, a fair portion of the real estate license exam is made up of math problems.

A. APPROACH TO SOLVING MATH PROBLEMS

While the prospect of mathematical computations arouses fear in the hearts of many of us, the math principles you will need to know are actually very basic. Solving math problems can be simplified by using a step-by-step approach. The most important step is to thoroughly understand the problem. You must know what answer you want before you can successfully work any math problem. Once you have determined what it is you are to find (for example, interest rate, loan-to-value ratios, or amount of profit), you will know what formula to use.

Then you must choose the correct mathematical formula. The formulas you will most likely be using will be explained in this chapter.

The next step is to substitute the numbers you know into the formula. In many problems you will be able to substitute the numbers into the formula without any additional steps. However, in many other problems, it will be necessary to take one or more preliminary steps; for instance, converting fractions to decimals.

Once you have substituted the number into the formula, you will have to do some computations to find the unknown. Most of the formulas have the same basic form ($A = B \times Q$). You will need two of the numbers (or the information that enables you to find two of the numbers) and then you will have to either divide or multiple them to find the third number—the answer you are seeking.

B. THE BASIC MATHEMATICAL FORMULA

Though it may not seem like it, the formulas we apply when solving routine real estate math problems are the same ones we use over the course of an ordinary day; for instance, when balancing the check book or budgeting for groceries. The numbers may be larger and the situations different, but the formulas are the same.

To illustrate the basic mathematical formula, let's solve this simple equation:

$2 \times 3 = ?$

Most of us learned our multiplication tables (at least I through 10) in the third or fourth grade, so we can quickly answer the above problem without too much trouble:

$2 \times 3 = 6.$

But what if we are looking for something else: $? \times 3 = 6.$

Again, you know without picking up a pencil that the answer is two. But what is significant here is that we have transformed a multiplication problem into a division problem: $6 \div 3 = 2$. Likewise, if the question is $2 \times ? = 6$, the problem is solved by division: $6 \div 2 = 3$.

Now let's work the same kind of problem but use larger numbers: $186 \times 1,412 = ?$

The answer is $186 \times 1,412 = 262,632$. If we rearrange the equation, we get $? \times 1,412 = 262,632$.

Answer: $262,632 \div 1,412 = 186$.

The numbers above are larger than $2 \times 3 = 6$, but the formula is the same. In the first instance we have a simple multiplication problem; in the second and third instance we have simple division problems. Now let's look at some typical real estate math problems.

II. Percentage Rates

The basic formula for a percentage rate problem is: the percentage of the total equals the part, or percent x total = part.

$$\% \; x \; T = P$$

Let's look at some real estate math problems using this formula:

1. A lender made an $86,000 loan at 13% interest. What is the annual interest?

   % x T = P
   13% x $86,000 = ?
   .13 x 86,000 = $11,180
       or

2. A lender made a loan at 13% annual interest which yielded $11,180. What was the loan amount?

   % x T = P
   13% x ? = $11,180
   11,180 ÷ .13 = $86,000
       or

3. A lender made a loan of $86,000 which yielded $11,180 annual interest. What was the interest rate?

   % x T = P
   ? x $86,000 = $11,180
   $11,180 ÷ 86,000 = 13%

Now let's compare the real estate math equations with our initial simple equation.

   2 x 3 = ?   *13% x 86,000 = ?*
   2 x 3 = 6   *.13 x $86,000 = $11,180*

   ? x 3 = 6   *? x $86,000 = $11,180*
   6 ÷ 2 = 3   *$11,180 ÷ $86,000 = .13*

   2 x ? = 6   *13% x ? = $11,180*
   6 ÷ 2 = 3   *$11,180 ÷ .13 = $86,000*

As you can see in the above examples, the formulas are the same:

   – if the unknown in the equation is on the **right**, it is a **multiplication** problem;

   – if the unknown is in the **center** or to the **left**, it is a **division** problem.

DIFFERENT CIRCUMSTANCES, SAME FORMULA

Even if the circumstances change, the formulas do not. For example:

1. A lender made a $95,000 loan which yielded $8,250. What was the interest rate?

or

2. A real estate broker sold a house for $95,000 and earned a commission of $8,250. What was the commission rate?

or

3. An investor earned $8,250 from an investment of $95,000. What was the investor's rate of return?

or

4. Based on an apartment's annual net income of $8,250, an appraiser estimated the property's worth to be $95,000. What capitalization rate did she use?

The circumstances in each of the above problems are different and may appear to require different solutions. But they don't—in every instance the formula is the same.

> $? \times 3 = 6$ $? \times \$95,000 = \$8,250$
> $6 \div 3 = 2$ $\$8,250 \div \$95,000 = .086842$ or 8.7%

Problems involving percentages or rates (e.g., interest rates, commission rates, rates of return, etc.) can almost always be solved by a variation of the $2 \times 3 = 6$ formula. Invariably, percentage rate problems are made up of three parts: two known parts and one unknown part. Armed with two of the three-piece "percentage rate puzzle," it is easy to find the missing part.

ARRANGING THE EQUATION IN THE PROPER ORDER

Many students have trouble arranging the numbers that make up a $2 \times 3 = 6$ equation in the proper sequence. For example, you know that a bank made a $48,000 loan and collected $5,280 in annual interest. You want to discover the interest rate. You know the two necessary numbers to solve the problem and you know how to plug them into the percentage rate formula:

> $\% \times T = P$
> $? \times \$48,000 = \$5,280$

Because the unknown number is on the left, you know you must rearrange the formula into a division problem. But in what order should they be arranged? If you have an aptitude for math, you will easily determine the proper sequence. But such an inclination, like the ability to carry a tune or paint a picture, is not possessed by everyone. Fortunately, while you may not instinctively know how to set up the problem properly, you can do it easily by following the steps outlined below.

Step 1: Set up the equation by the "x" and signs. (The x always comes before the = sign: ___ x ___ = ?)

Step 2: Using the percentage formula, plug in the numbers you know:
$\% \times T = P$
$? \times \$48,000 = \$5,280$

Step 3: The unknown quantity always goes after the equal sign. In this case it is the interest rate that is unknown. So we must rearrange the equation so that the interest rate portion of the equation comes after the equal sign. Remember that when the unknown factor is on the left side of the equal sign, the problem becomes a division problem: ___ ÷ ___ = ? *(interest rate)*.

Step 4: Use the appropriate variation of the *2 x 3 = 6* formula to determine the proper sequence of numbers.

? x 3 = 6   *? x $48,000 = $5,280*
6 ÷ 3 = 2   *$5,280 ÷ $48,000 = .11 or 11%*

Exercise: A real estate broker negotiated the sale of a properly. The commission was $7,150. The commission rate was 5%. What was the sales price?

Step 1:

Step 2:

Step 3:

Step 4:

Solution:

Step 1:   *? x ?*   =   *?*
Step 2.   *.05 x ?*   =   *$7,150*
Step 3:   *? ÷ ?*   =   *? (total unknown)*
Step 4:   *$7,150 ÷ .05*   =   *$143,000*
                Sales price: =   *$143,000*

PROFIT OR LOSS PROBLEMS

A variation of the typical percentage rate problem is the profit or loss problem. An example of a profit or loss problem is shown below:

Example: Jones bought a property and sold it nine years later for $92,000. This represented a 23% profit. What did Jones originally pay for the property?

The formula for solving this problem is the same as for any other percentage rate problem:

2 x 3 = 6
2 x ? = 6
1.23 x ? = $92,000

As you probably noticed, the figure placed in the equation is not .23 (23%) but 1.23 (123%). This is because the selling price ($92,000) is 123% (not 23%) of the original purchase price. Jones sold the property for 123% of what was originally paid for it. If the property would have sold for 23% of the original price, Jones would have sustained a substantial loss.

> *1.23 x ? = $92,000*
> *$92,000 ÷ 1.23 = $74,797*

Look what would happen if you placed .23 in the equation instead of 1.23:

> *.23 x ? = $92,000*
> *$92,000 ÷ .23 = $400,000 (incorrect)*

In the question it is stipulated that $92,000 represented a profit. Jones could hardly have paid $400,000 for the properly, sold it for $92,000 and claimed a profit.

At this point, many of us might ask: "Why can't we just take 23% of $92,000 and subtract it to find the original purchase price?"

Because we are looking for 23% of the unknown (original purchase price) and not 23% of $92,000.

> *$92,000 x .23 = $21,160*
> *$92,000 - $21,160 = $70,840 (incorrect)*

Now let's try a loss problem. Suppose Abernathy sold Blackacre for $69,000, which was 17% less than the purchase price. To find out the original purchase price, your equation would read as follows:

> *.83 x ? = $69,000*
> *$69,000 ÷ .83 = $83,133*

As you might have guessed, you always **add or subtract the percentage of gain or loss from 100%**.

If you buy and sell for the same price, you receive 100% of what you paid for the property. If you sell for an 11% profit, you receive 111% of what you paid for the property. If you sell for an 11% loss, you get 89% of what you paid. For the sake of working a profit or loss problem, add the percentage of profit to, or subtract the percentage of loss from, 100%.

QUIZ - PERCENTAGE RATE PROBLEMS

1. Jones paid $98,500 for his home in 1987, but lost his job one year later and was forced to sell the property quickly. Acting under pressure, he settled for 9% less than what he had paid one year earlier. What was the selling price?

    a. $88,000
    b. $90,411
    c. $89,635
    d. $86,841

2. Mary bought a small apartment in 1984 for $142,000. In late 1987, she sold it for $163,655. What was her percentage of profit?

    a. 12.5%
    b. 13.23%
    c. 14.61%
    d. 15.25%

3. Carmichael bought a rental home four years ago. Recently he accepted an offer of $119,500 for the property because it represented a 25% profit over the original purchase price. What did he first pay for the property?

    a. $90,150
    b. $95,600
    c. $89,625
    d. $93,500

4. Jones bought an apartment building two years ago. Under her management, monthly income from the apartment has gone up from $4,500 to $6,300. What is the percentage of increase?

    a. 71%
    b. 35%
    c. 40%
    d. 120%

5. First National loaned Smith $73,500. The year interest payments amounted to $7,715.50. What was the interest rate charged on the loan?

    a. 10.5%
    b. 11%
    c. 9.5%
    d. 10%

6. On the sale of his house, John took back a second mortgage for $15,000, with payments of interest only at 10.5% per annum during the first three years. How much interest will John receive in the first year?

    a. $131
    b. $1,575
    c. $1,500
    d. $4,725

MATH

7. If property values have increased by 27% over the past five years, what is the current value of a home that sold for $92,000 five years ago?

    a. $119,000

    b. $127,000

    c. $116,840

    d. $72,441

8. A $20,000 investment yielded $3,000 in profit during the first year. What was the percent of return on the investment?

    a. 15%

    b. 17%

    c. 20%

    d. 30%

ANSWERS TO PERCENTAGE RATE PROBLEMS

1. **c.** $98,500 x .91 = ?

      $98,500 x .91 = $89,635

2. **d.**   ? x $142,000 = $163,655

      $163,655 ÷ $142,000 = 1.1525

      1.1525 = .1525 or 15¼% profit

3. **b.**   1.25 x ? = $119,500

      $119,500 ÷ 1.25 = $95,600

4. **c.**   ? x $4,500 = $6,300

      $6,300 ÷ 4,500 = 1.40

      1.40 = .40 or 40% increase

5. **a.**   ? x $73,500 = $7,715.50

      $7,715 ÷ 73,500 = .105 or 10.5%

6. **b.**   .105 x $15,000 = ?

      .105 x $15,000 = $1,575

7. **c.**   1.27 x $92,000 = ?

      1.27 x $92,000 = $116,840

8. **a.**   ? x $20,000 = $3,000

      $3,000 ÷ $20,000 = ?

      $3,000 ÷ $20,000 = 15%

III. Interest

ANNUAL RATES

Most interest problems involve calculating simple interest over a period of time. Interest rates are almost always annual rates. Thus, unless otherwise stated, if a lender quotes an 11% rate of interest, he or she means 11% per year. However, sometimes an interest problem will refer to semi-annual, biannual, semi-monthly or bimonthly interest payments. You should know what each term means.

Semi-annually: twice a year
Biannually: also twice a year
Semi-monthly: twice a month
Bimonthly: once every two months

30-DAY MONTHS; 360-DAY YEARS

Ordinarily, interest calculations are based on **30-day months** and **360-day years**. This means that with respect to interest computations, there are no 28- or 31-day months. This is done merely to simplify calculations.

SIMPLE INTEREST

Most interest problems involve simple interest.

SIMPLE INTEREST - *the interest paid only on the principal amount of the loan and not on accumulated interest*. Most personal and real estate loans call for simple interest.

COMPOUND INTEREST ("interest on interest") - *interest paid on both the principal and the accumulated unpaid interest*. For example:

First year
12% (rate) x $115,000 (loan) = $13,800 (interest)
Second year
12% (rate) x $128,800 ($115,000 + $13,800) = $15,456 (compound interest)

Unless the problem specifies that the interest is compound, it is always presumed to be simple interest.

COMPUTING ANNUAL INTEREST

To determine annual interest you need only multiply the amount of the debt by the annual interest rate.

rate of interest x principal loan amount = interest amount
r x p = i
12% (rate) x $115,000 (loan) = $13,800 (annual interest)

If you want the monthly interest, you divide annual interest by 12 (months).

$13,800 ÷ 12 = $1,150 (monthly interest)

To determine the daily interest cost you divide the annual interest by 360 (days) or the monthly interest by 30 (days).

> *$13,800 ÷ 360 = $38.33*
> *$1,150 ÷ 30 = $38.33*

BASIC INTEREST PROBLEMS

Let's start with a relatively easy interest problem.

> **Example:** Jones borrowed $12,400 at 13½% interest. How much interest did Jones pay?
> **Formula:** *r x p = i*
> *.1350 x $12,400 = $1,674*

But the problem might be posed a little differently.

> **Example:** Jones obtained a loan at 13½% interest. After one year Jones had paid $1,674 in interest. What was the loan amount?
> **Formula:** *r x p = i*
> *2 x ? = 6   .135 x ? = $1,674*
> *6 ÷ 2 = 3 $1,674 ÷ .135 = $12,400*

Once again, it's the *2 x 3 = 6* formula. Another way to present the problem is as follows:

> **Example:** Jones borrowed $12,400 and paid $1,674 annual interest. What was the interest rate?
> **Formula:** *r x p = i*
> *? x 3 = 6   ? x $12,400 = $1,674*
> *6 ÷ 3 = 2 $1,674 ÷ $12,400 = 13½%*

Occasionally, the problem will be complicated with a preliminary problem.

> **Example:** Jones borrowed $12,400 and paid the loan back after 90 days. Interest paid during that period was $418.50. What was the loan's interest rate?

Since the problem gives you the amount of interest for a 90-day period but asks for the annual rate of interest, the preliminary problem is to determine the amount of annual interest. If interest calculations are based on a 360-day year, 90 days would be one-fourth of a year. Therefore:

> *$418.50 (¼ annual interest) x 4 = $1,674 (annual interest)*

Once you have the annual interest, the rest is easy.

> *? x 3 = 6   ? x $12,400 = $1,674*
> *6 ÷ 3 = 2 $1,674 ÷ $12,400 = .135 or 13 ½%*

COMPUTING DAILY AND MONTHLY INTEREST

Earlier it was explained that annual interest divided by 360 (days) equals the daily interest, or divided by 12 (months) equals the monthly interest. This information can be very useful in solving certain problems.

Example: Your buyer seeks a temporary loan in the amount of $62,000 to help finance the purchase of a home. Her present home has been sold and the sale is expected to close in 45 days. She plans to use the proceeds from the sale to repay the temporary loan. You locate a lender who is willing to make the loan at 14¾% interest. Your buyer wants to know how much interest she will have to pay over the 45-day period.

Solution:

1. .1475 (rate) x $62,000 (loan) = $9,145 (annual interest)
2. $9,145 ÷ 360 = $25.40 (per day interest charge)
3. $25.40 (per day charge) x 45 (days) = $1,143 (interest payable)

If the closing was delayed 4 days and it took your buyer 49 days to repay the loan, how much interest did she pay?

49 x $25.40 = $1,244.60

Example: Jones borrowed $98,500 for five years with interest-only payments. After 18 months, she pays off the loan and learns that during this period she has paid $21,054.38 in interest. What was the interest rate?

Solution:

1. Determine monthly interest charge
   $21,054.38 ÷ 18 = $1,169.69 (monthly interest)
2. Multiply monthly interest by 12 for annual interest
   12 x $1,169.69 = $14,036.28 (annual interest)
3. ? x 3 = 6? x $98,500 = $14,036.28
   6 ÷ 3 = 2 $14,036.28 ÷ $98,500 = 14.25%

QUIZ - PERCENTAGE AND INTEREST RATE PROBLEMS

1. What is the annual interest rate on a $16,000 loan when the required interest payments are $160.00 per quarter? At least:

    a. 6%, but less than 7%
    b. 5%, but less than 6%
    c. 4%, but less than 5%
    d. 3%, but less than 4%

2. An FHA borrower secured a loan in the amount of $57,250 to purchase a home. This loan was based upon 97% of the first $25,000 of the purchase price and 95% of the remaining balance. The purchase price of the property was most nearly:

    a. $59,737
    b. $54,397
    c. $57,890
    d. $60,120

3. Jones purchased a property for $200,000, paying 25% in cash and obtaining a purchase money loan for 75% of the purchase price. After 10 years, the property had doubled in value. Disregarding any equity build-up on the purchase money loan, what is Jones' initial cash investment now worth?

a. $120,000
b. $250,000
c. $100,000
d. $200,000

4. Mr. Adams and Mr. Hart each borrowed $75,000, using their homes as security. Mr. Adams' loan was for 20 years and Mr. Hart's loan was for 30 years. Adams' payments were $865.37, including 12¾% interest. Mr. Hart's payments were $815.03, including 12¾% interest. If both loans were paid over their full terms, Adams' interest payments would be approximately what percentage of the total paid by Hart?

a. 36%
b. 61%
c. 39%
d. 164%

5. A few months ago, a real estate investor purchased a property for $40,000. He made a $4,000 down payment and assumed a $36,000 trust deed against the property. No principal or interest payments are required during the first year. Soon after he resells for double the original purchase price. What is each dollar of his original cash investment now worth?

a. $10.00
b. $11.00
c. $1.00
d. $9.00

6. An investor paid $36,000 for a four-unit apartment house. Each apartment rents for $85 per month. The investor figures that by good management a profit of 45% of gross rentals could be made. If this is true, what rate of return will the investor realize on her investment?

a. 11.33%
b. 5.5%
c. 5.06%
d. 5.1%

7. The annual income from a property with a $120,00 building is $9,600. This represents a 6% return on the total investment. The indicated value of the land is:

a. 50% of the building value
b. 33% of the building value
c. 25% of the building value
d. 20% of the building value

8. An owner of an apartment building containing 20,000 square feet of living space wants to carpet 60% of the living space. If the carpet costs $6.00 per square yard, the total cost of carpeting would be most nearly:

    a. $8,000
    b. $13,333
    c. $15,050
    d. $72,000

9. Craft, who needed $3,000 to buy a new car, hired Broker Denton to negotiate a loan for him. Craft gave the lender a note for $3,600 secured by a second deed of trust against his home. The note was payable $77 per month including 10% interest per annum over a 3 year term. Craft signed a mortgage loan disclosure statement which showed that he would receive an estimated $3,000 from the completed transaction. The total principal amount which Craft must pay to the lender is:

    a. $3,600
    b. $3,000
    c. $3,100
    d. $3,492

10. There are five units in a condominium. Jones paid $12,600; Smith paid $13,500; Adams paid $13,750; Able paid $14,400; and Clark paid $15,250. There is a $1,800 annual maintenance fee and each owner must pay a proportionate share based upon the ratio of his or her unit purchase price to the total purchase price of all units. Mr. Jones' monthly share will be approximately:

    a. $28.12
    b. $27.17
    c. $36.00
    d. $32.40

11. If the value of a property is estimated to be $190,000 and the net income is $13,680, the capitalization rate must be:

    a. 7.2%
    b. 6.5%
    c. 7.5%
    d. 7%

12. An investor purchased property for $10,000 a few months ago, paying $1,000 in cash, with the seller taking back a trust deed for the balance of the purchase price. Soon thereafter, she sold the property for $20,000 before any payments had been made on the trust deed note. Under these circumstances, each dollar invested was worth:

    a. $100.00
    b. $11.00
    c. $1.10
    d. $10.00

13. An investor held a 5-year Trust Deed and Note which was recently paid in full at 7.2% interest per annum. If the total interest received from the borrower was $4,140, what was the approximate original amount of the loan?

    a. $11,500
    b. $57,500
    c. $29,700
    d. $5,900

14. In connection with a personal loan, a borrower paid $100 interest during a 90-day period. If the loan amount is $5,000, what was the interest rate?

    a. 8%
    b. 10%
    c. 5%
    d. 11%

15. Mr. Painter owns a parcel of land which is valued at $10,000. There is an existing first deed of trust in the amount of $9,000 which bears an annual rate of interest of 6%. Painter receives an 8% return on the property value after the standard operating expenses have been deducted. What would the return on his investment be?

    a. 80%
    b. 8%
    c. 26%
    d. None of the above

16. After deducting a $140.00 escrow fee and a commission equal to 6% of the sales price, the seller receives $13,584. What is the selling price?

    a. $14,540
    b. $14,440
    c. $12,770
    d. $14,600

17. Investor purchased a property for 20% below the listed price and later sold the property for the original listed price. What was the percentage of profit?

    a. 25%
    b. 40%
    c. 10%
    d. 20%

18. Astor sold his residence which was free and clear of any liens. Deductions made in escrow amounted to $215.30 plus a broker's commission of 6% of the selling price. The selling price was the only credit item. Astor received a $15,290 check from escrow. The selling price was most nearly:

    a. $16,495
    b. $16,430
    d. $16,200
    d. $16,266

19. A bank agreed to lend a property owner a sum equal to 66 2/3% of her property's appraised value. The interest rate charged on the amount borrowed is 15% per annum. The first year's interest amounted to $9,500. What was the value placed on the property by the bank?

   a. $75,000
   b. $85,000
   c. $100,000
   d. $95,000

20. Adams bought a property for $15,000, paying $2,000 cash and the balance on a $13,000 note. At the end of the first year, before any payments were made on the note, she sold the property for twice the amount paid. Each dollar of original investment would be worth:

   a. $7.50
   b. $11.00
   c. $8.50
   d. $6.50

21. How much money must be invested at 6% interest to generate an income of $125 per month?

   a. $50,000
   b. $25,000
   c. $20,000
   d. $9,000

22. Smith borrowed $750 and signed a straight note bearing interest at the rate of 6% per annum. If he paid $67.50 interest during the life of the note, what was its term?

   a. 20 months
   b. 24 months
   c. 18 months
   d. 12 months

23. A beneficiary is collecting interest-only payments on a first deed of trust. If the first payment of interest was $245, what is the loan balance if the interest rate is 12½% per annum?

   a. $20,000
   b. $23,520
   c. $24,260
   d. $25,000

24. If the total amount of interest paid over a five-year period came to $5,450 and the annual rate of interest was 8.4%, what was the original amount of the loan?

   a. $12,976
   b. $15,000
   c. $11,000
   d. $9,550

25. An investor bought two lots for a total of $3,000. Later he divided the lots into three lots and sold each for $2,400. His percent of profit was:

    a. 240%
    b. 140%
    c. 40%
    d. 20%

26. A husband and wife own a retirement unit in a resort area. The annual taxes on the property are $400,000. If the total taxes do not exceed 1% of the full cash value of the property, the "full cash value" would be:

    a. $40,000
    b. $20,000
    c. $80,000
    d. $10,000

ANSWERS TO PERCENTAGE AND INTEREST PROBLEMS

1. c.   Convert quarterly payments to annual payments ($160 x 4 = $640)
    ? x $16,000 = $640
    $640 ÷ $16,000 = 4%

2. a.   .97 x $25,000 = $24,250
    .95 x ? = $33,000
    $33,000 ÷ .95 = $34,737
    $25,000 + $34,737 = $59,737

3. b. $200,000 less $50,000 (25% initial cash investment = $150,000 loan
    $200,000 x 2 = $400,000 present value
    $400,000 - $150,000 = $250,000 present value of initial cash investment monthly share

4. b.   Adams will make 240 payments (20 yrs x 12 months) of $865.37
    $865.37 x 240 = $207,688.80
    $207,688.80 - $75,000 loan = $132,688.80 (interest)
    Hart will make 360 payments (30 yrs x 12 months) of $815.03
    $815.03 x 360 = $293,410.80
    $293,410.80 - $75,000 loan = $218,410.80 (interest)
    ? x $218,410.80 (Hart) = $132,688.80 (Adams)
    $132,688.80 ÷ $218,410.80 = .6075 or 61%

5. b. $40,000 x 2 = $80,000 sales price
    $80,000 - $36,000 = $44,000 equity
    $44,000 ÷ $4,000 (cash investment) = $11 value of each dollar invested

6. d. $85 (unit rent) x 4 (units) = $340 monthly rent
    $340 x 12 (mos.) = $4,080 gross annual rent
    $4,080 x .45 = $1,836 profit
    $1,836 profit ÷ $36,000 = .051 or 5.1%

7. **b.**   .06 x ? (property value) = $9,600
      $9,600 ÷ .06 = $160,000 property value
      $160,000 - $120,000 (building) = $40,000 land value
      $40,000 ÷ $120,000 = .3333 or 33%

8. **a.**   .60 x 20,000 = 12,000 sq. ft. to be carpeted
      12,000 sq. ft. ÷ 9 (convert to sq. yards) = 1,333.33 Sq. Yards
      1,333.34 x $6.00 = $8,000.04

9. **a.**   Craft signed a promissory note for $3,600 and that is the principal amount to be paid. The rest of the information is not relevant to the question.

10. **b.** $12,600 + $13,500 + $13,750 + $14,400 +
      $15,250 = $69,500 total purchase price of all units
      $12,600 ÷ $69,500 = .18 or 18% which is the ratio of Jones' unit price to total purchase price of all units
      $1,800 (maintenance fee) x .18 = $324 (Jones' annual share)
      $324 ÷ 12 = $27 (Jones' approximate monthly share)

11. **a.**   ? x $190,000 = $13,680
      $13,680 ÷ $190,000 = .072 or 7.2%

12. **b.** $20,000 resale price - $9,000 (trust deed) = $11,000 equity
      $11,000 ÷ $1,000 = $11 present value of each dollar invested

13. **a.** $4,140 ÷ 5 = $828 annual interest
      7.2% x ? = $828
      $828 ÷ .072 = $11,500 loan amount

14. **a.** $100 x 4 = $400 annual interest
      ? x $5,000 = $400
      $400 ÷ $5,000 = .08 or 8%

15. **c.**   .08 x $10,000 = $800 gross return
      $9,000 x .06 = $540 interest paid
      $800 - $540 = $260 (net return)
      $10,000 - $9,000 = $1,000 invested
      ? x $1,000 = $260
      $260 ÷ $1,000 = .26 or 26%

16. **d.**   .94 x ? = $13,724 ($13,584 + $140)
      $13,724 ÷ .94 = $14,600

17. **a.**   .80 x 100% = 80%
      80% x ? = 100%
      100% ÷ 80% = 1.25 or 125% or 25% profit

MATH

Example:
$100,000 (asking price) x .80 = $80,000 (sales price)
$80,000 x ? = $100,000 (resale price)
$100,000 - $80,000 = $20,000 profit
$20,000 ÷ $80,000 = .25 or 25%

18. a. .94 x ? = $15,505.30 ($15,290 + $215.30)
$15,505.30 ÷ .94 = $16,495

19. d. Determine the loan amount first:
.15 x ? = $9,500
$9,500 ÷ .15 = $63,333 loan amount
Relate loan amount to appraised value
.6666 x ? = $63,333
$63,333 ÷ .6666 = $95,009 value

20. c. $15,000 x 2 = $30,000 sales price
$30,000 - $13,000 = $17,000 equity
$17,000 ÷ $2,000 (cash investment) = $8.50 present value of each dollar invested

21. b. $125 x 12 = $1,500 annual income
.06 x ? = $1,500
$1,500 ÷ .06 = $25,000 investment

22. c. Determine annual interest:
.06 x $750 = $45 annual interest
$67.50 ÷ $45 = 1.5 year term of loan
1.5 years = 18 months

23. b. .125 x ? = $2,940 ($245 x 12)
$2,940 ÷ 125 = $23,520

24. a. $5,450 ÷ 5 = $1,090 annual interest
.084 x ? = $1,090
$1,090 ÷ .084 = $12,976

25. b. 3 x $2,400 = $7,200
? x $3,000 = $7,200
$7,200 ÷ $3,000 = 2.4 or 240%
Investor sold lots for 240% of what was paid for them; the profit is 140%

26. a. .01 x ? = $400
$400 ÷ .01 = $40,000

IV. Area and Volume

At some point in your exam you will probably be asked to compute the area of a lot or building. Area is the total surface as measured in square units, e.g., square feet or square yards. You may also have to measure the volume of something, like a building, which is the amount of space occupied in three dimensions, referred to as the cubic contents, i.e., cubic feet or cubic yards.

HOW TO FIND AREAS

Rectangles. A rectangle is a four-sided figure with four right angles. The opposite sides are equal in length and parallel to each other.

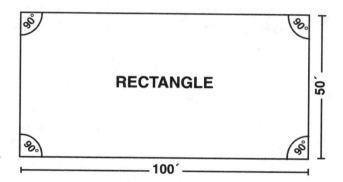

Formula: To find the area of a rectangle, multiply the length of one side of the rectangle by the length of an adjoining side. For example:

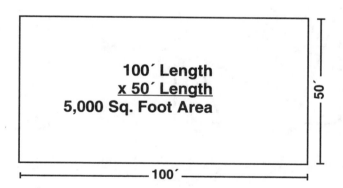

Keep in mind, in a real estate problem the rectangle will likely be an area of land or a building, and the length of any given side will probably be referred to as the width, frontage, depth, etc.

Square. A square is a four-sided figure with four right angles. All sides are equal and parallel to each other.

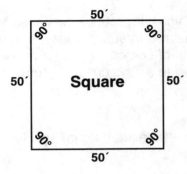

Formula: As with a rectangle, to find the area of a square, multiply the length of one side by the length of an adjoining side. For example:

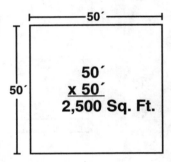

Triangles. A triangle is any three-sided figure.

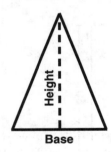

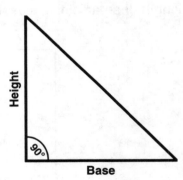

Formula: To find the area of a triangle, multiply 1/2 the base by the height to find the area. For example:

30' (height) x 10' (1/2 of base) = 300 sq. ft.

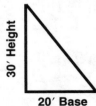

Trapezoids. A trapezoid is a four-sided figure with two sides that are parallel to each other and two sides which are not. The parallel sides are unequal in length, but the non-parallel sides are equal in length. For example:

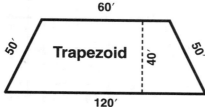

Formula: The average of the parallel sides is multiplied by the height to determine the area. For example:

60' + 120' = 180' ÷ 2 = 90'
90' average x 40' height = 3,600 sq. ft.

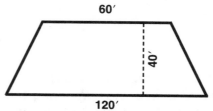

FINDING THE MISSING DIMENSION

In many cases, you are given the area and one of the dimensions and are asked to compute the missing dimension.

Example: The area of a rectangle is 4,000 square feet. The base is 80'. What is the height?

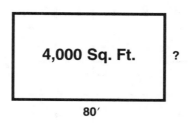

Solution: Using the always handy 2 x 3 = 6 formula, you can quickly determine the answer. To find the solution to the above problem simply divide the area by the known dimension:

4,000 sq. ft. ÷ 80' = 50' missing dimension

Missing Dimension - Right Triangles. If the area and either the base or height of a right triangle is known, the missing dimension can be computed by dividing the area by half of the known dimension. For example:

900 ÷ 15' (30 ÷ 2) = 60' base

Area = 900 Sq. Ft.

SOLVING AREA PROBLEMS INVOLVING GOVERNMENT SURVEY LEGAL DESCRIPTION

The government survey system is also called the **rectangular survey** system, or simply the **township and range** system. The basic unit of measurement in the government survey system is the **township**, an area of land six miles square (36 square miles).

6 Miles

6	5	4	3	2	1
7	8	9	10	11	12
18	17	16	15	14	13
19	20	21	22	23	24
30	29	28	27	26	25
31	32	33	34	35	36

36 Square Miles

6 Miles

Township

A township is divided into **36 sections**. Each section is 1 mile by 1 mile. The sections are numbered as indicated below. As you can see, the numbering scheme begins in the northeast corner snaking back and forth until it ends with section 36 in the southeast corner. The numbering system is the same for every township.

Township Divided Into Sections

NW — 640 Acres — 1 Mile — NE

6	5	4	3	2	1
7	8	9	10	11	12
18	17	16	15	14	13
19	20	21	22	23	24
30	29	28	27	26	25
31	32	33	34	35	36

6 Miles   6 Miles

SW   SE

One section of land contains **640 acres**. Each section can be divided in a number of ways. For instance, here it is shown divided into quarters. A quarter section contains **160 acres**.

NW¼ 160 Acres	NE¼ 160 Acres
SW¼ 160 Acres	SE¼ 160 Acres

**Section
640 Acres**

The SE¼ of section 27 contains 160 acres and is situated in a standard township as indicated below:

21	22	23	24
28		26	25
33	34	35	36

As previously mentioned, a section can be subdivided into smaller parcels. In this diagram, a parcel is divided in 1/4 of a quarter section. How many acres does the parcel contain?

Answer: 40 acres; ¼ of a quarter section (160 acres) is 40 acres.

20	21	22	23	24
29	28		26	25
32	33	34	35	36

LOCATING THE DESCRIBED LAND

To locate land described by government survey, **start at the end of the description and read backwards** to the beginning. Let's use the following description as an example.

The N½ of the SE¼ of the SW ¼ of section 12, township 7 north, range 3 east, Mt. Diablo meridian.

1. The first step is to locate the meridian. If a government survey description failed to include the meridian, it would be defective. The Mt. Diablo meridian is in central California.

2. Next identify the correct township by counting seven townships north of the baseline and three east of the meridian.

*The N½ of the SE¼ of the SW¼ Section 12, **Township 7 North, Range 3 East**, Mt. Diablo meridian.*

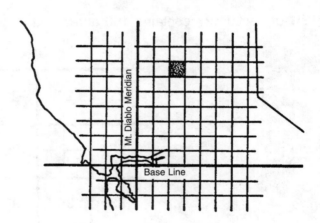

3. Locate Section twelve.

*The N½ of the SE¼ of the SW¼ of **Section 12**, Township 7 North, Range 3 East, Mt. Diablo meridian.*

6	5	4	3	2	1
7	8	9	10	11	12
18	17	16	15	14	13
19	20	21	22	23	24

4. Find the SW¼ of section twelve.

*The N½ of the SE¼ of the **SW¼** of Section 12, Township 7 North, Range 3 East, Mt. Diablo meridian.*

4	3	2	1
9	10	11	
16	15	14	13

5. Then find the SE¼ of the SW¼ of section twelve.

*The N½ of the **SE¼** of the SW¼ of Section 12, of Township 7 North, Range 3 East, Mt. Diablo meridian.*

4	3	2	1
9	10	11	
16	15	14	13

6. Finally, identify the N½ of the SE¼ of the SW¼ of section twelve in township 7 north range 3 east, Mt. Diablo meridian.

4	3	2	1
9	10	11	
16	15	14	13

DETERMINING NUMBER OF ACRES

Determining the number of acres in a government survey description is relatively simple. There are always 640 acres in a section, so start with the portion of the description that refers to the section and work backwards to the beginning. It is so easy you can do the calculations in your head.

> **Example:** The N½ of the E½ of the NE¼ of the SW¼ of the NE¼ of section 13, township 15 north, range 10 east, Humboldt meridian.

The township and range numbers and the name of the meridian are irrelevant to your computations. There are 640 acres in any section, including section 13, and that is all you need to know.

> *(2 1/2 acres)   (5 acres) (10 acres)   (40 acres)*
> North½ of the East½ of the NE¼ of the SW¼ of the
> *(160 acres) (640 acres)*
> NE¼ of section 13 (remainder of description irrelevant to computations)

As you can see, there are 2½ acres in the described parcel. The answer was achieved in seconds. To determine the number of square feet in the parcel, multiply the number of acres by 43,560 (square feet in an acre).

> *43,560 sq. ft. in an acre x 2.5 acres = 108,900 sq. ft. in parcel*

Caution: Very often a parcel will be situated in two sections. For example, "the southeast quarter of section 14 and the northeast quarter of section 22." When this happens, the acreage contained in each section is computed separately and then added together.

> *(160 acres)   (160 acres)*
> The SE¼ of section 14 **and** the NE¼ of section 22
>
> 160 acres in section 14
> +160 acres in section 22
> 320 acres in described parcel

Another variation of an area problem that pertains to government survey descriptions is where the described parcel is entirely contained within one section but is situated in more than one quarter section. For instance, "the South ½ of the Northwest ¼ **and** the Northeast ¼ of the Southwest ¼ of Section 11."

How many acres are in the described parcel?

>   (80 acres)   (160 acres)   (40 acres)
> The South ½ of the Northwest ¼ and the Northeast ¼ of
>   (160 acres)   (640 acres)
> the Southwest ¼ of Section 11.

>   80 acres
> $\pm\underline{40}$ acres
>   120 acres in the described parcel

The key in both of the preceding examples (parcel situated in more than one section or more than one quarter section) is the word "**and**" in the body of the description. The word "and" divides the description into parcels which must be computed separately and then added together.

Exercise: Find the number of acres contained in the following descriptions. Convert the acres into square feet.

1. The NE¼ of the SW¼ of the NW¼ of Section 6.

2. The W½ of the SW¼ of the NW¼ of the NW¼ of Section 22.

3. The S½ of the E½ of the SW¼ of the SE¼ of the NE¼ of Section 31.

4. The SE¼ of the SW¼ of the SE¼ of Section 20 and the N½ of the NW¼ of the NE¼ of Section 29.

5. The S½ of the SE¼ of the SW¼ of the NW¼ and the E½ of the NE¼ of the NW¼ of the SW¼ of Section 5.

Answers:

1. 10 acres x 43,560 = 435,600 square feet
The NE¼ (10) of the SW¼ (40) of the NW¼ (160) of Section 6 (640).

2. 5 acres x 43,560 = 217,800 square feet
The W½ (5) of the SW¼ (10) of the NW¼ (40) of the NW¼ (160) of Section 22 (640).

3. 2½ acres x 43,560 = 108,900 square feet
The S½ (2½) of the E½ (5) of the SW¼ (10) of the SE¼ of (40) the NE¼ (160) of Section 31 (640).

4. 30 acres x 43,560 = 1,306,800 square feet
The SE¼ (10) of the SW¼ (40) of the SE¼ (160) of Section 20 (640) **and** the N½ (20) of the NW¼ (40) of the NE¼ (160) of Section 29 (640).

5. 10 acres x 43,560 = 435,600 square feet
The S½ (5) of the SE¼ (10) of the SW¼ (40) of the NW¼ (160) and the E½ (5) of the NE¼ (10) of the NW¼ (40) of the SW¼ (160) of Section 5 (640).

Exercise: Find the number of acres contained in the shaded areas in the sections below.

1.

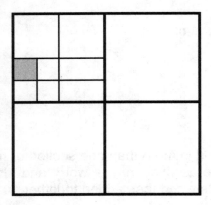

2.

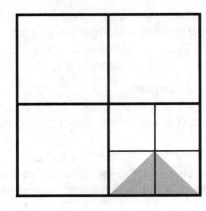

3.

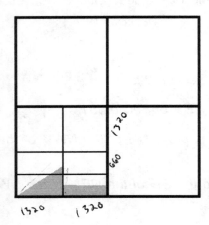

4.

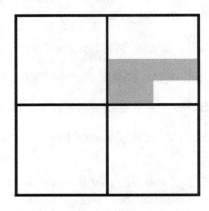

Answers:

1. **10 acres.** *It is the NW¼ of the SW¼ of the NW¼ of the section.*

2. **40 acres.** *The triangle has dimensions of 2,640 x 1,320. Half the base times the height. 1,320 x 1,320 = 1,742,400 square feet; divide by 43,560 = 40 acres.*

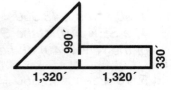

3. **25 acres.** *There is one triangle and one rectangle. Half the base times the height for the triangle: 660 x 990 = 653,400 square feet; divide by 43,560 = 15 acres. Base times the height for the rectangle: 1,320 x 330 = 435,600 square feet, divide by 43,560 = 10 acres. 15 acres + 10 acres = 25 acres.*

4. **60 acres.** *There is one square and one rectangle. 1,320' x 1,320' = 1,742,400 square feet, divide by 43,560 = 40 acres. 1,320' x 660' = 871,200 square feet; divide by 43,560 = 20 acres. 40 acres + 20 acres = 60 acres.*

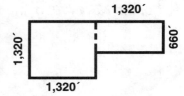

HOW TO FIND VOLUMES

Volume is always in cubic measurements. When recalling the difference between area and volume, think of the surface of one of a box's sides (area) and the airspace contained within the box (volume).

Unlike squares or rectangles, which have two dimensions, cubes are three-dimensional.

Example:

Rectangle	Cube
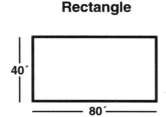	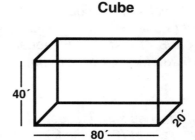

Contractors, engineers, and material suppliers frequently quote prices in cubic terms, e.g., $6.82 per cubic foot or $21.84 per cubic yard.

Formula: Find the area at the base of the cube, just as you would for any two-dimensional figure, then multiply the area by the third dimension.

Example:

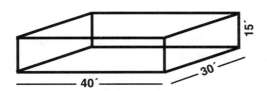

1. 30' x 40' = 1,200 sq. ft. area

2. 1,200 sq. ft. area
x15 3rd dimension
18,000 cubic ft. volume

Converting Different Measures. Real estate practitioners measure **distances** by the inch, foot, yard, or mile. **Areas** are usually measured by the square inch, square foot, square yard, or square mile. **Volumes** are measured by the cubic inch, cubic foot, or cubic yard.

When you add, subtract, divide, or multiply for distances, areas, or volumes, the measurements must be identical. For example, you cannot multiply 12 inches by 6 feet. You must first convert one or the other (inches to feet or feet to inches).

12 inches x 6 feet = 1 foot x 6 feet = 6 square feet

Measurements.

Length:

> 12 inches = 1 foot
> 3 feet = 1 yard
> 5,280 feet = 1 mile

Area:

> 12 inches x 12 inches (144 square inches) = 1 square foot
> 3 feet x 3 feet (9 square feet) = 1 square yard
> 208.71 feet x 208.71 feet (43,560 square feet) = 1 acre
> 5,280 feet x 5,280 feet = 1 square mile

Volume:

> 12 inches x 12 inches x 12 inches = 1 cubic foot
> 3 feet x 3 feet x 3 feet (27 cubic feet) = 1 cubic yard

Example: ACME Concrete is employed to lay a sidewalk in front of the new ABC Bakery Shop. The sidewalk is to be 5 feet wide, 15 yards long and 6 inches deep. How many cubic feet of concrete will be required to finish the sidewalk?

Answer: You can't multiply feet by yards by inches, so some conversions must be made before calculating the answer:

> 5 feet x 45 feet (3 x 15 yards) x .5 (6 inches = ½ foot = .5)
> 5 feet x 45 feet = 225 sq. feet (area)
> 225 feet x .5 = 112.5 cubic feet (volume)

Area and Volume Problems are Often Preliminary. Frequently, identifying the area or volume of something is only a first step towards solving a real estate math problem. In fact, more often than not the answer being sought involves money. For instance, in the preceding example, the question might have been, "If the concrete costs $1.50 per cubic foot, what would be the total cost of the sidewalk?"

> 5 feet x 45 feet = 225 sq. feet (area)
> 225 sq. feet x .5 feet = 112.5 cubic feet (volume)
> 112.5 x $1.50 = $168.75

Converting Square Yards and Cubic Yards. As indicated earlier, a square yard is 3 feet by 3 feet, a cubic yard is 3 feet by 3 feet by 3 feet.

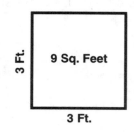

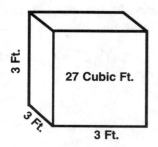

How To Pass The Real California Estate Exam

Conversions from square feet to square yards or cubic feet to cubic yards, and vice versa, are relatively simple.

1. Square feet to square yards. To convert square feet to square yards, simply divide by 9.

> **Example:** Foss owned a building which contained 12,640 square feet. How many square yards did it contain?
>
> *12,640 square feet ÷ 9 = 1,404.44 square yards*

2. Square yards to square feet. To do the reverse, convert square yards to square feet, multiply by 9.

> **Example:** Jones sold a building that had a roof surface area of 712 square yards. How many square feet were contained on the roof's surface?
>
> *712 square yards x 9 = 6,408 square feet*

3. Cubic feet to cubic yards. To convert cubic feet to cubic yards, divide by 27.

> **Example:** Johnson received a quote from an excavation contractor for the removal of 14,826 cubic feet of soil. How many cubic yards of soil were to be removed?
>
> *14,826 cubic feet ÷ 27 = 549.11 cubic yards*

4. Cubic yards to cubic feet: For this conversion, multiply by 27.

> **Example:** Smith purchased 1,842 cubic yards of land fill. How many cubic feet were included in the land fill?
>
> *1,842 cubic yards x 27 = 49,734 cubic feet*

MATH

QUIZ - AREA AND VOLUME PROBLEMS

Area Problems

1. A building has a floor space that measured 24' x 30'. If the walls are 6" thick, how many square feet would the building take up?

    a. 720 square feet
    b. 775 square feet
    c. 735 square feet
    d. 732 square feet

2. To identify the number of square feet in a square 40-acre parcel, you would multiply which of the following dimensions?

    a. 5,280' x 5,280'
    b. 1,320' x 1,320'
    c. 660' x 660'
    d. 2,640' x 2,640'

3. If a salesperson sold a parcel with 500 front feet at $400 a front foot and was to receive 40% of the broker's 6% commission, the salesperson would receive:

    a. $3,200
    b. $4,800
    c. $12,000
    d. None of the above

4. "Beginning at a point located 45' from the south-west comer of the intersection of 10th and Main Streets, follow a line due east 500', thence at a right angle due south 735', thence at a right angle due west 599', thence back to the point of beginning," is a legal description which contains approximately how many acres?

    a. 9
    b. 7
    c. 10
    d. 8

5. A parcel of land, which is rectangular in shape, has a canal running diagonally from one corner to the other. It divides the land into two equal lots. One lot measures 550 feet across and has a depth of 840 feet. Approximately how many acres are contained in the entire parcel?

    a. 4.7
    b. 8.3
    c. 5.3
    d. 10.6

6. The number of linear feet on each side of an acre of land that is almost square would be closest to:

    a. 199'
    b. 208'
    c. 255'
    d. 290'

7. What is the approximate square footage of the house in the drawing?

a. 2,200
b. 1,655
c. 1,433
d. 1,615

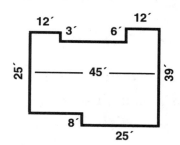

8. How many acres are contained in the triangle illustrated below?

a. 30
b. 40
c. 20
d. 10

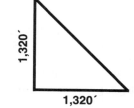

9. A parcel of land 660 feet wide by 1,320 feet deep totals:

a. 40 acres
b. 30 acres
c. 20 acres
d. 10 acres

10. 1,320 feet by 1,320 feet is:

a. 80 acres
b. 20 acres
c. 40 acres
d. 60 acres

11. An investor paid $193,000 for a lot on which he intended to build an apartment complex. If the lot was 200 feet deep and cost $4.40 per square foot, the cost per front foot was:

a. $960
b. $440
c. $220
d. $880

12. A rectangle shaped lot contains 45,100 square feet and has a depth of 410 feet. The owner wants to add onto the lot by buying the two lots on each side of it. If each adjoining lot contains 12,300 square feet, what will be the combined front footage of all three lots after the purchase?

a. 210 feet
b. 130 feet
c. 200 feet
d. 170 feet

13. A lot in a commercial subdivision contains 1,320 square feet. If the lot is rectangular and has a 45-foot frontage, what is the depth of the lot as expressed in feet?

    a. 31 feet
    b. 28 feet
    c. 29 feet
    d. 30 feet

14. The number of acres in the parcel of land illustrated below is:

    a. 80
    b. 160
    c. 120
    d. 180

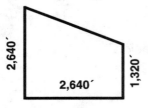

15. An individual owns a corner lot that measures 100 feet by 100 feet. She wants to install a six foot sidewalk within the lot limits along the two sides bordering the streets, and cement costs $1.70 per square foot. What will the sidewalk cost?

    a. $1,020.21
    b. $2,040.00
    c. $2,816.46
    d. $1,978.80

16. Hinckle owns a parcel of land ¼ mile wide and ½ mile long. He wants to clear a 50' wide area the length of the property plus 3 evenly divided 50' wide areas across the parcel. If he is charged $60 per acre to clear this strip, what will it cost?

    a. $455
    b. $540
    c. $444
    d. $450

17. Smith purchased a 3/4 acre lot with a depth of 100 feet for the purpose of subdividing it into 82.5' wide parcels. Before doing so, she elected to acquire the adjoining parcel which contained the same depth but had only 2/3 as much land. The cost of the second parcel was $1,400. She plans to divide the two parcels and sell them for $750 per lot. If on resale she nets 50% profit over what she paid for the parcels initially, what was the cost of the first parcel?

    a. $3,100
    b. $1,600
    c. $3,000
    d. $2,500

18. A lot that measures 1,740 feet by 1,740 feet represents approximately how many acres?

    a. 60
    b. 70
    c. 50
    d. 40

19. A square acre of land is divided into four lots of equal dimensions. The depth of each lot is approximately 209 feet. What is the total front footage of each lot?

    a. 218 feet
    b. 50 feet
    c. 52 feet
    d. 55 feet

20. Mr. Carlson owned a parcel of land free and clear of any liens. The property consisted of 397,440 square feet. Recently he decided to sell all of the property, except a 60' x 90' segment which he would keep for his own use. He received $1,250 per acre for the land that was sold. What was the sales price?

    a. $9,375.00
    b. $7,091.00
    c. $11,250.00
    d. $8,461.12

21. A road that runs the full length of the south half of a section is one side of a rectangular parcel. If the parcel contains 3 acres in area, its width is nearest to:

    a. 40 feet
    b. 30 feet
    c. 50 feet
    d. 20 feet

22. How many linear feet of single-strand wire would be necessary to fence the parcel described as the NW¼ of the NW¼ of the NW¼ of section 6?

    a. 1,230
    b. 2,640
    c. 5,280
    d. 660

23. How many acres of land would be contained in the following? "The N½ of the W½ of the W½ of the NW¼ of Section 5 and the E½ of the NE¼ of the NE¼ of Section 6."

    a. 60 acres
    b. 50 acres
    c. 40 acres
    d. 20 acres

24. If an easement for a road runs across the entire south side of a section and the total area covered by the easement is four acres, the width of the road would be:

    a. 45'
    b. 35'
    c. 55'
    d. 25'

MATH

25. What is the total area contained in the following description? "The S½ of the SE¼ of Section 15 and the NE¼ of the NE¼ of Section 22 and the W½ of the NW¼ of Section 23."

    a. 220 acres
    b. 240 acres
    c. 160 acres
    d. 200 acres

Volume Problems

1. A two-story commercial building measures 46' x 80' at its base. The height of the first story is W and the height of the second story is 14'. Replacement cost of the first story is calculated at $4.40 per cubic foot; the second story cost is $3.20 per cubic foot. Based on the above, the replacement cost of the building would be:

    a. $518,144
    b. $329,728
    c. $416,211
    d. $423,936

2. How many board feet of wood are there in a board that is nine feet long and four inches by four inches?

    a. 8
    b. 6
    c. 12
    d. 4

3. How many cubic yards of cement are there in a driveway 30' x 34' x 4"?

    a. 1224
    b. 408
    c. 15
    d. None of the above

4. What is the replacement cost of the driveway if the concrete slab 4" thick costs $15.00 a cubic yard with labor totaling $272.00.

    a. $460.85
    b. $838.67
    c. $4,320
    d. $7,072

5. How man square feet of concrete would be required to construct a sidewalk 6" deep and 7' wide around the outside of a 60' x 90' corner lot?

    a. 1,099 square feet
    b. 1,050 square feet
    c. 1,001 square feet
    d. None of the above

6. How many board feet of lumber in a piece 2" x 4" x 12"?

    a. 12 board feet
    b. 8 board feet
    c. 6 board feet
    d. 4 board feet

ANSWERS TO AREA AND VOLUME PROBLEMS

Area Problems

1. b. The 6 inch walls add 1 foot to the base and 1 foot to the height (see illustration).

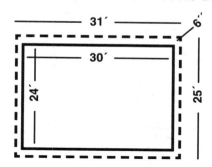

25' x 31' = 775 sq. feet

2. b. 40 acres (see illustration below)

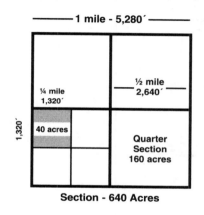

Section - 640 Acres

3. b. 500 x $400 = $200,000 (sales price)
$200,000 x 6% = $12,000 (commission)
$12,000 x .40 = $4,800 (salesperson's share)

4. a. Divide the parcel into a rectangle and a triangle as indicated below. Compute the area of the rectangle, the area of the triangle, add them together and divide by 43,560.

735' x 500' = 367,500 sq. feet
735' x 49.5 = 36,382.5 sq. feet
367,500 + 36,382.5 = 403,882.5 sq. feet in parcel
403,882.5 ÷ 43,560 = 9.27 acres

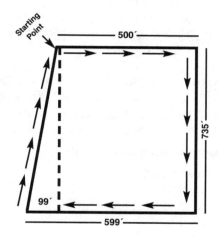

5. d. With or without the canal, the two parcels form a rectangle with dimensions of 550' x 840'.

840' x 550' = 462,000 sq. ft.
462,000 ÷ 43,560 = 10.6 acres

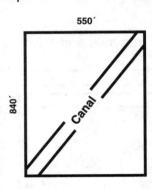

6. b. An acre that is square is 208.7' by 208.7'

7. c. 1,433 square feet. By drawing dotted lines as indicated below, you can form four rectangles with known dimensions:

3' x 12' = 36 sq. ft.
6' x 12' = 72 sq. ft.
8' x 25' = 200 sq. ft.
25' x 45' = 1,125 sq. ft.
Total = 1,433 sq. ft.

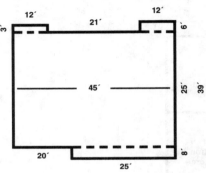

8. c. ½ base times height
660' x 1,320' = 871,200 sq. ft.
871,200 ÷ 43,560 = 20 acres

9. c. 660' x 1,320' = 871,200 sq. ft.
1,742,400 ÷ 43,560 = 40 acres

10. c. 1,320' x 1,320' = 1,742,400 sq. ft.
1,742,400 ÷ 43,560 = 40 acres

11. d. 1. Determine the area of land: $193,000 ÷ $4.40 = 43,864 sq. ft.
2. Determine front footage: 43,864 ÷ 200' = 219.32 front foot
3. $193,000 ÷ 219.32 = $879.99 or $880 per front foot

12. d. You have a large rectangle with a total area of 69,700 sq. ft. (12,300 + 45,100 + 12,300). Presuming the depth of all three lots is the same (410'), the frontage can be determined by dividing area by depth.

69,700 ÷ 410 = 170 frontage

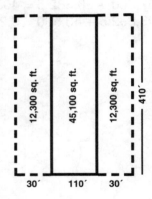

13. **c.** Area divided by frontage equals depth.

1,320 ÷ 45 = 29.33 depth

14. **c.** Once again, divide the parcel into a rectangle and a triangle, compute their areas, add them together, and divide by 43,560.

2,640 x 1,320 = 3,484,800 sq. ft.
2,640 x 660 = 1,742,400 sq. ft.
3,484,800 + 1,742,400 = 5,277,200 sq. ft.
5,277,200 ÷ 43,560 = 120 acres

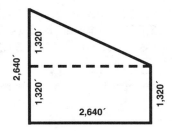

15. **d.** By looking at the illustration you can see that the dimensions of the sidewalk are 6' x 94' and 6' x 100'.

6' x 100' = 600 sq. ft.; 6' x 94' = 564 sq. ft.
600 sq. ft. + 564 sq. ft. = 1,164 sq. ft.
1,164 x $1.70 = $1,978.80

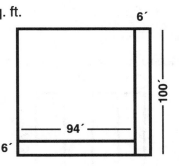

16. **c.** Again, as you can see from the illustration, the lengths of the "3 evenly divided" areas across the parcel should only be 1,270' (not 1,320') because of the 50' wide strip that is cleared for the length of the property.

50' x 2,640' = 132,000 sq. ft.
150' x 1,270' = 190,500 sq. ft.
132,000 + 190,500 = 322,500 sq. ft.
322,500 ÷ 43,560 = 7.40 acres
7.40 x $60 = $444

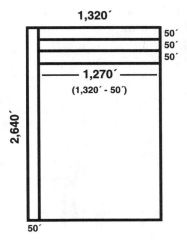

17. **b.** 1. Establish the area of the two parcels: the first parcel is 3/4 acres (43,560 x .75 = 32,670 sq. ft.); the second parcel is 2/3 of the first parcel (32,670 x .6666 = 21,780 sq. ft.);
32,670 + 21,780 = 54,450 total sq. ft.
2. Establish the total frontage (54,450 ÷ 110' depth = 495')
3. Determine how many 82.5' parcels can be obtained with 495' frontage (495 ÷ 82.5 = 6)
4. Multiply 6 (parcels) x $750 (selling price) = $4,500
5. 1.50 x ? (amount paid for the 2 lots) = $4,500
6. $4,500 ÷ 1.50 = $3,000 (amount paid for the two lots)
7. $3,000 - $1,400 (cost of second lot) = $1,600 (cost of first lot)

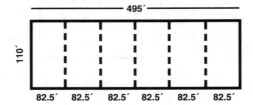

18. **b.** 1,740' x 1,740' = 3,027,600 sq. ft.
3,027,600 ÷ 43,560 = 69.5

19. **c.** Since the parcel is square, the width must also be 209'. Divide 209' by 4 = 52.25.

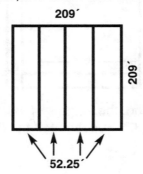

20. **c.** 397,440 sq. ft. - 5,400 sq. ft. (the 60'x 90' segment) = 392,040 sq. ft. that was sold.
392,040 ÷ 43,560 = 9 acres
9 x $1,250 = $11,250

21. **c.** You have the length of the rectangle, 2,640, and the area (3 x 43,560 = 130,680 sq. ft.)
130,680 ÷ 2,640 = 49.5 width

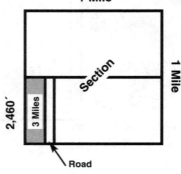

156

22. **b.** The described parcel is 1/8 mile on each of its 4 sides. 4 x 1/8 = 4/8 or 1/2 mile or 2,640'

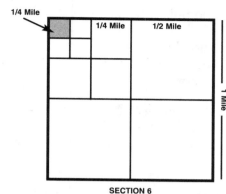

SECTION 6

23. **c.**
(20)   (40)   (80)

The N½ of the W½ of the W½ of the
(160)   (640)   (20)

NW¼ of Section 5 AND the E½ of the
(40)   (160)   (640)

NE¼ of the NE¼ of Section 6.

20 acres + 20 acres = 40 acres

24. **b.** 1. 4 x 43,560 = 174,240 sq. ft. area
2. 174,240 ÷ 5,280' = 33' width
This is the closest answer.

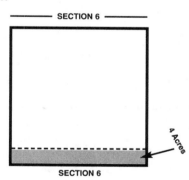

SECTION 6

SECTION 6

4 Acres

25. **d.**
(80)   (160)   (640)

The S½ of the SE¼ of Section 15 AND the
(40)   (160)   (640)

NE¼ of the NE¼ of Section 22 AND
(80)   (160)   (640)

the W½ of the NW¼ of Section 23.

80 acres + 40 acres + 80 acres = 200

Volume Problems

1. **d.** Determine area of first floor and multiply by the height.
   46' x 80' = 3,680 square feet
   3,680 sq. ft. x 16' = 58,880 cubic feet on first floor
   Second floor area the same as first floor: 3,680 sq. ft.
   Multiply by height: 3,680 x 14' = 51,520 cubic feet

   Multiply cubic feet on each floor by respective costs and add together:
   58,880 x $4.40 = $259.072
   51,520 x $3.20 = $164,864
   $423,936

2. **c.** A board foot of lumber is any combination of three dimensions totaling 144 cubic inches.
   (e.g., 12" x 12" x 1").
   Convert 9 feet to inches: 9' x 12" = 108"
   108" x 4" = 432 sq. inches x 4" = 1,728 cubic inches
   1,728 ÷ 144 = 12 board feet

3. **d.** 30' x 34' = 1,020 sq. ft. x 1/3 (convert inches to feet) = 340 cubic feet
   340 ÷ 27 = 12.59 cubic yards

4. **b.** Refer to the previous problem. 12.59 cubic yards x $15 = $188.85
   $1,888.85 + $272 (labor) = $460.85

5. **a.** You multiply 67' x 7' because there is an additional 7' at the corner due to the width of the sidewalk; then you multiply 90' x 7'.
   67' x 7' = 469 sq. ft.
   90' x 7' = 630 sq. ft.
   1,099 sq. ft.

   The 6" depth referred to in the question is irrelevant because you were asked for square feet rather than cubic feet.

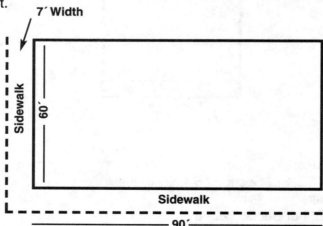

6. **b.** 2" x 4" = 8 sq. inches x 144 inches (convert feet to inches) = 1,152 cubic inches
   1,152 ÷ 144 (cubic inches in a board foot) = 8 board feet

V. Commission

Most commission problems are solved through the use of the 2 x 3 = 6 formula.

Example: Broker Jones sells a home for $82,000 and a 6% commission. What is the amount of the commission?

2 x 3 = ?
$82,000 x .06 = ?
$82,000 x .06 = $4,920

Example: Broker Jones earns a commission of $6,150, which was 7% of the selling price. What was the selling price?

? x 3 = 6
? x .07 = $6,150
$6,150 ÷ .07 = $87,857

Example: Broker Jones sells a home for $118,000 and earns a $7,080 commission. What was the rate of commission?

2 x ? = 6
$118,000 x ? = $7,080
$7,080 ÷ $118,000 = .06 or 6%

The arithmetic involved when computing commissions is usually quite simple. However, a commission problem can appear more difficult if the circumstances surrounding the problem are unfamiliar to us or if the problem contains information we do not recognize as irrelevant.

Example: Broker Herold negotiates a five-year lease calling for monthly payments of $2,850. The commission rate is 5%. What is the amount of the commission?

$2,850 x 60 (months) = $171,000
$171,000* x .05 = $8,550 commission

> **Lease commissions are usually based on the full amount of the lease (e.g., total lease payments over 5 years).*

Example: Broker Wells negotiates an eight year warehouse lease calling for payments of $4,200 a month. The agreed commission was 6% for the first two years, 3% for the next three years, and 1% for the last three years. What was the amount of the commission?

$4,200 x 24 (months) $100,800 x .06 = $6,048
$4,200 x 36 (months) $151,200 x .03 = $4,536
$4,200 x 36 (months) $151,200 x .01 = $1,512
Commission $12,096

Example: Broker Henderson listed a property for $162,000. Salesperson Smith from ABC Realty sold it one week later for $141,000. The commission was 7% and the two offices agreed to a 50/50 split. ABC Realty had an agreement with Smith to pay 28% of its share of the commission. How much did Smith receive?

$141,000* x .07 = $9,870 total commission
$9,870 x .50 = $4,935 to ABC Realty
$4,935 x .28 = $1,381.80 to Smith

*The asking price is irrelevant. The commission is based on the actual selling price.

QUIZ - COMMISSION PROBLEMS

1. A lot was sold for $14,500 and the seller paid a commission of 6% of the selling price. If the listing salesperson received 25% of the total commission, how much did the selling salesperson receive?

    a. $217.50
    b. $304.50
    c. $652.50
    d. None of the above

2. A real estate salesperson sold a lot for $31,000. If the broker's commission was 6% and the salesperson was to receive 45% of the total commission for selling the property, the salesperson would receive:

    a. $1,001.00
    b. $1,860.00
    c. $959.95
    d. $837.00

3. An owner listed her home at a price which would leave her $18,800 after she paid the broker a 6% commission. If the broker sold the property at the listed price, how much commission would be paid?

    a. $1,200
    b. $1,064
    c. $1,088
    d. $1,193

4. Mr. Smith listed a lot for sale for $18,300. The broker later presented an offer to Mr. Smith for much less than the listed price. Mr. Smith and the broker discussed the situation and agreed to counter offer at 6% below the asking price, provided the broker agreed to reduce her commission by 16 2/3%. Initially the broker's commission was to be 6% of the sales price. What would the seller receive for his property, assuming the only deduction from the selling price would be the broker's commission?

    a. $16,170
    b. $17,202
    c. $18,300
    d. $16,300

5. You sell a home for $100,000. The listing calls for a 6% commission on the sale. If your broker splits the commission 60/40 (40% for you), how much will you receive?

    a. $6,000
    b. $4,000
    c. $3,600
    d. $2,400

6. A broker earned a commission of $7,500 on the sale of a house. If the commission rate was 6%, what was the sales price?

    a. $125,000
    b. $100,000
    c. $130,000
    d. $150,000

7. A broker earns a commission of $6,650 on the sale of a property for $95,000. What is the rate of commission?

    a. 5%
    b. 6%
    c. 6.5%
    d. 7%

ANSWERS TO COMMISSION PROBLEMS

1. c. $14,500 x .06 = $870 commission
       $870 x (1.00 - .25) .75 = $652.50 commission to selling salesperson

2. d. $31,000 x .06 = $1,860 total commission
       $1,860 x .45 = $837 to salesperson

3. a.   ? x .94 = $18,800
       $18,800 ÷ .94 = $20,000
       $18,800 is 94% (100% - 6%) of $20,000
       $20,000 - $18,800 = $1,200

4. d. $18,300 x .94 (asking price less 6%)
       $17,202 (sales price)
       $17,202 x .06 = $1,032.12 (6% of sales price)
       $1,032.12 x .83333 (100% - 16.6666%)
       $860.10 (broker's commission)
       $17,202 - $860.10 = $16,341.90 (net to seller)

5. d.   .06 x $100,000 = ?
       .06 x $100,000 = $6,000 total commission
       .4 x $6,000 = ?
       .4 x $6,000 = $2,400

MATH

6.**a.** .06 x ? = $7,500
$7,500 ÷ .06 = ?
$7,500 ÷ .06 = $125,000

7.**d.** ? x $95,000 = $6,650
$6,650 ÷ $95,000 = ?
$6,650 ÷ $95,000 = 7%

VI. Amortization

To amortize a loan is to structure the payments of principal and interest so that they will retire the debt completely at the conclusion of the loan term.

HOW AMORTIZATION WORKS

Payments made on amortized loans include both principal and interest. In the early years of a long-term real estate loan, the majority of the payment is interest, and only a small part is applied to the principal. Nonetheless, with each payment the loan balance is lowered by the principal portion of the payment, and the next month's interest is calculated on the reduced balance.

> **Example:** A $110,000 loan at 12½% is amortized over 30 years. The monthly payment is set at $1,173.98. The interest portion of the first payment is $1,145.83
>
> $1,173.98 total payment
> - 1,145.83 interest payment
> $28.15 portion of 1st payment applied to principal

The debt is thus reduced by $28.15

> $110,000.00 original loan
> - 28.15
> $109,971.85 loan balance before second payment

The amount of all succeeding principal and interest payments will remain constant throughout the term of the loan, but since the debt is reduced with each payment, the interest portion diminishes steadily while the principal portion increases. In the last years of the loan, since the debt is significantly lower, most of each payment is principal with only a small part being applied to interest.

CALCULATING PRINCIPAL AND INTEREST PORTIONS OF EACH PAYMENT

There are two quick and easy ways to determine loan balances. The best way is to purchase and learn to use a pocket calculator that has the capacity to compute loan balances as quickly as you can feed it the necessary data—original loan amount, interest rate, term, and age of loan. The second way is to refer to printed amortization (loan progress) charts that can be obtained from most lenders. You cannot take loan progress charts into a license examination.

You can solve amortization problems without the help of a sophisticated calculator or loan progress charts, but the process is more time consuming. In order to compute a loan balance after a specified number of payments, you must know (1) the loan balance, (2) the annual interest rate, and (3) the total principal and interest payment. This data will be contained in a license examination question. A typical examination question will be answered to help explain the amortization process.

Amortization Formula

> **Example:** Abernathy obtained a $67,500 30-year loan at 11¾% interest. The principal and interest payments were $681.35. After making just three payments, she was transferred and had to sell the home. What was her loan balance after three payments?

Step 1: Calculate the interest for the initial loan amount.

> $67,500 *initial loan*
> x .1175 *(11¾%)*
> $7,931.25 *annual interest*

Step 2: Determine the monthly interest.

> $7,931.25 ÷ 12 *(months)* = $660.94 *monthly interest*

Step 3: Deduct the monthly interest from the monthly principal and interest payment.

> $681.35 *principal and interest payment*
> - 660.94 *interest portion of payment*
> $20.41 *principle portion of payment*

Step 4: Subtract the first principal payment from the original loan amount.

> $67,500.00 *original loan amount*
> - 20.41 *1st principal payment*
> $67,479.59 *principal balance after 1st payment*

You repeat this four-step process as many times as necessary to solve the problem. Our sample problem called for the loan balance after the third payment, so you repeat the process two more times.

Remember, the **interest portion of the next payment is based on the declining principal balance**. Thus, the interest for the second payment is computed on the basis of the $67,479.59 balance after the first payment.

Amortization procedure continued...

Step 1: Calculate the interest for the balance after the first payment.

> $67,479.59 *loan balance after 1st payment*
> x .1175
> $7,928.85 *annual interest*

Step 2: Determine the monthly interest.

> $7,928.85 ÷ 12 = $660.74 *monthly interest*

Step 3: Deduct the monthly interest from monthly principal and interest payment.

> $681.35 *principal and interest payment*
> -660.74
> $20.61 *principal portion of payment*

Step 4: Subtract the principal portion of payment from the loan balance after the first payment.

> $67,479.59 *balance after 1st payment*
> -20.61
> $67,458.98 *balance after 2nd payment*

Now repeat the process one more time.

Step 1: Calculate the interest for the balance after the second payment.

> $67,458.98 *balance after 2nd payment*
> x .1175
> $7,926.43 *annual interest*

Step 2: Determine the monthly interest.

> $7,926.43 ÷ 12 = $660.54 *monthly interest*

Step 3: Deduct the monthly interest from the monthly principal and interest payment.

> $681.35 *principal and interest payment*
> -660.54
> $20.81 *principal portion of interest*

Step 4: Subtract the principal portion of the payment from the loan's balance after the second payment.

> $67,458.98 *balance after 2nd payment*
> -20.81
> $67,438.17 *balance after 3rd payment*

Obviously the amortization process is tedious in the absence of loan progress charts or the more sophisticated pocket calculators, and the likelihood of an examination question asking for a loan balance after the third or fourth payments is minimal.

Example: How much interest will Abernathy pay over the entire 30-year loan term?

Answer: Multiply the monthly principal and interest payment by the number of months contained in a 30-year loan for the total principal and interest payments, then deduct the principal loan amount. The difference is the interest.

> 1.   30 *years*
>   x 12 *months*
>   360 *months in loan term*

> 2. $681.35 *monthly P & I payment*
>   x360
> $245,286 *total P & I payments*

> 3. $245,286 *total payments*
>   -67,500 *loan amount*
> $177,786 *total interest payments*

QUIZ - AMORTIZATION PROBLEMS

1. A second trust deed of $1,000 was to be paid in annual installments of $300 plus 9% interest, with a balloon payment of the balance at the end of the third year. The loan balance after the second annual installment had been paid was:

    a. $400.00
    b. $424.00
    c. $515.60
    d. $561.10

2. A $5,000 land contract of sale is payable on a principal reduction plan of $50 per month with interest at 10% per annum. Based on these figures, how long will it take to amortize the loan?

    a. 100 months
    b. 7 years
    c. 10 years and 8 months
    d. The answer cannot be determined

3. Jim Carlson, a licensed real estate broker, obtained an offer from Ms. Green on a vacant lot for $6,000 on the following terms: $2,000 down with the balance secured by a purchase money trust deed and note, payable at $70 per month, including interest at 7.2%. The offer was accepted by the seller. What is the loan balance after the first three monthly payments?

    a. $3,861.17
    b. $3,790.00
    c. $3,466.83
    d. $3,186.18

4. If a purchase and sale agreement called for the buyer to execute a second trust deed in favor of the seller in the amount of $2,500, payable at $30 per month, including interest at 8%, the first month's principal payment would be:

    a. $16.67
    b. $30.00
    c. $20.00
    d. $13.33

5. The following information pertains to an exclusive authorization and right to sell: Ending at noon on June 5, 1987. Selling Price: $85,000 including ww/cpts and drapes. Terms: $28,000 cash or more. Buyer to assume existing 1st deed of trust and note of approximately $57,000 payable in monthly installments of $447.51 including 9% interest, with all unpaid principal and interest due and payable in full on March 1, 1993, or upon resale of the property, whichever comes first. If the property was sold on May 10, 1987, what would the seller's loan balance be at the time of sale if the listing was signed by the seller April 27, 1987 and all payments including taxes are current?

    a. $56,979.99
    b. $56,982.44
    c. $57,552.49
    d. $56,552.49

6. If a note in the amount of $112,450 specified monthly payments over a period of 30 years at 11.3% interest per annum, what is the first month's interest payment?

    a. $1,016.12
    b. $1,058.90
    c. $1,082.41
    d. $998.72

7. Mr. Jones purchased a home and financed it with a 1st deed of trust and note in the amount of $20,000 payable at $143.90 per month, including 7.2% interest. Five years later, he sold the home for cash. The loan balance at the time of sale as $18,000. There was a prepayment penalty of 2% of the original loan amount. Based only upon the figures provided, how much did the loan cost Mr. Jones if he sold his property for $20,000?

    a. $7,034
    b. $8,634
    c. $9,034
    d. $9,067

8. Ms. Adams bought a home for $75,000. She paid $15,000 cash and financed the balance for 30 years with amortized payments of $529.36 per month including 10.2% interest. If all payments were made when due, what is the percentage of interest costs to the original purchase price?

    a. 154%
    b. 57%
    c. 75%
    d. 174%

9. A house cost $120,000. The cash down payment was $25,000. The purchaser executed a first deed of trust for the balance of the purchase price payable at $896.83 per month including interest at 11% per annum for 30 years. The interest cost for this loan is what percentage of the selling price?

    a. 169%
    b. 69%
    c. 190%
    d. 59%

MATH

ANSWERS TO AMORTIZATION PROBLEMS

1.a. The key to this question is the term "plus interest," which tells you that the $300 principal payments do not include interest. There are two annual principal installments made in the amount of $300, plus interest. $1,000 - $600 = $400

2.a. Again, the question specifically states that the contract is based on "a principal reduction plan of $50 a month." $5,000 ÷ $50 = 100 months

3.a. $6,000 - $2,000 = $4,000 trust deed
$4,000 x .072 = $288 (annual interest)
$288 ÷ 12 = $24 (1st month's interest)
$70 payment - $24 interest = $46 1st month's principal
$4,000 - $46 = $3,954 balance after 1st payment
$3,954 x .072 = $284.69 annual interest
$284.69 ÷ 12 = $23.72 2nd month's interest
$70 - $23.72 = $46.28 2nd month's principal
$3,954 - $46.28 = $3,907.72 balance after 2nd payment
$3,907.72 x .072 = $281.36 annual interest
$281.36 ÷ 12 = $23.45 3rd month's interest
$70 - $23.45 = $46.55 3rd month's principal
$3,907.72 - $46.55 = $3,861.17 balance after 3rd payment

4.d. $2,500 x .08 = $200 annual interest
$200 ÷ 12 = $16.67 1st month's interest
$30 - $16.67 = $13.33 1st month's principal payment

5.a. The seller would have made one principal and interest payment between the date of the listing (4/17) and the date of sale (5/10).
$57,000 x .09 = $5,130 annual interest
$5,130 ÷ 12 = $427.50 interest portion of May payment
$447.51 - $427.50 = $20.01 principal portion of May payment
$57,000 - $20.01 = $56,979.99 new loan balance

6.b. $112,450 x .113 = $12,706.85 annual interest
$12,706.85 ÷ 12 = $1,058.90

7.a. $143.90 x 60 (mos) = $8,634 principal and interest payments over 5 years
$8,634 - $2,000 (principal paid) = $6,634 interest
$20,000 (original loan) x .02 (prepayment penalty) = $400
$6,634 + $400 = $7,034 cost of loan

8.d. $529.36 x 360 (mos) = $190,569.60 total principal and interest payments
Loan amount is $60,000 ($75,000 - $15,000)
$190,569.60 - $60,000 = $130,569.60 interest paid over term of loan
$75,000 (purchase price) x ? = $130,569.60
$130,569.60 ÷ $75,000 = 1.74 or 174%

9.c. $896.83 x 360 (mos) = $322,858.80 total principal and interest payments
Loan amount is $95,000 ($120,000 - $25,000)
$322,858.80 - $95,000 = $227,858.80 interest paid over term of loan
$120,000 (purchase price) x ? = $227,858.80
$227,858.80 ÷ $120,000 = 1.898 or 190%

VII. Discounting Loans - Points

To discount a loan is to deduct interest in advance from the face amount of the promissory note. For example:

$50,000 loan at 12% interest with a 5% discount

$50,000 loan amount
x .05 discount rate
$2,500 amount of discount

In the above example, the borrower would sign a promissory note calling for repayment of $50,000 at 12% interest, and yet the actual amount received from the lender would only be $47,500 ($50,000 - $2,500). The discount amount ($2,500) would be additional profit for the lender.

Discounts are commonplace in loan transactions today. In the past they applied almost exclusively to FHA and VA transactions, but are now used regularly in connection with conventional loan transactions as well. The effect of points is to increase the lender's yield over and above the interest rate stated in the promissory note.

When a lender discounts a loan, it is sometimes referred to as **charging points**. The term "point" is a contraction of the larger term, "percentage point." Each point represents 1% of the loan amount. If a lender charges six points, the loan is discounted by 6%. Sometimes the loan origination fee, which is the handling charge assessed by the lender at the time the loan is made, is also referred to in terms of points (i.e., a 2% loan fee might be referred to as two points).

Another type of "discounting" a loan occurs when the lender sells the loan to a third party investor. For instance, Seller Brown sold her home and took back a second mortgage on her property from Buyer Smith in the amount of $10,000. Now Brown needs some cash and decides to sell the second mortgage to Mortgage Investments, Inc. However, Mortgage Investments, Inc. will not pay Brown the entire face value of the second mortgage, but will discount it in order to take into account transaction costs, risk of default, and profit. Mortgage Investments may offer to pay Brown only 60% of the face value, or $6,000. From Brown's point of view, $6,000 is better than no cash at all, so she accepts the offer. Brown's mortgage has been "discounted" by 40%.

MATH

QUIZ - DISCOUNTING LOANS

1. The Johnsons sold their home and had to carry back a second trust deed and note of $5,310 at 11½% interest. If they sold the note for $3,823.20 before any payments had been made, the discount rate came to:

    a. 54%
    b. 25%
    c. 72%
    d. 28%

2. Mr. Clay is interested in purchasing a loan that bears 14½% interest for one year with the unpaid balance due at the end of that year. The borrower is to pay $296.04 per month for twelve months. Mr. Clay plans to offer the beneficiary 60% of the face value of the loan. If this is a straight loan, how much should Mr. Clay offer?

    a. $13,500
    b. $14,100
    c. $14,650
    d. $14,700

3. A bank customarily charges four points on their loans and then later sells these loans at a 3.5% discount. If the bank received $14,475 when it sold one of its loans at the discounted rate, what was the original amount of the loan?

    a. $14,500
    b. $15,000
    c. $15,500
    d. $14,900

4. A $5,000 note is to be paid off at the end of twelve months. It bears an interest rate of 6% per annum and is purchased by an investor for $4,500. What is the rate of return on the principal amount invested?

    a. 16%
    b. 17.8%
    c. 20%
    d. 10%

5. Mary sold her house and took back a note for $4,200, secured by a second deed of trust. She promptly sold the note for $2,730. This represents a discount of:

    a. 65%
    b. 55%
    c. 35%
    d. 28%

6. It is generally noted that 6 discount points equal 1% interest. What can the seller be expected to pay on a $24,000 FHA loan at 9% if comparable conventional loans bear interest at the rate of 9¾% and the lender wants to increase the effective yield of the FHA loan to that of the conventional loan?

    a. $2,400
    b. $1,080
    c. $240
    d. None of the above

7. Able purchased a 2nd deed of trust and note for 80% of its $1,500 face value. The loan was scheduled to fully amortize in one year and called for payments of $131 per month, including 9% interest. If Able held the note for the full year and the borrower paid according to the terms of the contract, what was the yield on Able's original investment?

    a. 25%
    b. 29%
    c. 35%
    d. 31%

ANSWERS TO DISCOUNT PROBLEMS

1. d. $5,310 x ? = $3,823.20
    $3,823.20 ÷ $5,310 = .72 or 72%
    $3,823.20 is 72% of $5,310, which means the note was discounted by 28%.

2. d.   A straight note calls for payments of interest only.
    $296.04 x 12 (mos.) = $3,552.48 annual interest
    ? (loan amount) x .145 = $3,552.48
    $3,552.48 ÷ .145 = $24,499.86 or $24,500 loan amount
    $24,500 x .60 = $14,700 discounted amount

3. b.   If a lender discounts a loan by 3½ points (3½%), he is actually advancing 96½ cents on the dollar.
    ? (loan amount) x .965 = $14,475
    $14,475 ÷ .965 = $15,000 loan amount

4. b. $5,000 - $4,500 = $500 discount
    $5,000 x .06 = $300 interest
    ($500 + $300) = $800
    $4,500 (amount paid for note) x ? = $800
    $800 ÷ $4,500 = .1777 or 17.8%

5. c. $4,200 x ? = $2,730
    $2,730 ÷ $4,200 = .65 or 65%
    $2,730 is 65% of $4,200
    Discount rate is 35% (100% - 65% = 35%)

6. b.   6 points = 1%
    4½ points = ¾% (6 points x .75 = 4½ points)
    $24,000 x .045 = $1,080

7. d.　$1,500 x .80 = $1,200 amount paid
　　　　$131 (payments) x 12 (mos.) = $1,572
　　　　$1,572 (collected) - $1,200 (paid) = $372 profit
　　　　$1,200 x ? = $372
　　　　$372 ÷ $1,200 = 31% return

VIII. Capitalization

Capitalization is a method of appraising real property by converting into present value the anticipated future net income from the property. The capitalization rate is the rate used in the capitalization method or income approach to appraising property. The capitalization formula is:

property value x capitalization rate = net income
$$V \times R = I$$

To an appraiser, the unknown quantity in the equation is usually the property value. The appraiser can identify the net income by analyzing, among other things, the property's income and expense statement. The capitalization rate can be selected by direct comparison (which is the most common method), the band of investment method, or the summation method. With the capitalization rate and net income in hand, the appraiser can, with acceptable accuracy, estimate the value of the property.

Example: An appraiser determined a 12-unit apartment house was netting approximately $92,000 annually. By direct comparison she concluded 11% was a competitive capitalization rate. What is her estimate of the property's value?

Answer: *V x R = I*
? x .11 = $92,000
$92,000 ÷ .11 = $836,364

You probably recognized the 2 x 3 = 6 formula. In the above case, the unknown is the equivalent of 2.

? x 3 = 6   *? x .11 = $92,000*
6 ÷ 3 = 2   *$92,000 ÷ .11 = $836,364*

Suppose the value of the property and the net income are known but the capitalization rate is unknown.

Example: An appraiser determined a property's net income was $57,000, and on the basis of this estimated the property's value to be $456,000. What capitalization rate did the appraiser use?

Answer: *V x R = I*
2 x ? = 6   *$456,000 x ? = $57,000*
6 ÷ 2 = 3   *$57,000 ÷ $456,000 = .125 or 12½%*

ANNUAL FIGURES

Frequently, capitalization questions will be compounded by the use of monthly rather than annual figures.

Example: A property generates $1,650 net income a month. Using a capitalization rate of 10½%, what is the value of the property?

All figures, including earnings and expenses, must be converted to annual figures. **No exceptions**.

Answer: *$1,650 x 12 (mos.) = $19,800 annual net income*
? x .105 = $19,800
$19,800 ÷ .105 = $188,571

INCOME PROPERTY OPERATING STATEMENT

Refer to the income approach to value in the appraisal chapter of your real estate principles textbook for an explanation of earnings and expenses as they relate to the capitalization process. In some instances, capitalization questions might present preliminary problems (such as determining net income) before the primary problem (estimating the property's value) can be answered.

Example: A 36-unit apartment house is under appraisement. Twenty of the units rent for $350 a month; ten rent for $425 a month; the remaining six rent for $450 a month. The property's annual taxes are $28,800. Utilities are estimated $2,416 a month. The annual insurance premium is $5,300. Maintenance expenses run consistently around $1,850 a month. The cost of managing the property is $37.50 per unit per month. The appraiser determines by market analysis that a 6% bad debt/vacancy factor is realistic, and by the same method concludes a 9¼% capitalization rate is a competitive rate. What will be the estimate of value?

Answer: Convert all the numbers to annual figures, and from the gross income deduct the bad debt/vacancy factor and operating expenses to arrive at the net income. Then divide the net income by the capitalization rate for the estimated value.

Step 1: Determine gross income

$350 x 20 units x 12 mos. = $84,000
$425 x 10 units x 12 mos. = $51,000
$450 x 6 units x 12 mos.   = $32,400
Gross income $167,400

Step 2: Determine annual expenses

Utilities: $2,416 x 12 mos.   = $28,992
Maintenance: $1,850 x 12 mos.   = $22,200
Management: $37.50 x 12 mos. x 36 units   = $16,200

Step 3: Determine bad debt/vacancy factor

$167,400 x .06 = $10,044

Step 4: Determine net income

Gross income $167,400
Less bad debt/vacancy   -10,044
Effective gross income $157,356
Less operating expenses
Property taxes $28,800
Utilities   28,992
Insurance   5,300
Maintenance   22,200
Management   -16,200
Net income $55,864

Step 5: Calculate value

$55,864 ÷ .0925 = $603,935 estimated value

NOTE: Principal and interest payments on a mortgage or trust deed, also called **debt service payments**, are not deducted from gross earnings to determine net income because principal and interest payments are not considered operating expenses. After identifying net income and capitalizing it into the property's value, deduct the principal and interest payments from the net income to determine the **cash flow**.

CAPITALIZATION RATE AND VALUE

If the capitalization rate goes up, the value goes down and vice versa. The capitalization rate is, in part, influenced by the degree of risk presented by the investment property. In its simplest form a capitalization rate is an interest rate, and if the risk is high the capitalization (interest) rate will go up. Conversely, if the risk is low the capitalization rate will go down.

For examination purposes, the degree of risk is usually reflected in the quality of an income-producing property's tenants.

> **Example:** You are asked to appraise two buildings that are side by side. Both are approximately the same size and condition and generate the same amount of money. One has a hardware store for a tenant, the other is leased by the U.S. Postal Service. To which one will you likely give the higher value estimate?

The answer is the building with the Postal Service tenant. Why? Because the Post Office is the more stable and reliable of the two tenants.

Let's presume both buildings generate $31,800 a year net income. But, because the hardware store is a lower quality tenant, you decide to use a 10% capitalization rate with the hardware store and only a 9% rate with the Post Office building (the lower the risk, the lower the capitalization rate). Look at how the different capitalization rates affect the buildings' values.

Post Office: ? x .09 = $31,800
$31,800 ÷ .09 = $353,333 value
Hardware Store: ? x .10 = $31,800
$31,800 ÷ .10 = $318,000 value

QUIZ - CAPITALIZATION PROBLEMS

1. An appraiser was appraising a rented single-family residence. Another similar home in the immediate neighborhood recently sold for $84,000 and was renting for $525 per month. If the property being appraised rents for $575 per month, the value set by the appraiser would most nearly be:

    a. $97,500
    b. $118,000
    c. $108,000
    d. $92,000

2. Jones wants to make an investment in real property and is considering buying a vacant lot on which she will build a structure which will house a hardware business. This represents an accurate projection of the highest and best use of the land: The improvements will cost $150,000. The rental income will be $2,500 per month and the estimated annual expenses are $6,000. If the appraiser uses a 12% capitalization rate, what can Jones reasonably expect to pay for the land?

    a. $36,000
    b. $60,000
    c. $50,000
    d. It would not be profitable for her to build

3. An income property was appraised for $100,000 using a 6% capitalization rate. If an appraiser used an 8% capitalization rate, the value of the property would be:

    a. $85,000
    b. $75,000
    c. $90,000
    d. $70,000

4. A 20-unit apartment building was valued at $250,000 using a 10% capitalization rate. A new owner bought the property and raised each apartment's rent by $10 per month, without an increase in the operating expenses. If he used a 12% capitalization rate, the property would now be worth approximately:

    a. $260,000
    b. $240,000
    c. $230,000
    d. $220,000

5. The real property taxes on an income property increased $900 in one year. All other expenses and income remained the same. Using a 10% capitalization rate, the value of the property would change by which of the following amounts?

    a. $90 decrease
    b. $9,000 decrease
    c. $900 decrease
    d. There would be no change in value

6. An investment property is appraised at $400,000 with a net income of $36,000 and a 9% capitalization rate. What would be the value of the property if you used a 12% capitalization rate?

    a. $423,000
    b. $450,000
    c. $300,000
    d. $250,000

7. Mr. Adams owns an income property in which he deducts $27,000 in operating expenses from his gross income. If the operating expenses are 30% of the gross income, the value of the property, using a 12½% capitalization rate, is:

    a. $504,000
    b. $270,000
    c. $216,000
    d. $397,000

8. Mr. Able invested in a 20-unit apartment building several years ago. Recently, a new freeway was constructed near the property. Because of the closeness of the freeway, Able estimates that he loses $200 a month in rent. If comparable buildings in the area are figured at a capitalization rate of 12%, what is the monetary loss in value to the property?

Same as #9

    a. $2,400
    b. $20,000
    c. $2,000
    d. $24,000

9. An apartment building's operating statement reveals the following:

    Annual gross income: $10,000
    Vacancy factor: 10%
    Annual operating expenses: $4,000
    Principal and interest payments per month: $250
    Using a 10% capitalization rate, what is the property's value?

Good one

    a. $20,000
    b. $30,000
    c. $50,000
    d. $60,000

10. A property is valued at $200,000 using a capitalization rate of 8%. If the appraiser used a 10% rate, the estimated value would be:

    a. $160,000
    b. $150,000
    c. $120,000
    d. $180,000

11. The value of a 20-unit property has been determined to be $240,000. An analysis of the market has confirmed that the owner would be justified in applying a 10% capitalization rate when anticipating the property's net income. Should the owner increase the gross rentals $10 per unit per month and experience no increase in the expense of operation and should the capitalization rate be advanced to 12%, what would be the estimated value of the property?

   a. $264,000
   b. $240,000
   c. $220,000
   d. $200,000

12. Johnson bought an apartment building with 24 apartments. In 1987 all the apartments were rented for $85, and there were no vacancies. In 1988 Johnson rented the apartments for $95 each but experienced a 10% vacancy factor. Which of the following statements is true?

   a. both years were equal
   b. more was earned in 1988
   c. more was earned in 1987
   d. less was earned in 1988

13. The income of an improved property is $16,000 and this amounts to an 8% return on the current value. If the improvements are valued at $120,000 and have an economic life of 50 years, the value of the land is:

   a. $20,000
   b. $40,000
   c. $30,000
   d. $80,000

14. A prospect is considering the purchase of an income property. The property's operating statement shows $94,500 in expenses deducted from gross income to arrive at the net income. The deductions amount to 60% of the gross income. If an appraiser uses a 12½% capitalization rate, what is the value of the property?

   a. $620,000
   b. $504,000
   c. $196,000
   d. $182,000

15. Jones owns an income property in which $47,000 was deducted from gross income for operating expenses. If the operating expenses are 30% of gross income, the value of the property, using a 12½% capitalization rate, is:

   a. $804,000
   b. $496,000
   c. $877,336
   d. $396,000

ANSWERS TO CAPITALIZATION PROBLEMS

1. d. This is actually a "gross multiplier" problem. The gross multiplier method is an income method often applied to residential properties.
$84,000 (value of comparable) ÷ $525 (monthly rent) = 160 monthly multiplier
$575 (subject prop. rent) x 160 = $92,000 subject property value

2. c. $2,500 x 12 = $30,000 annual income
$30,000 - $6,000 = $24,000 net income
$24,000 ÷ .12 = $200,000 value of entire property
$200,000 - $150,000 = $50,000 land value

3. b. $100,000 x .06 = $6,000 net income
$6,000 ÷ .08 = $75,000

4. c. $250,000 x .10 = $25,000 net income
Increase rent for 20 units by $10 each = $200 a month or $2,400 a year
$25,000 + $2,400 = $27,400 increased rent
? x .12 = $27,400
$27,400 ÷ .12 = $228,333 new value

5. b. The $900 increase in taxes reduced the net income by that amount. Losses are capitalized like income: divide the loss in earnings by the capitalization rate for the loss in value.
$900 ÷ .10 = $9,000 value lost

6. c. $400,000 x .09 = $36,000
? x .12 = $36,000
$36,000 ÷ .12 = $300,000
If the capitalization rate increases and the income stays the same, the value decreases.

7. a. Determine the gross income with the following formula:
? x .30 = $27,000 expenses
$27,000 ÷ .30 = $90,000 gross income
$90,000 - $27,000 = $63,000 net income
? ÷ .125 = $63,000
$63,000 ÷ .125 = $504,000 value

8. b. Capitalize losses as you would income
$200 x 12 = $2,400 annual loss
$2,400 ÷ .12 = $20,000 value loss

9. c. Gross income $10,000
- vacancy factor $1,000
- operating expenses $4,000
Net income $5,000
$5,000 ÷ .10 = $50,000 value
(Do not deduct principal and interest payments to determine net income.)

MATH

10.a. $200,000 x .08 = $16,000
        ? x .10 = $16,000
        $16,000 ÷ .10 = $160,000 new value

11.c. $240,000 x .10 = $24,000 net income
        20 x $10 = $200 increase per month, $2,400 per year
        $24,000 + $2,400 = $26,400 revised income
        $26,400 ÷ .12 = $220,000 revised value

12.b.   1987: $85 x 24 x 12 = $24,480 annual income
        1988: $95 x 24 x 12 = $27,360 annual rent
        $27,360 x .90 (100% - 10% vacancy) = $24,624 annual income

13.d.   ? x .08 = $16,000
        $16,000 ÷ .08 = $200,000
        $200,000 - $120,000 = $80,000 land value

14.b.   ? x .60 = $94,500 expenses
        $94,500 ÷ .60 = $157,500 gross income
        $157,500 - $94,500 = $63,000 net income
        $63,000 ÷ .125 = $504,000 value

15.c.   ? x .30 = $47,000 expenses
        $47,000 ÷ .30 = $156,667 gross income
        $156,667 - $47,000 = $109,667 net income
        $109,667 ÷ .125 = $877,336 value

IX. Profit and Loss

If a property sells for more than it originally cost, it has been sold for a profit. If it sells for less than it originally cost, it has been sold at a loss. The formula for determining profit or loss is:

Value Before x percent of profit or loss = value after (**VB x % = VA**)

In profit and loss problems, **100%** is a key figure because it represents the value of a property before profit or loss, usually the price paid for the property.

Example: Smith sold her property for $50,000, which was 100% of what she paid for it. How much did she originally pay for the property?

Value Before x 100% = $50,000
$50,000 ÷ 1.00 = $50,000 value before

Now let's change the details a little. (Remember that the percent of profit is added to 100% and the percent of loss is deducted from 100%.)

Example: Smith sold her property for $83,000, which was 25% more than she paid for it. How much did she originally pay for the property?

VB x % = VA
? x 3 = 6   ? x 1.25 (100% + 25%) = $83,000
6 ÷ 3 = 2 $83,000 ÷ 1.25 = $66,400 value before

As you can see, once again we are working with the 2 x 3 = 6 formula. Watch what happens if Smith sells for a loss.

Example: Smith sold her property for $88,000, which amounted to a 10% loss. How much did she originally pay for the property?

VB x .90 (100% - 10%) = $88,000
$88,000 ÷ .90 = $97,778 value before

QUIZ - PROFIT AND LOSS PROBLEMS

1. Smith bought a property for $16,500. Now she intends to sell the property and figures her selling expenses will total 12%. If this is true, how much would Smith have to obtain for her property to just break even, not realizing a loss or gain?

    a. $18,480
    b. $14,520
    c. $19,800
    d. $18,750

2. A lot sold for $16,350, which was 9% more than its original cost. The original cost was:

    a. $14,715.00
    b. $14,878.50
    c. $15,000.00
    d. $16,000.00

3. A husband and wife sold their home for $17,200. This represents 9% more than what they paid for it. The original cost of the home was most nearly:

    a. $15,825
    b. $15,800
    c. $16,000
    d. $15,652

4. A homeowner sold her house for $23,000, which represented a 15% profit over what she had originally paid for the house. What was the original price of the home?

    a. $27,000
    b. $19,550
    c. $20,000
    d. None of the above

5. Sarah purchased some land for $62,000 and later sold it for a 15% profit. What was the sales price?

    a. $71,300
    b. $72,200
    c. $73,100
    d. $74,000

6. Honus realized a loss of 8% when he sold his property for $141,000. What did he originally pay for the property?

    a. $151,261
    b. $152,280
    c. $153,261
    d. $153,280

7. Twenty years ago, Luann paid $80,000 for her property. What is the percent of increase in the property's value if it is now worth $225,000?

    a. 345%

    b. 245%

    c. 365%

    d. 281%

MATH

ANSWERS TO PROFIT AND LOSS PROBLEMS

1.d. ? x .88 = $16,500
$16,500 ÷ .88 = $18,750
$16,500 is 88% of $18,750

2.c. ? x 1.09 = $16,350
$16,350 ÷ 1.09 = $15,000

3.b. ? x 1.09 = $17,200
$17,200 ÷ 1.09 = $15,799.82 or $15,800

4.c. ? x 1.15 = $23,000
$23,000 ÷ 1.15 = $20,000

5.a. $62,000 x 1.15 = ?
$62,000 x 1.15 = $71,300

6.c. ? x .92 = $141,000
$141,000 ÷ .92 = ?
$141,000 ÷ .92 = $153,261

7.d. $80,000 x ? = $225,000
$225,000 ÷ $80,000 = ?
$225,000 ÷ $80,000 = 2.81 or 281% increase

X. Depreciation/Appreciation

Appreciation is a rise in value or price. The term depreciation has different uses, but in any case it means some kind of loss in value due to any cause. To an appraiser, depreciation will represent an **actual loss in value** that will affect the appraised value of the property. To an accountant, depreciation is a **hypothetical loss in value** that affects an owner's financial status and has income tax consequences.

For examination purposes, you will find that land and improvements can depreciate or appreciate at different rates and that most of the problems will involve **straight line depreciation**, which means that the property depreciates in equal annual amounts during its useful life.

> **Example:** The useful life of a building is 20 years. The building will depreciate at a rate of 1/20, or 5% each year.
>
> *100% ÷ 20 years = 5% annual rate of depreciation*

> **Exercise:** Solve the following problems.
>
> 1. A home has an estimated useful life of 40 years. What is its annual rate of depreciation?
>
> 2. A warehouse has an economic life of 15 years. How much will it have depreciated after 3 years?
>
> 3. A barn is expected to be functional for 50 years. What is the anticipated depreciation after 8 years?

> **Answers:** *1. 100% ÷ 40 = 2.5% annual rate of depreciation*
> *2. 100% ÷ 15 = 6.667% annual rate of depreciation*
> *6.667% x 3 = 20% after 3 years*
> *3. 100% ÷ 50 = 2% annual rate of depreciation*
> *2% x 8 = 16% depreciation after 8 years*

Appreciation problems work the same way, except value is added to, rather than subtracted from, the property value.

> **Example:** If a property has appreciated 4% a year for the past six years, how much appreciation has occurred?
>
> *4% x 6 (years) = 24%*

HANDLE LIKE A PROFIT AND LOSS PROBLEM

If a property has depreciated a total of 22%, it is worth 78% of its original value (100% - 22% = 78%). Conversely, if the property has appreciated in value by a total of 19%, it is worth 119% of its original value. Use the same formula as you used for profit and loss problems:

> *Value before x gain or loss = Value after*

> **Example:** Jones bought a home that had an estimated useful life of 40 years. After 8 years of straight line depreciation, the depreciated value was estimated at $94,500. What did Jones originally pay for the property?

Answer: This is a two-part problem. First, determine the amount of depreciation.

    1. 100% ÷ 40 = 2.5% annual rate of depreciation
    2. 2.5% x 8 = 20% total accrued depreciation

Next, treat the problem like any other profit or loss problem. In this case, the depreciated value was 80% of the original value (100% - 20% = 80%).

    3. ? x .80 = $94,500
    4. $94,500 ÷ .80 = $118,125 original purchase price

LOT APPRECIATES/BUILDING DEPRECIATES

Sometimes the building will lose value while the lot is actually gaining in value.

Example: It cost $74,000 to build a house six years ago. The lot at that time was worth $21,000. If the house has been depreciating at 2.5% a year and the lot has been appreciating at 5% a year, what is the value of the property today?

Answer: Depreciate the house and appreciate the lot separately, then add your conclusions together.

    1. 25% x 6 = 15% total house depreciation
    2. $74,000 x .85 = $62,900 present house value
    3. 5% x 6 = 30% total lot appreciation
    4. $21,000 x 1.30 = $27,300 present lot value
    5. $62,900 + 27,300 = $90,200 present property value

QUIZ - DEPRECIATION/APPRECIATION PROBLEMS

1. Carlson bought a property for $200,000, paid $150,000 cash down, and executed a $50,000 first trust deed and note for the balance. The land was valued at $50,000, and the building had a salvage value of $15,000. The basis for computing straight-line depreciation for the life of the property would be:

   a. $200,000
   b. $165,000
   c. $150,000
   d. $135,000

2. A property supporting a six-plex was purchased at a total cost of $173,000. The land was valued at $23,500. At the time of purchase, the purchaser estimated 3% of the building cost for salvage value. Based on a 50-year economic life, what would the property's book value be at the end of the seventh year?

   a. $148,780.00
   b. $148,212.90
   c. $144,310.00
   d. $152,697.90

3. A small factory was constructed on a lot which cost $25,000. The cost of the land and improvements was $160,000. The estimated economic life of the improvements was 30 years. Using straight-line depreciation, the book value of this property at the end of the twelfth year is:

   a. $106,000
   b. $81,000
   c. $85,000
   d. $119,000

4. A property was purchased for $122,500, which included a land value of $24,500. The economic life of the improvements was set at 40 years. Using the straight-line method of depreciation, what was the book value of the property after 14 years?

   a. $79,625
   b. $63,700
   c. $88,200
   d. $42,875

5. Smith paid $24,200 for a freezer for a grocery store. For depreciation purposes, the economic life is 15 years and the salvage value is $4,500. Based upon the straight-line schedule, what would the book value be at the conclusion of the sixth year?

   a. $16,320
   b. $14,250
   c. $9,680
   d. $7,880

MATH

6. A commercial property cost $190,000. The land was valued at $30,000, and the salvage value of the building was estimated at $10,000. Which of the following figures would the owner use when establishing a depreciation schedule?

    a. $180,000
    b. $150,000
    c. $190,000
    d. $160,000

7. An investment property is purchased for a total price of $200,000, including $27,500 attributable to the land. The economic life of the property is set at 40 years. What would be the book value of the improvements at the end of the fourth year if the straight-line method of depreciation is used?

    a. $180,000
    b. $172,000
    c. $155,250
    d. $182,750

8. The cost of an improved property is $200,000. The land is valued at $50,000. There is an existing first lien of $50,000, and it is anticipated there will be salvage value of $10,000. What would the property's book value be at the end of the first year, presuming an economic life of 40 years?

    a. $186,500
    b. $196,500
    c. $136,500
    d. $146,500

9. An investor bought a property valued at $160,000 which depreciated over a 30 year period. The land was valued at $30,000 and after 11 years of depreciation on a straight-line basis, the depreciated value of the property is most nearly:

    a. $131,000
    b. $101,000
    c. $82,000
    d. $112,000

10. The replacement cost of a home is $114,500, less 14 years of accrued depreciation at the rate of 1½% per year. The lot is currently valued at $20,000. What is the current value of the property?

    a. $94,500
    b. $110,455
    c. $90,455
    d. $101,270

11. The following information was presented to you by the buyer for analysis. The price of a building was $160,000, excluding the lot. Fifteen years remain to be depreciated and the building is 37½% depreciated.

    a. The building has depreciated for 10 years
    b. The book value is now $120,000
    c. The depreciation exceeds 4% per year
    d. None of the above

ANSWERS TO DEPRECIATION/APPRECIATION PROBLEMS

MATH

1. a. The down payment and trust deed amounts are irrelevant to the problem. The "basis" is the price paid, $200,000. To determine the amount and rate of depreciation, deduct the land value and the salvage value from the price. Then divide by the anticipated economic life (e.g., 30, 40, 50 years).

2. d. $173,000 - $23,500 (land value) = $149,500 value of improvements
$149,500 x .97 (improvement value minus 3% salvage value) = $145,015 amount to be depreciated
$145,015 ÷ 50 (years) = $2,900.30 annual depreciation
$2,900.30 x 7 = $20,302.10 depreciation after 7 years
$173,000 - $20,302.10 = $152,697.90 depreciated property value

3. a. $160,000 - $25,000 = $135,000 improvement value
$135,000 ÷ 30 = $4,500 annual depreciation
$4,500 x 12 = $54,000 total depreciation
$160,000 - $54,000 = $106,000 depreciated value of property

4. c. $122,500 - $24,500 = $98,000 improvement value
$98,000 ÷ 40 = $2,450 annual depreciation
$2,450 x 14 = $34,300 annual depreciation
$122,500 less $34,300 = $88,200 depreciated value of property

5. a. $24,200 - $4,500 = $19,700 amount to be depreciated
$19,700 ÷ 15 = $1,313.33 annual depreciation
$1,313.33 x 6 = $7,880 total depreciation
$24,200 - $7,880 = $16,320 book value

6. b. $190,000 - $30,000 = $160,000 improvement value
$160,000 - $10,000 = $150,000 depreciable portion of property

7. c. $200,000 - $27,500 = $172,500 value of improvements
$172,500 ÷ 40 = $4,312.50 annual depreciation
$4,312.50 x 4 = $17,250 total depreciation
$172,500 - $17,250 = $155,250 depreciated value of improvements

8. b. The existing first lien of $50,000 is irrelevant to the problem
$200,000 - $50,000 = $150,000 improvement value
$150,000 - $10,000 = $140,000 to be depreciated
$140,000 ÷ 40 = $3,500 annual depreciation
$200,000 - $3,500 = $196,500 property value after one year

9. d. $160,000 - $30,000 = $130,000 improvement value
$130,000 ÷ 30 = $4,333.33 annual depreciation
$4,333.33 x 11 = $47,666.67 total depreciation
$160,000 - $47,666.67 = $112,333.33

10. **b.** $114,500 x .015 = $1,717.50 annual depreciation
$1,717.50 x 14 = $24,045 total depreciation
$114,500 - $24,045 = $90,455 depreciated value of improvements
$90,455 + $20,000 = $110,455 depreciated value of property

11. **c.** The unknown is the building's economic life. If 15 years of economic life remain, they represent 62½% of the total economic life (100% - 37½%). Arrange your equation as follows:

> ? x .625 = 15 years
> 15 ÷ .625 = 24 years
> 100% of the building value ÷ 24 = .04166 or 4.17% annual rate of depreciation

XI. Proration

To prorate is to divide and allocate an expense equally or proportionately according to time or use. When a transaction is ready to close, certain settlement expenses must be charged to the buyer, to the seller, or proportionately to both. Included among these expenses are hazard insurance premiums, property taxes, interest on mortgages, and installment payments on special assessments.

The process of accurately allocating these charges between the buyer and seller involves three steps:

1. **Determine the annual charge.** What are the annual taxes? Annual interest? Annual insurance premium?

2. **Divide annual charge by 360 (days).** Prorations are based on 360-day years, 30-day months. By dividing the annual charge by 360, you determine the per day cost—called the **per diem**.

3. **Count the days for which the buyer or seller is responsible and multiply by the per diem.** For instance, if a buyer owes 14 days' taxes and the per diem is $3.15, multiply $3.15 x 14 = $44.10.

Example: Jones has paid the year's property taxes of $1,052. He sells his home and the deal closes on March 20. What is the amount of Jones' credit for property taxes at closing?

Answer: Jones is responsible for the property taxes through March 19. The buyer assumes responsibility for the taxes from the date of closing forward. As such, the buyer must be charged, and Jones credited, for the property taxes from March 20 through June 30.*

Step 1. Determine the annual charge. Already established at $1,052.

Step 2. Divide by 360 days.
$1,052 ÷ 360 = $2.92 per diem.

Step 3. Count the days and multiply by per diem.

March 11
April 30
May 30
June 30
101 days
x 2.92 per diem
$294.92 charge to buyer and credit to seller

*Note: Tax year runs from July 1 to June 30.

QUIZ - PRORATION PROBLEMS

1. Mr. Johnson paid his taxes of $390.60 for the year. On May 1, he sells his home. What is the amount of the remaining pre-paid portion?

    a. $118.82
    b. $246.41
    c. $52.60
    d. $65.10

2. A 3-year fire insurance policy was purchased on January 1, 1987, for $470. If the house was sold on July 16, 1988, what was the unused portion?

    a. $181.45
    b. $121.25
    c. $141.25
    d. $228.53

3. A house is sold on January 16. The taxes of $846 for the year have been paid. The fire insurance premium of $122 for the calendar year has also been paid. How much will the buyer pay the seller at closing?

    a. $927.67
    b. $520.82
    c. $505.05
    d. $945.90

4. Jones sold her apartment building to Brown on the 13th of the month. She had already collected $8,450 in rent, plus $1,250 in back rent for the previous month. How much does she owe Brown at closing for prorated rental payments?

    a. $5,070
    b. $7,620
    c. $6,140
    d. $3,751

5. A seller has prepaid her homeowner's insurance for the first half of the calendar year. The six month premium is $180. If the sale closes on June 10 and the buyer assumes the seller's policy, how much will the buyer owe the seller for insurance?

    a. $19
    b. $20
    c. $21
    d. $22

6. Adele is buying a triplex from Byron. Byron has already collected rents from tenants for the month of September. If the monthly rents are $2,700 and the sale closes on September 18, how much will Byron owe Adele for prepaid rents?

    a. $1,140
    b. $1,170
    c. $1,200
    d. $1,300

7. A seller of real estate has paid money into a reserve account with a lender to cover property tax payments of $11,600 per year. There is currently enough in the account to cover all taxes accruing through August. If the property is sold on April 8, what will be the seller's refund of tax reserves?

    a. $4,080
    b. $4,226
    c. $4,422
    d. $4,608

MATH

ANSWERS TO PRORATION PROBLEMS

1. **d.** Taxes have been paid for the year in the amount of $390.60. The period in question is from May 1st to June 30 (two months). Bear in mind that in this context, the date of sale means the date the deed is given and accepted. The buyer assumes the responsibility for the taxes on the day the deed is accepted, in this case, May 1st.

   $390.60 ÷ 12 = $32.55 per month
   $32.55 x 2 (months) = $65.10

2. **d.** The policy is paid for, so the period in question is from the selling date to the end of the policy. January 1, 1987 to July 16, 1988 = 18½ months the policy is in force.
   $470 ÷ 36 months = $13.06 monthly premium
   36 (mos.) - 18½ (mos.) = 17½ months of unused policy
   $13.06 x 17.5 = $228.55 unused portion of premium

3. **c.** Taxes and insurance have been prepaid, but for different time periods, so the number of days has to be computed separately for each.

   Taxes: Jan. 15
           Feb. 30
           Mar. 30
           Apr. 30
           May 30
         June <u>30</u>
             165 days

   Insurance: 360 (days in year) - 15 (days in Jan.) = 345 days
   $846 ÷ 360 = $2.35 per diem
   $2.35 x 165 = $387.75 in taxes

   $122 ÷ 360 = .34 per diem
   .34 x 345 = $117.30 in insurance

   $387.75 + $117.30 = $505.05 total payment to seller

4. **a.** The back rent belongs to the seller; it is only the current rent that needs to be prorated.

   $8,450 ÷ 30 (days) = $281.67
   $281.67 x 18 (days) = $5,070

5. **c.** June 10 through June 30 = 21 days
   $180 ÷ 180 = $1 per diem
   21 x $1 = $21

6. **b.** Sept. 18 through Sept. 30 = 13 days
   $2,700 ÷ 30 = $90 per diem
   13 x $90 = $1,170

7. **d.** April 8 through August 30 (use 30-day months) = 143 days
   $11,600 ÷ 360 = $32.22 per diem
   143 x $32.22 = $4,608 (rounded)

Section 9
Real Estate Terms

A

ALTA Title Policy (American Land Title Association): A type of title insurance policy issued by title insurance companies which expands the risks normally insured against under the standard type policy to include unrecorded mechanic's liens, unrecorded physical easements, facts a physical survey would show, water and mineral rights, and rights of parties in possession, such as tenants and buyers, under unrecorded instruments.

ALTA Owner's Policy (Standard Form B1962, as amended 1969): An owner's extended coverage policy that provides buyers or owners the same protection the ALTA policy gives to lenders.

Abatement of Nuisance: Extinction or termination of a nuisance.

Absolute Fee Simple Title: Absolute or fee simple title is one that is absolute and unqualified. It is the best title one can have.

Abstract of Judgment: A condensation of the essential provisions of a court judgment.

Abstract of Title: A summary or digest of the conveyances, transfers, and any other facts relied on as evidence of title, together with any other elements of record which may impair the title.

Abstraction: A method of valuing land. The indicated value of the improvement is deducted from the sale price.

Acceleration Clause: Clause in trust deed or mortgage giving lender the right to call all sums owed to him to be immediately due and payable upon the happening of a certain event.

Acceptance: When the seller's or agent's principal agrees to the terms of the agreement of sale and approves the negotiation on the part of the agent and acknowledges receipt of the deposit in subscribing to the agreement of sale, that act is termed an acceptance.

Access Right: The right of an owner to have ingress and egress to and from his property.

Accession: Gaining title when property is added to a property by another or by a natural action.

Accretion: An addition to land from natural causes as, for example, from gradual action of the ocean or river waters.

Accrued Depreciation: The difference between the cost of replacement (new) as of the date of the appraisal and the present appraised value.

Accrued Items of Expense: Those incurred expenses which are not yet payable. The seller's accrued expenses are credited to the purchaser in a closing statement.

Acknowledgment: A formal declaration before a duly authorized officer by a person who has executed an instrument that such execution is his act and deed.

Acoustical Tile: Blocks of fiber, mineral, or metal, with small holes or rough textured surface to absorb sound, used as covering for interior walls and ceilings.

Acquisition: The act or process by which a person procures property.

Acre: A measure of land equaling 160 square rods, 4,840 square yards, 43,560 square feet, or a tract about 208.71 feet square.

Adjustments: A means by which characteristics of a residential property are regulated by dollar amount or percentage to conform to similar characteristics of another residential property.

Affiant: A person who has made an affidavit.

Administrator: A person appointed by the probate court to administer the estate of a person deceased.

Ad Valorem: A Latin phrase meaning, "according to value." Usually used in connection with real estate taxation.

Advance: Transfer of funds from a lender to a borrower, in advance, on a loan.

Advance Commitment: The institutional investor's prior agreement to provide long-term financing upon completion of construction.

Advance Fee: A fee paid in advance of any services rendered.

Adverse Possession: Claiming based on the open and notorious possession and occupancy, usually under an evident claim or right, in denial or opposition to the title of another claimant.

Affidavit: A statement or declaration reduced to writing sworn to or affirmed before some officer who has authority to administer an oath or affirmation.

Affidavit of Title: A statement in writing, made under oath by seller or grantor, acknowledged before a Notary Public, in which the affiant identifies himself and his marital status, certifying that since the examination of title on the contract date there are no judgments, bankruptcies, divorces, unrecorded deeds, contracts, unpaid repairs, improvements, or defects of title known to him, and that he is in possession of the property.

Affirm: To confirm, to aver, to ratify, to verify.

AFLB: Accredited Farm and Land Broker.

Agency: The relationship between principal and agent that arises out of a contract, either expressed or implied, written or oral, wherein the agent is employed by the principal to do certain acts dealing with a third party.

Agent: One who represents another from whom he has derived authority.

Agreement of Sale: A written agreement or contract between seller and purchaser in which they reach a meeting of minds on the terms and conditions of the sale.

Air Rights: The rights in real property to use the air space above the surface of the land.

Alienation: The transferring of property to another; the transfer of property and possession of lands or other things, from one person to another.

Allodial Tenure: A real property ownership system in which ownership may be complete except for those rights held by government. Allodial is in contrast to feudal tenure.

Alluvion: (Alluvium) Soil deposited by accretion. Increase of earth on a shore or bank of a river.

Amenities: Satisfaction of enjoyable living to be derived from a home; conditions of agreeable living or a beneficial influence arising from the location or improvements.

AMO: Accredited Management Organization.

Amortization: The liquidation of a financial obligation on an equal installment basis; also, recovery over a period, of cost or value.

Amortized Loan: A loan that is completely paid off, interest and principal, by a series of regular payments that are equal or nearly equal. Also called a Level Payments Loan.

Annuity: A series of assured equal or nearly equal payments to be made over a period of time or it may be a lump sum payment to be made in the future.

Anticipation, Principle of: Affirms that value is created by anticipated benefits to be derived in the future.

Appraisal: An estimate and opinion of value; a conclusion resulting from the analysis of facts.

Appraiser: One qualified by education, training, and experience who is hired to estimate the value of real and personal property based on experience, judgment, facts, and use of formal appraisal processes.

Appurtenance: A right, privilege, or improvement belonging to, and passing with, the land. For example, a barn, dwelling, garage, orchard, or easement passes with the land.

TERMS

Architectural Style: Generally the appearance and character of a building's design and construction.

ASA: American Society of Appraisers.

Asbestos: A fibrous insulation and construction material that causes serious lung problems.

Assessed Valuation: A valuation placed upon property by a public officer or board, as a basis for taxation.

Assessed Value: Value placed on property as a basis for taxation.

Assessment: The valuation of property for the purpose of levying a tax, or the amount of the tax levied.

Assessor: The official who has the responsibility of determining assessed values.

Assignment: A transfer or making over to another of the whole of any property, real or personal, in possession or in action, or of any estate or right therein.

Assignor: One who assigns or transfers property.

Assigns/Assignees: Those to whom property shall or has been transferred.

Assumption Agreement: An undertaking or adoption of a debt or obligation primarily resting upon another person.

Assumption Fee: A lender's charge for changing over and processing new records for a new owner who is assuming an existing loan.

Assumption of Mortgage: The taking of title to property by a grantee, wherein he assumes liability for payment of an existing note secured by a mortgage or deed of trust against the property, becoming a co-guarantor for the payment of a mortgage or deed of trust note.

Attachment: Seizure of property by court order, usually done to have it available in the event a judgment is obtained in a pending suit.

Attest: To affirm to be true or genuine; an official act establishing authenticity.

Attorney in Fact: One who is authorized to perform certain acts for another under a power of attorney; power of attorney may be limited to a specific act or acts, or be general.

Avulsion: The sudden tearing away or removal of land by action of water flowing over or through it.

Axial Growth: City growth which occurs along main transportation routes. Usually takes the form of star-shaped extensions outward from the center.

B

Backfill: The replacement of excavated earth into a hole or against a structure.

Balloon Payment: When the final installment payment on a note is greater than the preceding installment payments and pays the note in full, such final installment is termed a balloon payment.

Bargain and Sale Deed: Any deed that recites a consideration and purports to convey the real estate; a bargain and sale deed with a covenant against the grantor's acts is one in which the grantor warrants that he himself has done nothing to harm or cloud the title.

Baseboard: A board placed against the wall around a room next to the floor.

Base and Meridian: Imaginary lines used by surveyors to find and describe the location of private or public lands.

Base Molding: Molding used at top of baseboard.

Base Shoe: Molding used at junction of baseboard and floor. Commonly called a *carpet strip*.

Batten: Narrow strips of wood or metal used to cover joints, interiorly or exteriorly; also used for decorative effect.

Beam: A structural member transversely supporting a load.

Bearing Wall or Partition: A wall or partition supporting any vertical load in addition to its own weight.

Bench Marks: A location indicated on a durable marker by surveyors.

Beneficiary: (1) One entitled to the benefit of a trust; (2) One who receives profit from an estate, the title of which is vested in a trustee; (3) The lender on the security of a note and deed of trust.

Bequeath: To give or hand down by will; to leave by will.

Bequest: That which is given by the terms of a will.

Betterment: An improvement upon property which increases the property value and is considered as a capital asset, as opposed to repairs or replacements that do not change the original character or cost.

Bill of Sale: A written instrument given to pass title of personal property from vendor to the vendee.

Binder: An agreement to consider a down payment for the purchase of real estate as evidence of good faith on the part of the purchaser. Also, a notation of coverage on an insurance policy issued by an agent and given to the insured prior to issuing of the policy.

Blacktop: Asphalt paving used in streets and driveways.

Blanket Mortgage: A single mortgage which covers more than one piece of real estate.

Blighted Area: A declining area in which real property values are seriously affected by destructive economic forces, such as encroaching inharmonious property usages, infiltration of lower economic inhabitants, and/or rapidly depreciating buildings.

Board foot: A unit of measurement of lumber: one foot wide, one foot long, one inch thick, 144 cubic inches.

Bona Fide: In good faith, without fraud.

TERMS

Bond: An obligation under seal. A real estate bond is a written obligation issued on security of a mortgage or trust deed.

Bracing: Framing lumber nailed at an angle in order to provide rigidity.

Breach: The breaking of a law, or failure of duty, either by omission or commission.

Breezeway: A covered porch or passage, open on two sides, connecting the house and garage or two other parts of the house.

Bridge Loan: (Gap Loan-Swing Loan) short-term loan between construction loan and permanent financing.

Bridging: Small wood or metal pieces used to brace floor joists.

Broker: A person employed by another to carry on any of the activities listed in the license law definition of a broker, for a fee.

B.T.U. (British Thermal Unit): The quantity of heat required to raise the temperature of one pound of water one degree Fahrenheit.

Building Code: A systematic regulation of construction of buildings within a municipality. Established by ordinance or law.

Building Line: A line set by law a certain distance from a street line in front of which an owner cannot build on his lot. (A **Setback Line**)

Building Paper: A heavy waterproofed paper used as sheathing in wall or roof construction as protection against air passage and moisture.

Built-in: Cabinets or similar features built as part of the house.

Bundle of Rights: Beneficial interests or rights.

Buy-Down Loan: A loan in which the seller pays points to a lender so that the lender can offer below market financing.

Buyer's Agent: An agent representing the buyer rather than the seller.

C

CCIM: Certified Commercial Investment Member.

CC&Rs: Abbreviation for covenants, conditions and restrictions.

CPM: Certified Property Manager, a designation of the Institute of Real Estate Management.

Capital Assets: Assets of a permanent nature used in the production of an income, such as land, buildings, machinery, and equipment. Under income tax law, it is usually distinguishable from "inventory," which comprises assets held for sale to customers in the ordinary course of the taxpayer's trade or business.

Capital Gain: Income from the sale of an asset rather than from general business activity. Capital gains are generally taxed at a lower rate than ordinary income.

Capitalization: In appraising, determining value of property by considering net income and percentage of reasonable return on the investment. Thus, the value of an income property is determined by dividing annual net income by the capitalization rate.

Capitalization Rate: The rate of interest that is considered a reasonable return on the investment, used in the process of determining value based upon net income. It may also be described as the yield rate that is necessary to attract the money of the average investor to a particular kind of investment. In the case of land improvements which depreciate, to this yield rate add another factor to take into consideration the annual amortization factor necessary to recapture the initial investment in improvements.

Casement Window: Frames of wood or metal, which swing outward.

Cash Flow: The net income generated by a property before depreciation and other non-cash expenses.

Caveat Emptor ("Let the Buyer Beware"): The buyer must examine the goods or property and buy at his own risk.

Certificate of Reasonable Value (CRV): The federal Veterans Administration appraisal commitment of property value.

Chain: A unit of measurement used by surveyors. A chain consists of 100 links equal to 66 feet.

Chain of Title: A history of conveyances and encumbrances affecting the title from the time the original patent was granted, or as far back as records are available.

Change, Principle of: Holds that it is the future, not the past, which is of prime importance in estimating value.

Characteristics: Distinguishing features of a (residential) property.

Chattel Mortgage: A claim on personal property (instead of real property) used to secure or guarantee a promissory note. (See definition of Security Agreement and Security Interest.)

Chattel Real: A personal property interest related to real estate, such as a lease on real property.

Chattels: Goods or every type of property, movable or immovable, which are not real property.

Circuit Breaker: An electrical device which automatically interrupts an electric circuit when an overload occurs; may be used instead of a fuse to protect each circuit and can be reset.

Civil Rights Act of 1866: The first fair housing act (applied to race only).

Civil Rights Act of 1968: Our fair housing act.

Clapboard: Overlapping boards, usually thicker at one edge, used for siding.

Closing Statement: An accounting of funds, made separately, to the buyer and seller.

TERMS

Cloud on the Title: Any conditions revealed by a title search that affect the title to property. Usually relatively unimportant items, but cannot be removed without a quitclaim deed or court action.

Collar Beam: A beam that connects the pairs of opposite roof rafters above the attic floor.

Collateral: This is the property subject to the security interest. (See definition of Security Interest.)

Collateral Security: A separate obligation attached to a contract to guarantee its performance; the transfer of property or of other contracts, or valuables, to insure the performance of a principal agreement.

Collusion: An agreement between two or more persons to defraud another of his rights by the forms of law, or to obtain an object forbidden by law.

Color of Title: That which appears to be good title but which is not title in fact. Example: title under a forged deed.

Commercial Acre: A term applied to the remainder of an acre of newly subdivided land after the area devoted to streets, sidewalks, curbs, etc. has been deducted from the acre.

Commercial Paper: Bills of exchange used in commercial trade.

Commission: An agent's compensation for performing the duties of his agency; in real estate practice, a percentage of the selling price of property, percentage of rentals, etc.

Commitment: A pledge, promise, or firm agreement.

Common Law: The body of law that grew from customs and practices developed and used in England "since the memory of man runneth not to the contrary." (Based on court decisions, **not** statutes.)

Community: A part of a metropolitan area that has a number of neighborhoods that have a tendency toward common interests and problems.

Community Property: Property accumulated during marriage that is owned equally by husband and wife. (**Community Property States**)

Compaction: Ability of the soil to support a structure. Compaction tests are important as to filled land.

Comparable Sales: Sales which have similar characteristics as the subject property and are used for analysis in the appraisal process.

Compensator Damages: Damages to reimburse an injured party for the actual loss suffered.

Competent: Legally qualified.

Competition, Principle of: Holds that excess profits tend to breed competition.

Component: One of the features making up the whole property.

Compound Interest: Interest paid on original principal and also on the accrued and unpaid interest which has accumulated.

Conclusion: The final estimate of value, realized from facts, data, experience, and judgment.

Condemnation: The act of taking private property for public use. Also a declaration that a structure is unfit for use.

Condition: A qualification of an estate granted which can be imposed only in conveyances. They are classified as conditions precedent and conditions subsequent.

Condition Precedent: A condition that requires certain action or the happening of a specified event before the estate granted can take effect. **Example:** Most installment real estate sale contracts require all payments to be made at the time specified before the buyer may demand transfer of title.

Condition Subsequent: When there is a condition subsequent in a deed, the title vests immediately in the grantee, but upon breach of the condition the grantor has the power to terminate the estate if he wishes to do so. **Example:** A condition in the deed prohibiting the grantee from using the premises as a liquor store.

Conditional Commitment: A commitment of a definite loan amount for some future unknown purchaser of satisfactory credit standing.

Condominium: A system of individual fee ownership of units in a multifamily structure, combined with joint ownership of common areas of the structure and the land. (Sometimes referred to as a vertical subdivision.)

Conduit: Usually a metal pipe in which electrical wiring is installed.

Conduits: Individuals or firms that purchase loans from originators to resell to investors.

Confession of Judgment: An entry of judgment upon the debtor's voluntary admission or confession.

Confirmation of Sale: A court approval of the sale of property by an executor, administrator, guardian, or conservator.

Confiscation: The seizing of property without compensation.

Conforming Loans: Loans that meet the purchase requirement of Fannie Mae and Freddie Mac.

Conformity, Principle of: Holds that the maximum value is realized when a reasonable degree of homogeneity of improvements is present.

Conservation: The process of utilizing resources in such a manner that minimizes their depletion.

Consideration: Anything of value given to induce entering into a contract; it may be money, personal services, or anything having value.

Constant: The percentage which, when applied directly to the face value of a debt, develops the annual amount of money necessary to pay a specified net rate of interest on the reducing balance and to liquidate the debt in a specified time period. For example, a 6% loan with a 20-year amortization has a constant of approximately 8½%. Thus, a $10,000 loan amortized over 20 years requires an annual payment of approximately $850.00.

Contingent Remainder: A remainder interest that can be defeated by the happening of an event.

TERMS

Construction Loans: Loans made for the construction of homes or commercial buildings. Usually funds are disbursed to the contractor-builder during construction and after periodic inspections. Disbursements are based on an agreement between borrower and lender.

Constructive Eviction: Breach of a covenant of warranty or quiet enjoyment; e.g., the inability of a lessee to obtain possession because of a paramount defect in title, or a condition making occupancy hazardous. A lessee can treat it as cause to void a lease.

Constructive Notice: Notice given by the public records.

Consummate Dower: A widow's dower interest which, after the death of her husband, is complete or may be completed and become an interest in real estate.

Contour: The surface configuration of land.

Contour Lines: Lines on a map that indicate elevation. When lines are close together, it indicates a steep stoop, but if the lines are far apart, it indicates the land is relatively level.

Contract: An agreement, either written or oral, to do or not to do certain things.

Contribution, Principle of: Holds that maximum real property values are achieved when the improvements on the site produce the highest (net) return commensurate with the investment.

Consumer Goods: These are goods used or bought for use primarily for personal, family, or household purposes.

Conventional Mortgage: A mortgage securing a loan made by investors without governmental underwriting, i.e., which is not F.H.A. insured or V.A. guaranteed.

Conversion: Change from one character or use to another. Also, the wrongful appropriation of funds of another.

Conveyance: This has two meanings. One meaning refers to the process of transferring title to property from one person to another. In this sense it is used as a verb. The other meaning refers to the document used to effect the transfer of title (usually some kind of deed). In this last sense, it is used a noun.

Cooperative Ownership: A form of apartment ownership. Ownership of shares in a cooperative venture that entitles the owner to use, rent, or sell a specific apartment unit. The corporation usually reserves the right to approve certain actions such as a sale or improvement.

Corner Influence Table: A statistical table that may be used to estimate the added value of a corner lot.

Corporation: A group or body of persons established and treated by law as an individual or unit with rights and liabilities or both, distinct and apart from those of the persons composing it. A corporation is a creature of law having certain powers and duties of a natural person. Being created by law, it may continue for any length of time the law prescribes.

Corporeal Rights: Possessory rights in real property.

Correction Lines: A system compensating for inaccuracies in the Government Rectangular Survey System due to the curvature of the earth. Every fourth township line, 24-mile intervals, is used as a correction line on which the intervals between the north and south range lines are remeasured and corrected to a full 6 miles.

Correlate the Findings: The interpretation of data and value estimates to bring them together to a final conclusion of value.

Correlation: To bring the indicated values developed by the three approaches into mutual relationship with each other.

Correlative User: Rights of an owner to reasonable use of nonflowing underground water.

Cost: A historical record of past expenditures, or an amount which would be given in exchange for other things.

Cost Approach: One of three methods in the appraisal process. An analysis in which a value estimate of a property is derived by estimating the replacement cost of the improvements, deducting the estimated accrued depreciation, then adding the market value of the land.

Counterflashing: Sheet metal used around chimneys, at roof line, and in roof valleys to prevent moisture entry.

Covenant: Agreements written into deeds and other instruments promising performance or nonperformance of certain acts, or stipulating certain uses or nonuses of the property.

CPM: Certified Property Manager. IREM's highest designation.

Crawl Hole: Exterior or interior opening permitting access underneath a building, as required by building codes.

CRB: Certified Residential Broker.

CRE: Counselor of Real Estate. Members of American Society of Real Estate Counselors.

CRS: Certified Residential Specialist (A NAR designation).

Cubage: The number or product resulting by multiplying the width of a thing by its height and by its depth or length.

Curable Depreciation: Items of physical deterioration and functional obsolescence which are customarily repaired or replaced by a prudent property owner.

Curtail Schedule: A listing of the amounts by which the principal sum of an obligation is to be reduced by partial payments and of the dates when each payment will become payable.

Curtesy: The right which a husband has in a wife's estate upon her death.

D

Damages: The indemnity recoverable by a person who has sustained an injury, either in his person, property, or relative rights, through the act or default of another.

Data Plant: An appraiser's file of information on real estate.

Debenture: Bonds issued without specific security.

Debtor: This is the party who "owns" the property which is subject to the Security Interest.

Deciduous Trees: Lose their leaves in the autumn and winter. (Regarded as hardwoods.)

Deck: Usually an open porch on the roof of a ground or lower floor, porch, or wing.

Dedication: A conveyance of land by its owner for some public use, accepted for such use by authorized public officials on behalf of the public.

Deed: Written instrument which, when properly executed and delivered, conveys title.

Deed in Lieu of Foreclosure: Mortgagor gives a quitclaim deed to mortgagee. There could be a problem as to Junior Liens.

Deed Restrictions: This is a limitation in the deed to a property that dictates certain uses that may or may not be made of the property.

Default: Failure to fulfill a duty or promise or to discharge an obligation; omission or failure to perform any act.

Defeasance Clause: The clause in a mortgage that gives the mortgagor the right to redeem his property upon the payment of his obligations to the mortgagee.

Defeasible Fee: Sometimes called a base fee or qualified fee; a fee simple absolute interest in land that is capable of being terminated upon the happening of a specified event.

Deferred Maintenance: Existing but unfulfilled requirements for repairs and rehabilitation.

Deficiency Judgment: A judgment given when the foreclosure sale of the security pledge for a loan does not satisfy the debt.

Depreciation: Loss of value in real property brought about by age, physical deterioration, or functional or economic obsolescence. Broadly, a loss in value from any cause.

Depth Table: A statistical table that may be used to estimate the value of the added depth of a lot.

Desist and Refrain Order: An order directing a person to desist and refrain from committing an act in violation of the real estate law.

Desk Cost: The cost of operation of a real estate office expressed on a per-salesperson basis.

Deterioration: Impairment of condition. One of the causes of depreciation and reflecting the loss in value brought about by wear and tear, disintegration, use in service, and the action of the elements.

Devisee: One who receives a bequest made by will.

Devisor: One who bequeaths by will.

Directional Growth: The location or direction toward which the residential sections of a city are destined or determined to grow.

Discount: An amount deducted in advance from the principal before the borrower is given the use of the principal (see **Point[s]**).

Disintermediation: The relatively sudden withdrawal of substantial sums of money that savers have deposited with savings banks, commercial banks, and mutual savings banks. This term can also be considered to include life insurance policy purchasers borrowing against the value of their policies. The essence of this phenomenon is financial intermediaries losing, within a short period of time, billions of dollars, as owners of funds held by those institutional lenders exercise their prerogative of taking them out of the hands of these financial institutions.

Disposable Income: The after-tax income a household receives to spend on personal consumption.

Dispossess: To deprive one of the use of real estate.

Documentary Transfer Tax: A state enabling act allowing a county to adopt a tax to apply on all transfer of real property located in the county. Notice of payment is entered on the face of the deed or on a separate paper filed with the deed.

Dominant Tenement: Estate benefited by an easement right of use.

Donee: A person to whom a gift is made.

Donor: A person who makes a gift.

Dower: The right which a wife has in her husband's estate upon his death.

Dual Agency: An agent who has agency duties to both buyer and seller.

Duress: Unlawful constraint exercised upon a person whereby he is forced to do some act against his will.

E

Earnest Money: Down payment made by a purchaser of real estate as evidence of good faith.

Easement: Created by grant or agreement for a specific purpose, an easement is the right, privilege, or interest one party has in land of another. (**Example:** right of way.)

Easement by Necessity: Easement granted when lands were formerly under a single owner and there is not other ingress or egress.

Easement by Prescription: An easement obtained by open, notorious, and hostile use.

Easement In Gross: An easement created for the benefit of others who do not own adjoining or attached lands. For example, a utility company granted the right to run gas lines across your property.

Eaves: The protruding underpart of a roof overhanging exterior walls.

Economic Life: The period over which a property will yield a return on the investment, over and above the economic or ground rent due to land.

Economic Obsolescence: A loss in value due to factors away from the subject property, but adversely affecting the value of the subject property.

TERMS

Economic Rent: The reasonable rental expectancy if the property were available for renting at the time of its valuation.

Effective Age of Improvement: The number of years of age that is indicated by the condition of the structure.

Effective Date of Value: The specific day the conclusion of value applies.

Effective Interest Rate: The percentage of interest that is actually being paid by the borrower for the use of the money.

Electromagnetic Fields: Possible harmful magnetic fields surrounding high capacity electrical transmission lines.

Emancipated Minor: A person under the age of 18 years who has the contractual rights of an adult. The three ways that a minor becomes emancipated are:

1. Through marriage.
2. Member or former member of the armed forces.
3. Declared to be self-supporting by the courts.

Eminent Domain: The right of the government to acquire property for necessary public or quasi-public use by condemnation; the owner must be fairly compensated. The right of the government to do this and the right of the private citizen to get paid is spelled out in the 5th Amendment to the United States Constitution.

Encroachment: Trespass; the building of a structure or construction of any improvements partly or wholly on the property of another.

Encumbrance: Anything that affects or limits the fee simple title to property, such as mortgages, easements, or restrictions of any kind. Liens are special encumbrances that make the property security for the payment of a debt or obligation, such as mortgages and taxes.

Environmental Impact Report (EIR): A report as to the effect of a proposed development on the environment.

Equity: The interest or value that an owner has in real estate over and above the liens against it; the branch of remedial justice by and through which relief is afforded to suitors in courts of equity.

Equity of Redemption: The right to redeem property during or after the foreclosure period, such as a mortgagor's right to redeem within a set period after foreclosure sale (some states).

Erosion: The wearing away of land by the action of water, wind, or glacial ice.

Escalation: The right reserved by the lender to increase the amount of the payments and/or interest upon the happening of a certain event.

Escalator Clause: A clause in a contract or lease providing for the upward or downward adjustment of payments.

Escheat: The reverting of property to the state when heirs capable of inheriting are lacking.

Escrow: The deposit of instruments and funds with instructions to a third neutral party to carry out the provisions of an agreement or contract. When everything is deposited to enable carrying out the instructions, it is called a complete or perfect escrow.

Estate: As applied to the real estate practice, the term signifies the quantity of interest, share, right, equity, of which riches or fortune may consist, in real property. The degree, quantity, nature, and extent of interest that a person has in real property.

Estate of Inheritance: An estate which may descend to heirs. All freehold estates are estates of inheritance, except estates for life.

Estate for Life: A freehold estate, not of inheritance, but which is held by the tenant for his own life or the life or lives of one or more other persons, or for an indefinite period that may endure for the life or lives of persons in being and beyond the period of life.

Estate from Period-to-Period: An interest in land where there is no definite termination date but the rental period is fixed at a certain sum per week, month, or year. Also called a periodic tenancy.

Estate at Sufferance: An estate arising when the tenant wrongfully holds over after the expiration of his term. The landlord has the choice of evicting the tenant as a trespasser or accepting such tenant for a similar term and under the conditions of the tenant's previous holding. Also called a tenancy at sufferance.

Estate of Will: The permissive occupation of lands and tenements by a tenant for an indefinite period without a rental agreement.

Estate for Years: An interest in lands by virtue of a contract for the possession of those lands for a definite and limited period of time. A lease with a definite termination date may be said to be an estate for years.

Estate Tax: Inheritance tax.

Estimate: To form a preliminary opinion of value.

Estimated Remaining Life: The period of time (years) it takes for the improvements to become valueless.

Estoppel: A doctrine which bars one from asserting rights that are inconsistent with a previous position or representation.

Ethics: The system or code of moral science, idealism, justness, and fairness that a member of a profession or craft owes to the public, to his clients or patrons, and to his professional brethren or members.

Eviction: Dispossession by process of law. The act of depriving a person of the possession of lands, in pursuance of the judgment of a court.

Exclusive Agency Listing: A written instrument giving one agent the right to sell property for a specified time, but reserving the right of the owner to sell the property himself without the payment of a commission.

Exclusive Right to Sell Listing: A written agreement between owner and agent giving agent the right to collect a commission if the property is sold by anyone during the term of his agreement.

Execute: To complete, to make, to perform, to do, to follow out; to execute a deed, to make a deed, including especially signing, sealing, and delivery; to execute a contract is to perform the contract; to follow out to the end, to complete.

TERMS

Executor: A person named in a will to carry out its provisions as to the disposition of the estate of a person deceased.

Expansion Joint: A fiber strip used to separate units of concrete to prevent cracking due to expansion as a result of temperature changes.

Expenses: Certain items which may appear on a closing statement in connection with a real estate sale.

F

Facade: Front of a building.

Facilitator: A person who acts to bring parties to an agreement but is the agent of neither.

Farmers Home Administration: An agency of the Department of Agriculture. Primary responsibility is to provide financial assistance for farmers and others living in rural areas where financing is not available on reasonable terms from private sources.

Fair Market Value: The amount of money that would be paid for a property offered on the open market for a reasonable period of time with both buyer and seller knowing all the uses to which the property could be put and with neither party being under pressure to buy or sell.

Federal Deposit Insurance Corporation (FDIC): Agency of the federal government that insures deposits at commercial banks and savings banks.

Federal Housing Administration (FHA): An agency of the federal government that insures mortgage loans.

Federal National Mortgage Association (FNMA): "Fannie Mae" a private, shareholder-owned company whose primary function is to buy and sell FHA and VA mortgages in the secondary market.

Fee, Estate in: An estate of inheritance in real property.

Fee Simple: In modern estates, the terms "Fee" and "Fee Simple" are substantially synonymous. The term "Fee" is of Old English derivation. "Fee Simple Absolute" is an estate in real property, by which the owner has the greatest power over the title that it is possible to have, being an absolute estate. In modern use, it expressly establishes the title of real property in the owner's name, without limitation or end. He or she may dispose of it by sale, trade, or will as he or she chooses.

Fee Simple Determinable: An estate that ends automatically when a condition is breached.

Feudal Tenure: A real property ownership system where ownership rests with a sovereign who, in turn, may grant lesser interests in return for service or loyalty. In contrast to allodial tenure where ownership is complete.

Feuds: Grants of land.

Fidelity Bond: A security posted to ensure the honesty of a person.

Fiduciary: A person in a position of trust and confidence, as between principal and broker; broker as fiduciary owes certain loyalty that cannot be breached under the rules of agency.

Filtering Down: The process of housing passing down to successively lower income groups.

Financial Intermediary: Financial institutions such as commercial banks, savings banks, and life insurance companies that receive relatively small sums of money from the public and invest them in the form of large sums. A considerable portion of these funds are loaned on real estate.

Financing Statement: This is the instrument which is filed in order to give public notice of the security interest in personal property and thereby protect the interest of the secured parties in the collateral. See definitions of **Security Interest** and **Secured Party**.

Finder's Fee: A fee for introducing the parties to a transaction.

Finish Floor: Finish floor strips are applied over wood joists and plywood before finish floor is installed; finish floor is the final covering on the floor: wood, linoleum, cork, tile, or carpet.

Fire Stop: A horizontal board between studs placed to prevent the spread of fire and smoke through such a space.

First Mortgage: A legal document pledging collateral for a loan (see "mortgage") that has first priority over all other claims against the property except taxes and bonded indebtedness.

Fiscal Controls: Federal tax and expenditure policies used to control the level of economic activity.

Fixity of Location: The physical characteristic of real estate that subjects it to the influence of its surroundings.

Fixtures: Appurtenances attached to the land, or improvements which usually cannot be removed without agreement as they become real property. Example: plumbing fixtures built into the property.

Flashing: Sheet metal or other material used to protect a building from seepage of water.

Footing: The base or bottom of a foundation wall, pier, or column.

Foreclosure: Legal procedure whereby property pledged as security for a debt is sold to pay the debt in event of default in payments or terms.

Forfeiture: Loss of money or anything of value due to failure to perform.

Foundation: The supporting portion of a structure below the first floor construction, or below grade.

Franchise: A specified privilege or right awarded by a government or business firm to operate a public utility, etc. or private dealership.

Fraud: The intentional and successful employment of any cunning, deception, collusion, or artifice used to circumvent, cheat, or deceive another person, whereby that person acts upon it to the loss of his property and to his legal injury.

Freehold: An estate of indeterminable duration; e.g., fee simple or life estate.

Frontage: Land bordering a street.

Front Foot: Property measurement for sale or valuation purposes; the property measures by the front foot on its street line—each front foot extending the depth of the lot.

Front Money: The minimum amount of money necessary to initiate a real estate venture.

Frostline: The depth of frost penetration in the soil. Varies in different parts of the country. Footings should be placed below this depth to prevent movement.

Fructus Naturales: Naturally growing plants and trees.

Functional Obsolescence: A loss of value due to adverse factors built into the structure which affect the utility of the structure.

Funding Fee: A fee paid to the Department of Veterans Affairs for a VA loan.

Furring: Strips of wood or metal applied to a wall or other surface to even it, to form an air space, or to give the wall an appearance of greater thickness.

Future Benefits: The anticipated benefits the present owner will receive from his property in the future.

G

Gable Roof: A pitched roof with sloping sides.

Gambrel Roof: A roof with two slopes on each side, the lower steeper than the upper, which form the ridge.

General Lien: A lien on all the property of a debtor.

General Warranty Deed: The warranty deed where the seller guarantees that the title is marketable.

Gift Deed: A deed for which the consideration is love and affection and where there is no material consideration.

Girder: A large beam used to support beams, joists, and partitions.

Grade: Ground level at the foundation.

Graduated Lease: Lease which provides for a varying rental rate, often based upon future determination; sometimes rent is based upon result of periodical appraisals; used largely in long-term leases.

Grant: A technical term made use of in deeds of conveyance of lands to import a transfer.

Grant Deed: A deed in which "grant" is used as the word of conveyance. The grantor impliedly warrants that he has not already conveyed to any other person, and that the estate conveyed is free from encumbrances done, made, or suffered by the grantor or any person claiming under him, including taxes, assessments, and other liens.

Grantee: The purchaser; a person to whom a grant is made.

Grantor: Seller of property; one who signs a deed.

GRI: Graduate, Realtors® Institute.

Grid: A chart used in rating the borrower risk, property, and the neighborhood.

Gross Income: Total income from property before any expenses are deducted.

Gross Domestic Product (GDP): The total value of all goods and services produced in a economy during a given period of time.

Gross Rate: A method of collecting interest by adding total interest to the principal of the loan at the outset of the term.

Gross Rent Multiplier: A figure which, times the gross income of a property, produces an estimate of value of the property.

Ground Lease: An agreement for the use of the land only, sometimes secured by improvements placed on the land by the user.

Ground Rent: Earnings of improved property credited to earnings of the ground itself after allowance is made for earnings of improvements; often termed economic rent.

Growing Equity Mortgage (GEM): A mortgage with payments that increase in steps resulting in a rapid payback.

H

Habendum Clause: The "to have and to hold" clause in a deed.

Hard Money Loan: A cash loan by a noninstitutional lender.

Header: The horizontal beam above doors or windows.

Highest and Best Use: An appraisal phrase meaning that use which, at the time of an appraisal, is most likely to produce the greatest net return to the land and/or buildings over a given period of time; that use which will produce the greatest amount of amenities or profit. This is the starting point for appraisal.

Hip Roof: A pitched roof with all sides sloping to the eaves.

Holder in Due Course: One who has taken a note, check, or bill of exchange in due course that:
1. Appears good on its face;
2. was taken before it was overdue;
3. was taken in good faith and for value;
4. was taken without knowledge that it has been previously dishonored and without notice of any defect at the time it was negotiated to him.

Holdover Tenant: Tenant who remains in possession of leased property after the expiration of the lease term.

TERMS

Homestead: A home upon which the owner or owners have recorded a Declaration of Homestead. As provided by statutes in some states, it protects home against judgments up to specified amounts.

Hundred Percent Location: A city retail business location which is considered the best available for attracting business.

Hypothecate: To give a thing as security without the necessity of giving up possession of it.

I

Impounds: A trust-type account established by lenders for the accumulation of funds to meet taxes and future insurance policy premiums required to protect the lenders' security. Impounds are usually collected with the note payment.

Inchoate Right of Dower: A wife's interest in the real estate of her husband during his life which, upon his death, may become a dower interest.

Income Approach: One of the three methods in the appraisal process; an analysis in which the estimated net income from the subject residence is used as a basis for estimating value by dividing the net by a capitalization rate.

Incompetent: A person who, because of old age, disease, weakness of mind, or any other cause, does not have the capacity to enter into a contract.

Incorporeal Rights: Nonpossessory rights in real estate.

Increment: An increase. Most frequently used to refer to the increase of value of land that accompanies population growth and increasing wealth in the community. The term "unearned increment" is used in this connection since values are supposed to have increased without effort on the part of the owner.

Indenture: A formal written instrument made between two or more persons.

Indorsement: The act of signing one's name on the back of a check or note, with or without further qualification. (Also spelled "endorsement.")

Injunction: A writ or order issued under the seal of a court to restrain one or more parties to a suit or proceeding from doing an act which is deemed to be inequitable or unjust in regard to the rights of some other party or parties in the suit or proceeding.

Input: Data or information that is fed into a computer or other system.

Installment Contract: Purchase of real estate wherein the purchase price is paid in installments over a long period of time; title is retained by seller and upon default, the payments are forfeited. Also known as a **Land Contract**.

Installment Note: A note which provides that payments of a certain sum or amount be paid on the dates specified in the instrument.

Installment Reporting: A method of reporting capital gains by installments for successive tax years to minimize the impact of the totality of the capital gains tax in the year of the sale.

Instrument: A written legal document created to effect the rights of the parties.

Interest: The charge in dollars for the use of money for a period of time. In a sense, the "rent" paid for the use of money.

Interest Rate: The percentage of a sum of money charged for its use.

Interim Loan: A short-term loan until long-term financing is available.

Intermediate Theory: States that a mortgage is a lien but title transfers to mortgagee automatically upon default.

Interstate Land Sales Full Disclosure Act: Disclosure requirements for unimproved land sales made in interstate commerce.

Intestate: A person who dies having made no will, or one that is defective in form, in which case the estate descends to his or her heirs at law or next of kin.

Involuntary Alienation: Involuntary transfer, such as foreclosure for eminent domain.

Involuntary Lien: A lien imposed against property without consent of an owner. Examples: taxes, special assessments, and federal income tax liens.

Inwood Tables: Concept of using present value of income in a perpetuity table to help appraisers.

IREM: Institute of Real Estate Management. Part of the National Association of Realtors® (NAR).

Irrevocable: Incapable of being recalled or revoked; unchangeable.

J

Jalousie: A slatted blind shutter or window, like a venetian blind, but used on the exterior to protect against rain as well as to control sunlight.

Jamb: The side post or lining of a doorway, window, or other opening.

Joint Note: A note signed by two or more persons who have equal liability for payment.

Joint Tenancy: Joint ownership by two or more persons with right of survivorship; all joint tenants own equal interest and have equal rights in the property and are formed at the same time by the same instrument.

Joint Venture: Two or more individuals or firms joining together on a single project as partners.

Joist: One of a series of parallel horizontal beams to which the boards of a floor and ceiling laths are nailed and supported in turn by larger beams, girders, or bearing walls.

Judgment: The final determination of a court of competent jurisdiction of a matter presented to it; money judgments provided for payment of claims presented to the court, or for damages, etc.

Judgment Lien: A legal claim on all of the property of a judgment debtor in the county where recorded, which enables the judgment creditor to have the property sold for payment of the amount of the judgment.

Junior Mortgage: A mortgage second in lien to a previous mortgage.

Jurisdiction: The authority by which judicial officers take cognizance of and decide causes; the power to hear and determine a cause; the right and power which a judicial officer has to enter upon the inquiry.

L

Laches: Delay or negligence in asserting one's legal rights.

Land Contract: A contract ordinarily used in connection with the sale of property in cases where the seller does not wish to convey title until all or a certain part of the purchase price is paid by the buyer. Often used when property is sold on small down payment.

Landlord: One who rents his property to another.

Lateral Support: The support which the soil of an adjoining owner gives to his neighbors' land.

Lath: A building material of wood, metal, gypsum, or insulating board fastened to the frame of a building to act as a plaster base.

Lead-Based Paint Disclosure: Federally mandated disclosure for residential property built prior to 1978.

Lease: A contract between owner and tenant, setting forth conditions upon which tenant may occupy and use the property, and the term of the occupancy.

Leasehold Estate: A tenant's right to occupy real estate during the term of the lease. This is a personal property interest.

Legal Description: A description recognized by law; a description by which property can be definitely located by reference to government surveys, metes and bounds, or approved recorded maps.

Lessee: One who contracts to rent property under a lease contract.

Lessor: An owner who enters into a lease with a tenant.

Level Payment Mortgage: A loan on real estate that is paid off by making a series of equal (or nearly equal) regular payments. Part of the payment is usually interest on the loan and part of it reduces the amount of the unpaid balance of the loan. Also sometimes called an **Amortized Mortgage**.

Leverage: Maximizing net by using borrowed funds.

Lien: A form of encumbrance which usually makes property security for the payment of a debt or discharge of an obligation. Examples: judgments, taxes, mortgages, deeds of trust, etc.

Lien Theory: A mortgage theory that a mortgage creates only a lien.

Life Estate: An estate or interest in real property which is held for the duration of the life of some certain person.

Limited Partnership: A partnership composed of some partners whose contribution is financial, and liability is limited to their investment.

Lintel: A horizontal board that supports the load over an opening such as a door or window.

Lis Pendens: "Suit pending"; usually recorded so as to give constructive notice of pending litigation.

Liquidated Damages: A sum agreed upon by the parties to be full damages rewarded if an agreement is breached.

Listing: An employment contract between principal and agent authorizing the agent to perform services for the principal involving the latter's property; listing contracts are entered into for the purpose of securing persons to buy, lease, or rent property. Employment of an agent by a prospective purchaser or lessee to locate property for purchase or lease may be considered a listing.

Loan Administration: Also called loan servicing. Mortgage bankers not only originate loans, but also "service" them from origination to maturity of the loan.

Loan Application: The loan application is a source of information on which the lender bases his decision to make the loan and defines the terms of the loan contract; gives the name of the borrower, place of employment, salary, bank accounts, and credit references; and describes the real estate that is to be mortgaged. It also stipulates the amount of loan being applied for and repayment terms.

Loan Closing: When all conditions have been met, the loan officer authorizes the recording of the trust deed or mortgage. The disbursal procedure of funds is similar to the closing of a real estate sales escrow. The borrower can expect to receive less than the amount of the loan, as title, recording, service, and other fees may be withheld, or he can expect to deposit the cost of these items into the loan escrow. This process is sometimes called **Funding** or **Settlement**.

Loan Commitment: Lender's contractual commitment to a loan based on the appraisal and underwriting.

Loan To Value Ratio (LTV): The percentage of a property's value that a lender can or may loan to a borrower. For example, if the ratio is 80% this means that a lender may loan 80% of the property's appraised value to a borrower.

Long-Term Gain: Capital gain on sale of property held over 18 months.

Louver: An opening with a series of horizontal slats set at an angle to permit ventilation without admitting rain, sunlight, or vision.

M

MAI (Member, Appraisal Institute): Designates a person who is a member of the Appraisal Institute.

TERMS

Manufactured Home: Sometimes incorrectly referred to as a "mobile home," this type of home is constructed to the HUD Code in a factory and transported on its own chassis to its final location.

Margin of Security: The difference between the amount of the mortgage loan(s) and the appraised value of the property.

Marginal Land: Land that barely pays the cost of working or using.

Market Data Approach: One of the three methods in the appraisal process. A means of comparing similar type residential properties, which have recently sold, to the subject property.

Market Price: The price paid, regardless of pressures, motives, or intelligence.

Market Value: (1) The price at which a willing seller would sell and a willing buyer would buy, neither being under abnormal pressure; (2) as defined by the courts, the highest price estimated in terms of money which a property will bring if exposed for sale in the open market, allowing a reasonable time to find a purchaser with knowledge of the property's use and capabilities for use.

Marketable Title: Merchantable title; title free and clear of objectionable liens or encumbrances.

Material Fact: A fact is material if it is one which the agent should realize would be likely to affect the judgment of the principal in giving his consent to the agent to enter into the particular transaction on the specified terms.

Mechanic's Lien: A lien created by statute which exists against real property in favor of persons who have performed work or furnished materials for the improvement of the real estate.

Meridians: North-south surveyor lines that intersect base lines to form a starting point for the measurement of land.

Metes and Bounds: A term used in describing the boundary lines of land, setting forth all the boundary lines together with their terminal points and angles.

Mid-Term Gain: Gain on sale of property held over one year but less than 18 months.

Mile: 5,280 feet.

Mineral, Oil, and Gas Rights: The right to minerals, oil, and gas in the ground and the implied easement to enter to mine or drill.

Minor: All persons under 18 years of age who are not emancipated.

Misplaced Improvement: Improvements on land which do not conform to the most profitable use of the site.

Mitigation of Damages: Duty of lessor to attempt to rent to keep defaulting tenant's damages down.

Modular: A building composed of modules constructed on an assembly line in a factory. Usually, the modules are self-contained.

Moldings: Usually patterned or curved strips used to provide ornamental variation of outline or contour, such as cornices, bases, windows, and door jambs.

Monetary Controls: Federal Reserve tools for regulating the availability of money and credit to influence the level of economic activity.

Monument: A fixed object and point established by surveyors to establish land locations.

Moratorium: The temporary suspension, usually by statute, of construction or the enforcement of a debt.

Mortgage: An instrument recognized by law by which property is hypothecated to secure the payment of a debt or obligation; procedure for foreclosure in event of default is established by statute.

Mortgage Guaranty Insurance: Insurance against financial loss available to mortgage lenders from Mortgage Guaranty Insurance Corporation (MGIC), a private company organized in 1956.

Mortgage Loan Broker: A broker who charges borrowers for loans arranged.

Mortgagee: One to whom a mortgagor gives a mortgage to secure a loan or performance of an obligation; a lender. (See definition of **Secured Party**.)

Mortgagor: One who gives a mortgage on his property to secure a loan or assure performance of an obligation; a borrower. (See definition of **Debtor**.)

Multiple Listing: A listing, usually an exclusive right to sell, taken by a member of an organization composed of real estate brokers, with the provision that all members will have the opportunity to find an interested client; a cooperative listing.

Mutual Water Company: A water company organized by or for water users in a given district with the object of securing an ample water supply at a reasonable rate; stock is issued to users.

N

NAREB: National Association of Real Estate Brokers, or "Realtist." A national organization of brokers with a predominance of Afro-American members, although membership is by no means limited to Afro-Americans.

NAR: National Association of Realtors®. The national trade association for all the state associations and local boards of Realtors® in the United States.

Narrative Appraisal Report: A summary of all factual materials, techniques, and appraisal methods used by the appraiser in setting forth his or her value conclusion.

Negative Amortization: Loan payments that do not cover the interest due, thus increasing the loan principal.

Negative Declaration: A statement that a development will not adversely affect the environment.

Negotiable: Capable of being negotiated; assignable or transferable in the ordinary course of business.

Net Listing: A listing which provides that the agent may retain as compensation for his services all sums received over and above a net price to the owner. (Illegal in many states.)

TERMS

Nominal Interest Rates: The percentage of interest that is stated in loan documents.

Notary Public: An appointed officer with authority to take the acknowledgment of persons executing documents, to sign the certificate and affix his or herl seal.

Note: A signed, written instrument acknowledging a debt and promising payment.

Notice: Actual knowledge acquired by being or knowing of the occurrence.

Notice of Nonresponsibility: A notice provided by law designed to relieve a property owner from responsibility for the cost of work done on the property or materials furnished therefor; when contracted by a tenant or vendee on a land contract notice must be verified, recorded, and posted.

Notice to Quit: A notice to a tenant to vacate rented property.

Obligating Advance: Required advance on a construction loan as work progresses.

Obsolescence: Loss in value due to reduced desirability and usefulness of a structure because its design and construction become obsolete.

Occupancy Permit: Required from building inspector prior to occupancy of a new unit.

Offset Statement: Statement by owner of property or owner of lien against property, setting forth the present status of liens against said property.

Open-end Mortgage: A mortgage containing a clause which permits the mortgagor to borrow additional money without rewriting the mortgage.

Open Housing Law: See Civil Rights Act of 1968.

Open Listing: An authorization given by a property owner to a real estate agent wherein said agent is given the non-exclusive rights to secure a purchaser. Open listings may be given to any number of agents without liability to compensate any except the one who first secures a buyer ready, willing, and able to meet the terms of the listing, or secures the acceptance by the seller of a satisfactory offer.

Opinion of Title: An attorney's evaluation of the condition of the title to a parcel of land after his examination of the abstract of title to the land.

Option: A right given for a consideration to purchase or lease a property upon specified terms within a specified time.

Oral Contract: A verbal agreement; one which is not reduced to writing.

Orientation: Placing a house on its lot with regard to its exposure to the rays of the sun, prevailing winds, privacy from the street, and protection from outside noises.

Overhang: The part of the roof extending beyond the walls, to shade buildings and cover walks.

Over Improvement: An improvement that is not the highest and best use for the site on which it is placed by reason of excess size or cost. An improvement that will not reasonably contribute to income or market value.

P-Q

Packaged Mortgage: A mortgage covering both real and personal property.

Parquet Floor: Hardwood flooring laid in squares or patterns.

Participation: In addition to base interest on mortgage loans on income properties, a percentage of ownership is given to the lender.

Partition Action: Court proceedings by which co-owners seek to sever their joint ownership.

Partnership: A partnership as between partners themselves may be defined to be a contract of two or more persons to unite their property, labor, or skill (or some of them) in prosecution of some joint or lawful business, and to share the profits in certain proportions.

Party Wall: A wall erected on the line between two adjoining properties that are under different ownership, for the use of both properties.

Patent: Conveyance of title to government land.

Penalty: An extra payment or charge required of the borrower for deviating from the terms of the original loan agreement. Usually levied for being late in making a regular payment or for paying off the loan before it is due.

Penny: The term, as applied to nails, serves as a measure of nail length and is abbreviated by the letter "d."

Percentage Lease: Lease on the property, the rental for which is determined by amount of business done by the lessee; usually a percentage of gross receipts from the business with provision for a minimum rental.

Perimeter Heating: Baseboard heating, or any system in which the heat registers are located along the outside walls of a room, especially under the windows.

Personal Property: Any property which is not real property.

Physical Deterioration: Impairment of condition. Loss in value brought about by wear and tear, disintegration, use, and actions of the elements.

Pier: A column of masonry, usually rectangular in horizontal cross section, used to support other structural members.

Pitch: The incline or rise of a roof.

Planned Unit Development (PUD): A land use design with private unit ownership, but having common areas.

Plate: A horizontal board placed on a wall or supported on posts or studs to carry the trusses of a roof or rafters directly; a shoe or base member of a partition or other frame; a small flat horizontal board placed on or in a wall to support girders, joists, rafters, etc.

Pledge: The depositing of personal property by a debtor with a creditor as security for a debt or engagement.

Pledgee: One who is given a pledge or a security. (See definition of **Secured Party**.)

Pledgor: One who offers a pledge or gives security. (See definition of **Debtor**.)

Plottage Increment: The appreciation in unit value created by joining smaller ownerships into one large single ownership.

Plywood: Laminated wood made up in panels; several thickness of wood glued together with grain at different angles for strength.

PMI (Private Mortgage Insurance): A policy usually required for a conventional loan where the down payment is less than 20 percent.

POB (Point of Beginning): Beginning point for a metes and bounds description.

Points: Each point is one percent of the loan. They are charged by lenders to make the loan more attractive. For buyers they are treated as prepaid interest.

Police Power: The right of the state to enact laws and regulations and enforce them for the order, safety, health, morals, and general welfare of the public.

Power of Attorney: An instrument authorizing a person to act as the agent of the person granting it, and a general power authorizing the agent to act generally in behalf of the principal. A special power limits the agent to a particular or specific act as: a landowner may grant an agent special power of attorney to convey a single and specific parcel of property. Under the provisions of a general power of attorney, the agent having the power may convey any or all property of the principal granting the general power of attorney.

Prefabricated House: A house manufactured and sometimes partly assembled before delivery to building site.

Prepaid Items of Expense: Prorations of prepaid items of expense which are credited to the seller in the closing statement.

Prepayment: Provision made for loan payments to be larger than those specified in the note.

Prepayment Penalty: Penalty for the payment of a mortgage or trust deed note before it actually becomes due if the note does not provide for prepayment.

Present Value: The lump sum value today of an annuity. A $100 bill to be paid to someone in one year is worth less than if it were a $100 bill to be paid to someone today. This is due to several things, one of which is that the money has time value. How much the $100 bill to be paid in one year is worth today will depend on the interest rate that seems proper for the particular circumstances. For example, if 6% is the appropriate rate, the $100 to be paid one year from now would be worth $94.34 today.

Presumption: A rule of law that courts and judges shall draw a particular inference from a particular fact or from particular evidence, unless and until the truth of such inference is disproved.

Prima Facie: Presumptive on its face.

Principal: This term is used to mean either the employer of an agent or the amount of money borrowed, or the amount of the loan.

Principal Note: The promissory note that is secured by the mortgage or trust deed.

Prior Appropriation: The superior rights of the first user of flowing water (in some states).

Privity: Mutual relationship to the same rights of property; contractual relationship.

Procuring Cause: That cause originating from series of events that, without break in continuity, results in the prime object of an agent's employment producing a final buyer.

Progression, Principle of: The worth of a lesser valued residence tends to be enhanced by association with many higher valued residences in the same area.

Promissory Note: Following a loan commitment from the lender, the borrower signs a note, promising to repay the loan under stipulated terms. The promissory note establishes liability for its repayment.

Property: The rights of ownership. The right to use, possess, enjoy, and dispose of a thing in every legal way and to exclude everyone else from interfering with these rights. Property is generally classified into two groups: personal property and real property.

Proprietary Lease: The lease that goes with stock in a cooperative, authorizing occupancy of a specific unit.

Proration: Adjustments of interest, taxes, and insurance, etc., on a prorated basis as of the closing date. Fire insurance is normally paid for in advance. If a property is sold during this time, the seller is entitled to a refund on that portion of the advance payment that has not been used at the time the title to the property is transferred.

Proration of Taxes: To divide or prorate the taxes equally or proportionately to time of use.

Proximate Cause: That cause of an event is that which, in a natural and continuous sequence unbroken by any new cause, produced that event, and without which the event would not have happened. Also, the procuring cause.

Public Trustee: The county public official whose office has been created by statute, to whom title to real property in certain states, e.g., Colorado, is conveyed by Trust Deed for the use and benefit of the beneficiary, who usually is the lender.

Punitive Damages: Damages in excess of compensatory damages to punish the wrongdoer for an outrageous action.

Purchase and Installment Sale-Back: Involves purchase of the property upon completion of construction and immediate sale-back on a long-term installment contract.

Purchase of Land, Leaseback, and Leasehold Mortgages: An arrangement whereby land is purchased by the lender and leased back to the developer with a mortgage negotiated on the resulting leasehold of the income property constructed. The lender receives an annual ground rent, plus a percentage of income from the property.

TERMS

Purchase and Leaseback: Involves the purchase of property subject to an existing mortgage and immediate leaseback.

Purchase Money Mortgage or Trust Deed: A trust deed or mortgage given as part or all of the purchase consideration for property. In some states the purchase money mortgage or trust deed loan can be made by a seller who extends credit to the buyer of property or by a third party lender (typically a financial institution) that makes a loan to the buyer of real property for a portion of the purchase price to be paid for the property. (In many states there are legal limitations upon mortgagees and trust deed beneficiaries collecting deficiency judgments against the purchase money borrower after the collateral hypothecated under such security instruments has been sold through the foreclosure process. Generally no deficiency judgment is allowed if the collateral property under the mortgage or trust deed is residential property of four units or less with the debtor occupying the property as a place of residence.)

Quantity Survey: A highly technical process in arriving at cost estimate of new construction, and sometimes referred to in the building trade as the "price takeoff method." It involves a detailed estimate of the quantities of raw material lumber, plaster, brick, cement, etc., used, as well as the current price of the material and installation costs. These factors are all added together to arrive at the cost of a structure. It is usually used by contractors and experienced estimators.

Quarter Round: A molding that presents a profile of a quarter circle.

Quiet Enjoyment: Right of an owner to the use of the property without interference of possession.

Quiet Title: A court action brought to establish title; to remove a cloud on the title.

Quitclaim Deed: A deed to relinquish any interest in property which the grantor may have, without claiming to have an interest.

R

Radiant Heating: A method of heating, usually consisting of coils or pipes placed in the floor, wall, or ceiling.

Radon: A colorless, odorless, naturally occurring hazardous gas.

Rafter: One of a series of boards of a roof designed to support roof loads. The rafters of a flat roof are sometimes called roof joists.

Range: A strip of land six miles wide determined by a government survey, running in a north-south direction.

Ratification: The adoption or approval of an act performed on behalf of a person without previous authorization.

Real Estate Board: An organization whose members consist primarily of real estate brokers and salespeople.

Real Estate Settlement Procedures Act: A federal disclosure law effective June 20, 1975, requiring new procedures and forms for settlements (closing costs) involving federally related loans.

Real Estate Trust: A special arrangement under federal and state law whereby investors may pool funds for investments in real estate and mortgages and yet escape corporation taxes.

Realtist: A real estate broker holding active membership in a real estate board affiliated with the National Association of Real Estate Brokers.

Realtor®: A real estate broker holding active membership in a real estate board affiliated with the National Association of Realtors®.

Recapture: The rate of interest necessary to provide for the return of an investment. Not to be confused with interest rate, which is a rate of interest on an investment.

Reconveyance: The transfer of the title of land from one person to the immediate preceding owner. This particular instrument of transfer is commonly used when the performance or debt is satisfied under the terms of a deed of trust, when the trustee conveys the title he has held on condition back to the owner.

Recording: The process of placing a document on file with a designated public official for everyone to see. This public official is usually a county officer known as the **County Recorder**. She designates the fact that a document has been given to her by placing her stamp upon it indicating the time of day and the date when it was officially placed on file. Documents filed with the Recorder are considered to be placed on open notice to the general public of that county. Claims against property usually are given a priority on the basis of the time and the date they are recorded, with the most preferred claim status going to the earliest one recorded and the next claim going to the next earliest one recorded, and so on. This type of notice is called **Constructive Notice** or **Legal Notice**.

Redemption: Buying back one's property after a judicial sale.

Refinancing: The paying off of an existing obligation and assuming a new obligation in its place.

Reformation: An action to correct a mistake in a deed or other document.

Rehabilitation: The restoration of a property to satisfactory condition without drastically changing the plan, form, or style of architecture.

Release Clause: This is a stipulation that upon the payment of a specific sum of money to the holder of a trust deed or mortgage, the lien of the instrument as to a specific described lot or area shall be removed from the blanket lien on the whole area involved.

Release Deed: An instrument executed by the mortgagee or the trustee reconveying to the mortgagor the real estate which secured the mortgage loan after the debt has been paid in full. Upon recording it cancels the mortgage lien created when the mortgage or trust deed was recorded.

Reliction: The addition to land by the permanent recession of water.

Remainder: An estate which takes effect after the termination of the prior estate, such as a life estate.

Remainder Depreciation: The possible loss in value of an improvement which will occur in the future.

Replacement Cost: The cost to replace the structure with one having utility equivalent to that being appraised, but constructed with modern materials and according to current standards, design, and layout.

Reproduction Costs: The cost of replacing the subject improvement with one that is the exact replica, having the same quality of workmanship, design, and layout.

Request for Notice of Default: Recorded request so junior lienholder will be notified of foreclosure action.

Request for Notice of Delinquency: When filed, mortgagee must notify junior lienholder that mortgagor is delinquent in payments.

Required Provider: A lender requiring particular service providers.

Rescission of Contract: The abrogation or annulling of contract; the revocation or repealing of contract by mutual consent by parties to the contract, or for cause by either party to the contract.

Reservation: A right retained by a grantor in conveying property.

RESPA (Real Estate Settlement Procedures Act): A law for the sale or transfer of 1-to-4 residential units requiring specific procedures and forms for settlements (closing costs) involving most home loans from financial institutions with federally insured deposits, including FHA and VA loans.

Restriction: The term as used relating to real property means the owner of real property is restricted or prohibited from doing certain things relating to the property, or using the property for certain purposes. Property restrictions fall into two general classifications—public and private. Zoning ordinances are examples of the former type. Restrictions may be created by private owners, typically by appropriate clauses in deeds, or in agreements, or in general plans of entire subdivisions. Usually they assume the form of a covenant or promise to do or not to do a certain thing. They cover a multitude of matters including use for residential or business purposes; e.g. houses in tract must cost more than $150,000.

Retrospective Value: The value of the property as of a previous date.

Reversion: The right to future possession or enjoyment by the person or his heirs, creating the preceding estate.

Reversionary Interest: The interest which a person has in lands or other property, upon the termination of the preceding estate.

Ridge: The horizontal line at the junction of the top edges of two sloping roof surfaces. The rafters at both slopes are nailed to a ridge board at the ridge.

Ridge Board: The board placed on edge at the ridge of the roof to support the upper ends of the rafters; also called roof tree, ridge piece, ridge plate, or ridgepole.

Right of First Refusal: A right to buy or lease only if an owner wishes to sell or lease to another party. (Rights holder must match the offer.)

Right of Survivorship: Right to acquire the interests of a deceased joint owner; distinguishing feature of a joint tenancy.

Right of Way: A privilege operating as an easement upon land, whereby the owner does by grant or by agreement, give to another the right to pass over his land, to construct a roadway, or use as a roadway, a specific part of his land, or the right to construct through and over his land telephone, telegraph, or electric power lines, or the right to place underground water mains, gas mains, sewer mains, etc.

Riparian Rights: The right of a landowner to flowing water on, under, or adjacent to his land.

Riser: The upright board at the back of each step of a stairway. In heating, a riser is a duct slanted upward to carry hot air from the furnace to the room above.

Risk Analysis: A study made, usually by a lender, of the various factors that might affect the repayment of a loan.

Risk Rating: A process used by the lender to decide on the soundness of making a loan and to reduce all the various factors affecting the repayment of the loan to a qualified rating of some kind.

S

Sales Contract: A contract by which buyer and seller agree to terms of a sale.

Sale-Leaseback: A situation where the owner of a piece of property wishes to sell the property and retain occupancy by leasing it from the buyer.

Sandwich Lease: A leasehold interest which lies between the primary lease and the operating lease.

Sash: Wood or metal frames containing one or more window panes.

Satisfaction: Discharge of mortgage or trust deed lien from the records upon payment of the evidenced debt.

Satisfaction Piece: An instrument for recording and acknowledging payment of an indebtedness secured by a mortgage.

Scribing: Fitting woodwork to an irregular surface.

Seal: An impression made to attest to the execution of an instrument (document) in some states.

Secondary Financing: A loan secured by a second mortgage or trust deed on real property. These can be third, fourth, fifth, sixth—on and on ad infinitum.

Secured Party: The party having the security interest. Thus the mortgagee, the conditional seller, the beneficiary, etc., are all now referred to as the secured party.

Security Agreement: An agreement between the secured party and the debtor which creates the security interest.

Security Interest: A term designating the interest of the creditor in the personal property of the debtor in all types of credit transactions. It thus replaces such terms as the following: chattel mortgage, pledge, trust receipt, chattel trust, equipment trust, conditional sale, inventory lien, etc.

Section: A section of land is established by government survey and contains 640 acres.

Seizin: Possession of real estate by one entitled thereto.

Separate Property: Property owned by a husband or wife which is not jointly owned.

Septic Tank: An underground tank in which sewage from the house is reduced to liquid by bacterial action and drained off.

Servicing: Supervising and administering a loan after it has been made. This involves such things as: collecting the payments, keeping accounting records, computing the interest and principal, foreclosure of defaulted loans, and so on.

Servient Tenement: The estate being used by an easement holder.

Setback Ordinance: An ordinance prohibiting the erection of a building or structure between the curb and the setback line.

Severalty Ownership: Owned by one person only. Sole ownership.

Shopping Center, Regional: A large shopping center with 250,000 to 1,000,000 or more square feet of store area, serving 200,000 or more people.

Shake: A handsplit shingle, usually edge grained.

Sharing Appreciation Mortgage: A loan where a lender shares in the value appreciation. It usually requires a sale or appraisal at a future date.

Sheathing: Structural covering, usually boards, plywood, or wallboards, placed over exterior studding or rafters of a house.

Sheriff's Deed: Deed given by court order in connection with sale of property to satisfy a judgment.

Short-Term Gain: Gain on sale where property was held for one year or less.

Sill: The lowest part of the frame of a house, resting on the foundation and supporting the uprights of the frame (mud sill). The board or metal forming the lower side of an opening, as a door sill, window sill, etc.

Sinking Fund: Fund set aside from the income from property which, with accrued interest, will eventually pay for replacement of the improvements.

SIOR (Society of Industrial and Office Realtors®): An international organization whose members specialize in a variety of commercial real estate activities.

Soft Money Loan: Seller financing where cash does not change hands.

Soil Pipe: Pipe carrying waste out from the house to the main sewer line.

Sole or Sole Plate: A member, usually a 2 by 4, on which wall and partition studs rest.

Span: The distance between structural supports such as walls, columns, piers, beams, girders, and trusses.

Special Assessment: Legal charge against real estate by a public authority to pay cost of public improvements such as: street lights, sidewalks, street improvements, etc.

Special Warranty Deed: A deed in which the grantor warrants or guarantees the title only against defects arising during his ownership of the property and not against defects existing before the time of his ownership.

Specific Liens: Liens which attach to only a certain specific parcel of land or piece of property.

Specific Performance: An action to compel performance of an agreement, e.g., sale of land.

Standard-Depth: Generally the most typical lot depth in the neighborhood.

Standby Commitment: The mortgage banker frequently protects a builder by a "standby" agreement, under which he agrees to make mortgage loans at an agreed price for many months in the future. The builder deposits a "standby fee" with the mortgage banker for this service. Frequently, the mortgage banker protects himself by securing a "standby" from a long-term investor for the same period of time, paying a fee for this privilege.

Starker Exchange: A delayed tax deferred exchange.

Statute of Frauds: State law which provides that certain contracts must be in writing in order to be enforceable at law. Examples: A real property lease for more than one year; an agent's authorization to sell real estate.

Statutory Warranty Deed: A short form warranty deed which warrants by inference that the seller is the undisputed owner and has the right to convey the property and that he will defend the title if necessary. This type of deed protects the purchaser in that the conveyor covenants to defend all claims against the property. If he fails to do so, the new owner can defend said claims and sue the former owner.

Straight-Line Depreciation: A method of computing depreciation for income tax purposes in which the difference between the original cost and no salvage value is deducted in installments evenly over the life of the asset.

Strict Foreclosure: Foreclosure without a sale if the debt has not been paid after statutory notice. The court transfers title to the mortgagee. (Used in a few states.)

String, Stringer: A timber or other support for cross members. In stairs, the diagonal support on which the stair treads rest.

Studs or Studding: Vertical supporting timbers in the walls and partitions.

Subjacent Support: The duty of an excavator or miner to support the surface.

Subject to Mortgage: When a grantee takes a title to real property subject to mortgage, he is not responsible to the holder of the promissory note for the payment of any portion of the amount due. The most that he can lose in the event of a foreclosure is his equity in the property. See also *Assumption of Mortgage*. In neither case is the original maker of the note released from his responsibility.

Sublease: A lease given by a lessee.

Subordinate: To make subject to, or junior to.

Subordination Clause: Clause in a junior or a second lien permitting retention of priority for prior liens. A subordination clause may also be used in a first deed of trust permitting it to be subordinated to subsequent liens as, for example, the liens of construction loans.

TERMS

Subpoena: A process to cause a witness to appear and give testimony.

Subrogation: The substitution of another person in place of the creditor, to whose rights he succeeds in relation to the debt. The doctrine is used very often where one person agrees to stand surety for the performance of a contract by another person.

Substitution, Principle of: Affirms that the maximum value of a property tends to be set by the cost of acquiring an equally desirable and valuable substitute property, assuming no costly delay is encountered in making the substitution.

Sum of the Years Digits: An accelerated depreciation method.

Supply and Demand, Principle of: Affirms that price or value varies directly, but not necessarily proportionally with, demand and inversely, but not necessarily proportionately, with supply.

Surety: One who guarantees the performance of another: **Guarantor**. A surety bond guarantees contract performance.

Surplus Productivity, Principle of: Affirms that the net income that remains, after the proper costs of labor, organization, and capital have been paid, is imputable to the land and tends to fix the value thereof.

Survey: The process by which a parcel of land is measured and its area is ascertained.

Syndicate: A partnership organized for participation in a real estate venture. Partners may be limited or unlimited in their liability.

T

Tacking: Adding or combining successive periods of continuous use of real property by adverse possessors. Used to establish a claim of adverse possession for an entire statutory period even though that person has not been in possession for the entire period.

Takeout Loan: The permanent loan arranged by the owner or builder/developer for a buyer. The construction loan made for construction of the improvements is usually paid from the proceeds of this loan.

Tax-Free Exchange: An exchange of one income property for another for which no capital gains tax payment is due.

Tax Roll: Total of taxable property assessments in taxing district.

Tax Sale: Sale of property by a taxing authority after a period of nonpayment of taxes.

Tax Shelter: Use of depreciation to shelter income from taxation.

Teaser Rate: An initial rate on an adjustable rate loan less than the index figure plus margin. It is usually only given for a relatively short period of time.

Tenancy in Common: Ownership by two or more persons who hold undivided interest without right of survivorship. Interests need not be equal.

Tenants by the Entireties: Under certain state laws, ownership of property acquired by a husband and wife during marriage that is jointly owned and cannot be separately transferred. Upon death of one spouse, it becomes the property of the survivor.

Tentative Map: The Subdivision Map Act requires subdividers to initially submit a tentative map of their tract to the local planning commission for study. The approval or disapproval of the planning commission is noted on the map. Thereafter, a final map of the tract embodying any changes requested by the planning commission is required to be filed with the planning commission.

Tenure in Land: The mode or manner by which an estate in lands is held.

Termites: Ant-like insects that feed on wood.

Termite Shield: A shield, usually of noncorrodible metal, placed on top of the foundation wall or around pipes to prevent passage of termites.

Testator: One who leaves a will in force at his death.

Threshold: A strip of wood or metal beveled on each edge and used above the finished floor under outside doors.

Third Party Originator: A party that prepares loan packages for borrowers for submission to lenders.

Time Is the Essence: A requirement that performance be punctual and that any delay will breach the contract.

Title: Evidence that the owner of land is in lawful possession thereof; an instrument evidencing such ownership.

Title Insurance: Insurance written by a title company to protect property owner against loss if title is imperfect.

Title Report: A report which discloses condition of the title, made by a title company prior to the issuance of title insurance.

Title Theory: Mortgage arrangement whereby title to mortgaged real property vests in the lender.

Topography: Nature of the surface of land; topography may be level, rolling, or mountainous.

Torrens Title: System of title records provided by state law (no longer used in California).

Tort: A wrongful act; wrong, injury; violation of a legal right.

Township: A division by government survey that is six miles long, six miles wide and containing 36 sections, each one mile square.

Trade Fixtures: Articles of personal property annexed to real property, but which are necessary to the carrying on of a trade and are removable by the owner.

Treads: Horizontal boards of a stairway on which one steps.

Trim: The finish materials in a building, such as moldings, applied around openings (window trim, door trim) or at the floor and ceiling (baseboard, cornice, picture molding).

Trust Account: An account separate and apart and physically segregated from broker's own funds, in which broker is required by law to deposit all funds collected for clients.

Trust Deed: Just as with a mortgage, this is a legal document by which a borrower pledges certain real property or collateral as guarantee for the repayment of a loan. However, it differs from the mortgage in a number of important respects. For example, instead of there being two parties to the transaction, there are three. There is the borrower who gives the trust deed and who is called the trustor. There is the third, neutral party (just as there is with an escrow) who receives the trust deed and is called the trustee. And finally there is the lender who is called the beneficiary, since he is the one who benefits from the pledge arrangement in that in the event of a default, the trustee can sell the property and transfer the money obtained at the sale to him as payment of the debt.

Trustee: One who holds property in trust for another to secure the performance of an obligation.

Trustor: One who deeds his property to a trustee to be held as security until he has performed his obligation to a lender under terms of a deed of trust.

U-V

Under Improvement: An improvement which, because of its deficiency in size or cost, is not the highest and best use of the site.

Underwriting: The technical analysis by a lender to determine if a borrower should receive a loan.

Undue Influence: Taking any fraudulent or unfair advantage of another's weakness of mind, distress, or necessity.

Unearned Increment: An increase in value of real estate due to no effort on the part of the owner; often due to increase in population.

Uniform Commercial Code (UCC): Establishes a unified and comprehensive scheme for regulation of security transactions in personal property, superseding the existing statutes on chattel mortgages, conditional sales, trust receipts, assignment of accounts receivable, and others in this field.

Unit-In-Place Method: The cost of erecting a building by estimating the cost of each component part, i.e. foundations, floors, walls, windows, ceilings, roofs, etc. (including labor and overhead).

Urban Property: City property; closely settled property.

Usury: On a loan, claiming a rate of interest greater than that permitted by law.

Utilities: Refers to services rendered by utility companies, such as: water, gas, electricity, telephone.

Utility: The ability to give satisfaction and/or excite desire for possession.

Valid: Having force, or binding force; legally sufficient and authorized by law.

Valley: The internal angle formed by the junction of two sloping sides of a roof.

Valuation: Estimated worth or price; estimation. The act of valuing by appraisal.

Vendee: A purchaser; buyer.

Vendor: A seller; one who disposes of a thing in consideration of money.

Veneer: Thin sheets of wood glued to other wood products to form a surface.

Vent: A pipe installed to provide a flow of air to or from a drainage system or to provide a circulation of air within such system to protect trap seals from siphonage and back pressure.

Verification: Sworn statement before a duly qualified officer to correctness of contents of an instrument.

Vested: Bestowed upon someone; secured by someone, such as a title to property.

Vested Remainder: A certain remainder interest.

Void: To have no force or effect; that which is unenforceable.

Voidable: That which is capable of being adjudged void, but is not void unless action is taken to make it so.

Voluntary Lien: Any lien placed on property with consent of, or as a result of, the voluntary act of the owner.

W-Z

Wainscoting: The covering of an interior wall with wood (usually panels), tiles, etc., from the floor to a point about half way to the ceiling. The remaining portion is painted, wallpapered, or covered with another material different from the lower portion.

Waive: To relinquish, or abandon; to forego a right to enforce or require anything.

Warranty Deed: A deed used to convey real property that contains warranties of title and quiet possession, and the grantor thus agrees to defend the premises against the lawful claims of third persons. It is commonly used in many states, but in others the grant deed has supplanted it due to the practice of securing title insurance policies which has reduced the importance of express and implied warranty in deeds.

Waste: An improper use or abuse of a property by person holding a less-than-freehold interest in a property (i.e., tenant, life tenant, mortgagor, or vendee). The value of the land or the interest of the person holding title or reversionary rights is usually impaired by such waste.

Water Table: Distance from surface of ground to a depth at which natural groundwater is found.

Wrap Around Mortgage: A second trust deed with a face value of both the new amount it secures and the balance due under the first trust deed. A wrap-around can take the form of a land contract or a deed of trust.

Yield: The interest earned by an investor on his investment (or bank on the money it has lent). Also called **Return**.

Yield Rate: The yield expressed as a percentage of the total investment. Also called **Rate of Return**.

Zone: The area set off by the proper authorities for specific use; subject to certain restrictions or restraints.

Zoning: Act of city or county authorities specifying type of use to which property may be put in specific areas.

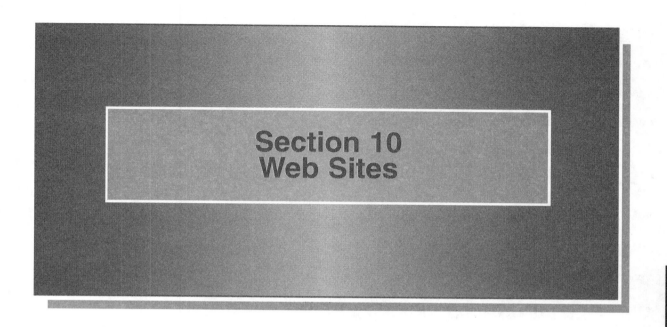

Section 10
Web Sites

GENERAL

www.etcbooks.com (Educational Textbook Company)

www.dre.ca.gov (Department of Real Estate - Homesite)

www.dre.ca.gov/licstats.htm (Department of Real Estate - License Status)

http://lcweb2.loc.gov/ammem/cbhtml/cbintro.html (California History)

www.thomas.com (Thomas Guide)

www.sbaonline.sba.gov (Starting Your Business)

www.car.org (California Association of Realtors®)

www.realtor.com (National Association of Realtors® - NAR)

www.nareb.org/index.htm (National Association of Real Estate Brokers - "Realtist")

www.nahrep.org (National Association of Hispanic Real Estate Professionals)

www.inman.com (Inman News Features)

SERVICES

www.ipix.com (Internet Pictures Corp. - Virtual Home Tours)

www.behere.com (Be Here Corp. - ivideo)

www.evox.com (Evox Productions - Interactive Imagining)

www.virtualproperties.com (Panoramic Images)

SOFTWARE

www.enroute.com (Immersive Imaging)

www.mgisoft.com (Digital Imagining)

www.smoothmove.com (Immersive Video)

MULTIPLE LISTING SERVICES (MLS)

www.ca.realtor.com (California Living Network)

www.car.org (California Association of Realtors®)

www.sucasa.net (Spanish Version)

www.homestore.com

www. themls.com (Combined L.A./Westside MLS)

LISTING SITES

http://sucasa.net (Listings in Spanish)

www.homeseekers.com (Residential Listings)

www.baynet.com (San Francisco Area Listings)

http://listinglink.com (Homescape - Buying, Renting, Selling, etc.)

FRANCHISE SITES

www.remax.com (Remax Real Estate)

www.lyonrealty.com (Lyon and Associates Realtors®)

www.century 21.com (Century 21)

www.mcguirere.com (Maguire Real Estate)

www.mm4re.com (Mason-Duffie Regional Franchise)

CONTRACTS

www.calbar.org (State Bar of California)

www.leginfo.ca.gov/calaw.html (California Law - The 29 Codes)

www.leginfo.ca.gov/statute.html (State Statutes)

www.courtinfo.ca.gov (California Courts)

www.ca9.uscourts.gov (9th Circuit Court of Appeals)

LANDLORD - TENANT

www.ca-apartment.org (California Apartment Association)

http://search.yahoo.com/search?p=California+rental (Rentals and Roommates)

http://tenant.net/Other_Areas/Calif (California Tenants' Rights)

www.irem.org (Institute of Real Estate Management - IREM)

ESCROWS AND TITLE INSURANCE

www.conejohomes.com/escrow.htm (Understanding Escrow)

www.dca.ca.gov (DCA/Structural Pest Control Board)

www.clta.org (California Land Title Association)

www.alta.org (American Land Title Association)

www.ceaescrow.org (California Escrow Association)

FINANCING

www.careermosaic.com (Careers in Finance and Accounting)

www.bankrate.com (Current Interest Rates)

http://latimes.partner.mortgagequotes.com/calc.htm (Mortgage Calculator)

www.relist.com/mortcalc.html (Mortgage Calculator)

www.loanpage.com (Independent Loan Information)

www.loanshop.com (Independent Loan Information)

www.countrywide.com (Large Home Lender)

www.wellsfargo.com (Wells Fargo Bank)

www.bog.frb.fed.us (Federal Reserve Board)

www.ustreas.gov (U.S. Treasury)

WEB SITES

www.occ.treas.gov (Office of the Comptroller of the Currency)

www.frbsf.org (Federal Reserve Bank of San Francisco - 12th District)

www.fdic.gov (Federal Deposit Insurance Corporation - FDIC)

www.ncua.gov (National Credit Union Administration [NCUA])

www.hud.gov/index.html (Housing and Urban Development)

www.hud.gov/oig/oigindex.html (Office of The Inspector General - OIG)

www.comerica.com/comeria/default.html (Comerica - Independent FHA Lender)

www.fix.net/~chase/fha.html (AMFiNet - Independent FHA lender)

www.va.gov (VA Loans)

www.cdva.ca.gov (Cal-Vet Loans)

www.chfa.ca.gov (California Housing Finance Agency)

www.fanniemae.com (Fannie Mae Home Site)

www.ginniemae.gov (Ginnie Mae Home Site)

www.freddiemac.com (Freddie Mac Home Site)

APPRAISAL

www.iami.org/narea.html (National Association of Real Estate Appraisers)

www.appraisalinstitute.org (Appraisal Institute - AI)

http://naifa.com (National Association of Independent Fee Appraisers - NAIFA)

www.nahb.com (National Association of Home Builders)

www.bhwc.com (Buyers Home Warranty Company)

www.aicanada.org (The Appraisal Institute of Canada)

www.marshallswift.com (Marshall and Swift - Cost Engineers)

www.orea.cahwnet.gov (Office of Real Estate Appraisers)

www.appraisers.org (American Society of Appraisers - ASA)

www.asfmra.org (American Society of Farm Managers and Rural Appraisers - ASFMRA)

www.iaao.org (International Association of Assessing Officers - IAAO)

www.irwaonline.org (International Right of Way Association - IRWA)

www.masterappraisers.com (National Association of Master Appraisers - NAMA)

SUBDIVISION AND GOVERNMENT CONTROL

www.dre.ca.gov/subs_sub.htm (DRE - Subdivisions, Public Report)

www.consrv.ca.gov/dmg (Dept. of Conservation - California Division of Mines & Geology)

TIMESHARES

www.ired.com/dir/timeshar.htm (Ired Timeshare)

http://galaxymall.com/market/time2/index.html (Travels World Marketplace)

www.tug2.net (The Timeshare Users Group)

www.timeshare-resorts.com (Timeshare Resorts, International)

TAXATION

www.co.la.ca.us/assessor (L. A. County Assessor)

www.cacttc.org/start.html (List of Assessors)

www.irs.ustreas.gov (Internal Revenue Service)

www.co.sacramento.ca.us/ccr/index.html (County Clerk - Recorder for Sacramento County)

LICENSING AND EDUCATION

www.ca.gov (Welcome to California - Online Services)

http://registry.yosemite.cc.ca.us (California Community Colleges)

www.dre.ca.gov (Department of Real Estate Home Page)

www.dre.ca.gov/salesqs.htm (Salesperson Examination Content and Test Questions)

www.corp.ca.gov (Department of Corporations)

www.census.gov (U.S. Census Bureau)

www.sbaonline.sba.gov (Small Business Administration)

www.abc.ca.gov (Alcoholic Beverage Control)

www.car.org (California Association of Realtors® - CAR)

www.car/org/newsstand/cre/index.html (California Real Estate Magazine)

www.nareb.com (National Association of Real Estate Brokers)

www.nahrep.org (National Association of Hispanic Real Estate Professionals)

WEB SITES

NAR AFFILIATES

www.realtor.com (NAR) (All these affiliates can be accessed here)

www.ccim.com (Commercial Real Estate Network)

www.crb.com (Real Estate Brokerage Managers Council)

www.cre.org (The Counselors of Real Estate)

www.sior.com (Society of Industrial and Office Realtors®)

BOARD OF REALTORS®

www.bhbr.com (Beverly Hills/Greater Los Angeles Association of Realtors®)

www.abr.org (Altlanta, Georgia, Board of Realtors®)

www.hicentral.com (Hawaii Real Estate Central)

www.vbr.net (Vail, Colorado, Board of Realtors®)

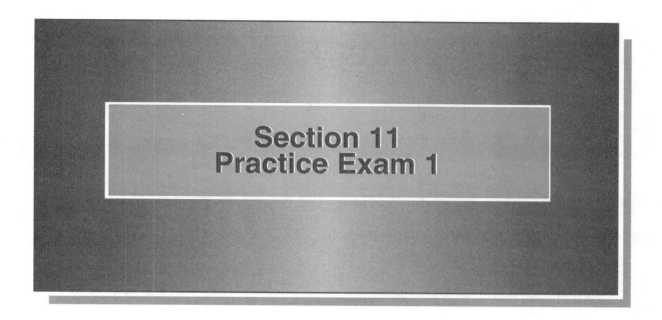

Section 11
Practice Exam 1

1. Broker A accepted a deposit from Buyer B with an offer on a property, and promptly deposited the Buyer's check into his Trust Account. Seller rejected the offer and Buyer demanded the deposit back—immediately. Broker wrote check to Buyer from Trust Account, but later learned that Buyer's original check had not cleared due to insufficient funds. Which of the following statements is correct?

    a. Broker violated Real Estate Law by refunding Buyer's deposit before receiving notice it had cleared.
    b. Broker has shortages in his Trust Account.
    c. Broker should have given Buyer a postdated check.
    d. All of the above.

      ANSWER: b.   *This was poor judgment on the part of the broker.*

2. The resale of which of the following would NOT require a notice to the Department of Real Estate (DRE)?

    a. 2 units in a planned development
    b. 5 units in a condominium project
    c. 5 lots in a standard subdivision
    d. 5 units in a stock cooperative

      ANSWER: a.   *The DRE requires a noticee to be filed for the resale of 5 lots or more in a planned unit development (PUD).*

3. A real estate broker lends his own money to Buyer to aid in purchasing a home. The note is for $4,000, and will be secured by a trust deed on the purchased property. The note interest rate is 12% per year, with monthly payments of $40. Final payoff will be on the 48th month payment. Which of the following is true?

    a. Broker holds legal title to property.
    b. Broker is in violation of usury.
    c. Final amount of payoff on the 48th month will be $4,040.
    d. None of the above.

    ANSWER: c.   *Payments are "interest only," resulting in no principal reduction. The final month payment PLUS the $4,000 principal is due at that time.*

4. National Fair Housing principles are founded on:

    a. First Amendment to the Constitution.
    b. Unruh Act.
    c. 13th Amendment to the Constitution.
    d. Rumford Act.

    ANSWER: c.   *The 13th Amendment and Title 8 of the Civil Rights Act of 1968 both provide for fair housing on a national level.*

5. If Notification of Default was filed on July 15th and publication of sale was started on Oct. l5th, the right of the Trustor after Oct. 15th is:

    a. pay the back payments and late charges and fees.
    b. pay the balance due, including all penalties and late charges.
    c. neither a nor b.
    d. either a or b.

    ANSWER: b.   *Prior to Oct. 15th - bring current; After Oct. 15 - full payoff is required.*

6. What is NOT required to be disclosed under the Truth-in-Lending Law?

    a. Annual percentage rate (APR)
    b. Length of loan
    c. Monthly payment
    d. Total finance charge in purchase of single-family, owner-occupied dwelling

    ANSWER: d.   *Only the APR, length of loan, and monthly payments are required.*

7. Over and above the strictly legal relationship, the Real Estate Commissioner feels that the relationship between the salesperson and the client should be like that higher and more important relationship of:

    a. vendor to vendee.
    b. broker to salesperson.
    c. trustee to beneficiary.
    d. attorney to client.

    ANSWER: c.   *Trustee has a "fiduciary" relationship with the beneficiary.*

8. The expression "A Bundle of Rights" best describes:

    a. a Lessee's rights to quiet and complete freedom of possession of the leased property.
    b. a Vendee's rights in a Land Contract agreement.
    c. rights or interest which an owner has in the thing he/she owns—the right to possess, use, encumber, dispose of, and to exclude.
    d. none of the above describes a "bundle of rights."

      ANSWER: c.   *Best describes a "Bundle of Rights."*

9. What landmark case of the U.S. Supreme Court affected fair housing by prohibiting discrimination?

    a. Shaffer v. Beinhorn
    b. Jones v. Mayer
    c. Weinhoff v. Morgan
    d. None of the above.

      ANSWER: b.   *Jones v. Mayer (after the Civil War) was the landmark case that helped create Title VIII of the Federal Civil Rights Act of 1968.*

10. A broker obtained an exclusive listing to sell a piece of property. He spent much time, money, and energy. The seller refused to allow the broker to proceed under the agreement. The broker should:

    a. consider the seller's refusal a breach and sue for damages.
    b. consider the seller's refusal a breach and claim the amount of commission as liquidated damages.
    c. ignore the seller and proceed.
    d. relieve seller of liability, and work on improving relationship so as to enable retaining future business.

      ANSWER: a.   *When seen from a technical point of view. In reality, sometimes "d" would result in more favorable and profitable end results.*

11. In a period of tight money, the Federal Reserve Bank can increase the supply of money by:

    a. raising the discount rate charged to member banks.
    b. increasing member bank reserve requirements.
    c. selling bonds on the open market.
    d. lowering member bank reserve requirements.

      ANSWER: d.   *The resulting surplus reserve funds would increase money available for customers to borrow from member banks. Answers "a," "b," & "c" would result in decreasing available funds.*

EXAM 1

12. Mr. Traveler needs money to go on a trip. He possesses a $10,000 note and T.D. on the Mayor's farm. Mr. Banks offers to loan Mr. Traveler the $4,000 he needs, providing he can hold the $10,000 note and T.D. as security. If all agree, this would be an example of a:

   a. real chattel agreement.
   b. purchase money trust deed agreement.
   c. subordination agreement.
   d. negotiated pledge agreement.

   ANSWER: d.   *This is a negotiated pledge agreement—Mr. Traveler has pledged the note and T.D. as security.*

13. An investor purchased a $140,000 four-unit apartment building. For a "Cap Rate" of 10%, what would the owner have to get monthly from each of the two bedroom units?

   a. $342
   b. $292
   c. $252
   d. $272

   ANSWER: b.   *Value x Rate = Income; $140,000 x 10% = $14,000 Gross Annual Income; $14,000 ÷ 4 ÷ 12 months = $292 per unit per month.*

14. Buyer purchased a home with a standard policy of title insurance. After moving in, she discovers that the roof eave is only two feet from the property line. The zoning requirements are five feet minimum. In this situation, the buyer may collect:

   a. price of repair minus attorney fees.
   b. price of damages plus cost to repair.
   c. price of the property plus treble damages.
   d. nothing.

   ANSWER: d.   *Standard title insurance policy (CLTA) does NOT provide **on-site inspection**. Extended coverage (ALTA) would have covered this type of defect, but a property inspection would have been made prior to policy issuance anyway.*

15. A broker arranges the sale of a home. There is a purchase money T.D. from the lender. The broker is NOT required to see that the T.D. is recorded if the:

   a. buyer instructs him not to record.
   b. buyer and seller select not to have an escrow.
   c. broker is not involved financially in the loan procurement.
   d. the beneficiary instructs him not to record the T.D.

   ANSWER: d.   *Only a lender (beneficiary) can decide whether a promissory note and trust deed are to be recorded.*

16. Value levels in a residential neighborhood are influenced more by social characteristics of its present and prospective occupants than by any other factor. What would maintain high values in a given neighborhood?

    a. Everybody purchasing with comparable down payments.
    b. Everybody having approximately the same income levels.
    c. Both a and b.
    d. None of the above.

    ANSWER: c.   *Neighborhoods generally have similar physical structures based on common social, economic, and political characteristics.*

17. In is unlawful for any person to effect the sale of any franchise that is regulated by the Franchise Investment Law, unless such person has made an application to the Corporation Commissioner, and is licensed by the:

    a. Franchise Tax Board.
    b. Corporation Commissioner.
    c. Real Estate Commissioner.
    d. Real Estate Commissioner or Corporation Commissioner.

    ANSWER: d.   *A license from one of these two is required.*

18. Mr. E purchased property for $150,000 (Improvement 80%: Land Ratio 20%). If he used the straight-line method of depreciation with 35 years remaining life, what would be the adjusted basis of the property after 10 years?

    a. $85,408
    b. $106,760
    c. $110,204
    d. $115,714

    ANSWER: d.   *$150,000 - 20% = 150,000 - 30,000 = $120,000 improvement value. $120,000 ÷ 35 years = $3,428.57 x 10 years = $34,285.71 accrued depreciation. Adjusted Basis (10 yrs later) = $150,000 - $34,286 = $115,714.*

19. Mr. A sold Mr. B an option for $500 for a 60-day period starting March 13th. In the event the option was exercised, the buyer would be required to complete a 30-day escrow commencing on the day the option was exercised, paying all cash for the property. Mr. B assigned his option to Mr. C for $1,000 consideration. On April 30th, Mr. C informed Mr. A that he would pay cash for the property on May 7th. Mr. A claimed that the option was void. The option was:

    a. void, because the original buyer sold it without permission.
    b. void, because the proposed purchase date would not be within the 60-day option period.
    c. void, even though original holder had sold the option—however, the purchase day was beyond the required date of sale.
    d. valid, and the Assignee (Mr. C) would be able to purchase the subject property on May 7th.

    ANSWER: d.   *Option assignment was legal (without prohibition stated in the original document), and the escrow period commenced within the option period and did not run beyond the prescribed 30-day period.*

20. You have taken an exclusive right to sell listing to assist an owner in selling his home. The owner could lease the property for a maximum of:

    a. as long as he wishes, with consent of broker.
    b. not more than 99 years, with or without the broker's consent.
    c. not beyond the listing period, without the broker's consent.
    d. the owner cannot lease the property without the consent of the broker, as is clearly spelled out in the listing agreement.

    ANSWER: b. The owner can do as he wishes, with or without the consent of the broker. However, violation of the listing agreement could create a condition whereby the owner was liable to the broker for a full commission. Under no circumstances can the owner lease for a period in excess of the 99 years maximum allowed by law.

21. If on a grant deed the manner of taking title is NOT indicated after the names of the two grantees, the courts would rule:

    a. severalty.
    b. joint tenancy.
    c. tenants in common.
    d. community property.

    ANSWER: c. There are two grantees, so it cannot be severalty (sole ownership); There is no mention of right of survivorship, so no joint tenancy; There is no mention of marriage, so no community property.

22. A real estate broker negotiates the sale of a residential property, which involves execution of a new first trust deed. Under what circumstances would the broker be excused from the recording the trust deed?

    a. When he has a financial interest in the trust deed.
    b. When the buyer instructs him not to record.
    c. When the escrow officer "promises" that she/he will see that the trust deed is properly recorded.
    d. None of the above.

    ANSWER: d. Only when the lender (beneficiary) instructs the broker not to record the trust deed is he excused, by law.

23. Five people hold undivided interest as tenants in common. Which is always true?

    a. Each has an equal interest.
    b. Each acquired their interest at the same time.
    c. Each cannot identify their respective part of the property.
    d. Each has an unequal interest.

    ANSWER: c. Each tenant in common owns an "undivided interest" in the property.

24. In the event there is an encroachment on another's property, legal action must commence within:

   a. 6 months.
   b. 1 year.
   c. 3 years.
   d. 5 years.

   ANSWER: c.   *Per statute of frauds.*

25. Which of the following restrictions, set up by the developer of a subdivision (based on experience), would be the least likely to be enforced?

   a. Height restrictions (including number of floors).
   b. Minimum dollar amount expended for improvements on each lot.
   c. Limitations on lot size.
   d. Limitations on minimum square footage for improvement on each lot.

   ANSWER: b.   *Inflationary trends that vary make dollar amount limitations meaningless in a very short time, and therefore impossible to enforce.*

26. A tax that the city could levy against a real estate brokerage firm, based on its gross receipts, would be:

   a. documentary tax stamps.
   b. a business license tax.
   c. a sales tax.
   d. a use tax.

   ANSWER: b.

27. Which of the following is smaller than a section?

   a. 1/36 of a township
   b. Sixteen 40 acre parcels
   c. 27,000,000 sq. ft.
   d. Lot 5000' X 6000'

   ANSWER: c.   *27,000,000 ÷ 43,560 = 620 acres. A section = 640 acres.*

28. When selling a reasonably priced, well established home in a classy, suburban neighborhood, the broker would probably gain the most interest in:

   a. prestige.
   b. tax advantage.
   c. investment.
   d. need.

   ANSWER: a.   *Probably the best "guess" knowing so little about buyer motivations.*

29. A property is owned by five persons in "joint tenancy." Which of the following actions would destroy the respective tenancy relationship?

    a. One tenant wills his interest to another.
    b. Judgment and writ of execution is rendered against a tenant.
    c. Another of the joint tenants places a trust deed against her interest.
    d. Lender completes a foreclosure action against a joint tenants, issuing a trustee's deed to the highest bidder.

      ANSWER: d.   *The new deed "breaks" two of the unities—TIME and TITLE. New owner with trustee's deed is **tenant in common**.*

30. A salesperson brought in an offer on an office lot listing for $18,500. The broker, when taking the listing, was informed by the seller that they would take $18,000. What must the broker do?

    a. Do nothing and close the deal at $18,000.
    b. Inform the buyer of the $18,000 acceptable price.
    c. Say nothing to the seller, and split the $500 equally with the selling salesperson.
    d. Present the $18,500 offer to the sellers for approval.

      ANSWER: d.   *A salesperson must present all reasonable offers to the seller.*

31. Jurisdiction over practices of unfair or discriminatory acts in housing matters belongs to the:

    a. Real Estate Commissioner.
    b. Labor Commission.
    c. Department of Housing.
    d. Fair Employment Practices Commission.

      ANSWER: d.

32. A property for sale is listed at $120,000 and has an outstanding assessment bond of $1,200. At time of sale, for tax purposes, the basis for taxes would be:

    a. $121,200.
    b. $118,000.
    c. $120,000.
    d. indeterminable from information.

      ANSWER: c.   *Acquisition price sets basis. Assessment bond merely provides one way of financing a small part of purchase price.*

33. By definition, a planned development is where:

    a. owners of separately owned lots have another ownership in common in one or more additional lots in the development.
    b. owners of separately owned lots (home and site) also own in common with other owners in the development the common grounds, facilities, parking lots, etc. through an "owners association."
    c. a development having been totally approved throughout the entire city/county planning department.
    d. none of the above.

      ANSWER: b.

34. Which of the following is a "penalty payoff"?

    a. VA loan origination fee.
    b. FHA loan origination fee.
    c. 2% fee on Cal-Vet loan.
    d. All of the above.

    ANSWER: c.   VA and FHA loans have no prepayment penalty provisions. Cal-Vet does allow a prepayment penalty charge of 2% of the outstanding loan balance, if the loan is paid in full within 2 years of its origin.

35. The Real Estate Commissioner has the power to investigate, suspend, or revoke the license of a licensee when that person has been found guilty of:

    a. using a false or fictitious name, knowingly made false statements in any application for registration of a manufactured home as a vehicle.
    b. submitting a check, draft, or money order to the Dept. of Motor Vehicles for any obligation or fee due the State, which was thereafter dishonored or payment refused upon presentation.
    c. both a and b.
    d. none of the above.

    ANSWER: c.

36. The following are all correct concerning a valid homestead, except:

    a. the declarant must reside on property at time of declaring.
    b. the declarant must give a description of the property.
    c. the declarant must be married at the time of declaring.
    d. all of the above.

    ANSWER: c.   The declarant need NOT be married to file/declare.

37. All of the following are essential elements to claim an easement by prescription, except:

    a. payment of taxes for 5 years.
    b. open and notorious use for 5 years.
    c. use is hostile to owner.
    d. claim or right.

    ANSWER: a.   Payment of taxes is tied to taking title by "Adverse Possession."

EXAM 1

38. Broker "U" receives a $5,000 deposit with an offer to purchase one of your personal listings priced at $100,000. The escrow is to close in only one week. The seller has previously agreed to pay you a $5,000 commission for any sale he can get on this property. Seller now instructs you to place the deposit into escrow. You (broker) should:

    a. put the $5,000 into escrow with instructions to escrow to pay this amount back to you at closing.

    b. put $5,000 into your broker trust account.

    c. keep the $5,000 in the office (locked in your desk drawer) until the seller comes by to sign papers related to the sale.

    d. put $5,000 into escrow.

    ANSWER: d.   *Only one obvious solution. When in doubt, follow directions of the principal.*

39. When an appraiser is concerned about "equilibrium" and "decline," he is working with one of the three sub-principles of which of the following?

    a. Principle of Substitution

    b. Principle of Supply and Demand

    c. Principle of Highest and Best Use

    d. Principle of Change

    ANSWER: d.   *Relative to the Sub-Principle of Integration and Disintegration, (1) Integration (development); (2) Equilibrium (static state); (3) Disintegration (decline or decay).*

40. An easement held by the power company for erecting poles and lines as required is an easement:

    a. personal.

    b. appurtenant.

    c. in gross.

    d. prescriptive.

    ANSWER: c.

41. For a buyer in a new subdivision, which of the following would provide the least amount of protection against loss in value in the subdivision?

    a. Zoning

    b. Newness

    c. Natural barriers

    d. Private restrictions.

    ANSWER: d.   *Typically, by limiting use, etc.*

42. You wish to purchase 2 acres of property for which you will pay up to $1.13 per square foot. The purchase price (maximum) would be:

   a. $87,650.
   b. $984,456.
   c. $98,445.60.
   d. $49,222.80.

   ANSWER: c.   2 acres x 43,560 = 87,120 sq. ft.
   87,120 sq. ft. x $1.13 per sq. ft. = $98,445.60

43. A request for a "Notice of Default" on a first trust deed is for the benefit of the:

   a. trustor.
   b. vendee.
   c. trustee.
   d. beneficiary.

   ANSWER: d.   A beneficiary of any junior note and trust deed would benefit from such a notice, in a timely fashion, so that he will have sufficient time to take necessary measures to protect himself during the reinstatement period.

44. All of the following are used in the purchase of residential properties, except:

   a. Cal-Vet.
   b. VA approved lenders.
   c. Commercial banks.
   d. FHA approved lenders providing insured FHA Title I and Title II loans.

   ANSWER: d.   FHA Title I loans are for home improvement.

45. An owner of a business property sold the property and then "leased it back." Which of the following factors was most advantageous for the owner/lessee?

   a. Was relieved of property management.
   b. Has an improved tax situation, with all rent payment being deductible from income.
   c. Does not have to be concerned about property taxes on the building in the future.
   d. Now has more working capital at his disposal.

   ANSWER: d.   Probably the best answer in most situations.

46. An option is given to an optionee for a $1,000 consideration. All the following are true statements, except:

   a. the optionee has a legal interest in the property.
   b. the consideration is valid.
   c. the optionor must sell the property.
   d. the optionee has no obligation to purchase.

   ANSWER: a.   The optionee merely has the right to buy the property under agreed upon conditions.

EXAM 1

47. In a partnership, if one of the partners dies, the surviving partner:

    a. cannot transact any partnership business by himself until heirs of the estate are able to assume responsibility.

    b. becomes a partner with the heirs.

    c. cannot transact any partnership business as death conceals the partnership.

    d. becomes exclusive manager of the partnership business, and retains the title to the partnership property until he winds up the partnership business.

    ANSWER: d.

48. The primary reason for maintaining funds in a trust account separate from the broker's general account is to:

    a. insure the future control of funds.

    b. make the bank liable in the event of fraud.

    c. provide easier and more simplified record keeping.

    d. protect funds in the event of a civil suit against broker.

    ANSWER: d. A broker must NOT commingle funds.

49. A parcel of land 500 ft. x 300 ft. is bisected into two equal sized rectangles by a row of eucalyptus trees. How many acres are there in each portion?

    a. 3.44

    b. 1.72

    c. 0.34

    d. 15.0

    ANSWER: b.   Total area = 500' x 300' = 150,000 sq. ft.
    150,000 ÷ 43,560 = 3.44 acres total ÷ 2 = 1.72 acres each.

50. In the appraising of real estate, there are several "principles of value." Of the following, which most clearly describes the "Principle of Change"?

    a. Less desirable properties enhance the values of more desirable properties.

    b. More desirable properties are adversely affected by less desirable properties in their midst.

    c. Tomorrow evolves out of today which came out of yesterday.

    d. None of the above.

    ANSWER: c.   Principle of Change: (1) Development; (2) Static; (3) Decline.

51. Which of the following most clearly describes the "Principle of Regression"?

    a. Less desirable properties enhance the value of more desirable properties.

    b. More desirable properties are adversely affected by less desirable properties in their midst.

    c. Tomorrow evolves out of today, which came out of yesterday.

    d. None of the above.

    ANSWER: b.

52. A real property security endorsement is valid for:

    a. as long as the broker's license is valid, and it needs no further endorsement.
    b. multiples of 4 years.
    c. one year.
    d. the term of the broker's license to which the endorsement is affixed.

    ANSWER: d.

53. One way to jointly hold title to real property is "joint tenancy." Another way would be:

    a. tenancy in common.
    b. community property.
    c. tenancy in partnership.
    d. all of the above.

    ANSWER: d.

54. In real estate, the word "tenancy" means:

    a. a device.
    b. a tenacious person.
    c. two or more persons joined in an enterprise.
    d. a mode of holding ownership.

    ANSWER: d.

55. By recording a deed with the County Recorder's Office, one:

    a. validates the document so recorded.
    b. makes it possible for the new owner to be able to sell the property.
    c. gives actual notice of interest in real property.
    d. establishes precedence over subsequently recorded instruments.

    ANSWER: d.   Creates priorities between various instruments.

56. A loan of $200,000 is placed on a fourplex which has a tax basis of $150,000. Which of the following applies?

    a. The basis is increased by the amount of the loan.
    b. The basis is decreased to the amount of the loan.
    c. There is no tax due on the transaction.
    d. The basis is increased to the extent that the loan exceeds the basis.

    ANSWER: c.   The tax basis is affected only by: (1) the addition of capital improvements, or (2) the deduction of depreciation.

EXAM 1

57. A building has two separate sections, each with internal dimensions of 25' width by 80' depth. The dividing center wall, running from front to back, is 12" thick, and all exterior walls are 6" thick. How much land does the building cover?

    a. 4,043 sq. ft.
    b. 4,061 sq. ft.
    c. 4,212 sq. ft.
    d. 4,366 sq. ft.

    ANSWER: c.   *Width = 6" + 25' + 12" + 25' + 6" = 52'*
                      Depth = 6" + 80' + 6" = 81'
                      Gross sq. ft. = 52' x 81' = 4,212 sq. ft.

58. A "land project" is best defined as:

    a. 50 or more unimproved lots in a rural area.
    b. ownership of an undivided interest in land coupled with the right of exclusive occupancy of any apartment thereon.
    c. ownership of an undivided interest in common in a portion of property, together with a separate interest in space in a residential, industrial, or commercial building.
    d. ownership of an undivided interest in land.

    ANSWER: a.

59. When interest rates on real property loans increase, capitalization rates on income properties tend to:

    a. be affected inversely.
    b. remain the same
    c. increase
    d. decrease.

    ANSWER: c.

60. Assume the streets in a subdivision were financed through the issuance of 1911 Street Improvement Act Bonds. When he prepares his income tax return, the:

    a. owner of the liened lot can deduct principle and interest payments on the bonds.
    b. owner of liened lot can deduct only principal payments.
    c. bond holder must report principle payment received as taxable income.
    d. bond holder need not declare the interest as income.

    ANSWER: d.   *Bonds are tax exempt; therefore, income generated is not taxed.*

61. A corporation issued a deed to real property. The president and secretary both signed the deed and affixed the corporate seal. These actions would probably be sufficient to pass marketable title if:

    a. the deed is executed in connection with the dissolution of the corporation.
    b. the transaction involved is within the ordinary scope of business of the corporation.
    c. the transferor is a religious organization or church.
    d. all of the assets of the corporation are included in the transfer.

    ANSWER: b.

62. When a tenant who had rightfully come into possession of a property by means of a lease agreement retains possession after the expiration of said lease without permission of the owner, it is called a(n):

    a. estate for years.
    b. estate at sufferance.
    c. periodic tenancy.
    d. estate at will.

    ANSWER: b.   Also, an estate at sufferance does NOT require a notice of termination.

63. "Placement of a Home" would best match up with which of the following?

    a. Prescription
    b. Subordination
    c. Orientation
    d. Novation.

    ANSWER: c.

64. An FHA appraisal report includes the abbreviation "MPR" This refers to:

    a. Maximum Property Requirements.
    b. Multiple Property Ratio.
    c. Maximum Price Ratio.
    d. Minimum Property Requirements.

    ANSWER: d.   Minimum Property Requirements

65. A Licensee would have the least chance of receiving a commission in which of the following circumstances?

    a. A sale of personal property without written authorization.
    b. Failing to reveal the amount of profit under a net listing.
    c. An exchange of businesses under verbal authorization.
    d. Negotiating a lease of one year or less, not in writing.

    ANSWER: b.

EXAM 1

66. The term on a listing agreement is dated January 7, 1988, through April 5, 1988. This agreement would be for a term of:

    a. 3 months
    b. 90 days
    c 91 days
    d. 92 days

      ANSWER: b.   *Jan. = 25 days + Feb. = 29 days + Mar. = 31 days + Apr. = 5 days Total number of days = 90 days.*

67. The secondary money market refers to:

    a. participation in California real estate financing by out-of-state lenders.
    b. transfers of notes and T.D.s between mortgagees for value.
    c. junior loans.
    d. transfers of loans and T.D.s between mortgagors for value.

      ANSWER: b.   *Transfers between lenders as well as agencies set up for the purpose of buying and selling notes and T.D.s, i.e. "Fannie Mae," etc.*

68. When interest rates increase but net income remains unchanged, the value of an owner's equity tends to:

    a. increase.
    b. decrease.
    c. remains the same.
    d. none of the above.

      ANSWER: b.   *An owner's equity will decrease when net income remains the same while interest rates increase.*

69. An appraiser's definition of "Value" would be:

    a. present worth of all rights to future benefits arising out of ownership.
    b. the ability of one commodity to command other commodities in exchange.
    c. relationship between the thing desired and the potential purchaser.
    d. all of the above.

      ANSWER: d.   *These are elements of value.*

70. The members of the National Association of Real Estate Brokers are called:

    a. Realtors®.
    b. Consolidated Brokers.
    c. Realtists.
    d. None of the above.

      ANSWER: c.

71. The following are essential to the creation of an "agency" relationship, except:

    a. parties are competent.
    b. agreement to pay consideration.
    c. agreement between principal and agent.
    d. fiduciary relationship.

    ANSWER: b.   "Gratuitous agent" would NOT necessitate consideration.

72. On FHA and VA loans, the lender is allowed to charge the borrower a fee (percentage of the loan) as an initial service fee. This is generally referred to as a(n):

    a. subordination fee.
    b. accommodation fee.
    c. acceleration fee.
    d. origination fee.

    ANSWER: d.

73. To "rescind" is the same as to:

    a. revise.
    b. transfer.
    c. resale.
    d. revoke.

    ANSWER: d.   To revoke, or take away a license. (The Real Estate Commissioner has this power.)

74. Three of the following are closely related. Which one is NOT?

    a. Judgment
    b. Claim
    c. Real estate taxes
    d. Easement

    ANSWER: b.   Claim is associated with insurance, whereby the others are types of encumbrances.

75. "Domicile" most frequently means:

    a. semi-circled ceiling.
    b. relationship of parties.
    c. home or residence.
    d. none of above.

    ANSWER: c.

EXAM 1

76. An unlawful detainer action may be filed by a landlord in all but one of the following. Which is it?

    a. Tenant holds over after termination of lease.
    b. Tenant fails to pay rent.
    c. Tenant exercises lease option agreement, but fails to make payment as required.
    d. Tenant breaches lease by permitting nuisance on the property.

    ANSWER: c.   *By process of elimination, this is the exception. The others are three of five lawful situations for exercising this action, the others being: (4) failure to perform any lease covenant, and (5) failure to give up possession when he had previously given written notice of intention to do so.*

77. A home sold for $150,000 on which seller was to pay a 6% brokerage fee. Additional costs were: 2% prepayment penalty on existing loan balance of $102,800, escrow fees of $210, new loan discount fee of $534. The seller's cost of sale will be what percent of gross equity?

    a. 20.5%
    b. 25%
    c. 23.4%
    d. 228%

    ANSWER: b.

Commission = $150,000 x 6% = 150,000 x .06	=	*$9,000*
Escrow Fees..	=	*210*
New Loan Discount Fee.....................................	=	*534*
Prepayment Penalty = 2% x $102,800.............	=	*2,056*
Total Seller Costs	=	*$11,800*
Equity = Sale Price minus 1st loan = $150,000 - $102,800	=	*$47,200*
Costs as "%" of Equity = $11,800 ÷ 47,200 x (100)	=	*25%*

78. An "agreement in a deed" would best match up with:

    a. option.
    b. prescription.
    c. covenant.
    d. subrogation.

    ANSWER: c.

79. A homestead offers NO protection against which of the following?

    a. Real property taxes
    b. Mechanic's liens
    c. Prior recorded liens
    d. All of the above

    ANSWER: d.

80. Real estate brokers and salespeople are authorized to engage in listing and selling certain manufactured homes which have been registered with the Department of Motor Vehicles for a minimum of:

a. 18 months.
b. 6 months.
c. 1 year.
d. 2 years.

ANSWER: c. *No minimum time limit if manufactured home has been converted into real property.*

81. Occasionally a property owner will realize a taxable gain when his property is destroyed or taken through condemnation. This is know as:

a. trading up.
b. depreciation.
c. owner's amenities.
d. involuntary conversion.

ANSWER: d. *The conversion of real property to personal property (money).*

82. Which of the following statements will incorrectly complete this phrase? A subdivider who is not a licensee of the DRE:

a. may not sell or offer for sale any lots in a subdivision prior to issuance of the Commissioner's Public Report.
b. may sell all lots in a subdivision himself.
c. may make any improvements on the land prior to receiving the public report.
d. may employ licensed real estate salespeople to sell lots in a subdivision.

ANSWER: d. *Only a broker can hire or employ salespeople to sell real estate. The subdivider would have to employ a broker, who in turn would hire salespeople.*

83. A property offered for sale for $88,000 has been appraised for a new FHA loan at an appraised value of $87,500. How large a loan can be obtained if the FHA down payment is 3% of the first $25,000 of the appraised value plus 5% of the remainder of $25,000?

a. $84,100
b. $83,625
c. $84,338
d. $84,125

ANSWER: b. *Loan calculation must use the APPRAISED value*

Appraised Value	=	*$87,500*
Down Payment Requirements: 3% x $25,000	=	*$750*
5% x 62,500	=	*3,125*
Total Down Payment	=	*$3,875*
Sale Price - Down Payment = Loan = $87,500 - 3,875	=	*$83,625*

84. Which of the following groups represent ALL specific liens?

    a. Lien for descendants debts, vendor's lien
    b. Mechanics' liens, tax liens, assessment liens
    c. Federal income tax liens, attachments, state inheritance tax liens
    d. Corporate franchise tax liens, federal estate tax liens, judgment liens

    ANSWER: b.   *All liens in this group are against one property.*

85. Which of the following would complete this (true) statement? Property is:

    a. real if movable.
    b. personal if a fixture.
    c. personal if not real.
    d. real if tangible.

    ANSWER: c.

86. Market value is:

    a. assessed value.
    b. book value.
    c. highest price in terms of money.
    d. all of the above.

    ANSWER: c.   *Market value is the highest price a buyer will pay and a owner will accept.*

87. A business opportunity is sold under the Bulk Sales Law and included in the sale is the entire stock and inventory of the vendor. Which of the following statements is NOT correct?

    a. The seller pays the tax in his final quarterly statement.
    b. The tax is paid to the State Board of Equalization.
    c. The tax will be waived under most circumstances.
    d. None of the above.

    ANSWER: c.   *Taxes are NOT waived. This is a wrong statement.*

88. Following is a quote from California Real Estate Law which partially defines "in the Business": "The sale or exchange with the public of eight (8) or more real property sales contracts or promissory notes, secured directly or collaterally by liens on real property during a calendar year..." As used in this section of the law, "collaterally" refers to:

    a. subdivision lots encumbered by liens of equal precedence.
    b. liens secured by other loans.
    c. blanket encumbrances.
    d. junior liens.

    ANSWER: b.   *Refers to liens secured by other loans which have as security the titles to other pieces of real property.*

89. A rectangular lot is divided diagonally into two (2) parcels by a small stream. The dimensions of the lot are 300' x 600'. How many acres are there in each of the resultant triangularly shaped lots?

   a. 6.2
   b. 4.1
   c. 2.1
   d. 3.8

      ANSWER: c.   *Total lot area = 300' x 600' = 180,000 sq. ft.; Acreage = 180,000 sq. ft. ÷ 43,560 = 4.13 acres (rectangular lot). Since the stream cuts the larger lot into two equal parcels, each would have:*
                180,000 ÷ 43,560 ÷ 2 = 2.07 (approx. 2.1 acres).

90. An investor (unlicensed) purchased five (5) notes secured by trust deeds. He sold these within the next three months. During the following eight (8) months, he purchased eight (8) more such notes and T.D.s and sold six (6) of these. Which of the following statements is true?

   a. Each transaction is legal and the investor is not required to be licensed.
   b. The law has not been violated, since no more than six (6) notes and T.D.s were sold at any one time.
   c. A real estate license would not be required because the instruments were bought and sold within one year.
   d. The investor is in violation of California Real Estate Law.

      ANSWER: d.   *The law requires that anyone—principal or agent—who ACQUIRES for "resale" to the public, and not as an investment, eight (8) or more security devices during a calendar year, must be licensed by the Real Estate Commissioner.*

91. An apartment building has a land value set at $30,000. The investor recently bought the property for $150,000. Assuming an economic life for the improvement to be 35 years, using the straight-line approach, what would be the value of the property after 14 years?

   a. $77,143
   b. $102,000
   c. $93,635
   d. $112,840

      ANSWER: b.   *Improvement Value = $150,000 - $30,000 = $120,000*
                Allowable annual depreciation = $120,000 ÷ life (35 years) = $3,428.57
                Amount depreciated over 14 years = $3,428.57 x 14 yrs = $48,000
                Value of property after 14 years = 150,000 - 48,000 = $102,000

92. All of the following statements concerning options are correct, except:

   a. the optionee has no obligation to purchase the property.
   b. taking the property off the market is consideration upon the part of the optionor.
   c. the distinguishing characteristic of an option is the initial lack of mutuality of the obligation created.
   d. the optionee has a legal interest in the property.

      ANSWER: d.   *The optionee has no legal interest in the property until she exercises option.*

EXAM 1

93. "Offering land to the public" would best match up with:

    a. novation.
    b. ethnic.
    c. arbitration.
    d. dedication.

    ANSWER: d.

94. The initial step in the appraisal process is:

    a. establish the commission.
    b. estimate the square footage.
    c. establish the fee.
    d. define the problem.

    ANSWER: d.   Nothing can happen until the problem is defined.

95. You own a ranch that is 12 miles square. How many townships would lie within the boundaries of your ranch?

    a. 36
    b. 24
    c. 12
    d. 4

    ANSWER: d.   12 mi. x 12 mi. = 2 townships x 2 townships = 4 townships.

96. Which of the following maintains inspection controls over wood-destroying organisms?

    a. Ecology Board
    b. Real Estate Commissioner
    c. Structural Pest Control Board
    d. Animal Regulation

    ANSWER: c.   The State Structural Pest Control Board maintains control over termites and other wood destroying pests or organisms.

97. The Grant Deed provided by the Developer to buyers on a new subdivision contained restrictions prohibiting the placement of any "For Sale" signs on any of the properties. This restriction is unenforceable since:

    a. it infringes on the police power.
    b. it infringes on the owners' power of alienation.
    c. it infringes on the owners' power of hypothecation.
    d. none of the above.

    ANSWER: b.   "...unenforceable and void, as this is an unreasonable restraint upon the power of alienation."

98. The second installment of real property taxes become delinquent on:

    a. Dec. 31.
    b. Feb. 10.
    c. Apr. 10.
    d. Mar. 15

       ANSWER: c. *It becomes delinquent after 5pm on April 10th.*

99. A family sold their home through a broker. Escrow charges were $500 and Title Insurance policy premium was $400. They paid the broker a 7% commission and miscellaneous costs were $500. The sellers received a check from escrow in the amount of $40,100. The selling price was the only credit item on the sellers' closing statement. The current loan balance on the sellers' home was $98,000. What did the sellers receive for their home (sale price)?

    a. $140,000
    b. $145,000
    c. $150,000
    d. $155,000

       ANSWER: c. *Add all debit items known:*

Existing loan balance	=	*$98,000*
Escrow charges	=	*500*
Title Insur. Premium	=	*400*
Misc. Expenses	=	*500*
Check from Escrow	=	*40,000*
Total Debits	=	*$139,000 (not include commission)*

    Total Debits divided by 93% of Sale Price
    Commission   = 7% of Sale Price
    Therefore, Sale Price   = Total Debits ÷ 93% = $139,500 ÷ .93 = $150,000
    and commission   = $150,000 x 7% = 150,000 x .07 = $10,500

100. Sam purchased a $10,000 straight note through a broker at a 25% discount. The note called for all interest (@12% per year simple) plus principal to be paid back on the 48th month. What is the approximate (simple interest) percentage return per year on the **original** invested amount?

    a. 18.3%
    b. 21.3%
    c. 24.3%
    d. 27.3%

       ANSWER: c. *Discount Profit = $10,000 x 25% (.25) = $2,500*
    Investment = 10,000 - 2,500 = $7,500
    Interest Income (Profit) for 4 years = $10,000 x 12% x 4 yrs = $4,800
    Total 4 yr. Profit = $2,500 + $4,800 = $7,300
    Rate of Return = Total 4 yr. Profit x (100) divided by Investment
    = Percentage Return (4 years)
    *= 7,300 x 100 = 730,000 ÷ 7,500 = 97.3% (4 years) ÷ 4 = **24.33% per year***

EXAM 1

101. A real estate broker, licensed only in California, agreed verbally to share a commission with a broker licensed in Florida. This would be:

  a. a violation of California real estate law.
  b. permissible, but the California broker must first obtain the approval of the DRE in California.
  c. unenforceable in the California court, because the agreement was not in writing as required by the Statute of Frauds.
  d. permissible.

  ANSWER: d.   *Verbal agreements between brokers are permissible, although a written agreement is always the best course of action.*

102. Broker A and Broker B both took open listings for the sale of property owned by Seller. Broker A showed the property to Buyer A who liked the property but could not make up his mind. Two weeks later, Broker B showed the property to Buyer A. Buyer A then purchased the property from Broker B. Under these circumstances, who is entitled to the commission?

  a. Broker A and Broker B receive 50% each.
  b. Broker B full commission.
  c. Full commission to each broker.
  d. No commission paid to either broker.

  ANSWER: b.   *Generally, unless specifically noted, an open listing provides that the broker who makes the sale is entitled to the commission. Broker A's only protection might have been that he could have effectively used a "safety clause," but we had no knowledge of such.*

103. The person who receives personal property under the terms of a will is the:

  a. claimant.
  b. devisor.
  c. grantee.
  d. legatee.

  ANSWER: d.

104. Regarding an outstanding loan, $200 interest was paid during a three month term. If the loan was for $10,000, the interest rate was:

  a. usurious.
  b. 10%.
  c. 8%.
  d. 5%.

  ANSWER: c.   *$200 ÷ $10,000 x 100 x (12 ÷ 3) = 8.0%.*

105. A broker has shown a prospective buyer one of his own listings (open listing). After showing the property, he should:

   a. write a memo to the seller disclosing facts of his showing (client registration).
   b. phone the seller to notify him of the showing.
   c. introduce the two parties.
   d. write a memo to his office disclosing the showing.

   ANSWER: a. Safety clauses are only safe when in writing.

106. "A" deeded a home to "B" for the duration of "C's" life.

   a. C holds a life estate and B an estate in remainder.
   b. B holds a fee simple estate and C a life estate.
   c. B holds a life estate and A an estate in reversion.
   d. B holds a life estate and A an estate in remainder.

   ANSWER: c.

107. Which of the following sale prices would probably NOT be used when appraising a single family residence using the market data approach?

   a. Smaller residences in the neighborhood.
   b. Similar homes in the neighborhood soled over six months ago.
   c. Similar home in a different neighborhood.
   d. Similar home in neighborhood, sold under much pressure or by forced sale.

   ANSWER: d. This would not be a good source for comparable sales.

108. "A right to future possession of the property" would best match up with:

   a. reconveyance.
   b. alienation.
   c. subrogation.
   d. reversion.

   ANSWER: d.

109. Under Regulation "Z" (Truth in Lending Law), all borrowers have the right to rescind before midnight of the third business day following consummation of the contract when:

   a. security for the loan is real property and the principle residence of the borrower.
   b. lien is not the first lien to purchase the property.
   c. both a and b.
   d. neither a nor b.

   ANSWER: c.

110. All of the following are considered contracts, except:

    a. mortgages.
    b. open listing.
    c. grant deed.
    d. escrow instructions.

    ANSWER: c.   *A contract is an agreement to perform or not to perform a certain act or service. A grant deed transfers title, it is NOT a contract.*

111. The Real Estate Commissioner's authority over the sale of a subdivision would include which of the following?

    a. Alignment of the street within the subdivision.
    b. Design and improvements for storm drain systems.
    c. Financial arrangements to insure completion of community facilities.
    d. All of the above.

    ANSWER: c.   *Concerned about the sale, leasing, or financing aspects of the project.*

112. Ezzy received notification from the DRE that he had passed his real estate salesperson's exam, taken on December 18th. Ezzy worked at his old job for another year, retiring on the last day of that year. He mailed in an application to the DRE, with appropriate fees, for his license. What kind of license will Ezzy receive from the DRE as the result of this application?

    a. Brokers.
    b. 3 year salesperson's license.
    c. 4 year salesperson's license.
    d. None of the above.

    ANSWER: d.   *The DRE requires that a candidate who successfully passes the State examination must apply for the corresponding license within one (1) year of the exam date. Otherwise, reexamination is required.*

113. Which of the following is a proper disbursement from the broker's trust account?

    a. To pay a bond for a fiduciary agent who will be authorized to withdraw money from the account.
    b. To pay advertising bills for the broker's office.
    c. To pay plumbing bills of a commercial building which he manages.
    d. To pay the gas bill for the broker's office.

    ANSWER: c.   *The other three are all forms of "conversion."*

114. A broker sold a home to a young married couple. The deed was recorded before records revealed that the two were both under 18 years of age. The contract they had executed was:

    a. valid.
    b. illegal.
    c. unenforceable.
    d. voidable.

    ANSWER: a.   *Emancipated minors are "legal."*

115. A broker was leaving his office to present an offer he had written on one of his office listings. The first offer met the terms as listed. The second offer provide for a larger cash investment, with more favorable financing terms for the sellers, but the price was $1,000 under the listed price. The listing broker would submit:

   a. only the second offer if he feels the initial offer is a bad risk.
   b. both offers at the same time.
   c. both offers in the order received.
   d. only the first offer.

   ANSWER: b.

116. "The relationship of the thing desired to potential purchaser..." is a definition of:

   a. "utility" as definition of value.
   b. need.
   c. the economic man.
   d. value.

   ANSWER: d. According to the reference book on appraisals, used by the MAI group.

117. The general rule for establishing whether house numbers will be odd or even is:

   a. north or west side of the street odd: South or east side even.
   b. north or west side even: south or east side odd.
   c. north or east side odd: south or west side even.
   d. none of the preceding.

   ANSWER: a. Statement of fact. **STUDENT NOTE: SEE** *- South, East, Even; and* **NOW** *- North, Odd, West.*

118. With respect to probate court disposition of property, which of the following is NOT true?

   a. The minimum bid a court will accept must be within 10% of court appraisal.
   b. The executor of an estate may enter into an open listing with a broker.
   c. Commissions for brokers negotiating sales are set by the California Probate Code according to selling price of the property.
   d. A representative may make an offer subject to the court approval.

   ANSWER: d.

119. The California real estate law would be found in the:

   a. Civil Code.
   b. Uniform Commercial Code.
   c. Business and Professions Code.
   d. Administrative Procedure Act.

   ANSWER: c. And enforced by the Commissioner.

120. The act of recording instruments which transfer or encumber real property has all the following effects, except:

    a. gives priority over subsequently recorded instruments.
    b. creates a presumptive delivery.
    c. presents creation of a forged (wild) document.
    d. gives notice of the contents of the instrument.

    ANSWER: c.

121. The "FED" (Federal Reserve Board) controls the flow of money by:

    a. selling bonds.
    b. raising the discount rate it charges member banks who borrow money.
    c. increase member bank reserve requirements
    d. all of the above.

    ANSWER: d.   The FED controls the flow of money by all these methods.

122. Which of the following would most likely lower the value of a single-family residence?

    a. Age-life ratio
    b. Obsolescence
    c. Depreciation
    d. Deferred maintenance

    ANSWER: d.   Existing, but unfulfilled requirements for repairs/maintenance.

123. "Moral science" would best match up with:

    a. alienation.
    b. ethnic.
    c. dedication.
    d. ethics.

    ANSWER: d.

124. Violation of California anti-discrimination laws could result in which of the following?

    a. Loss of license.
    b. Exposure for damages.
    c. Fine of up to $1,000.
    d. All of the above.

    ANSWER: d.   All answers are correct.

125. According to Article 7 (Loan Brokers Law), the maximum "cost and expenses" that can be charged by a broker for negotiating a $10,000 second loan (hard money) is:

    a. actual expenses.
    b. $500, which is 5% of loan.
    c. $350.
    d. either a or c, as appropriate.

    ANSWER: d.   *"c" is the maximum limit, as long as the actual is not less.*

126. From the above question, what is the maximum commission the broker can charge if the loan was to be repaid in 30 months?

    a. $1,000
    b. $500
    c. $1,500
    d. none of the above

    ANSWER: d.   *The law does not set a maximum in this case, since the loan was for $10,000. The restrictions are for loans UNDER $10,000; therefore, broker can charge what the market will bear.*

127. A lien that will take priority over all other liens, regardless of the date it was created, is called a:

    a. subordinated lien.
    b. legal lien
    c. superior lien.
    d. junior lien.

    ANSWER: c.   *Note: it referred to date of creation, NOT recordation.*

128. In a subdivision, which of the following is considered an "off-site" improvement?

    a. Septic tank.
    b. Private well.
    c. Streets and curbs.
    d. Barn.

    ANSWER: c.   *Off-site improvements generally add to a parcel's usefulness and sometimes its value. All other choices are "on-site" improvements.*

129. The most important rights a tenant has are:

    a. privacy and subletting privileges.
    b. quiet enjoyment and possession.
    c. privacy and cancellation privileges.
    d. choice of neighbors and possession.

    ANSWER: b.   *These are part of the "Bundle of Rights."*

EXAM 1

130. An "oral" agreement for the sale of real property may be enforced where:

  a. a neutral depository is used.
  b. the broker guarantees performance.
  c. the purchaser takes possession and makes valuable improvements to the property.
  d. the consideration paid is a minimum of $2,500.

  ANSWER: c.

131. Which of the following statements regarding notes and trust deeds is true?

  a. T.D. outlaws before the note.
  b. Upon conflict in provisions regarding the maturity of debt, the T.D. will prevail.
  c. The T.D. is more important than the note.
  d. The lien of the T.D. is merely incidental to the debt.

  ANSWER: d.   T.D. is NOT more important than the note and outlaws after the note.

132. A verbal acceptance of an offer for the purchase of real estate with a broker would constitute a contract that was:

  a. valid.
  b. invalid.
  c. unenforceable.
  d. enforceable.

  ANSWER: c.   The Statute of Frauds requires real estate contracts to be in writing; however, the contract which fails to comply is NOT void, just unenforceable.

133. Where land values of an area are well known and much data available from recent lot sales, which method of appraising property in that area would be *least* likely used?

  a. Comparison
  b. Property residual direct capitalization
  c. Building residual
  d. Land residual straight-line

  ANSWER: d.   Land does NOT "depreciate."

134. A condominium owner and apartment dweller have many things in common. Which of the following is true for both?

  a. Estate of inheritance
  b. Fee simple
  c. Less than freehold
  d. Estate in real property

  ANSWER: d.   Both are estates in real property.

135. A lease agreement written for a definite period of time with prescribed payment conditions is:

    a. real property.
    b. personal property.
    c. estate property.
    d. none of the above.

    ANSWER: b.   *The lease agreement is a "chattel real"—an <u>interest</u> in real property. Therefore, it is personal property.*

136. Under which of the following situations would the beneficiary have the best opportunity to secure a "deficiency judgment" in the event of a foreclosure?

    a. Note and T.D. taken back by subdivider as part of purchase price of unimproved lot.
    b. Second note and T.D. taken back by subdivider as part of purchase price of unimproved lot.
    c. Note and T.D. executed in favor of conventional lender, with proceeds being used to purchase a residence.
    d. Note and T.D. executed in favor of a conventional lender, with the proceeds being used to pay hospital bills.

    ANSWER: d.   *Not "purchase money" note and trust deed.*

137. On which of the following is sales tax charged?

    a. Sale of all tangible personal property
    b. Personal property used or consumed in the state, purchased outside the state
    c. Both a and b
    d. Neither a nor b

    ANSWER: a.   *"Use" tax would be imposed for "b."*

138. "The theory of Adverse Possession" would best match up with:

    a. dedication.
    b. conversion.
    c. prosecution.
    d. prescription.

    ANSWER: d.   *Prescription is an easement, or the right to use another's land.*

139. Three methods used by appraisers, architects, and contractors to estimate the cost of reproduction are:

    a. utility, unit-in-place, quantity survey.
    b. capitalization, utility, marketability.
    c. comparative square foot-cubic foot, capitalization, quantity survey.
    d. quantity survey, comparative square foot-cubic foot, unit-in-place.

    ANSWER: d.

140. From which of the following would reliable "selling price" information be available?

    a. Recorded deed
    b. Records of Department of Housing and Urban Development
    c. Lessee
    d. None of the above

    ANSWER: d.

141. In appraising a house, the shape (design) of a residence would affect the appraiser's estimate in regard to:

    a. economic obsolescence.
    b. replacement costs.
    c. income attributable to the property.
    d. none of the above.

    ANSWER: b.   Odd or peculiar design or shape should be taken into consideration for its replacement costs.

142. Which of the following would be a violation of the Real Estate Commissioner's regulations?

    a. Transferring earned commissions from the trust account to the broker's commercial account.
    b. Maintaining a "pre-numbered" account for trust fund checks.
    c. Maintaining a "pre-numbered" account for the cash journal.
    d. Immediate destruction of a "pre-numbered" check that was voided.

    ANSWER: d.   Keep all records.

143. Where the ratio of land and improvement cost is concerned, which offers the investor the largest depreciation basis?

    a. Farm property valued at $100,000.
    b. Apartment building valued at $100,000.
    c. Commercial building valued at $100,000.
    d. Industrial building valued at $100,000.

    ANSWER: b.   Typically, construction costs (improvements) for apartment buildings are much greater than for the other types mentioned.

144. What are "walkups"?

    a. Restaurants
    b. Drive-ins
    c. Apartments
    d. Hotels

    ANSWER: c.   Deals with buildings without elevators; multi-stories. Could be an example of functional obsolescence.

145. An example of an economic gain that is realized on an investment in real property, received in installments over a prescribed period of time, would be:

    a. rent.
    b. leverage.
    c. appreciation.
    d. amortization.

    ANSWER: a.

146. Based on the Civil Rights Act of 1968 (Title VIII), complaints must be filed within how many days of the violation?

    a. 30
    b. 60
    c. 90
    d. 180

    ANSWER: d.

147. Based on the California Fair Housing Act (Rumford Act), complaints must be filed within how many days of the violation?

    a. 30
    b. 60
    c. 90
    d. 180

    ANSWER: b.

148. Corporations would most likely raise equity investment capital by:

    a. issuing long-termed bonds.
    b. selling stock in the corporation
    c. borrowing from an insurance company.
    d. both a and b.

    ANSWER: d.

149. If a railroad company desired to build additional lines across property it did not own or have interest in, and the owners were not interested in selling, what course of action would the railroad company most likely take?

    a. Injunction
    b. Prescriptive easement by adverse possession
    c. Attachment
    d. Eminent domain

    ANSWER: d.   *Examples of public uses include: streets, railroads, etc.*

EXAM 1

150. A notice to creditors of bulk transfer would contain all of the following, except:

    a. location and general description of goods to be transferred.
    b. names and addresses of transferor and transferee.
    c. location and date on (or after) which the transfer will be consummated.
    d. names and addresses of all creditors.

    ANSWER: d.   *Creditors' names and addresses are NOT required.*

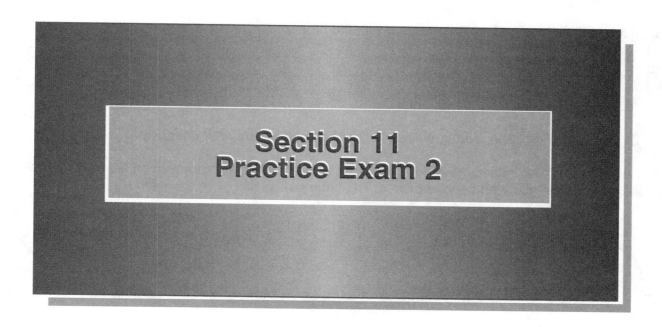

Section 11
Practice Exam 2

1. One month interest payment on a straight note amounts to $180. At 9% per annum interest rate, what is the face amount of the note?

   a. $26,000
   b. $20,000
   c. $24,000
   d. $27,000

> **ANSWER: c.** *Annual Interest = $180 x 12 = $2,160*
> *Interest amount divided by Rate = Principal Amount =*
> *$2,160 ÷ 9% = $24,000.*

2. A licensed real estate broker, buying and selling many properties for himself, may have his profits taxed as:

   a. long-term capital gains.
   b. short-term capital gains.
   c. deferred capital gains.
   d. ordinary income.

> **ANSWER: d.** *One who holds property "primarily for the sale to customers in the ordinary course of business" is considered a "dealer" and may have profits taxed as ordinary income.*

3. Which of these words does NOT belong with the others?

    a. Will
    b. Executor
    c. Sale
    d. Heir

    ANSWER: c.   *a, b, and d relate to disposition of property after death.*

4. The county building inspector would not approve a site ready for construction on a new residence until a "percolation" test had been approved. The latter deals with:

    a. the water table.
    b. runoff drainage.
    c. the septic tank.
    d. none of the above.

    ANSWER: c.   *Deals with the ability of earth to filter liquids from the septic tank.*

5. Demise deals with:

    a. transferability of an estate by lease or will.
    b. personal property left in a will.
    c. a "type" of will.
    d. none of the above.

    ANSWER: a.   *Not to be confused with "devise," a gift of real property by will.*

6. In a real property sales contract for the purchase of newly subdivided land, a clause prohibits the purchaser from prepaying principal during the first 12 months following the purchase. The buyer is to only make his normal monthly payments. If the buyer subsequently selects to pay off the contract, within the first 12 month period, the clause:

    a. is binding on the buyer.
    b. may be ignored by the buyer.
    c. is illegal and voids the contract.
    d. could have been waived by the buyer by sending such notification to the subdivider.

    ANSWER: b.   *"Lock-ins" are allowed only in private party financing.*

7. Two businessmen have been operating their businesses successfully in a community for a number of years. They have frequently made referrals between one another. Mr. E is an insurance broker; Mr. M is a real estate broker. They are considering joining forces, as partners – "E" & "M" Real Estate & Insurance. Which of the following statements is correct?

    a. Their partnership would be permissible, as the law allows brokers to form partnerships.
    b. They would be required to secure a partnership license and file their name with the Secretary of State.
    c. This is good as long as only Mr. E sells insurance.
    d. Mr. E would be required to secure a real estate broker's license.

    ANSWER: d.   *Although real estate brokers can form partnerships with unlicensed persons, only brokers' names are permitted as part of the firm's name.*

8. A buyer wishes to purchase a home through Broker Bob, making the following offer: Sale price is $100,000; Buyer to put $10,000 down and obtain a new FHA insured loan for $80,000; Buyer to execute a 2nd note and trust deed in favor of seller for $10,000. Broker should advise:

    a. transaction is okay.

    b. seller should not have the new 2nd trust deed recorded until after escrow has closed, so as not to alarm FHA.

    c. the Buyer that she cannot purchase in this manner, because FHA does not allow 2nd notes and trust deeds, but requires cash to the FHA loan.

    d. none of the above

    ANSWER: c.   This is an FHA requirement.

9. Regarding easements, which of the following is NOT correct?

    a. Easements can be created by reservation.

    b. Easements can be created by dedication.

    c. A lessee can give an easement for the duration of a lease to a third party.

    d. Deeds granting unlocated easements are invalid.

    ANSWER: d.   Easements do NOT have to be specifically located to be valid.

10. A home built in 1959 cost $14,500. The home is 32' x 48' and the attached garage is 18' x 20'. In 1983, the cost per square foot factors were $75 (house) and $15 (garage). If the improvement depreciated at 2% per year and the land value of the lot had risen to $25,000, what was the value of the property in 1983?

    a. $84,367

    b. $81,258

    c. $87,531

    d. $87,712

ANSWER: d.		
32' x 48' = 1,536 sq. ft. x $75...............	=	*$115,200*
18' x 20' = 360 sq. ft x $15....................	=	*5,400*
Cost new in 1983....................................	=	*120,600*
Minus 2% per year depreciation............	=	*- 57,888*
Improvement adjusted basis..................	=	*$62,712*
Land value...	=	*25,000*
Approximate value (1983) of property.....	=	*$87,712*

11. A business has been sold, and the State Board of Equalization has checked the records and found that all required taxes have been paid. The board will then issue to the buyer a:

    a. tax paid receipt.

    b. clearance receipt.

    c. successor's liability receipt.

    d. none of the above.

    ANSWER: b.   If the buyer does not get this clearance receipt from the board, the buyer is liable for any unpaid taxes the seller did not pay.

12. Which of the following would NOT qualify for an "on-sale" liquor license?

    a. A club that was six months old.
    b. A cafeteria that was six months old.
    c. 12-year-old restaurant.
    d. One year old hotel.

      ANSWER: a.   *Clubs must NOT have been in business for less than one year.*

13. The least important factor in a "sale-lease back" is:

    a. the credit rating of the lessee.
    b. a well designed general purpose building.
    c. a well located building.
    d. seller's book value of the building.

      ANSWER: d.   *Seller becomes lessee. The book value is not important any longer, for new owner will set up his own books for tax purposes.*

14. Fill in appropriately: "A trend in real estate _____ the recession trends of business, and _____ when business starts a swing upward."

    a. precedes, proceeds
    b. follows, lags behind
    c. lags behind, precedes
    d. precedes, lags behind

      ANSWER: d.   *Typical business cycle:*
                (1) Expansion...prosperity (good times)
                (2) Recession...turn around from prosperity (real estate precedes)
                (3) Depression...opposite from (1) above
                (4) Revival...turn around in prosperity (real estate lags)

15. The goal of the Fair Housing Act is for the purpose of:

    a. removing prejudice in every community.
    b. establishing selling practices that are "color blind."
    c. establishing selling practices where you do unto others as you would have them do unto you.
    d. all of the above.

      ANSWER: d.

16. A plot of land that is 30 miles square contains how many townships?

    a. 0.69
    b. 4
    c. 9
    d. 25

      ANSWER: d.   *The plot is 30 miles on a side and a township is six miles on a side. Therefore, the plot has five townships on a side, or 5 by 5 = 25.*

17. Which of the following would be considered an offer in a real estate transaction?

  a. Condition
  b. Covenant
  c. Performance
  d. Tender

  ANSWER: d. *Tender is an offer to perform.*

18. Which of the following phrases would best bind all parties to pay their debts?

  a. Jointly
  b. Individually
  c. Individually and severally
  d. Jointly and severally

  ANSWER: d. *All parties are held responsible collectively or individually for the entire obligation.*

19. If one person has the authority to act on matters for another, including the right to bind (sign for) on contractual matters, the person with that authority would be known as the:

  a. power of attorney.
  b. beneficiary.
  c. trustee.
  d. attorney-in-fact.

  ANSWER: d. *A step beyond that of agent. Can affix that other person's name to a contract. Signature: "Principal, by Agent Only, His Attorney-in-Fact."*

20. A real estate syndicate fails to disclose a true statement of the condition of title and all the encumbrances thereon. The penalty for this violation is:

  a. $5,000 judgment against officers.
  b. $5,000 fine and 10 years in jail.
  c. $10,000 fine and 10 years in jail.
  d. $5,000 fine and 5 years in jail.

  ANSWER: c.

21. Accountants and appraisers are interested in depreciation of real property from two different viewpoints.

  a. The appraiser is only interested in book value.
  b. The accountant is concerned with book depreciation and the appraiser deals with actual depreciation.
  c. The accountant is interested in the book value and the appraiser in the "theory of depreciation."
  d. The accountant is only interested in what caused the depreciation.

  ANSWER: b. *Accountant: For tax purposes, book depreciation.
  Appraiser: To establish "present value," actual depreciation.*

EXAM 2

22. An apartment house tenant was injured in the swimming pool of his apartment complex. He sued the obtained a judgment of $5,000. When recorded, the abstract of the judgment will create a lien that is:

    a. voluntary.
    b. general.
    c. specific.
    d. exclusive.

    ANSWER: b. Judgment liens are general liens.

23. A buyer offers to perform on his purchase contract. This is known as a:

    a. condition.
    b. tender.
    c. covenant.
    d. surrender.

    ANSWER: b.

24. When a lender refers to a "nominal" interest rate, it means:

    a. points will be required because of the lower than normal rate.
    b. the maximum rate of interest allowed.
    c. the rate of interest specified in the promissory note.
    d. that the final rate of interest granted will be greater than the original commitment.

    ANSWER: c. Usually, an annual amount, compounded more frequently, e.g., 15% compounded monthly, would deal with monthly payment periods.

25. An investor has purchased an apartment building. She reports income on a cash basis, and will be allowed deductions for all but which of the following?

    a. Cost or redecorating.
    b. Loss of rent due to vacancies.
    c. Interest payments on 2nd loan.
    d. Depreciation, even though the building is daily going up in value.

    ANSWER: b. Loss of rent due to vacancies is NOT allowed as a deduction.

26. In evaluating agriculture properties, an appraiser would consider the overall effects of our economic growth during the past 50 years upon such properties. All of the following statements would be true, except:

    a. farmers' investments in equipment and storage facilities have expanded considerably since the 1940s.
    b. stables with stanchion spaces for cows are being replaced with sheds and milking facilities.
    c. value of the various buildings—living quarters, barns, hay, and straw baling storage facilities, etc.— is expressed in terms of value added to the property being appraised.
    d. the average individually owned farm size has shown a steady downward trend since the 1940s.

    ANSWER: d. With modern equipment, the acreage that one man can farm effectively has increased farm sizes, and large corporations have affected farm sizes.

27. When looking for records regarding chattel liens, you should go to the:

    a. Secretary of State.
    b. County Recorder.
    c. either a or b.
    d. none of the above.

    > ANSWER: c.   *Chattel (mortgage) – County Recorder; Security Agreement – Secretary of State.*

28. An agent may represent both parties in a transaction, providing he:

    a. gets consent of both parties.
    b. informs both parties.
    c. discloses his commission agreement with both parties.
    d. all of the above.

    > ANSWER: d.   *These are all requirements for representing both the seller and buyer (dual agency).*

29. Which of the following would be an example of "economic obsolescence"?

    a. No bathroom on first level of multilevel residence.
    b. Eccentric design.
    c. High tax rate.
    d. Lack of normal, proper care.

    > ANSWER: c.   *High taxes, resulting from excessive local improvement needs, would be an "outside" or "extraneous" situation or factor.*

30. SBM & BL, MDM & BL, HM & BL are abbreviations which have meaning to:

    a. Small Business Administration.
    b. County Recorder.
    c. Secretary of State.
    d. Points of interest for surveyors.

    > ANSWER: d.   *The three principal "base and meridian" intersections in California.*

31. A broker is entitled to one-half of the commission plus all his costs when:

    a. a loan is denied due to the failure of a borrower to disclose pertinent factors relating to his qualifying.
    b. loan is not consummated due to failure of a lender to supply funds.
    c. never.
    d. none of the above.

    > ANSWER: a.

EXAM 2

32. FHA programs have caused the "quality" of homes to be improved because the FHA:

    a. grants quality home loans.
    b. insures home loans.
    c. requires "maximum building standards" (MBS).
    d. none of above.

    ANSWER: d.   *The FHA establishes minimum property requirements (MPRs) that, in most situations, are more demanding than State Housing Law or local building code requirements.*

33. Which of the following would be most like an easement appurtenant?

    a. Easement in gross
    b. Attachment
    c. Stock in a mutual water district.
    d. Lease.

    ANSWER: c.   *Easements appurtenant cannot be separated from the land, as the stock in a mutual water company cannot be split from ownership.*

34. An acquired right to use and enjoy that a person may have on land of another is known as a(n):

    a. easement.
    b. devise.
    c. lease.
    d. riparian right.

    ANSWER: a.

35. An investor purchased a property for 10% less than the listed price, then resold it for the previously listed price. What was the percentage profit?

    a. 9%
    b. 10%
    c. 11%
    d. 12%

    ANSWER: c.   *MADE divided by PAID = RATE*
          10% ÷ 90% = (.01) ÷ (.90) = (.1111) = 11%

36. In order to maximize return for his efforts during a tight money market, a real estate broker would best direct his efforts into:

    a. sale of single dwellings, with assumption of existing loans.
    b. property exchanging.
    c. sale of recreational properties.
    d. sale or leasing of income property.

    ANSWER: b.   *Exchanges most frequently would require minimal new, or refinancing, exchanging equities.*

37. A property was sold on a real estate sales contract. Subsequently, the buyer refused to make required payments, breaching the agreement. The seller may take which of the following courses of action?

    a. Unilateral rescission.
    b. Action for damages.
    c. Action for specific performance.
    d. All of the above.

    ANSWER: d. *All courses of action listed are open to the seller.*

38. A purchaser of a home could NOT complete a legal contract because of which of the following?

    a. Did not have sufficient cash for down payment and costs.
    b. Is not a citizen.
    c. Is not yet "of age" (is 17 years old).
    d. None of the above.

    ANSWER: c. *Lacks essential element of contract—capacity.*

39. Which of the following is NOT included in the "Principle of Balance"?

    a. Land
    b. Management
    c. Capital
    d. Depreciation

    ANSWER: d. *The 4 ingredients involved in the production of income are: labor, capital, management, and land.*

40. For a given loan amount, with a specified interest rate, which of the following would result in lower monthly costs to a borrower?

    a. FHA loan
    b. VA loan
    c. Conventional loan (90% of value) which requires an additional ¼% monthly private mortgage insurance
    d. None of the above

    ANSWER: b. *Both FHA and conventional loans require extra monies for insurance premiums; VA guarantees its loans, requiring no insurance for the borrower to pay.*

EXAM 2

41. Sellers sold their residence and closed escrow on Oct. 15th. Taxes on the property were $1,400 per year and had not been paid since payment of the last installment of the preceding tax year. What will their tax proration for this escrow be?

    a. Credit $408
    b. Credit $467
    c. Debit $408
    d. Debit $467

    ANSWER: c.   *Taxes were paid through June 30th. Sellers owe for 3½ months, namely July, Aug., Sept. and one-half of Oct. A charge is a "debit."*
    Amount = $1,400 ÷ 12 x 3.5 months = $408.33 = $408.

42. A piece of lumber 4˝ x 4˝ x 6´ is how many board feet?

    a. 6
    b. 8
    c. 10
    d. None of the above

    ANSWER: b.   *4˝ x 4˝ x 12˝ x 6´ ÷ 144 = 8.0 board feet.*

43. In a subdivision, which of the following would NOT be a blanket encumbrance?

    a. Trust Deed
    b. Subdivision lot improvement assessment
    c. Mechanic's lien
    d. None of the above

    ANSWER: b.   *Would be levied against each and every lot in the subdivision separately.*

44. The normal method of disposing of government property is by:

    a. sealed bids.
    b. negotiated sale.
    c. auction.
    d. predetermined prices.

    ANSWER: c.

45. A soil pipe is used in:

    a. irrigation.
    b. soil conservation.
    c. soil depletion.
    d. sewers.

    ANSWER: d.   *A soil pipe is used to carry waste and sewage from a property.*

46. California law opposes the practice of discrimination due to race, color, religion, national origin, or ancestry in public assisted housing accommodations. Discrimination in which of the following cases would be in violation of this code?

    a. In houses receiving tax exemptions (exception VA).
    b. On land purchased for less than value due to state or local sale pursuant to Federal Housing Act of 1949.
    c. Housing in multiple dwellings financed with federally insured or guaranteed funds.
    d. All of the above.

    ANSWER: d.   *Where government money is involved, NO discrimination of any kind is allowed.*

47. A real estate syndicate ownership may take the form of a:

    a. corporation.
    b. real estate investment trust.
    c. limited partnership.
    d. all of the above.

    ANSWER: d.   *"Syndicate" has NO precise legal significance, and organizational structure is setup by the syndicator. "Limited partnership" is most frequently used for real estate syndicates.*

48. H.U.D. has established certain factors (standards) that must exist before it will insure a home loan through one of its agencies. Known as MPRs, these are:

    a. Maximum Probability Ratio.
    b. Mortgage Protection Requirements.
    c. Market Price Rating.
    d. Minimum Property Requirements.

    ANSWER: d.   *The FHA is an agency of H.U.D. (Department of Housing and Urban Development).*

49. "The right of one or more persons to possess and use something to the exclusion of others" describes:

    a. discrimination.
    b. novation.
    c. ownership.
    d. equity.

    ANSWER: c.

50. A land project consists of:

    a. 50 or more parcels and less than 15,000 voters within two miles of the subdivision.
    b. 100 or more parcels and less than 1,500 voters within two miles of the subdivision.
    c. 50 or more parcels and less than 1,500 voters within two miles of the subdivision.
    d. none of the above.

    ANSWER: c.

EXAM 2

51. When the business cycle is in the prosperity phase, real estate cycle is in a phase of:

    a. high construction, high borrowing, high sales.
    b. low construction, little borrowing, low sales.
    c. low construction, high borrowing.
    d. high construction, low sales, high borrowing.

    ANSWER: a.

52. A conventional loan would differ from an FHA loan in that the conventional loan would have:

    a. lower monthly payments.
    b. lower interest rates.
    c. lower down payment requirements.
    d. lower loan-to-value ratio.

    ANSWER: d.   *FHA typically will loan a greater percentage of value to the borrower than a conventional lender, requiring a smaller down payment. The conventional lender does not have the "insurance" against loss that the FHA lender has and, therefore, is taking greater risks and must receive more down payment (equity) from the buyer/borrower.*

53. The owner of a large apartment complex was considering adding another swimming pool. An appraiser hired to do a study for the owner would use what basic principle of appraising to determine the feasibility of adding the pool?

    a. Substitution
    b. Competition
    c. Contribution
    d. Appreciation

    ANSWER: c.   *Would the addition of the pool contribute to the rent schedule?*

54. Code requirements for "studding" in single-family units is:

    a. 16˝ o.c.
    b. 18˝ o.c.
    c. 20˝ o.c.
    d. 24˝ o.c.

    ANSWER: a.   *In some areas, codes allow up to 24˝ on center, but the standard is 16˝ on center.*

55. You own the business you run and lease the building in which you operate. You hold a (an):

    a. remainder.
    b. interest in, but not an estate.
    c. less-than-freehold estate.
    d. freehold estate.

    ANSWER: c.   *With a less-than-freehold (leasehold) estate, there is NO direct ownership of real estate.*

56. When establishing value by "appraisal," it is necessary to recognize the difference between the function of the appraisal and:

    a. the appraisal process.
    b. amenities to the owner.
    c. principles of appraisal.
    d. the purpose for which the appraisal is being made.

        ANSWER: d.   *The purpose may be to estimate value for: (1) listing with a broker, (2) financing, (3) condemnation, or (4) an insurance settlement.*

57. An investor in an eight-year-old apartment building will be allowed by the IRS to calculate depreciation by which of the following methods?

    a. Income method
    b. Cost method
    c. Straight-line method
    d. None of the above

        ANSWER: c.   *Straight-line method. The others are types of appraisals.*

58. Which of the following is NOT associated with market value?

    a. Exchange value
    b. Reasonable value
    c. Material costs
    d. Objective value

        ANSWER: c.

59. Which one of the following is NOT classified as a subdivision?

    a. Community apartment project with 20 or more apartments.
    b. Condominium project with 10 or more units.
    c. Stock cooperative containing 10 or more units.
    d. Planned development containing four lots.

        ANSWER: d.   *A subdivision must have five or more units.*

60. When personal property becomes (by intent) a part of real property, it becomes a(n):

    a. attachment.
    b. inclusion.
    c. dedication.
    d. fixture.

        ANSWER: d.

EXAM 2

61. A bearing wall in a building:

    a. could be at any angle relative to a door.
    b. probably would not be removed during remodeling.
    c. would have structural integrity.
    d. all of the above.

       ANSWER: d.   *Such a wall bears much weight, supporting upper floor and/or roof loads.*

62. A purchaser in a sale-leaseback transaction would be least concerned about:

    a. the location of the property.
    b. general credit of the lessee.
    c. depreciated book value of the improvement.
    d. condition of improvements.

       ANSWER: c.   *Purchaser will set up his own depreciation schedule, and cares not about what the previous owner's book showed, with respect to depreciation.*

63. Which of the following is NOT necessary in a bill of sale?

    a. Date
    b. Mention of consideration
    c. Signature of vendor
    d. Acknowledgment

       ANSWER: d.

64. A family purchased a residence two years ago, financing through a mortgage company with a small down payment. Which of the following would be the most likely reason for refinancing?

    a. Small equity
    b. Rise in interest rates
    c. Decrease in interest rates
    d. Increased taxes

       ANSWER: c.   *If interest rates had dropped enough to make it more economical to refinance, the reduced monthly payments would compensate for the costs involved in such refinancing.*

65. Prior to granting a loan, a lender considers the ability of the borrower to repay the loan, the character of the property, and the terms of the requested financing. This is known as a:

    a. credit check.
    b. loan origination check.
    c. loan evaluation.
    d. mortgage discounting.

       ANSWER: c.   *This is loan evaluation.*

66. The value of an investment is as follows:

Total value = V(t)   = $300,000
Income attributable to building = $21,600
Reasonable "cap rate"   =   9%

What is value of the land?

a. $90,000
b. $80,000
c. $70,000
d. $60,000

ANSWER: d. Value (bldg.) = 1 (bldg.) divided by "cap rate" = $21,600 ÷ 9%
           = $21,600 ÷ (.09)   = $240,000
     Value (land) = Value (total) - Value (bldg.)
           = $300,000 - $240,000   = $60,000

67. A brother and sister own a property as joint tenants. The sister marries and then deeds one-half of her interest to her new husband. Which of the following is a true statement?

a. All three are now joint tenants.
b. Brother is joint tenant, sister and husband hold title as community property.
c. Brother holds in severalty, sister and husband hold as community property.
d. The joint tenancy is totally destroyed.

ANSWER: d. *Sister automatically eliminates her joint tenancy when she deeds to her husband. Brother cannot thereafter (as only one person) hold in joint tenancy. Therefore, he too loses joint tenancy.*

68. A contract of sale to an investor is conditioned upon the new prospective owner finding tenants for his building in advance. This agreement is:

a. unreal.
b. unenforceable.
c. enforceable.
d. void because it violates the statute of frauds.

ANSWER: c. *Contracts in which performance is made subject to buyer's approval of specific terms or conditions (as in this case, buyer finding satisfactory leases) have been upheld by most recent court decisions as valid and enforceable.*

69. Which of the following abbreviations are associated with the FHA?

a. NAR and CAR
b. CPM and CRV
c. MMI and MIP
d. MAI and MBA

ANSWER: c. *MMI - Mutual Mortgage Insurance; MIP - Mortgage Insurance Premium.*

70. If the taxes on a newly acquired property will amount to 1¼% of the purchase price, what will the first installment (6 months) bill for a home costing $125,500 be?

    a. $765.35
    b. $742.51
    c. $784.38
    d. $795.97

    ANSWER: c.   *$125,500 x (.0125) ÷ 2 = $784.38.*

71. SHE owns a single-family residence in which SHE lives. SHE trades HE for another residence which HE is renting to a tenant. Both parties intend to use their newly acquired properties for rental income. Which of the following is true?

    a. SHE can negotiate a tax-free (deferred) exchange.
    b. HE can negotiate a tax free (deferred) exchange.
    c. Both parties can negotiate tax-free exchanges.
    d. Neither can negotiate a tax-free exchange.

    ANSWER: b.   *HE is exchanging income property for the same—like-for-like; SHE is not.*

72. In which of the following would you use a "package mortgage"?

    a. When covering more than one parcel of land in a subdivision.
    b. When encumbering real property and using personal property as additional collateral.
    c. When securing additional financing from the lender at a later date without rewriting the original loan.
    d. None of the above.

    ANSWER: b.   *A loan that is secured by the basic lot and improvement, plus fixtures attached to the home (appliances, carpeting, drapes, air conditioning, and other kinds of personal property).*

73. The legal purpose of zoning restrictions is to:

    a. keep all types of commercial property out of residential neighborhoods.
    b. keep the land in every area as similar as possible.
    c. preserve or protect public health, safety, morals, or general welfare.
    d. none of the above.

    ANSWER: c.

74. Financial enhancement, as compared to comfort and safety when purchasing a home, is generally considered:

    a. absolute.
    b. primary.
    c. secondary.
    d. none of the above.

    ANSWER: c.

75. An investor who owned a 16-unit apartment complex has evaluated a newly installed freeway near his property, which has caused a decrease in monthly rent in the amount of $320. When an 11% "cap rate" for the area is applied, what is the resulting loss in value he has experienced due to the freeway?

    a. $45,000
    b. $40,908
    c. $34,909
    d. $32,468

        ANSWER: c.   *Yearly loss in income = $320 x 12 = $3,840*
                        Value Loss = Monthly Income Loss divided by "cap rate"
                        = $3,840 ÷ 11% (.11) = $34,909.

76. All the following statements are incorrect, except:

    a. a real property security can be created from a note on a home not located in any subdivision.
    b. real property securities are always secured by installment sales contracts.
    c. real property securities and real property sales contracts are interchangeable terms.
    d. out-of-state subdivisions offered in California for sale need not comply with Article 6 of the California Real Estate Law.

        ANSWER: a.   *All that is necessary would be the "guarantee" against loss, or a specific minimum yield, made by the selling broker.*

77. To whom is the Mutual Mortgage Insurance (MMI) premium on a VA loan paid?

    a. The broker
    b. The mortgage company
    c. The Veterans Administration
    d. To no one

        ANSWER: d.   *FHA has the requirement for such a premium, NOT the VA.*

78. Which of the following would constitute a proper delivery of a deed?

    a. Escrow mailing the deed to the Grantee after signed by seller, and after all other requirements of the escrow had been met, but also after the seller had died.
    b. After signing, seller gave to broker with instructions to give it to buyer.
    c. Escrow delivers deed to buyer without completed (signed) instructions.
    d. After signing the deed, Grantee personally delivers to Grantor.

        ANSWER: a.   *Death does NOT automatically terminate contract. If it can be proved that the seller intended to deliver to the buyer upon completion of requirements of escrow, it would be a valid delivery.*

EXAM 2

79. An owner has been found guilty of discrimination under the Health and Safety Code. What action can the aggrieved party take?

    a. May purchase the property in question, if still available.
    b. May purchase another like property, if the original property is not available.
    c. May be awarded $500 in damages if neither a nor b available.
    d. All of the above.

    ANSWER: d.

80. An apartment owner desires to carpet his units. The area to be covered is 60% of the total 15,000 sq. ft. living space in the building. If the total cost of the carpet (including installation) is $14 per sq. yd., what will be the owner's total expenditure?

    a. $12,000
    b. $14,000
    c. $16,000
    d. $18,000

    ANSWER: b.   *Area to be carpeted (yds) = 15,000 x 60% ÷ 9 sq. ft/sq yd*
                    = 15,000 x (.60) ÷ 9 = 1,000
                    Total cost = area x $14 = 1,000 sq. yds x 14 = $14,000.

81. A member of the Institute of Real Estate Managers would carry the designation:

    a. NAREM.
    b. MAI.
    c. CPM.
    d PMA.

    ANSWER: c.   *CPM - Certified Property Manager. The others are: NAREM - National Association of Real Estate Managers; MAI - Member of Appraisal Institute; and PMA - Property Manager's Association.*

82. An apartment house offered single garages. When a new unit was built nearby, offering double garages, the tenants all moved into the newer units. This is an example of:

    a. physical deterioration.
    b. economic obsolescence.
    c. social obsolescence.
    d. functional obsolescence.

    ANSWER: d.   *Refers to "outdated" condition.*

83. A personal, revocable, and unassignable permission of authority to do one or more acts on the land of another, without possessing any interest therein, is the definition of:

    a. license.
    b. easement.
    c. encroachment.
    d. option.

    ANSWER: a.   *Easement includes an "interest"; license just gives permission.*

84. Regarding a "Blanket Trust Deed," which of the following statements is correct?

    a. It covers more than just one property.
    b. It usually contains a "release clause" providing for release of a particular parcel upon the repayment of a specified portion of the loan.
    c. It is typically used with a tract of homes built on speculation.
    d. All of the above.

        ANSWER: d. *All the statements describe a blanket encumbrance, or trust deed.*

85. A person holding a judgment against a real estate broker seeking relief from the Recovery Fund could obtain a maximum of:

    a. $10,000.
    b. $15,000.
    c. $100,000.
    d. $20,000.

        ANSWER: d. *$20,000 per claimant, NOT to exceed that figure for all claimants in a single transaction. The $100,000 is the maximum for multiple transactions per one licensee.*

86. Under an "exclusive agency" agreement:

    a. the owner can sell property himself, without liability of commission to broker.
    b. the owner must pay commission to broker, no matter who sells property.
    c. the owner can sell to anyone the day after the listing expires, without being liable to broker for commission.
    d. the owner can subsequently give another broker a listing (at any time), which would have the effect of canceling the original listing agreement.

        ANSWER: a. *Answer (c) is incorrect, for most contracts utilized today have the safety clause, which would prohibit owner from selling to anyone registered by a broker.*

87. When water is returned to the "water table" by the percolation process, the water belongs to the:

    a. state.
    b. people.
    c. local water company.
    d. owner of the land directly above the water.

        ANSWER: b. *The land owner has only the right, in common with others, to take her share of water for her own beneficial use.*

88. Mr. Buyer has obtained approval for an FHA loan through a local mortgage company. He has been informed that the company will be charging him a 1% fee, which is called a:

    a. prepayment fee.
    b. tax.
    c. buyer discount fee.
    d. loan processing fee.

        ANSWER: d. *Also more commonly known as "loan origination fee."*

EXAM 2

89. Which of the following is an exception to the Map Act with respect to the definition of a subdivision?

    a. Any parcel of land divided into lots or parcels, each of a gross area of 40 acres or more.

    b. The whole parcel before subdivision contains less than 5 acres, each parcel created by the division abuts upon a public street or highway and no dedications or improvements are required by the governing body.

    c. Any parcel divided into lots or parcels, each of a gross area of 20 acres or more, and each of which has an approved access to a maintained public street or highway.

    d. All of the above.

    ANSWER: d.

90. A couple purchasing a $94,400 home are using an FHA insured loan to complete the purchase. All the following would be advantages created by this transaction, except:

    a. budgeted payments.
    b. conserving working capital.
    c. enforced savings.
    d. liquidity.

    ANSWER: d.   *Most consider real estate to be the least liquid of investments.*

91. A lease that designates that the lessee is to pay the real property taxes is usually a:

    a. gross lease.
    b. percentage lease.
    c. net lease.
    d. fixed rate lease.

    ANSWER: c.   *In addition to lease payment, lessee pays all variable costs, such as taxes, insurance, and maintenance.*

92. Escrow prorations are based on how many days in the year?

    a. 365
    b. 366
    c. 360
    d. 350

    ANSWER: c.   *30 days in each month; 30 x 12 = 360.*

93. On March 1, a buyer offered to purchase a listing for $120,000, closing escrow in 3 months. Buyer was to pay cash to and take over an existing VA guaranteed loan with a loan balance of approx. $95,855 payable at $1,028.61 per month (P+ I) at 12% annual interest. Seller sent in three payments during the escrow. At closing, the seller's equity in the property (excluding costs of sale) will be approximately:

    a. $22,000.
    b. $23,456.
    c. $25,689.
    d. $24,355.

    ANSWER: d.   *Additional seller payments. = $1,028.61 x 3 = $3,086 (P+ I)*
        3 months interest payments = $95,855 x 1% x 3 months = $2,876
        3 months principal payments = $3,086 - 2,876 = $210

        Loan balance at close of escrow = $95,855 - 210 = $95,645
        Seller equity at close of escrow = $120,000 - 95,645 = $24,355 (closing equity)

94. The simple interest on a $9,000 loan at 15% for 2 years, 5 months, and 23 days would be:

    a. $3,748.75.
    b. $3,548.75.
    c. $3,348.75.
    d. $3,148.75.

    ANSWER: c.   *Based on 360 days per year, the time would be = 2.4806 years*
        = 2 + 5/12 + 23/360 = 2.0 + 0.4167 + 0.0639 = 2.4806.

        Interest = Principal x Rate x Time = $9,000 x 15% x 2.4806
        = $9,000 x (0.15) x (2.4806) = $3,348.75.

95. A property is sold, a grant deed recorded and standard policy of title insurance issued. Which of the following warranties made by the seller is NOT insured by the title property?

    a. That the seller indeed owns the property.
    b. That there are no undisclosed liens that the seller has not disclosed.
    c. That there has not been forgery in the chain of title.
    d. That the grantor is competent.

    ANSWER: a.   *Not one of the two warranties in a grant deed.*

96. Which of the following are the 5 requisites for a "Conditional" or "Installment Land Sales Contract"?

    a. Seller/buyer agreement, legality, consideration, written performance
    b. Maturity, seller/ buyer agreement, legality, consideration, lawful object
    c. Mutuality, seller/buyer agreement, consideration, consent, written
    d. Mutuality, seller/buyer agreement, consideration, legality, written

    ANSWER: d.

EXAM 2

97. When comparing a 30-year loan to a 2-year loan, which of the following statements would be most correct regarding the 30-year loan?

    a. Interest is less.
    b. Interest rate must change.
    c. Monthly payment will be more.
    d. Monthly payment will be less.

      ANSWER: d.   *All other things remaining unchanged, the longer the term, the smaller the monthly payments.*

98. All of the following illustrate differences between mechanic's liens and judgments, except:

    a. mechanic's lien is a statutory lien.
    b. mechanic's lien may have priority over previously recorded lien.
    c. judgment is a voluntary lien.
    d. judgment must be recorded to be valid.

      ANSWER: c.   *Judgments are involuntary liens.*

99. A grant deed cannot be recorded until:

    a. it has been acknowledged by grantor.
    b. the documentary transfer tax has been paid.
    c. both a and b.
    d. neither a nor b.

      ANSWER: c.

100. How many acres are contained within an area measuring 330' x 330'?

    a. 5.0
    b. 7.5
    c. 2.5
    d. 2.0

      ANSWER: c.   *Area = 330' x 330' = 108,900 sq. ft.*
                    Acres = 108,900 sq. ft ÷ 43,560 = 2.5 acres.

101. A "Lis Pendens" notice is effective until:

    a. action is dismissed.
    b. time for appeal has past.
    c. final determination on appeal.
    d. all of the above.

      ANSWER: d.

102. State Housing Laws provide minimum construction and occupancy requirements for dwellings, apartment, houses, and hotels. Which of the following statements is NOT true regarding these laws?

   a. Construction requirements are handled by local building inspectors.
   b. Occupancy and sanitation regulations are enforced by local health officers.
   c. Local city or county authorities cannot impose more stringent requirements than those of the state.
   d. None of the above.

   ANSWER: c.   *Local authorities CAN impose more stringent requirements than those of the state.*

103. In California, the basis for prohibiting discrimination is the:

   a. State Reform Act.
   b. Business and Professions Code.
   c. Health and Safety Code.
   d. Civil Procedure Code.

   ANSWER: c.

104. Which of the following qualifies as a bulk transfer sale?

   a. Subdivider transfers entire 50 parcel unimproved subdivision.
   b. Lumber company transfers a substantial amount of lumber, not in the ordinary course of business.
   c. Judicial transfer of a business including stock used for resale, fixtures, licenses, and leases.
   d. All of the above.

   ANSWER: b.   *Key phrase "not in the ordinary course of business" should provide signal.*

105. Which of the following is generally the most advantageous regarding income taxes?

   a. Selling homes to customers.
   b. Selling property held for investment.
   c. Selling income property.
   d. Selling property used as a business.

   ANSWER: c.   *Income property (rentals and business sites) have the preferred tax treatment by the IRS: (1) Full deductions for losses; (2) Tax postponement measures for installment sales and exchanges. Classifications in "a," "b," and "d" (above) are NOT eligible for as many tax advantages.*

106. In which court division would one find the Probate Court?

   a. Appellate
   b. District
   c. Municipal
   d. Superior

   ANSWER: d.   *Probate is handled in Superior Court.*

EXAM 2

107. How is a commission to a broker calculated for a lease that he negotiated?

    a. Percentage of initial year lease amount.
    b. Percentage of total lease payments.
    c. Amount equal to any prepaid rent.
    d. None of the above.

      ANSWER: b. *Although commissions are negotiable between parties, (c) is the normal for industry.*

108. A real estate broker acting as a loan broker has arranged a loan for an owner. His disclosure statement has been prepared and signed by the borrower. Then the broker discovered a lien on the property that the owner failed to disclose to the broker. If the new loan cannot be arranged due to that "old" lien, the borrower would be liable for:

    a. no costs, expenses, or commission.
    b. cost and expenses of originating the loan which have either been paid or incurred.
    c. one-half of all costs, expenses, and commissions shown on the statement.
    d. all costs and expenses incurred or paid, plus one-half the commission charge.

      ANSWER: d.

109. A list of the improvements and buildings on a property are required with a:

    a. grant deed.
    b. contract of sale.
    c. CLTA policy of title insurance.
    d. none of the above.

      ANSWER: d. *Such a list is NOT required on any instrument.*

110. Which of the following could be an example of an institutional lender?

    a. Investment trust company.
    b. Mortgage company
    c. Insurance company.
    d. None of the above.

      ANSWER: c. *Insurance companies are always "institutional." Mortgage companies can be, but most commonly are loan representatives, and as such, are classified as noninstitutional lenders. Investment trust companies are always noninstitutional.*

111. Which of the following would appear as a "debit" on the seller's closing statement?

    a. Selling price
    b. Prepaid rent, received by seller
    c. Prepaid taxes
    d. None of the above

      ANSWER: b. *Unless the rent was for the period of time prior to the close of escrow, it would be passed on to the buyer, who would be the owner during the time rent applied.*

112. What insect is the most destructive to wood?

    a. Wood beetles
    b. Wood lice
    c. Termites
    d. None of the above

    ANSWER: c.

113. A buyer recently purchased a home and is already refinancing the property. Which of the following is most likely the reason for such action?

    a. Long-term loan
    b. Short-term loan
    c. Alienation clause
    d. Low equity in the property

    ANSWER: b.   *Generally indicates need to pay off short-term financing, i.e. a construction loan, or some form of interim financing.*

114. There are 50 units in a condominium project. Five Plan A's cost $105,000; 13 Plan B's cost $109,000; 17 Plan C's cost $111,00; 15 Plan D's cost $115,000. For a gross $4,600 monthly maintenance budget, and if each owner was to pay his proportionate share of this fee based on the ratio of his unit purchase price to the total purchase price of all units, the monthly maintenance assessment for an owner of a unit "B" would be:

    a. $86.96.
    b. $90.28.
    c. $91.93.
    d. $95.25.

    ANSWER: b.   *The other values are the other unit monthly fees, respectively.*

    NOTE: All dollar amounts are in ($1,000):

    Total Cost = (5) x (105) + (13) x (109) + (17) x (111) + (15) x (115)
    = $5,554
    Unit "B" = 109 ÷ 5,554 x (100) = (109 ÷ 5,554) x (100) = 1.963% (based on values)
    Monthly Fee for "B" = $4,600 x (1.963%) = 4.600 x (.01963) = $90,277

115. A single woman owned a number of properties as her separate property. After marrying, she executed a new deed, naming herself (new last name) as owner, as "a married woman." Which of the following statements would be true? This action probably would:

    a. mean that the remainder of her property would be considered community property.
    b. be invalid because, as sole owner she cannot deed to herself.
    c. permit her husband to execute a valid deed to this property.
    d. create a cloud on the title of this property.

    ANSWER: d.   *Not illegal, but could cause confusion with the "maiden" name as grantee on the original deed, and "married" name as grantor or grantee on the newer deed.*

116. Which of the following is correct regarding a five-year-old liquor license?

    a. Any amount can be charged when it is resold.
    b. $6,000 is the maximum allowed price on resale.
    c. A $250 transfer fee is required by the state.
    d. None of the above.

    ANSWER: b.   *Five years or less, limited to $6,000. To get more, it must be OVER five years old. Wait one more day!*

117. A broker is taking a listing on a church facility that is owned by an unincorporated association. In order to determine who is the proper authority to represent the group and sign documents, the broker should:

    a. contact the members and arrange to have a meeting for a majority vote.
    b. check the county recorder's records.
    c. contact the person who originally built the facilities.
    d. check the charter or bylaws of the group.

    ANSWER: d.   *Latest copies, representing the most recent authority.*

118. When a judgment of the court is recorded, it becomes a(n):

    a. superior lien.
    b. inferior lien.
    c. voluntary lien.
    d. involuntary lien.

    ANSWER: d.   *Most such actions are NOT voluntarily accepted.*

119. An appraiser, when asked to determine the value of real property, would give consideration to which of the following?

    a. Relationship of value of a property in exchange for another property.
    b. Desire of the person for the desired property.
    c. Effective demand, evidenced by purchasing power.
    d. All of the above.

    ANSWER: d.

120. The term "secondary market," as used in financing, refers to:

    a. transferring of loans by mortgagors.
    b. transferring of loans by sellers.
    c. second loans.
    d. transferring of loans by beneficiaries.

    ANSWER: d.

121. "Depression, expansion, prosperity, and recession" are all terms related to which of the following cycles?

    a. Capital market
    b. Mortgage market
    c. Real estate
    d. Business

    ANSWER: d.

122. The terms "special, qualified and limited" refer to:

    a. contracts.
    b. deeds.
    c. endorsements.
    d. liens.

    ANSWER: c.   Ways to "endorse" documents: blank, special, restrictive, qualified.

123. The Alcoholic Beverage Control Board (ABC) will NOT issue:

    a. a license to a seasonal resort.
    b. a license near a school.
    c. a license to a newly formed club.
    d. an off-sale license to an alien.

    ANSWER: c.   Private (bona fide) club must have been in operation for "at least one year."

124. Which of the following would most likely be personal property?

    a. A cause of action
    b. A chattel real
    c. An easement in gross
    d. All of the above

    ANSWER: d.

125. Of the following parcel descriptions, which is the largest?

    a. Two sections
    b. 1/10 of a township
    c. Two square miles
    d. Area 5280' x 6600'

    ANSWER: b.   1/10 x township = 1/10 x 36 sq. mi = 3.6 sq. mi
    Two sections = 2 sq. mi
    5280' x 6600' ÷ 43,560 ÷ 640 = 1.25 sq. mi

EXAM 2

126. Relative to a "balance sheet," which of the following would NOT be a definition of "net worth"?

    a. Net worth represents owner equity.
    b. Net worth = Assets + Liabilities.
    c. New Worth + Liabilities = Assets.
    d. Net worth is the difference between revenues and expenses for a given period of time.

    ANSWER: d.   Is a definition for net income – P & L Statement.

127. Adam dies, leaving no heirs, but he willed his "garden ranch" to Eva. Mr. Apple was in possession under a lease that had two years to run. During the probate of Adam's will, the court found it invalid. Therefore, title to the "garden" would;

    a. pass to Eva, since that was Adam's intent.
    b. pass to lessee Apple who is in possession.
    c. pass to Adam's estate.
    d. escheat to the state, subject to the lease with Mr. Apple.

    ANSWER: d.   Since Adam had no heirs nor will (it was invalid), the State would take the property by action of law.

128. A doctor owns an apartment building that showed a $3,000 operating loss for the year. For income tax purposes he:

    a. can deduct $1,000 per year for 3 years.
    b. may take 50% of the loss in the year the loss occurred.
    c. can take the entire $3,000 as a deductible against ordinary income.
    d. must apply the loss against capital gains.

    ANSWER: c.   An operative loss is treated, for tax purposes, as an ordinary loss, and may be used to offset ordinary income.

129. Planning commission members are:

    a. elected in both cities and counties.
    b. appointed in both cities and counties, and advise the city council.
    c. appointed in the county and elected in the city.
    d. appointed in the city and elected in the county.

    ANSWER: b.   The city council and board of supervisors members are elected. Planning commission members are appointed. Creation of a commission is required of counties, but optional for cities.

130. When is a property manager required to be "in residence"?

    a. For 16 or more units.
    b. For 5 or more units.
    c. For 12 or more units.
    d. Never.

    ANSWER: a.

131. A written listing contract in which the agent receives a right to a commission regardless of who sells the property, except the owner, is an:

    a. exclusive right to sell.
    b. exclusive agency.
    c. open listing.
    d. option.

        ANSWER: b.   With an exclusive agency, if the owner sells the property, the broker receives NO commission.

132. The metal used by builders to prevent seepage of water for certain joints in a building are called:

    a. drain joints.
    b. flashing.
    c. guttering.
    d. stoving.

        ANSWER: b.   Flashing is sheet metal used to protect against water seepage.

133. Of the following, who would be interested in knowing about the Soldier's and Sailor's Relief Act of 1940?

    a. Internal Revenue Service
    b. Parties to trust deed
    c. Parties to homestead
    d. Parties to a statutory suit

        ANSWER: b.   Designed to protect service men and women while serving in the armed services, as regarding financial debts they were unable to pay.

134. When using the "straight-line" method of depreciation, the initial year's depreciation on a property with an economic life of five years would be:

    a. 33%
    b. 66%
    c. 20%
    d. 25%

        ANSWER: c.   The initial year and remaining years will be 20% (100% ÷ 5).

135. The purpose of the California Franchise Investment Law is to:

    a. protect the franchisee against fraud or likelihood that the franchised promises would be fulfilled.
    b. protect the franchiser by providing a better understanding of relationships between parties with regard to their business relationship.
    c. compel franchiser to furnish a prospective franchisee with sufficient information to enable him to make an intelligent decision.
    d. all of the above.

        ANSWER: d.

EXAM 2

136. Which of the following would be classified as a "specific" lien?

    a. Assessment lien
    b. Mechanic's lien
    c. Property tax lien
    d. All of the above

    ANSWER: d.   *A specific lien is a lien against ONE property.*

137. The Notice to Creditors of a bulk transfer required by the Uniform Commercial Code (UCC) must contain all the following, except:

    a. names and business addresses of creditors.
    b. location at which transfer is to be consummated.
    c. names and addresses of the transferors and transferees.
    d. location of the property to be transferred.

    ANSWER: a.

138. A real estate broker desires to negotiate the sale of a property, the principal value of which consists of mineral and oil rights. To do so he or she:

    a. can conduct one sale per year under his broker license.
    b. must get a permit from the DRE.
    c. must advise the buyers to get an oil and gas quote from the U.S. Dept. of Interior.
    d. is not required to have any special permit or additional license.

    ANSWER: d.   *By statute, original Mineral, Oil, and Gas (MOG) broker licenses are no longer issued. However, real estate brokers may conduct mineral, oil, and gas transaction activities under their individual broker or real estate corporation license.*

139. Dr. J purchased a parcel of land that had a uniform depth of 110'. The area of the property was 2/3 acre. The following spring he was able to purchase the adjoining lot, which had the same depth of the initial lot (A). However, this lot (B) was only 1/2 the area of lot (A). He paid $13,750 for lot (B). Thereafter, he combined the two parcels, divided the whole acreage into smaller parcels, each having a uniform width of 66', and sold each for $11,000. This brought him a 60% profit over what he had paid for lots A & B combined. What was the cost of the initial parcel (lot A)?

    a. $13,750
    b. $17,500
    c. $27,500
    d. $23,750

    ANSWER: c.   *Acreage: Lot A = 2/3 ac; Lot B = 1/2 x 2/3 = 1/3 acre*
    Lot A + Lot B = 2/3 + 1/3 = 1.0 acre = 43,560 sq. ft.

    Therefore, width of (A+B) = 43,560 divided by 110' = 396'
    Total number of new lots = 396 ÷ 66' = 396/66 = 6 lots

    Total sales price (6 lots combined) = 6 x $11,000 = $66,000
    This represents a 60% gain over cost of lots (A+B), therefore
    Cost of (A+B) = $66,000 ÷ 160% = 66,000 ÷ 1.6 = $41,250
    If Lot A+Lot B = $41,250, then subtract cost of Lot B ($13,750)
    Cost of Lot A = $41,250 - $13,750 = $27,500

140. When asked to give an opinion as to the value of an unimproved lot for the purpose of building a single family residence, a real estate salesperson would use the:

    a. capitalization of net income approach.
    b. cost approach.
    c. replacement cost approach.
    d. comparative analysis approach.

    ANSWER: d.

141. A real estate broker is required to notify which of the following within 5 days after the sale of a manufactured home?

    a. Department of Motor Vehicles
    b. DRE
    c. Department of Housing and Community Development
    d. All of the above

    ANSWER: a.

142. To obtain a real estate salesperson's license, a person must be:

    a. 21 years of age.
    b. fingerprinted for the DRE.
    c. be a U.S. citizen.
    d. none of the above.

    ANSWER: b.   *Of the items on this list, only fingerprints is correct.*

143. An investor owns an industrial property for which he paid $300,000. The County Assessor valued the land at $63,000 and the improvement at $147,000. Using the Assessor's ratios, what would the investor use as a basis for depreciation on the property?

    a. $190,000
    b. $200,000
    c. $210,000
    d. $220,000

    ANSWER: c.   *Assessor's Ratios: Total value = $63,000 + 147,000 = $210,000*
                         Improvement ratio: 147,000 ÷ 210,000 x (100) = 70%
                         Therefore: Basis for depreciation = $300,000 x 70% = $210,000

144. In a trust deed foreclosure situation, who gives notice for the action to commence?

    a. Trustor to beneficiary
    b. Trustor to trustee
    c. Beneficiary to trustee
    d. Beneficiary to trustor

    ANSWER: c.   *Legally, the Trustee holds "bare naked title," given to Trustee by Trustor in the form of the trust deed. However, the instrument is retained with note by the beneficiary (lender) until such time as a foreclosure action must be initiated. At this time, the beneficiary will send the trust deed to the Trustee and request the foreclosure.*

EXAM 2

145. "A" borrowed $100,000 to purchase a residence. The loan was to be amortized over 30 years, and from an "amortization table," the factor to amortize $1,000 in 360 monthly payments was $10.2861. If "A" retains the property for the full 30 years, making the required 360 (P+I) payments, how much interest would he have paid throughout the loan period?

    a. $100,000
    b. $370,300
    c. $270,300
    d. None of the above

> ANSWER: c.   *Payment (P+I) = $10.2861 per $1,000 of loan amount*
> *= (10.2861) x (100) = $1,028.61 per month*
> *Total money paid in = $1028.61 x (360) = $370,300*
> *Deduct Principal amount = $370,300 - $100,000 = Interest Paid = $270,300.*

146. One person has been designated in an instrument (should be recorded) to act officially for another person. This is considered:

    a. principle.
    b. principal.
    c. fiduciary.
    d. attorney-in-fact.

> ANSWER: d.

147. California real estate law defines a "planned development" as which of the following?

    a. Condominium project
    b. Subdivision
    c. Cooperative apartment project
    d. Community apartment project

> ANSWER: b.   *Like the subject, answers a, c, and d are defined as subdivisions, providing there are five units involved in the project.*

148. An attachment lien may NOT be released by which of the following?

    a. Written release by the plaintiff.
    b. Satisfaction of judgment, if a judgment is entered in favor of the plaintiff.
    c. An order of the court.
    d. Death of the defendant.

> ANSWER: d.   *Heirs would be held liable.*

149. A salesperson leaves the services of his broker. The former broker must notify DRE:

    a. within 5 days.
    b. within 10 days.
    c. within 15 days.
    d. only in the case of terminating the salesperson for violation of California real estate law.

> ANSWER: b.   *New broker must notify within 5 days.*

150. A minimum of how many days must elapse between the first notice of sale and the actual date of the trustee's sale?

    a. 90

    b. 111

    c. 21

    d. None of the above

    ANSWER: c.   *This period comes after the "3 month waiting period."*

EXAM 2

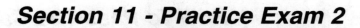

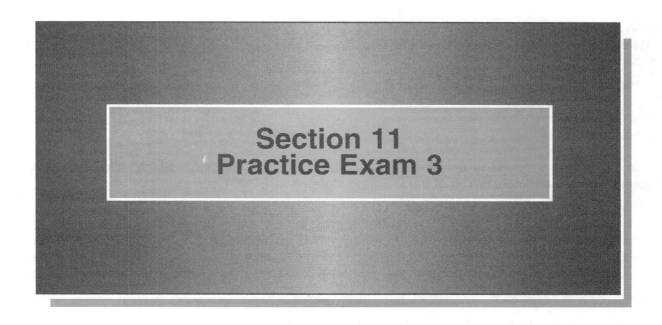

Section 11
Practice Exam 3

NOTE: For better self-testing, the answers to this exam have been moved to the end of the exam.

1. The appraiser's primary measure of the efficiency of an office building plan is:

    a. elevator capacity.
    b. corridor widths.
    c. parking.
    d. ratio of net rentable area to gross area.

2. Advertising regulations of the Truth-in-Lending Law apply to all of the following, except:

    a. homeowner who is advertising own home for purchase subject to the existing loan.
    b. homeowner advertising that loan may be assumed under certain terms.
    c. financing institution advertising to promote consumer credit.
    d. broker advertising a property with an annual percentage rate.

3. Regarding termination of estates in manufactured home parks, a tenant who has a tenancy in a manufactured home that cannot be legally moved without a permit, may not have the tenancy terminated without written notice of not less than:

    a. 30 days.
    b. 45 days.
    c. 60 days.
    d. 90 days.

4. An investor purchased a property, financing with a 75% loan-to-value ratio loan. Payments of interest only for the first 6 months was $6,000. Interest rate is 10%. What was the appraised value of the property?

    a. $170,000
    b. $160,000
    c. $150,000
    d. $140,000

5. An owner of a cooperative apartment project makes monthly payments which include principal, interest, taxes, insurance. Which of the following statements is NOT correct?

    a. Tax collector will render a separate tax bill to each owner.
    b. Assessment bond costs will be divided among the owners.
    c. Owner may deduct the amount of property taxes paid on his income tax return.
    d. If other owners fail to make payments, all owners could lose their equities, for a foreclosure action could be taken against the (single) blanket type loan, unless delinquencies were brought current.

6. According to the statute of frauds, all the following must be in writing to be enforceable, except:

    a. an agreement that (by its terms) is not to be performed within one year of execution of the agreement.
    b. an agreement that employs a broker to solicit, sell, lease, or exchange real property.
    c. a partnership agreement between two or more parties to engage in the sale or exchange of real property.
    d. an agreement for leasing real property for more than one year.

7. The California Commissioner of Real Estate has authority to:

    a. create laws to discipline licensees.
    b. promulgate reasonable rules and regulations.
    c. settle commission disputes.
    d. issue licenses for out-of-state licenses.

8. An option in a lease:

    a. is illegal.
    b. is valid only if recorded.
    c. normally passes with the assignment of lease, even if not mentioned in the assignment.
    d. none of the above.

9. Which of the following would NOT affect the basis of real property?

    a. Remodeling
    b. Maintenance
    c. New roof
    d. New concrete patio

10. On which of the following properties may one file a valid Declaration of Homestead?

    a. Fourplex
    b. House on 2-acre parcel
    c. Single-family dwelling
    d. All of the above.

11. A freehold estate is a(n):

    a. estate for years.
    b. estate at will.
    c. estate from period-to-period.
    d. fee simple estate.

12. In situations whereby real property taxes are not paid, the Tax Collector will effect a "Sold to the State" on which of the following dates?

    a. July 1st, following the unpaid year.
    b. June 30th, five years after the unpaid tax year.
    c. June 30th, the last day of the unpaid tax year.
    d. None of the above.

13. An investor needed cash for additional investments, and "took out" a loan against his property. His interest payment on this new loan was less than the net return he was realizing on the property. This is an example of:

    a. capital turnover.
    b. trading on equity.
    c. band of investment.
    d. deficit financing.

14. For federal income tax purposes, a taxpayer could adjust the basis of his residence with which of the following?

    a. Property taxes.
    b. Accrued depreciation.
    c. Addition of a patio.
    d. None of the above, for a personal residence basis cannot be adjusted for any reason.

15. In addition to being registered for a minimum of one year, manufactured homes sold by real estate licensees are vehicles designed for human habitation which are greater than:

    a. 8' wide and 20' long.
    b. 6' wide and 40' long.
    c. 12' wide and 30' long.
    d. 8' wide and 40' long.

16. Complaints involving violations of federal law must be filed within how many days of the violation?

    a. 90
    b. 120
    c. 150
    d. 180

17. To divide equally or proportionately to time of use is to:

    a. progress.
    b. probate.
    c. prorate.
    d. procrastinate.

EXAM 3

18. An owner offered his home to a buyer for $100,000 cash. The buyer paid the owner $100 cash to keep the offer open for two weeks. The owner accepted the $100. Ten days later, the owner notified the buyer that he was withdrawing his home from the sale. The next day the buyer tendered $100,000 cash to the owner. Under these conditions:

    a. the offer to sell was binding.

    b. seller violated the agreement to hold open the offer to sell, but did not have to sell to the buyer because the buyer had not promised in his original conversation to buy the property.

    c. seller rescinded, voiding the transaction.

    d. although the seller violated the agreement, he effectively prevented a binding contract from forming by withdrawing his property from the market.

19. The Truth-in-Lending Law would apply to which of the following?

    a. First trust deed and junior loans

    b. Construction loans

    c. All loan transactions

    d. None of the above

20. The primary activities of FNMA in the secondary money market involves:

    a. FHA loans only.

    b. VA and FHA loans.

    c. 2nd loans up to $22,000.

    d. all types of real estate loans.

21. A father needed money to send his son to college. He borrowed money from the bank, securing the loan with a first trust deed. Later, he sold the home subject to the first loan, and took back a 2nd trust deed from the buyer as a part of the purchase price. In the event of a default, which of the following would be true?

    a. The bank could obtain a deficiency judgment against the purchasers.

    b. The bank could obtain a deficiency judgment against the father.

    c. The father could get a deficiency judgment against the purchasers on the 2nd trust deed.

    d. None of the above.

22. Which of the following would be considered a "general lien"?

    a. Federal tax lien

    b. Franchise tax lien

    c. Judgment lien

    d. All of the above

23. Buyer purchased a new residence for $110,000, lived in the property for 3 years, and then sold the property. He then moved into an apartment, signing a 3-year lease agreement. If he does NOT purchase another residence within the next two years, what income tax obligation has he created?

    a. Nothing reportable from sale of residence

    b. Capital gains taxable

    c. Capital gains nontaxable

    d. None of the above

24. What is the written instrument used to create land use restrictions for the benefit of the owners in a new subdivision?

    a. Zoning ordinances
    b. Original subdivision deed
    c. Subdivision map
    d. Declaration of restrictions

25. Which of the answers makes the following statement true? No real estate salesperson may be licensed in the employ of a corporation real estate broker licensee, or perform acts for which a real estate license is required on behalf of the corporation, if:

    a. the salesperson, singly or together with other real estate salespersons licensed in the employ of the corporation, owns or controls, directly or indirectly, a majority of the outstanding stock of the corporation.
    b. the salesperson is a director or officer of the corporation.
    c. both a and b.
    d. none of the above.

26. A real estate broker discloses the race of a buyer to the seller upon request of that information. Is the broker in violation of the law?

    a. Yes, because of specific federal and state legislation.
    b. Yes, this is a violation of current civil rights legislation per state attorney general's office.
    c. No, because agent is required to disclose all matters to his principal.
    d. No, as this has not been made the subject matter for specific legislation.

27. A broker's loan statement protects the:

    a. broker.
    b. trustee.
    c. trustor.
    d. beneficiary.

28. What is the monthly impound account payment for fire insurance for the following?
    Insured value = $100,000; Rate = $0.40 per $100; 3 yr. premium = 2.5 times annual rate.

    a. $25.78
    b. $26.78
    c. $27.78
    d. $28.78

29. Concerning FHA loans, all of the following statements are correct, except:

    a. level payments required.
    b. monthly payments of taxes and insurance for impound account.
    c. monthly budgeted payments suitable to buyer's pocketbook.
    d. provides maximum building standards.

EXAM 3

30. If two lots were purchased for $9,900 each, then split into three lots and sold for $8,500 each, what is the percentage yield on the original purchase price?

    a. 26.79%
    b. 27.79%
    c. 28.79%
    d. 29.79%

31. The IRS considers a "dealer" as a person who holds interests in real property:

    a. for sale to customers.
    b. for investment.
    c. for production of income.
    d. none of the above.

32. When a real estate licensee has been accused of a Code violation, the initial step for the Commissioner in initiating the hearing procedure would be to:

    a. require complainant to file testimony at the hearing.
    b. bring charges against licensee.
    c. serve the accused licensee with the accusation.
    d. file a complaint against the licensee.

33. Which of the following would issue a CRV when asked to approve a new loan?

    a. Savings bank
    b. Department of Veterans Affairs
    c. FHA
    d. VA

34. Which of the following would be considered publicly assisted housing?

    a. Property purchased with FHA insured loan.
    b. Property purchased with government assistance.
    c. Property receiving tax exemption (other than Veterans).
    d. Both a and b.

35. A piece of lumber that is 2" x 12" x 24 ft. contains how many board feet?

    a. 36
    b. 48
    c. 60
    d. 72

36. When a deed is recorded:

    a. title always passes.
    b. possession is granted.
    c. presumption of delivery arises.
    d. none of above.

37. What is the area of the parcel described as follows: NW¼ of the SE¼ and the W½ of the NE¼ and the NE¼ of the NW¼ of Section 13; plus, to this add the SE¼ of the SW¼ and the SW¼ of the SE¼ of Section 14?

    a. 200 acres
    b. 160 acres
    c. 120 acres
    d. 240 acres

38. "Placement of a home on a lot" best matches:

    a. option.
    b. avulsion.
    c. dedication.
    d. orientation.

39. An owner, desiring to sell his residence, demands that the words "property is offered without respect to race, creed, national origin, etc." be omitted from his listing agreement. The broker should:

    a. ignore the seller's request and take the listing.
    b. suggest that under those terms, the seller should sell himself.
    c. refuse to show the property to minorities.
    d. none of the above.

40. Any person in whom the title of real estate is vested, who afterwards has a name change must:

    a. change all recorded documents to reflect the change, immediately.
    b. sign any subsequent conveyance with latest name, including maiden name.
    c. set forth the name in which such person derived title, in subsequent conveyances.
    d. none of the above.

41. Which of the following defines a "blind ad"?

    a. Neither sale price nor terms of property are included in the ad.
    b. Licensee does not include address of property in the ad.
    c. Licensee does not reveal that the ad was placed by licensee.
    d. None of the above.

42. Which of the following statements is NOT correct?

    a. A Cal Vet loan is a guaranteed loan.
    b. An FHA loan is an insured loan.
    c. A VA loan is a guaranteed loan.
    d. A conventional loan is not backed by any governmental agency.

43. Which of the following is primarily responsible for the considerable increase in low cost rental housing for low income groups?

    a. Federal Housing Administration
    b. Public Housing Administration
    c. State Housing Act
    d. Urban Renewal Service

EXAM 3

44. Adam purchased a residence for $180,000 and made $20,750 in capital improvements. He sold the house for $200,000 and moved into an apartment on a 3-year lease. What kind of tax effect would this sale have?

    a. Capital gain of $750
    b. Capital loss of $750
    c. Capital loss of one-half of the $750
    d. No effect

45. In determining local property taxes on a property:

    a. assess land and improvements separately, then multiply each by a different rate.
    b. assess separately and then multiply total by one tax rate.
    c. assess together, they multiply each by a different tax rate.
    d. assess together, then multiply by one tax rate.

46. Any persons who violate the "kickback" provisions of R.E.S.P.A. may be fined:

    a. not more than $10,000.
    b. by sentence of one year in prison.
    c. both a and b.
    d. none of the above.

47. California law requires a subdivider to notify the Real Estate Commissioner whenever there is a material change after the "final public report" has been issued. Which of the following would be considered a material change?

    a. Price increase
    b. Broker given exclusive listing
    c. Sale of six units to developer
    d. All of the above

48. An appraiser evaluated a building and reported to the owner that the $2,500 per month income was in line with other comparable properties in the area. Recent sales of some of those comparable properties brought $350,000. What monthly gross multiplier would he use in further evaluations?

    a. 130
    b. 140
    c. 150
    d. None of the above

49. A salesperson purchased a property listed through his broker's office. Later the sellers complained to the Commissioner that the salesperson had neglected to inform them he was a licensee. Which of the following is correct?

    a. Salesperson is not responsible, just the broker.
    b. Seller should have guessed that the buyer was licensed, due to his knowledge.
    c. Salesperson and broker are both subject to disciplinary action.
    d. No violation of real estate law.

50. An owner gives an "open listing" to many brokers, including "A" and "B." Broker A shows the home to a customer, but does not make a sale. Broker B later sells the home to the same customer. The seller is obligated to pay:

    a. "A" a full commission.
    b. "B" a full commission.
    c. "A" and "B", who split the commission.
    d. "A" and "B", who both receive full commissions.

51. Mr. Soldier wants to purchase a home on his VA entitlement. The asking price is $100,000. The VA "CRV" came back at $98,750. Which of the following statements is correct?

    a. Buyer can ask seller to reduce purchase price.
    b. Buyer can pay the extra $1,250 in cash and get the $98,750 loan.
    c. Buyer can request the VA to reevaluate the property (ask for re-appraisal), hoping to get the full value.
    d. All of the above.

52. A buyer has purchased a residence for $100,000 utilizing VA entitlement to finance the entire purchase price. The interest rate = 12%; combined monthly payments for 30 years will accumulate to be $370,300. What will be the initial month's principal payment?

    a. $128.61
    b. $78.61
    c. $28.61
    d. $0.00

53. A tenant is justified in abandoning a lease property if the landlord demonstrates constructive eviction. Which of the following acts would be considered constructive eviction?

    a. The property has been shown to another party that has entered into negotiations with the landlord.
    b. The landlord has failed to make needed repairs and maintain the property in the agreed manner.
    c. The landlord has altered the building to an extent that is no longer usable for its original purpose.
    d. All of the above.

54. Less-than-freehold estates consist of estates owned by:

    a. grantees of life estates.
    b. holders of easements.
    c. beneficiaries of trust deeds.
    d. lessees.

55. "Assignment of rents" in a loan or trust deed:

    a. provides for new buyer to pay rent until title passes.
    b. provides that the borrower pays.
    c. protects trustor or mortgagor.
    d. benefits mortgagee or beneficiary.

EXAM 3

56. Which of the following can contain the Real Estate Commissioner's recommendation for sales?

    a. Real Property Security
    b. Residential subdivision
    c. Syndicate security
    d. None of the above

57. Borrowing against a property with a loan interest rate less that the "equity yield" on the property:

    a. is unlawful.
    b. decreases equity yield.
    c. has no effect on equity yield.
    d. enhances equity yield.

58. An investor is considering buying a vacant property and building a building on it which will cost $170,000. Rental income will be $2,700 per month, and annual expenses will be $8,200. What is the maximum he can pay for the land if he uses an 11% capitalization rate?

    a. $60,000
    b. $50,000
    c. $40,000
    d. $30,000

59. All of the following are necessary for obtaining title to a property by "adverse possession," except:

    a. must possess under some evidence of color of title or claim of right.
    b. must pay taxes 5 years, before they become delinquent.
    c. must possess property continuously for 5 years.
    d. must occupy property hostile to recorded owner.

60. California real estate law considers manufactured homes:

    a. personal property.
    b. real property.
    c. both a and b.
    d. none of the above.

61. Market price is:

    a. what a property would bring in the open market.
    b. price offered by an informed purchaser.
    c. price asked for by an informed seller.
    d. price actually paid for property (escrow closed).

62. Deed restrictions are enforced by:

    a. consent decree.
    b. desist and refrain.
    c. indictment.
    d. injunction.

63. When appraising residential properties, an appraiser should carefully examine which of the following?

    a. Comparable homes currently for sale.
    b. Comparable homes recently for sale, but not sold.
    c. Comparable homes recently sold, escrow's being closed.
    d. All of the above.

64. Management of a condominium project, under control of and for the benefit of the owners, may acquire, hold, and sell:

    a. tangible personal property.
    b. tangible and intangible personal property.
    c. personal and real property.
    d. none of the above.

65. An "installment sale" contract is which of the following?

    a. A real properly sales contract in which a seller agrees to convey title to real property to the buyer, after the buyer has met certain conditions specified in the contract.
    b. Does not require conveyance of title until after one year.
    c. Will allow a seller to "stretch out" his tax liability over a longer period of time, thereby reducing the effective tax paid on a capital gain realized.
    d. All of the above.

66. In the real estate business, the buyer is commonly referred to as a(n):

    a. attorney-in-fact.
    b. fiduciary.
    c. client.
    d. customer.

67. An "agreement in a deed" best matches which of the following?

    a. Prescription
    b. Avulsion
    c. Covenant
    d. Option

68. A corporation listed a property with a broker, and subsequently the entire slate of officers were killed in a plane crash. The listing is:

    a. valid.
    b. void.
    c. voidable.
    d. invalid.

69. An investor group recently sold a parcel of land for $217,500, which was 45% more than they paid for it. The land is described as follows: N½ of the NW¼ of the SE¼ of Section 13 plus the W½ of the NE¼ of Section 13. What was the original price they paid per acre for the property?

    a. $1,500
    b. $1,200
    c. $1,000
    d $750

EXAM 3

70. The best source for establishing the age of a home would be the:

   a. assessor's office.
   b. building and safety department.
   c. county recorder's office.
   d. either a or b.

71. Examination of the records indicate there are conflicts between the local zoning restrictions and private restrictions contained within the deed that conveyed the property. Which of the following statements is true?

   a. The deed restrictions would prevail.
   b. The zoning restrictions would prevail.
   c. Since they are in conflict, the earlier restriction would prevail.
   d. The more restrictive of the two (deed vs. zoning) requirements would prevail.

72. The primary purpose of the Federal National Mortgage Association (FNMA) is to:

   a. provide large sums of money for the building industry.
   b. finance the construction of low cost residential housing.
   c. lend money in the residential marketplace lower than normal interest rates for lower income families.
   d. Expand available home loan funds by buying and selling VA, FHA, and conventional loans in the secondary money market.

73. On which of the following dates does California real property taxes become a lien on the subject property?

   a. Dec. 10th
   b. Apr. 10th
   c. Jul. 1st
   d. Mar. 1st

74. A true disadvantage of owning real property would be the lack of liquidity. Of the following, which would provide the greatest amount of liquidity to such an investment?

   a. Amortization
   b. Leaseback
   c. Leverage
   d. Syndication

75. Which of the following represents an essential part of a valid grant deed?

   a. Acknowledgment and recordation
   b. Offer and acceptance
   c. Parties capable of contracting
   d. Parties properly described

76. Which of the following properties could be purchased using FHA financing, but NOT VA financing? The purchase of:

   a. a business.
   b. a farm.
   c. farm equipment.
   d. income property.

77. Which of the following would NOT be considered a "fiduciary" relationship?

    a. Agent to seller
    b. Attorney-in-fact to principal
    c. Attorney to client
    d. Trustor to beneficiary

78. For an appraisal being conducted on a residence built in 1910, which of the following would an appraiser use?

    a. Original cost of construction.
    b. Original cost of materials multiplied by the change in the cost of living index since 1910.
    c. Today's cost of reproduction less depreciation.
    d. None of the above.

79. In appraising a residential property, the appraiser must consider the forces currently influencing the neighborhood. Boundaries of such a neighborhood are best established by:

    a. geographical situation.
    b. social composition.
    c. street pattern.
    d. traffic flow.

80. Involving the sale of a property, which of the following would be exempt from the "discrimination and unlawful acts" of the Health and Safety Code?

    a. Duplex financed by VA loan.
    b. Single family, owner-occupied residence financed by FHA.
    c. Single family, owner-occupied residence unencumbered.
    d. Twenty unit apartment financed by a conventional loan.

81. A corporation "seal" evidences the:

    a. authority of persons using the "seal."
    b. rights and privileges of recipient of document with "seal."
    c. proof of office of the presidency.
    d. none of above.

82. "Moral philosophy" best matches:

    a. ethnics.
    b. ethics.
    c. dedication.
    d. subordination.

83. The first and last months' rent payments were collected by the lessor, leasing a single family residence. The prepaid rents received would be reported on income tax:

    a. in year received totally.
    b. split between year received and year in which last month would occur.
    c. all in year which last month occurs.
    d. would not need to be reported because they were prepaid.

EXAM 3

84. The wording... "all monies paid on the property are to be held in trust until a release is obtained from the blanket encumbrance..." is required to protect the:

    a. holder of blanket encumbrance.
    b. broker.
    c. subdivider.
    d. purchaser.

85. Abe owned two parcels of land, "A" and "B." Abe sold lot "A" to Bob who, before escrow closed, had the escrow officer change the deed to read lot "B." Escrow closed and documents were recorded. Bob then sold lot "B" to Chuck, who recorded his deed. Subsequently, Abe sold "B" to Daren, who recorded his deed. Who is the owner of lot "B"?

    a. Abe
    b. Bob
    c. Chuck
    d. Daren

86. A deed of trust must contain which of the following clauses to be valid and enforceable? Requires the trustor to:

    a. keep the property in good condition and repair.
    b. keep property insured against fire and other hazards.
    c. pay taxes and assessments before they become delinquent.
    d. none of the above.

87. An investor is considering purchasing a property which has $88,400 in annual expenses. This represents 68% of the annual gross income of the property. If the investor requires a 10% return on investment, what could he pay for this property?

    a. $130,000
    b. $416,000
    c. $83,200
    d. $516,000

88. Most agency agreements between sellers and brokers are created by:

    a. estoppel.
    b. expressed agreement.
    c. implied agreement.
    d. ratified contract.

89. Considering the following types of financing, which pairs are the same?

    a. Construction vs. takeout loans
    b. Takeout loans vs. secondary financing
    c. Construction vs. interim loans
    d. Obligatory advances vs. installment loan

90. An escrow is closing October 1st. Sellers have not paid taxes for this tax year. Which of the following situations is true?

a. Seller owes buyer no tax rebate.
b. Seller owes buyer 3 months' tax rebate.
c. Buyer owes seller 2 months' tax reimbursement.
d. Buyer owes seller 3 months' tax reimbursement.

91. A home being appraised is 15 years old, but has an estimated economic life of forty years. The appraiser estimates the age, because of its obvious good upkeep and care, to be equal to comparable six-year-old homes in the neighborhood. Which of the following ages did the appraiser use in his evaluation?

a. Actual age
b. Chronological age
c. Effective age
d. Physical age

92. Which of the following statements is NOT correct?

a. All townships contain the same (exact) area.
b. Townships are bound on the sides by range lines (N-S) and by township lines (E-W).
c. A township equals 36 square miles.
d. A standard township contains 36 sections of land.

93. A buyer is purchasing a home which is to be financed with a new loan. The buyer is paying $100,000 for the property and has $50,000 cash to use as down payment. Buyer decides to put $10,000 down and obtain a new $90,000 FHA loan. All of the following are advantages for a buyer purchasing with a relatively small cash investment, except:

a. resale of the home could be easier with the large loan that could be assumed.
b. buyer keeps most of his funds more liquid for future unknowns.
c. trustor of maximum loan benefits when value of property goes down.
d. all of the above.

94. Real property CANNOT be:

a. alienated.
b. assessed.
c. hypothecated.
d. none of the above.

95. A buyer purchased the following parcel of land for $100,000. Description: SW¼ of the SW¼ of the NE¼ and the NW¼ of the NW¼ of the SE¼ and the N½ of the SW¼ of the NW¼ of the SE¼ of section 34. How much per acre did the buyer pay for the property?

a. $3,000
b. $4,000
c. $4,500
d. $5,000

96. In evaluating land to be utilized for industrial purposes, one would be least concerned about which of the following?

    a. Fertility
    b. Location
    c. Subsoil
    d. Topography

97. "Future rights to possession" best matches:

    a. orientation.
    b. prescription.
    c. reversion.
    d. subordination.

98. An attachment lien cannot be released by which of the following?

    a. Court order
    b. Death of defendant
    c. Satisfaction of judgment entered in favor of plaintiff
    d. Written release by plaintiff

99. An existing contract is replaced with an entirely new contract. This act is referred to as:

    a. rescission.
    b. assignment.
    c. novation.
    d. subordination.

100. An "assignment of rents" clause in a note and trust deed:

    a. protects the trustor.
    b. protects the lessee in the event of lessor default.
    c. permits beneficiary to collect lease payments directly from lessee, in the event of lessor default, and apply money to payment of the loan.
    d. protects the trustee.

101. In real estate financing, a "takeout" loan is:

    a. a blanket encumbrance.
    b. a construction loan.
    c. a long-term loan taken out after construction has been completed, paying off the short-term construction loan.
    d. the net amount of a loan after the discount points are taken out.

102. A real estate broker closes an escrow on the sale of residential property. Under what circumstances would he be excused from recording the newly executed first trust deed involved in the sale?

    a. When instructed by the buyer not to record.
    b. When instructed by the seller not to record.
    c. When instructed by the lender not to record.
    d. When instructed by the previous owner not to record.

103. Which of the following is true regarding taxes?

    a. Depreciation is considered return of investment and therefore not taxable.
    b. Interest income is considered as ordinary income and is so taxed.
    c. Both a and b.
    d. Neither a nor b.

104. For an income property, after paying the loan payment and all expenses, any money the owner has remaining is considered:

    a. cash flow.
    b. gross income.
    c. net taxable income.
    d. none of above.

105. For a corporation to obtain a valid real estate broker's license, all of the following must be true, except:

    a. the articles of incorporation are filed with the secretary of state.
    b. corporate applicant must pay the required license fee before the license can be issued.
    c. a real estate salesperson licensee will be employed by the corporation as an officer or director.
    d. the principal place of business must be in California.

106. A broker operating as an escrow agent on his own transactions is under which of the following jurisdictions?

    a. State Board of Equalization
    b. DRE
    c. Corporations Commissioner
    d. Escrow Commissioner

107. Which of the following would express the greatest ownership in real property?

    a. Ownership, security interest, and right of possession
    b. Freehold, estate at will
    c. Fee simple absolute
    d. Less-than-freehold estate, lease

108. Buyer obtained an $80,000 loan at 10% interest to finance the purchase of a residence. He paid a one point loan origination fee to obtain the loan. After 10 years, his loan balance was $72,750.42, having made 120 monthly $702.06 payments. He sold the home for cash, and had to pay a 2% prepayment penalty on the loan balance. Over the term of this loan, how much (approximately) did the lender make?

    a. $2,255
    b. $76,998
    c. $79,253
    d. $80,000

EXAM 3

109. Owner sells a property for $130,000 which has a first loan of $80,000 and a 2nd loan of $10,000 outstanding at close of escrow. The buyer desires to pay cash ($50,000) and take over the first loan. In what order will the documents be recorded to accomplish this sale?

    a. Reconveyance deed and 2nd trust deed
    b. A 2nd trust deed and grant deed
    c. Grant deed and 2nd trust deed
    d. Reconveyance deed and grant deed

110. Consider two homes built by the same builder, at the same time, with the same materials and quality construction, on adjacent lots. Both of the current (original) owners have provided comparable maintenance for their homes. However, the recent appraisals on these two homes indicate that one is worth more than the other. The depreciation experienced by the one of lesser value would most likely be attributed to:

    a. economic.
    b. functional.
    c. physical.
    d. social.

111. An owner of a small appliance store (toasters, mixers, blenders, etc.) needs to borrow money for business reasons. He cannot have his promissory note secured by:

    a. personal guarantee endorsement.
    b. security agreement on furniture and fixtures.
    c. security agreement on inventory held for sale.
    d. assigning accounts receivable.

112. "Adverse possession" best matches:

    a. avulsion.
    b. reversion.
    c. subordination.
    d. prescription.

113. An owner of an apartment building receives a net income of $5,000 per year. If the interest rate on his financing goes up, with no increase in rent, which of the following would be true?

    a. Equity increases
    b. Equity decreases
    c. Equity remains the same
    d. Events listed have nothing to do with equity

114. An investor holds a leasehold interest in a commercial building which has four more years remaining on the term. Current monthly payments are $1,000, with provisions for the payments to go up $100 per month each year. This is known as what type of lease?

    a. Revelation lease
    b. Step-down lease
    c. Indexed lease
    d. Graduated lease

115. In two adjoining townships, the section that is directly south of section 32 is section:

    a. 29
    b. 5
    c. 4
    d. 3

116. Which of the following would be required to have an active real estate broker's license?

    a. Attorney-in-fact for principal
    b. Divorce attorney selling home for divorcing couple
    c. Attorney who solicits real estate business
    d. Attorney-officer of a corporation selling corporate property

117. Which of the following is NOT a lien?

    a. Attachment for default
    b. Charges assessed for improvement (a bond)
    c. Unpaid property taxes
    d. Easement appurtenant

118. Of the following items required to create a valid contract, oral evidence of which one might be acceptable in a court hearing?

    a. Payment schedule
    b. Purchase price
    c. Names and signatures of parties
    d. Adequate description of property

119. A "trend" is defined by appraisers as:

    a. a series of related changes brought about by a chain of causes and effects.
    b. changes brought about by economic and political forces working in the market.
    c. a series of changes at the international level.
    d. observed changes in the appraising process.

120. A cul-de-sac is defined as a(n):

    a. French container.
    b. alley.
    c. "dead-end" street or passage way.
    d. none of the above.

121. An agency agreement can be created by all of the following, except:

    a. estoppel.
    b. expresses contract.
    c. ratification.
    d. subrogation.

EXAM 3

122. Placement of a residence relative to privacy, protection from traffic, exposure to sun, and prevailing winds, refers to:

   a. elevation.
   b. plottage.
   c. orientation.
   d. topography.

123. Duress is most closely associated with:

   a. agency.
   b. unenforceable contracts.
   c. endorsements.
   d. easement.

124. California law regulates where a real estate broker may have his place of business. An example of this would be that a broker may NOT operate an office where _____ manufactured homes are offered for sale unless he has a manufactured home dealer's license.

   a. ten or more
   b. five or more
   c. two or more
   d. one or more

125. Taxes paid on "fixtures" involved in the sale of a business opportunity would be:

   a. franchise tax.
   b. sales tax.
   c. transfer tax.
   d. use tax.

126. A property owner owns a building worth $500,000. The basis for the building is $370,000. The owner borrows $200,000 against the property. What amount of income tax would the owner have to pay on this transaction?

   a. $100,000
   b. $50,000
   c. $60,000
   d. None of the above

127. Upon the sale of a property in a tight money market, with an alienation clause in the existing trust deed on the property, which of the following would most likely occur?

   a. Seller would refinance
   b. Buyer would take "subject to"
   c. Buyer would assume the existing loan
   d. Buyer would refinance

128. The "summation" approach in appraising is the same as:

   a. comparative.
   b. cost.
   c. income.
   d. replacement.

129. A franchise being offered for sale in California need NOT be registered with the Corporations Commissioner providing the franchiser:

a. is a part of a company incorporated out-of-state.
b. has a net worth (consolidated basis) of not more than $1,000,000.
c. has a net worth (consolidated basis) of not more than $5,000,000.
d. is a subsidiary of another state corporation.

130. How many acres are there in the following parcel of land? S½ of the SW¼ of the SW¼ of the SE¼ of the NE¼ of Section 7?

a. 10 acres
b. 40 acres
c. 2.5 acres
d. 1.25 acres

131. For a long-term lease agreement, there are no arrangements for adjusting rents. If the economic rent is less than the contract rent, this would favor the:

a. lessee.
b. lessor.
c. occupant.
d. all of the above.

132. The sudden tearing away or removal of land by action of an adjacent stream is:

a. avulsion.
b. alluvium.
c. accretion.
d. accession.

133. All of the following are grounds for either suspension or revocation of a real estate license, except:

a. licensee fails to pay appropriate fees when due.
b. licensee violates any of the rules and regulations of the DRE for enforcement of California law.
c. licensee conducts himself in a manner which would have warranted denial of license.
d. licensee is negligent or incompetent in performing duties for which a license is required.

134. Broker has property listed for a client at $400,000 with a 10% commission. The owner has rejected several low offers. Broker presents new offer at full price on behalf of Ajax Company—a corporation owned by the broker and his salespeople. No disclosure of the latter relationship was made to the seller. Which of the following statements is true?

a. Broker and salespeople are in trouble with the DRE, with disciplinary action being most probable.
b. Disclosure to seller that buyers were licensees (without further identification) would not be sufficient.
c. The fact that the seller had rejected other offers did not excuse the buyers from full disclosure.
d. All of the above.

EXAM 3

135. Holder of a renewal license, who fails to renew it prior to the expiration of the period for which it was issued, has how long from expiration to renew?

    a. One year
    b. Two years
    c. 18 months
    d. 180 days

136. An "open-ended" loan would most benefit a borrower who:

    a. pays extra principal payments to pay off early.
    b. allows a new buyer to takeover the old loan.
    c. uses this loan to subordinate to another newer loan.
    d. borrows more money.

137. When appraising raw land, the initial step would be to determine:

    a. highest and best use.
    b. replacement cost.
    c. net potential income.
    d. residual value.

138. Fixing up an old apartment building without altering the interior or exterior designs would be an example of:

    a. modernization.
    b. reclamation.
    c. remodeling.
    d. rehabilitation.

139. A summary of all transfers, conveyances, and other facts relied on as evidence of title, showing continuity of ownership, together with any other elements of record which may impair title, is known as a(n):

    a. title insurance policy.
    b. preliminary title report.
    c. title company report.
    d. abstract of title.

140. Which of the following is a written instrument given to pass title to personal property from vendor to vendee?

    a. Inventory
    b. Sales contract
    c. Bill of sale
    d. Binder

141. Generally, the initial step in the appraisal process is to:

    a. define the appraisal problem.
    b. define the "answer" the requester needs from the appraisal.
    c. establish the costs to do the appraisal.
    d. classify the date.

142. The reverting of property to the state, when heirs capable of inheriting are lacking, is the definition of:

 a. novation.
 b. reversion.
 c. escheat.
 d. subordination.

143. An "unearned increment" is an increase in value of property resulting from all the following, except:

 a. decrease in taxes.
 b. improvement of nearby vacant property by others.
 c. over-improvement of subject property.
 d. appreciation due to new highway construction.

144. Which of the following is NOT correct?

 a. Township = 36 sections
 b. Township = 23,040 acres
 c. Township = 6 miles square
 d. Numbering of sections in townships begins in NW corner

145. Which of the following best completes the sentence for a "holder in due course"? One who has taken a note, check or bill of exchange in due course:

 a. before it was overdue.
 b. in good faith and for value.
 c. without knowledge of previous dishonor and without notice of any defect when received.
 d. all of the above.

146. Notice to creditors of bulk transfer must be recorded in the county where:

 a. goods to be transferred are located.
 b. transferee resides.
 c. transferor resides.
 d. sale is to be conducted.

147. Advertising is said to be anything that favorably influences people. Which of the following best depicts advertising?

 a. Advertisement that creates attention, interest, desire, and action
 b. Billboards
 c. Institutional Advertising
 d. Manufacturer promoting new product

148. A real estate salesperson asks another broker (other than his own) for a $1,000 advance against the commission to be paid to him from an escrow on a new sale of one of that broker's own listings. If the other broker pays the advance, he is:

 a. a good friend.
 b. committing conversion.
 c. in violation of law.
 d. within his rights as a broker.

EXAM 3

149. An individual who just purchased an apartment complex for investment is uncertain about depreciation allowances. If the previous owners had been depreciating the building while they owned it, the new owner:

    a. can ignore what the other owner did and establish his own schedule of depreciation.
    b. may use the "sum-of-the-digits" method.
    c. must use the same schedule the former owner used.
    d. can only depreciate the improvements based on the former owner's remaining life estimate.

150. A new homestead to be recorded would be invalidated if:

    a. improvements are destroyed.
    b. owner has a prior recorded homestead on another property, in which he previously resided.
    c. owner moves out of old homestead property.
    d. owner moves of out the state.

Practice Exam 3 Answers

1.   *d.*

2.   *a.*   Regulation "Z" requires that those who "extend credit" must make certain disclosures.

3.   *c.*

4.   *b.*   Annual Interest = $6,000 x 2 = $12,000
Principal Amount = $12,000 ÷ 10% (.10) = $120,000
Appraisal Value = Loan divided by (LTV Ratio) = $120,000 ÷ 75% (.75)
= $160,000

5.   *a.*   A stock cooperative receives one tax bill in the name of the corporation.

6.   *c.*   If this had been a limited partnership by definition, then it too must be in writing.

7.   *b.*   Does NOT create laws, but makes the rules and regulations that have the effect of law.

8.   *c.*   All terms of lease pass with lease, whether mentioned or not.

9.   *b.*   Refers to "cost basis or adjusted cost basis."

10.   *d.*   Requires "principle residence."

11.   *d.*   Freehold = Fee simple; Less than Freehold = Leasehold.

12.   *c.*   On the day just prior to the new tax year, the Collector effects a "book sale" of the property to the State. If not redeemed within 5 years, the on June 30th (end of 5th year following book sale), property is deeded to State. Sale or auction would follow.

13.   *b.*

14.   *c.*   Capital improvements are acceptable adjustments to basis.

15.   *d.*

16.   *d.*

17.   *c.*   Prorate is to divide, assess proportionately.

18.   *a.*   Seller has no option. By accepting the $100 payment, he entered into a binding agreement. Only the buyer has the privilege of deciding "to buy, or not to buy." That is what the $100 option money paid for.

19.   *a.*   Does NOT apply to ALL loans, i.e., construction loans to developers or builders.

20.   *b.*   The "key" word is the "primary" activity. FNMA can now deal with conventional loans, but still heavily works with VA and FHA loans.

EXAM 3

21. **b.** The father is liable on (hard money) first loan; purchasers are not, for they bought "subject to" the loan. The 2nd loan is a purchase money loan, and no deficiency judgment is attainable.

22. **d.**

23. **b.** Residence profit is capital gains, and is taxed as ordinary income. Could have deferred tax liability had he purchased another residence within 2 years of the last sale.

24. **d.** A developer uses the declaration of restrictions to create deed restrictions.

25. **a.** There is only a corporate broker license, but major stock holders can buy or sell corporate real property.

26. **b.**

27. **c.** Protects the borrower.

28. **c.** Annual premium = $100,000 x (0.40) = $400.00; 3 year premium = $400 x 2.5 = $1,000; Monthly impound payment = $1,000 ÷ 36 = $27.78.

29. **d.** FHA loans involve MPRs (minimum property requirements), NOT maximum building standards.

30. **c.** Original purchase price = $9,900 x 2 = $19,800
Sale price of lots = $8,500 x 3 = $25,500
Profit on sale = $25,500 - 19,800 = $5,700
Yield = $5,700 ÷ $19,800 x (100) = 28.79%

31. **a.** A broker who buys and sells real property as inventory may be considered a dealer by the IRS and pays ordinary income taxes on any profit or loss.

32. **c.**

33. **d.** CRV is a "certificate of reasonable value," a VA appraisal.

34. **d.** Generally, "public" assistance means "government" assistance.

35. **b.** 2" x 12" x (24 x 12) = 2 x 12 x 288 ÷ 144 = 48.

36. **c.** Deed must be delivered to be effective. It is logical the grantor intended delivery if he signed and had it acknowledged by a notary public.

37. **d.** Remembering that each section = 640 acres; (1) each quarter of that would equal 160 acres; (2) ½ a quarter = 80 acres; ¼ a quarter = 40 acres. Then: (Section 13) NW¼ of the SE¼ = 40 acres; W½ of the NE¼ = 80 acres; NE¼ of the NW¼ = 40 acres. (Section 14) SE¼ of the SW¼ = 40 acres; SW¼ of the SE¼ = 40 acres. Total Acres = 240.

38. **d.** Orientation is planning the most advantageous place on a parcel of land for an improvement to be located.

39. *b.*   A licensee must refuse to take a listing that discriminates.

40. *c.*   Must either grant title in the identical name originally taken, or refer to such former name. For example: Where a single woman received title as Mary Smith, and later marries, she should grant as "Mary Smith Jones, formerly Mary Smith."

41. *c.*   When agent advertises customer's home, but does not reveal the ad was placed by a licensee. Be safe, say, "Agent, 345-6789" or name the company.

42. *a.*   Cal Vet loans are "land contracts" with the state holding title.

43. *b.*

44. *d.*   Cannot declare loss on personal residence.

45. *b.*   Land value + Improvement value = Total Value Tax = Total Value x Tax Rate.

46. *c.*

47. *c.*   Upon sale of five (5) units or more, to same buyer, the subdivider and new purchaser must report this change to the Commissioner.

48. *b.*   Sale price divided by monthly income = $350,000 ÷ 2,500 (Monthly Gross Multiplier) = 140.

49. *c.*   Broker must exercise reasonable supervision over salesperson, and is required to sign all contracts within 5 days. Broker should have known that salesperson did not give proper disclosures.

50. *b.*   Generally, an open listing pays only to the salesperson who sells.

51. *d.*   The only thing the buyer cannot do is finance above the CVR.

52. *c.*   Monthly (P+I) = $370,300 ÷ (30 x 12) = $1,028.61
Initial month interest = $100,000 x 12% ÷ 12 = $1,000
Therefore, initial month principal amount = $1,028.61- $1,000 = $28.61.

53. *d.*   All define constructive eviction.

54. *d.*   A "freehold" estate is of indeterminable duration—fee simple or life estate. Therefore, "less-than-freehold" would be of determinable time or duration—a lease.

55. *d.*   At default, this would allow lender foreclosing on property to collect rents from tenant, and apply this money towards debts of borrower.

56. *d.*   Commissioner's office can "issue public reports" that might be favorable, but cannot make any recommendation to purchase.

57. *d.*   Referred to as "trading on equities."

EXAM 3

58. *b.*   Annual gross income = $2,700 x 12 = $32,400
Net annual income = $32,400 - 8,200 = $24,200
Value = Income divided by "cap" rate =
24,200 ÷ 11% (.11) = $220,000 (Total Value)
Total Value - Bldg. Value = Value of the Lot =
$220,000 - $170,000 = $50,000

59. *b.*   The word "delinquent" is NOT required by law; just pay the taxes for 5 years.

60. *c.*   Personal property, until (1) placed on foundation (with permit), (2) certificate of occupancy is issued, and (3) proper documents filed reflecting unit has been fixed to foundation.

61. *d.*   Others are just "ideas" of what price should be. The final sale sets the record straight.

62. *d.*   Is a writ or court order restraining named parties from doing an act which is deeded inequitable or unjust in the regards to the rights of other parties in the suit or proceedings.

63. *d.*   Although it is true that those homes for which the escrow has been closed provide "what the buyer will pay," the other data is of great value in establishing the ranges of value within which the subject property should fall.

64. *b.*

65. *d.*   All answers describe a real property sales contract.

66. *d.*   The seller is referred to as the "client."

67. *c.*   A promise to do, or not to do a specified thing. If breached, it may result in "dollar damages" only.

68. *a.*   The corporation did NOT die with the officers, it lives on.

69. *a.* $217,500 ÷ 145% (1.45) = $150,000 original price
Acreage: N½ of the NW¼ of the SE¼ = 20 acres
W½ of the NE¼ = 80 acres
Therefore, price per acre = $150,000 ÷ 100 = $1,500.

70. *d.*   Department of building and safety issues the final approval (completion documents) and the assessor's office receives those records upon completion.

71. *d.*   The more restrictive of conflicting zoning restrictions would prevail.

72. *d.*

73. *d.*   On the March 1st preceding the tax year, the lien is placed on the property. December and April dates above are dates taxes become delinquent for their respective periods, and July 1st is the beginning of the tax year.

74. **d.** A syndication participant would be able to convert property interests into cash, without having to sell the property.

75. **d.** The five essential elements of a valid deed are: (1) In writing; (2) Parties properly described; (3) Adequate property description; (4) Operative words (granting); (5) Signed by Grantor.

76. **d.** VA requires the veteran purchaser must "move into" the property being purchased as personal residence. The purchase of "units" (4 maximum) is allowed, if the veteran will be residing in one of the units.

77. **d.** Fiduciary relationship involves "trust and confidence." This is NOT required between trustor (borrower) and beneficiary (lender).

78. **c.** This is the replacement cost method (cost approach).

79. **b.** Theory: most people with mutual interest and desires usually group together in a given area (forming a neighborhood), creating market influences.

80. **d.** Law applies to: (1) owner-occupied, publicly assisted (gov't. financing program) single family dwellings; (2) Publicly assisted apartment units (3 or more); (3) Privately financed apartments (5 or more); and (4) Public housing projects.

81 **c.**

82. **b.**

83. **a.** For income tax purposes, the amount of rent paid in advance must be included in the landlord's income for that year.

84. **d.** This provision will assure the buyers that their money is safe, until such time the developer can get a release on the parcel of land involved with their purchase. Otherwise, without such "partial" release, no transfer of title could occur on various purchases until the encumbrance on the entire parcel developed was paid in full.

85. **d.** Alteration (unilaterally) of the deed in escrow voided that deed. Therefore, no transfer to Bob of lot "B," and subsequently, none to Chuck, for Bob did not have title to that lot. Abe's transfer to Daren was valid. Title insurance involvement in these transactions would have saved a lot of trouble and headaches.

86. **d.** A trust deed may contain any/all of these clauses, but none are required.

87. **b.** Gross Income = $88,400 ÷ 68% (.68) = $130,000
Net Income = $130,000 - 88,400 = $41,600
Property Value = Income divided by "cap" rate = $41,600 ÷ (.10) = $416,000

88. **b.** Expressed means in writing, and most agency agreements are created through written contract.

EXAM 3

89. *c.*   A construction loan, by definition, is an interim loan, which would be replaced after the construction is complete with some form of "takeout" loan, which would thereafter finance the property for the new purchasers.

90. *b.*   Seller owes buyer for months July, August, and September.

91. *c.*   Effective age reflects the condition of the building.

92. *a.*   Careful with this one. State exam may NOT use the word "exact" in this statement, but it considers the fact that, with the curvature of earth, all townships cannot be exactly equal in size. For all practical purposes, each is the same size.

93. *c.*   No owner, whether large loan or no loan, benefits when the value of the home goes down.

94. *d.*   Can be either of the three answers, therefore "d" is the most correct answer.

95. *b.*
Areas: SW¼ of SW¼ of NE¼	=	10 acres
NW¼ of NW¼ of SE¼	=	10 acres
N½ of SW¼ of NW¼ of SE¼	=	5 acres
Total Area	=	25 acres

Cost per acre = $100,000 ÷ 25 acres = $4,000 per acre.

96. *a.*   Fertility relates to farming.

97. *c.*   The estate held by the one to whom a property will "revert" to upon the happening of a certain thing...i.e., after the person on whom a life estate is based dies, the property rights revert to the holder of the "estate in Reversion."

98. *b.*   Death does NOT terminate, finalize, or release the defendant.

99. *c.*

100. *c.*

101. *c.*   A takeout loan is a long-term loan.

102. *c.*   The trust deed is protection for the lender.

103. *c.*   Interest is income; depreciation is an allowed "paper" expense, written off against income, allowing recapture of the investment.

104. *a.*

105. *d.*   By process of elimination, a, b, and d are all correct statements. Therefore "d" must be the answer. Likewise, there are no requirements that a prospective licensee live in the state of California in order to apply for the license.

106. *b.* If the broker had formed a legally incorporated escrow company, its activities would fall under the Corporations Commissioner. Since the broker is acting under his real estate license, his escrow activities are under the jurisdiction of the Real Estate Commissioner's office, which is the "DRE"—Department of Real Estate.

107. *c.* Greatest interest available, which is of indefinite duration, and without qualifications or limitations. Can be disposed of during owner's life, or after death.

108. *c.*

Origination fee (1% of new loan) = $80,000 x (.01)	=	$800.00
Total (P+I) payments = $702.06 x (120)	=	$84,246.87
Principal payment = $80,000 - 72,750.42	=	$7,249.58
Net Interest Payments (120 months)	=	$76,997.29
Prepayment on payoff = 2% x ($72,750.42)	=	$1,455.01
Total the lender made over the 10 yrs. on loan	=	$79,252.30

109. *d.* Initially, the old 2nd must be cleared (reconveyance deed); then the transfer of title (grant deed) must be accomplished.

110. *b.* Somehow, functionally, these homes must be different, i.e. floor plan, etc., which would explain the difference in value.

111. *c.* Uniform Commercial Code (UCC) prohibits owner using "stock in trade" for security for a loan.

112. *d.*

113. *b.* If the rent remains the same and interest costs go up, net income is reduced. With lower income, for a given "capitalization rate," the value of the investment will be less. Therefore, the equity will be less.

114. *d.* Provides for a flat rate payment, with step-changes (up/down) at specified times.

115. *b.*

116. *c.* Attorneys do NOT need to be licensed to perform the "law" duties unless they specifically solicit for the real estate business. The corporate officer is acting for the corporation, selling property that belongs to the company (as long as he does not receive special compensation for the selling act).

117. *d.* Easements are NOT liens; liens are used to collect debts or obligations.

118. *d.* On occasions, legal descriptions would be necessary. However, there are numerous situations where only "adequate" description is needed to properly take care of the matter at hand.

119. *a.*

120. *c.* A cul-de-sac lot faces the turnaround portion of a dead-end street.

EXAM 3

121. *d.*   Subrogation: replacing one person with another in regard to a legal right or obligation...i.e., insured and insurance company, whereby after paying claimant, the insurance company can take the place of the insured and go after the third party who caused the damage to the insured.

122. *c.*

123. *b.*   Duress is where one party is forced to do something he would not otherwise do. That would result in a voidable contract.

124. *c.*   Two or more manufactured homes for sale on a lot requires a manufactured home dealer's license.

125. *b.*   For the sale of such property, there would be sales taxes due.

126. *d.*   No tax liability created for borrowing money.

127. *d.*   Alienation clause would, upon transfer of title, require the old loan to become fully due and payable immediately. This would require refinancing.

128. *b.*

129. *b.*

130. *d.*   Working backward across this description...
SW½ of the SW¼ of the SW¼ of the SE¼ of the NE¼
1.25 acres   2.5 ac.   10 ac.   40 ac.   160 ac.

131. *a.*   Economic rent is what the property should rent for, and since it is lower than the contract rent, the lessor is losing – the lessee is happy.

132. *a.*   **Alluvium** - The gradual increase of earth on shore or bank resulting from action of water. **Accretion** - Accession by natural forces, i.e. Alluvium. **Accession** - Addition to property through efforts of man or by natural forces.

133. *a.*   Failure to pay on time is NOT grounds for suspension or revocation of license.

134. *d.*

135. *b.*   After 2 years, all license rights lapse, and for the person to be licensed, he or she must meet the same requirements as the original license applicant—retesting.

136. *d.*   The open-ended loan is one whereby the borrower is allowed to borrow additional money, applying it to the old amount—not creating a new loan with its extra costs.

137. *a.*   All others relate to improvements.

138. *d.*   The restoration of property to satisfactory conditions, without drastically changing the plan, form, or style of architecture.

139. *d.*

140. *c.*   *A bill of sale is used to pass personal property.*

141. *a.*   *Set the appraisal objectives.*

142. *c.*   **Novation** *– substitution of new for old by mutual consent.* **Subordination** *– allowing a senior lien to become junior to another.* **Reversion** *– future rights or interests, created by deed.*

143. *c.*   *Due to operation of social or economic forces rather than to personal efforts, intelligence, or initiative of owner.*

144. *d.*   *Begins at NE corner.*

145. *d.*   *All are required for a holder in due course.*

146. *a.*   *Where the goods (business) are located.*

147. *a.*   *Does everything it needs to do to get action.*

148. *c.*   *No broker can pay anything to another broker's salesperson.*

149. *a.*   *New owner now starts new depreciation schedule, regardless of what previous owner had, or had not done.*

150. *b.*   *Only one "homestead" at a time is allowed. Just moving out of the other property on which he had the old homestead does not terminate the old homestead.*

EXAM 3

 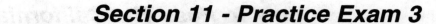

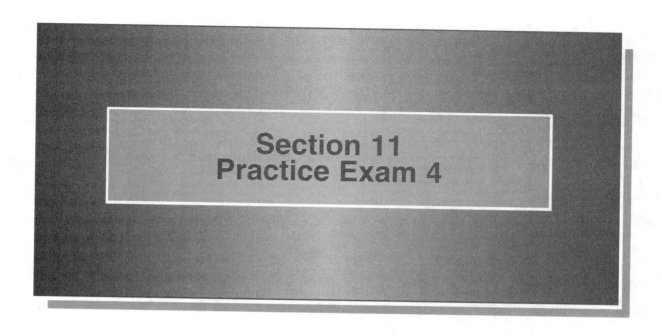

Section 11
Practice Exam 4

NOTE: For better self-testing, the answers to this exam have been moved to the end of the exam.

1. If the "demand" for homes goes up and the "supply":

    a. diminishes, the values will decrease.
    b. remains the same, the values go down.
    c. remains the same, the values will increase.
    d. goes up, the values will go up.

2. When taking a listing, what is the most important question to ask?

    a. Will you help finance the sale?
    b. What is your asking price?
    c. Why are you selling?
    d. What are your existing loans?

3. Which of the following would come first?

    a. Hereditament
    b. Writ of attachment
    c. Writ of Execution
    d. Judgment

4. With which of the following would appraisers least likely use the "gross income" appraisal technique?

    a. Residential apartments
    b. Industrial
    c. Commercial
    d. Public buildings

5. If a broker decided to add to his real estate business and handle the sale of trust deeds, what other kind of license would he have to get?

    a. Loan broker's license
    b. Securities dealer's license
    c. Business opportunity license
    d. None of the above

6. Which of the following would most likely appear in an appraiser's definition of "highest and best use"?

    a. Contract rent
    b. Ground rent
    c. Economic rent
    d. Net return

7. Which of the following types of depreciation would be difficult to eliminate?

    a. Economic obsolescence
    b. Functional obsolescence
    c. Physical depreciation
    d. Physical deterioration

8. The agency of a real estate broker is created by:

    a. estoppel.
    b. expressed contract.
    c. implied contract.
    d. ratification.

9. In California, the salesperson's commission is paid by the:

    a. seller.
    b. buyer.
    c. escrow holder.
    d. broker.

10. A real estate broker who negotiated a real property loan must record the trust deed:

    a. within 10 days of release of funds, provided lender authorizes prior release.
    b. before any funds are released.
    c. either a or b.
    d. none of the above.

11. The primary source of funds for junior loans is:

    a. the FHA.
    b. institutional lenders.
    c. noninstitutional lenders.
    d. private lenders.

12. A buyer purchasing a home financed by a new FHA loan should do all of the following, except:

    a. find a property that will meet FHA requirements.
    b. find a seller willing to sell under FHA terms.
    c. find a lender who makes FHA loans.
    d. contact FHA for an appraisal.

13. An auctioneer who sells a business on which a Notice of Sale was properly recorded and published:

    a. is personally liable for any losses to seller's creditors.
    b. must have a "Business Opportunity" license.
    c. must have a "Securities Dealer" license.
    d. only needs a Real Estate Broker's license.

14. Under a lease agreement, who holds the leasehold estate?

    a. Beneficiary
    b. Lessee
    c. Lessor
    d. None of the above

15. Which of the following types of financing generally does NOT require any down payment?

    a. Cal-Vet
    b. Conventional
    c. FHA
    d. VA

16. Regarding Conditions and Covenants, which are restrictions imposed upon grantees limiting property use, the enforcement of "conditions" would be considered:

    a. the same as for covenants.
    b. more stringent than for covenants.
    c. less stringent than for covenants.
    d. none of the above.

17. Sheet metal used to protect a building from water seepage is called:

    a. furring.
    b. flashing.
    c. footing.
    d. facade.

18. A licensed real estate broker desires to work as a salesperson. She should:

    a. apply to take salesperson's examination.
    b. inactivate broker license and apply for salesperson's license.
    c. apply for salesperson's license.
    d. enter into agreement (written) with employing broker and work as a salesperson.

EXAM 4

19. Characteristics of a particular lender are: prefers short-term loans; prefers interim loans; buyer costs are higher than other lenders; past relationships with borrowers are important. What kind of lender is this?

    a. Savings bank
    b. Insurance company
    c. Private individual
    d. Bank

20. A salesperson, working with buyers having limited cash available for down payment, finds a property listed at $96,000, cash to new loan. The buyers want the home. However, the maximum loan available is for 80% of value, requiring 20% cash investment. The buyers say that if the sellers would take back a 2nd note, maybe they could buy it. Sellers do not want to take back a note, per listing information. The salesperson should:

    a. not write any offer, since it will not be what sellers want.
    b. call the sellers to discuss their taking back a 2nd note.
    c. write the offer the buyers want to make and present it to the sellers.
    d. write an offer for cash to a new loan, and hope the buyers are lucky and obtain a cooperative lender.

21. Which of the following would NOT be considered one of the major forces influencing value?

    a. Building restrictions
    b. Economic adjustments
    c. Government regulations
    d. None of the above

22. For an exclusive listing, negotiations for a buyer should be conducted through the:

    a. seller.
    b. trustee.
    c. listing broker.
    d. none of the above.

23. The initial step in the appraisal process is to:

    a. collect the fee.
    b. correlate the data.
    c. define the problem.
    d. determine the fee.

24. Functional utility in a building is most dependent upon:

    a. conditions of heating-cooling systems.
    b. desires of occupants.
    c. floor plan and equipment.
    d. area zoning.

25. First time buyers are concerned as to how the lenders qualify prospective buyers regarding income. Lenders:

    a. look at the income of only the husband, even if the wife also works.
    b. look at husband's and half of the wife's income.
    c. look at half of husband's income and half of wife's income.
    d. look at all income from both husband and wife, including incomes other than from wages and salaries.

26. According to California law, real property securities include all of the following, except:

    a. any out-of-state subdivision offered for sale in California.
    b. promotional notes secured by any part of subdivision offered for sale in California.
    c. guaranteed notes or sales contracts.
    d. any transaction including real property as security for a loan.

27. An appraiser must be careful to distinguish the fundamental purpose of the appraisal from which of the following?

    a. Appraisal procedures to be used.
    b. Function for which the estimate of value is required.
    c. Techniques he will use to determine his opinion of value.
    d. All of the above.

28. If an out-of-state resident were to ask when the first installment of the county taxes becomes due, you should answer:

    a. December 10.
    b. November 1.
    c. March 1.
    d. July 1.

29. In a situation whereby a deposit with an offer to purchase was in the form of a promissory note instead of cash or check, which of the following is NOT true?

    a. The contract is just as binding at the time of acceptance by both parties as if it there were a cash deposit.
    b. Agent is required by law to make seller aware that he has received a nonnegotiable promissory note deposit, in lieu of cash or check.
    c. Failure of buyer to redeem note as required by purchase agreement is a violation of California real estate law.
    d. None of the above.

30. In real estate matters, the word "impound" most often means:

    a. attachment.
    b. judgment.
    c. principal and interest account with lender.
    d. reserve account for taxes and insurance with lender.

EXAM 4

31. Personal assets of principals of which of the following are available to creditors for satisfaction?

    a. Corporation
    b. Limited Partnership
    c. Partnership
    d. None of the above

32. Relative to requirements for establishing "planning commissions," they:

    a. may be established in cities, must be established in counties.
    b. must be in cities, may be in counties.
    c. must consist of members with experience in appraisal of real estate.
    d. both cites and counties must appropriate funds for establishing planning commissions.

33. Under the Manufactured Home Act, which of the following would NOT be grounds for disciplinary action?

    a. Agent fails to withdraw advertising on unit within 48 hrs. after receipt of notice of its sale.
    b. Agent advertises new manufactured home as used, since he can only work with units that have been registered with DRE for at least one year.
    c. Agent represents that the manufactured home is capable of being operated as a vehicle on California roads, if the unit does not meet all applicable equipment requirements for such operation.
    d. None of the above.

34. Who is responsible for properly working sewer systems in a community?

    a. Real Estate Commissioner
    b. Homeowner
    c. Subdivider
    d. Health officer

35. Which of the following represent the four unities of market value?

    a. Time, title, interest, possession
    b. Possession, encumber, will, sell
    c. Demand, utility, scarcity, transferability
    d. Location, demand, financing, interest

36. A land developer should initially:

    a. acquire the land.
    b. do a cost analysis.
    c. do a market analysis.
    d. determine the development costs.

37. At the time of his death, Broker "A," a licensed real estate broker, had 18 listings in his possession. He left his entire estate to a son, "B," who also is a licensed real estate broker. If "B" desires to collect any commissions on the sales of any of the 18 listings, he must:

    a. take "quiet title" court action to authorize collection.
    b. notify each owner that the commissions would be payable to him in lieu of his father.
    c. do nothing.
    d. renegotiate new listing contracts with each of the 18 owners.

38. Which of the following lenders tends to give the longest term on uninsured loans?

    a. Banks
    b. Insurance companies
    c. Private individuals
    d. Savings banks

39. A cattle rancher purchased the following two parcels of land for grazing pasture. How many feet of wire will be required to enclose the entire pasture? Descriptions: E½ of the SE¼ of the SE¼ of the NW¼ and the W½ of the SW¼ of the SW¼ of the NE¼ of Section 34.

    a. 4,620'
    b. 3,300'
    c. 2,640'
    d. 1,980'

40. A seller sold a property taking back a note and trust deed for $20,000 as a part of the purchase price. He later desired to purchase a lot on which he could build a home and needed $9,000 to buy the lot. He borrowed the money from the bank, giving the $20,000 note and T.D. as security, which was considered to be a:

    a. chattel mortgage.
    b. holding agreement.
    c. pledge.
    d. purchase money loan.

41. A borrower negotiates a $4,500 loan secured by a 2nd trust deed through a broker. The loan was to be for a term of 2 years. What is the maximum commission the broker can charge for services?

    a. $450
    b. $225
    c. $675
    d. None of the above

42. If a deposit receipt does NOT contain a legal description of the property to be purchased, it would be:

    a. illegal.
    b. unenforceable.
    c. voidable.
    d. none of the above.

43. A broker agrees to manage a client's investment portfolio ($85,000) of 1st trust deeds. If broker guarantees a return of 11% on the investments, he:

    a. must provide a bond.
    b. must obtain a loan broker's license.
    c. would be violating "Regulation Z."
    d. would be violating usury laws.

EXAM 4

44. A married woman purchased a business with separate funds, and subsequently decided to obtain a liquor license. She:

　　a. must apply to the Department of Alcoholic Beverage Control.
　　b. must apply to the Franchise Tax Board.
　　c. must apply, with her husband, to the Board of Equalization.
　　d. must apply, with her husband, to the Alcoholic Beverage Control Department.

45. For which of the following could a deduction for income tax purposes be taken when unimproved land is held for investment?

　　a. Depreciation
　　b. Loss on the sale of land
　　c. Short-term capital gains
　　d. None of the above

46. Which of the following can make withdrawals from the broker's trust account?

　　a. Sales associates employed by broker
　　b. Corporate officers of licensed real estate corporation
　　c. Bonded unlicensed employees of broker
　　d. All of the above

47. California State sales tax applies to:

　　a. food products.
　　b. real property.
　　c. tangible property.
　　d. all of the above.

48. All contracts to be valid must contain the following elements or characteristics, except:

　　a. competent parties.
　　b. consideration.
　　c. legal object.
　　d. must be in writing.

49. The series of parallel beams to which floorboards and ceiling laths are nailed, which are supported by large beams, girders, and bearing walls, are called:

　　a. braces.
　　b. plates.
　　c. joists.
　　d. guides.

50. A waiver is defined as a:

　　a. release from an attachment.
　　b. release from an injunction.
　　c. bilateral act that voluntarily relinquishes a known right or privilege.
　　d. all of above.

51. Of the following types of appraisal reports, which would be the most detailed?

   a. Certificate
   b. Form
   c. Letter
   d. Narrative

52. A property was leased to a lessee for a two-year period, with monthly lease payments to be $800. The lessor collected the first and last month payments. This agreement would most likely NOT include which of the following statements?

   a. Escalator clause
   b. Compliance with local laws
   c. Condemnation provisions
   d. Third-party liability clause

53. Considering the "Interstate Land Sales Full Disclosure Act," which of the following is NOT true?

   a. Controls subdivisions of 25 (or more) lots, unimproved at the time of sale.
   b. Developer must register subdivision with Office of Inter-Land Sales Registration (OILSR), and provide copy of "property report" to purchaser or lessee.
   c. Any contract to purchase or lease may be revoked by purchaser or lessee within 7 days of signing the contract.
   d. Violations are punishable by fines up to $50, imprisonment of up to 5 weeks, or both.

54. A property valued at $550,000 has a capitalization rate of 10%. The net income is $55,000. If the "cap rate" increased to 11%, what would be the adjusted value of the property?

   a. $495,000
   b. $500,000
   c. $480,000
   d. $450,000

55. A buyer recently purchased a property for $150,000. If the cost to sell the property would be 9% of sale price, how much must the property appreciate in value in order for the owner to sell and get his $150,000 out of the sale?

   a. $13,500
   b. $14,835
   c. 9%
   d. 109%

56. Which of the following would take the position of "senior" lien?

   a. Assessment bond
   b. First trust deed
   c. Homestead
   d. The one above which was first recorded

EXAM 4

57. Mr. and Mrs. "Z" own property in joint tenancy. The "Zs" each have a son by a previous marriage. Mrs. "Z" dies and leaves by will 2/3 of her property to her son and the other 1/3 to Mr. "Z's" son. The guys:

   a. hold title as tenants in common.
   b. hold title as joint tenants, with right of survivorship.
   c. may select to hold title in community property.
   d. none of the above.

58. When purchasing a "business opportunity" and using personal property acquired to secure a loan, which of the following is necessary to "perfect" the transaction?

   a. The contract developed to facilitate the sale.
   b. Filing of the security agreement.
   c. Filing of the financing statement.
   d. Recording the original contract.

59. Which of the following would NOT be constructive eviction of a tenant (lessee) by a landlord?

   a. During lease, landlord attempts to lease property to others.
   b. Landlord ousts tenants or allows third party to oust tenants.
   c. Landlord makes extensive, unwarranted alterations to the property.
   d. Landlord fails to repair excessive wear and tear to property caused by tenant's neglect.

60. A clothing store owner could NOT use which of the following as security for a loan?

   a. Accounts receivable
   b. Fixtures
   c. Personal note
   d. Stock

61. In the "income" approach to value, the recapture of capital invested in the improvements is provided for by:

   a. accruals for depreciation.
   b. cost to cure.
   c. observed conditions.
   d. observed depreciation.

62. Two single persons desire to take and hold title to property, with the ability to later will their portions to whomever they desire. They should take title as:

   a. joint tenants.
   b. tenants in common.
   c. community property.
   d. severalty.

63. Condominium ownership is an undivided interest in common areas with all other project owners, plus separate interest in the "air space" of a particular unit. Air space is:

   a. space within prescribed boundaries indicated by legal description of project.
   b. space between outer boundaries of buildings.
   c. space between painted exterior walls (inner surfaces) of prescribed unit.
   d. all of the above.

64. A buyer purchased a home for $85,000, putting $8,000 cash down, taking over a $75,000 first loan, and assuming the liability for paying a $2,000 outstanding sewer bond. This assessment is:

    a. part of the purchase price.
    b. a personal debt assumed by buyer for improvements on personal property.
    c. prepaid to offset future taxes.
    d. none of the above.

65. A broker has received a $5,000 personal check as deposit on an offer. Since the sellers are NOT home, broker deposits the buyer's check into his broker trust account. Buyer thereafter rescinds offer and demands return of deposit. Broker should:

    a. return the buyer's check.
    b. return the buyer's deposit in the form of a check drawn against the broker's trust account.
    c. wait until the buyer's check clears the bank, then return the deposit in the form of a check drawn against broker's trust account.
    d. none of the above.

66. A buyer purchased a residence for $225,000, with 12% down, and the seller is taking back a note and T.D. for the balance, payable at 12% per annum. Monthly payments were to be $520 principal plus interest. Taxes are $2,700 per year and hazard insurance is $804 per year. What will be the buyer's 1st monthly payment plus monthly amounts for impound account for taxes and insurance?

    a. $2,972
    b. $2,792
    c. $2,279
    d. $2,927

67. Buyer sells his residence for $200,000. He may defer capital gains realized if he purchases another residence of equal or greater value within how many months?

    a. 6
    b. 12
    c. 18
    d. 24

68. According to California law, legal closing occurs at which of the following times?

    a. When broker gets all required signatures and acceptance is acknowledged.
    b. When funds for loan are placed in escrow.
    c. When escrow disburses money (checks).
    d. When all instruments necessary to transfer title have been executed and recorded.

69. Which of the following is NOT a lien?

    a. Encumbrance
    b. Homestead
    c. Zoning
    d. All of the above

EXAM 4

70. "Gross multiplier" is used to determine value of certain types of income properties. It is determined by:

    a. dividing the gross rental income by the appraised value.
    b. multiplying the market price by the capitalization rate.
    c. dividing the verified sales price by the gross monthly rental.
    d. multiplying the gross monthly rental by a reasonable cap rate.

71. Three general partners borrowed money and agreed to be liable for the repayment, either individually or collectively. They signed the security instrument:

    a. jointly.
    b. singularly.
    c. jointly and collectively.
    d. jointly and severally.

72. For a straight-line schedule of depreciation:

    a. earlier years receive more weight.
    b. later years receive more weight.
    c. each year receives equal weight.
    d. none of the above.

73. In the development of a subdivision of single-family homes, which of the following would be the least economical?

    a. Cul-de-sacs
    b. Long blocks
    c. Right angle (90%) intersections into major streets
    d. Short blocks

74. For a "blanket encumbrance," the typical release clause requires the debtor to pay more to the lender than each released property is worth because:

    a. better lots are sold first.
    b. compensates for unsold lots.
    c. lender desires to increase security on overall loan.
    d. all of the above.

75. In contracting, if one of the parties enters the agreement under duress, the contract would be:

    a. valid.
    b. voidable.
    c. void.
    d. Illegal.

76. An owner acquires title to additional land on his river-front property when the river shifts its course. This is acquiring by:

    a. acclamation.
    b. accession.
    c. abstraction.
    d. alienation.

77. Under which of the following types of financing is a buyer required to purchase term life insurance?

    a. Cal-Vet
    b. Conventional
    c. FHA
    d. VA

78. In residential real estate lending, when lenders "soften" their requirements to allow less than qualified buyers to "qualify,":

    a. overall financing costs tend to remain the same.
    b. overall financing costs tend to decrease.
    c. overall financing costs tend to increase.
    d. overall financing costs are not affected.

79. All of the following instruments are used to convey an interest in real property, except:

    a. agreement of sale.
    b. bill of sale.
    c. deed.
    d. lease.

80. Which of the following is NOT related to a "will"?

    a. Bequeath
    b. Bequest
    c. Devise
    d. None of the above

81. According to R.E.S.P.A., on applicable loans, a lender is required to furnish a copy of a *Special Information Booklet* (prescribed by Housing and Urban Development) together with a "Good Faith Estimate" of closing costs to every person from whom it receives (or for whom it prepares) a written application for a federally related loan, within:

    a. 3 days.
    b. 12 days.
    c. 15 days.
    d. 21 days.

82. Which of the following would NOT be eligible for filing a mechanic's lien?

    a. Architect
    b. Handyman, if more than 75 days has elapsed since recording of notice of completion
    c. Subcontractor, if a notice of completion has been recorded within the past 29 days
    d. None of the above

83. Which of the following is NOT necessary in the formation of a contract?

    a. Acceptance
    b. Consideration
    c. Offer
    d. Performance

84. Which of the following would NOT be included in an "eminent domain" situation?

    a. Condemnation proceedings
    b. Fair consideration
    c. For public good
    d. Zoning regulations

85. The Uniform Commercial Code revised, combined, and replaced many statutes and laws, including:

    a. Uniform Conditional Sales Act.
    b. Uniform Negotiable Instruments Law.
    c. neither of the above.
    d. both a and b.

86. Which of the following best describes a "land project"?

    a. A subdivision of land located in a sparsely populated area, having less than 1,500 registered voters.
    b. Division of a parcel into 5 lots in an urban area.
    c. Division of land into 50 or more parcels, offered for sale for residential purposes, located in an area containing less than 1,500 registered voters within the subdivision, or within 2 miles of the subdivision.
    d. A condominium project or community apartment projects.

87. Which of the following types of properties would result in the lowest loan-to-value ratio?

    a. Agricultural
    b. Commercial
    c. Industrial
    d. Residential

88. According to California real estate law, a broker can:

    a. act for one or both parties in a transaction.
    b. collect commissions from one or both parties in a transaction.
    c. have an option in a sale, as long as she makes it known to all that she is a principal.
    d. all of the above.

89. Which of the following is incorrect with respect to a "metes and bounds" description?

    a. A neighbor's property line can be used as a boundary.
    b. "Metes" means boundaries, and "Bounds" means measurements.
    c. One can use lines or a specific number of feet from one point to another.
    d. One can use a tree or a permanent fence as a boundary.

90. In contracting, if one of the parties makes a mistake based on his own negligence, the contract would be:

    a. valid.
    b. voidable.
    c. void.
    d. illegal.

91. The statute of frauds is state law, based on old English law, requiring certain contracts to be:

    a. prepared by attorneys.
    b. a typed or printed form.
    c. in writing and signed in order to be enforceable at law.
    d. approved by the Real Estate Commissioner.

92. An investor owns two 12-unit apartment buildings. "A" rents for $500 per unit, per month, with no vacancies; "B" rents for $550 per unit, per month, with a 10% vacancy factor. Which statement is correct?

    a. "A" should raise rents to make as much as "B."
    b. "B" is the more profitable of the two buildings.
    c. "B" rents might be lowered slightly, reducing vacancy factors, and maybe becoming as much or more profitable as "A."
    d. None of the above.

93. Escrow operations and regulations are under the:

    a. DRE.
    b. Secretary of State.
    c. HUD.
    d. Corporations Commissioner.

94. Per the R.E.S.P.A., a federal law, the definition of "federally related institution" allows which of the following to be included?

    a. FHA, Title II guaranteed loans.
    b. Only federal savings banks.
    c. VA insured loans.
    d. Any loan made by an institution whose funds (deposits) are insured by the Federal government or FDIC.

95. Of the following types of purchases, which one would be permitted under conventional financing programs, but not by VA programs? The purchase of:

    a. a business.
    b. a farm.
    c. a residential rental.
    d. farm equipment.

96. Real estate brokers CANNOT hold escrows for compensation in connection with transactions:

    a. which involve properties listed and sold by other brokers.
    b. which involve their listings.
    c. which involve their sales.
    d. all of the above.

97. Relating to an "exclusive agency" listing agreement, the owner of a property can do which of the following, without creating a liability for commission to the listing broker?

    a. Personally advertise the property for sale.
    b. Give the property to a relative.
    c. Sell the property personally.
    d. Lease the property for more than one year.

98. A broker instructed his salespeople to: (1) seek listings in areas where minorities had recently purchased properties, and (2) to only take listings from "white" owners. With regard to these directions:

    a. item "1" is proper.
    b. item "2" is proper.
    c. items "1" and "2" are both proper.
    d. items "1" and "2" are in violation of discrimination laws.

99. A deed may be:

    a. assigned.
    b. foreclosed.
    c. signed with an "X" mark.
    d. none of the above.

100. How many square acres can be found in Section 13 along a highway that runs along the south border of the section? Approximately:

    a. 25
    b. 26
    c. 20
    d. 30

101. The shape of an acre is:

    a. square or rectangular.
    b. round or elliptical.
    c. irregular.
    d. none of the above.

102. The sealed bid received by the court in a probate sale was for $150,000, which met the minimum requirements of the court. At the confirmation hearing, the minimum to open the "overbidding" at the hearing would be:

    a. $158,000.
    b. $155,000.
    c. $160,000.
    d. none of the above.

103. Comparisons show that comparable single-family homes in a neighborhood rent for $750 per month and sell for an average of $125,000. What is the gross rent multiplier?

    a. 153
    b. 157
    c. 167
    d. 140

104. If a buyer desired to purchase a property using an FHA loan, you would send him to the:

    a. FHA regional office.
    b. FHA district office.
    c. FHA approved lender.
    d. local office of HUD (Housing and Urban Development).

105. In contracting, if the subject matter of the contract no longer exists and neither party has knowledge of this change, the contract would be:

a. valid.
b. voidable.
c. void.
d. illegal.

106. Which of the following would accounts payable be classified as:

a. an asset.
b. a liability.
c. a deferment.
d. part of "net worth."

107. An investor is considering purchasing a 10-unit apartment building and uncovers the following factors with which to evaluate his involvement in the investment: Age = 24 yrs.; Economic rent per unit = $300 per month, with 10% vacancy factor; Acceptable "cap rate" = 8%; Total annual expenses = $6,7600. How much should the investor pay for the property?

a. $300,000
b. $320,500
c. $350,000
d. $360,000

108. Under the "Truth-in-Lending" law, finance charges would include all of the following, except:

a. commission.
b. taxes.
c. finder's fee.
d. interest.

109. When a buyer assumes an existing loan in purchasing a home, the closing statement would show the old loan as a:

a. credit to beneficiary.
b. credit to seller.
c. debit to buyer.
d. debit to seller and credit to buyer.

110. Complaints involving alleged violations of California law prohibiting discrimination must be filed within how many days of the act?

a. 60
b. 90
c. 120
d. 180

111. Per IRS regulations, federal taxes on ordinary income are considered to be:

a. progressive.
b. proportional.
c. regressive.
d. regenerative.

112. A person appointed by the court to handle the estate of one who died intestate is called a(n):

    a. administrator.
    b. executor.
    c. trustor.
    d. vendor.

113. Probably the oldest method of appraising is the:

    a. cost approach.
    b. income approach.
    c. Inwood method.
    d. market data (comparison) approach.

114. "A" is deeded an interest in a property for the life of "B." "A" dies while "B" is still living. What happens to the interest?

    a. Passes to heirs of "A"
    b. Reverts back to grantor
    c. Passes to "B"
    d. Passes to state

115. Which of the following would terminate an offer to purchase?

    a. Ask buyer if he would approve a counter offer.
    b. Holding offer for evaluation (not beyond allowed time).
    c. Rejection by offeror.
    d. Revocation by offeror.

116. After consummating a valid purchase agreement, buyer desires to take an early possession. To do this, buyer must obtain permission from the:

    a. escrow.
    b. broker.
    c. lender.
    d. owner.

117. Of the following properties, which one would usually have the highest loan-to-value (LTV) ratio?

    a. Residential single-family "fixer-upper"
    b. Residential two-family rental
    c. Residential owner to occupy, adjacent to commercial or apartment complex
    d. Single-family owner to occupy in middle of nice conforming neighborhood

118. A deed that has been executed but NOT recorded is:

    a. invalid as between the parties and valid as to third parties.
    b. valid as between the parties and valid as to subsequent recorded interests.
    c. valid as between the parties and invalid as to subsequent recorded interests without notice.
    d. invalid as between the parties.

119. The right to possess, use, encumber, dispose of, and to exclude most accurately describes:

    a. tenancy.
    b. real estate.
    c. ownership.
    d. equity.

120. In real estate matters, to "execute" is to:

    a. kill a sale.
    b. complete, perform, follow-out.
    c. sign and deliver.
    d. both b and c.

121. Which of the following relates to time, title, interest, and possession?

    a. Adverse possession
    b. Community property
    c. Survivorship
    d. Severalty

122. In contracting, if a party to a contract purposely omitted a material fact, the contract would be:

    a. valid.
    b. voidable.
    c. void.
    d. illegal.

123. Which of the following is NOT considered real property?

    a. Basketball backboard bolted to the garage
    b. Easement appurtenant
    c. Leasehold interest
    d. Garage shelving nailed and screwed into the rafters and studs

124. An investor purchased a property, putting 35% down, and borrowing the balance at 11% interest (straight note) for ten years. If his annual interest payment is $50,050, what was the value of his purchase?

    a. $455,000
    b. $700,000
    c. $614,250
    d. None of the above

125. While examining a home in preparation of taking a listing, a salesperson notices a crack in the basement wall. It appears to be in the corner and runs out in two directions. Which of the following would be the most likely reason for the crack?

    a. Studs spaced too far apart
    b. Walls too thin
    c. Concrete deterioration
    d. Building is settling with age

126. An investor/builder is seeking a vacant lot on which he can build a building. His plans indicate the building will cost him $300,000, and annual income will be $50,000 less $10,000 yearly expenses. If he desires a 10% capitalization rate for investments, how much can he pay for the land?

    a. $100,000
    b. $95,000
    c. $90,000
    d. $87,000

127. Which of the following may use the "Realtor®" designation?

    a. Any person selling their property in a professional way.
    b. A person who has passed the state required testing, paid his required fees, and is a member of the National Association of Realtors®.
    c. An attorney representing a client.
    d. None of the above.

128. The approach in which income is projected to a future date and then discounted to today's rates to attract investors relates to a technique known as:

    a. capitalization.
    b. equity manipulation.
    c. future projection.
    d. unearned increments.

129. Which of the following would least likely be found in the conveyance or encumbrance of personal property?

    a. Deed restriction
    b. Financing statement
    c. Lease
    d. Security agreement

130. The major part of California laws relating to real estate comes from:

    a. the Business and Professions Code.
    b. legislature acts.
    c. the Real Estate Commissioner.
    d. the state constitution.

131. The Real Estate Commissioner administers California real estate law, including licensing. He may reject any application if the applicant CANNOT prove:

    a. he was acquitted of any crime brought against him.
    b. that any charge brought against him by the DRE was unfounded.
    c. he is of good moral character and reputation.
    d. none of the above.

132. How would a city hold title to property such as parks, schools, and recreational facilities?

    a. In common
    b. In joint tenancy
    c. In severalty
    d. In tenancy in partnership

133. In contracting, if two parties enter into a contract agreement and each party is ignorant of the fact that it is based upon a mistake in fact, the contract would be:

    a. valid.
    b. voidable.
    c. void.
    d. illegal.

134. An owner holds title to a large parcel of land recently vacated by a lessee farmer who was growing crops for sale. The owner plans to eventually build a race track on the property. The crops, also known as emblements, legally belong to whom?

    a. Owner's heirs
    b. Old lessee
    c. Beneficiary
    d. Real estate property manager

135. Which of the following is NOT one of the four basic elements that contribute to the production of income?

    a. Depreciation
    b. Capital
    c. Land
    d. Coordination

136. An appraiser owns 100 shares of a total outstanding 1,000,000 shares of XYZ Corporation. He is asked to appraise a property for the corporation. Upon disclosure of his ownership in stock, the president indicated he believed the appraiser could still do a professional job and that there were no conflict of interest difficulties. The appraiser should:

    a. make the appraisal, but disclose his holdings of stock in an appropriate place on the report.
    b. make the appraisal, not mentioning his stock holdings, since they were so small.
    c. refuse to do the appraisal.
    d. make the appraisal after placing stock in trust.

137. A creditor, attempting to collect an account receivable, would be most successful if he were the creditor of a:

    a. corporation.
    b. general partnership.
    c. joint tenant.
    d. limited partnership.

138. Metes and bounds descriptions are measured in degrees, minutes, and seconds from:

    a. north or south points.
    b. east or west points.
    c. north or east points.
    d. south or west points.

EXAM 4

139. A request for notice of default would be issued for the benefit of the:

    a. trustor on the first trust deed.
    b. trustee on the first trust deed.
    c. trustor on the second trust deed.
    d. beneficiary on the second trust deed.

140. "Procuring cause" is most often associated with a(n):

    a. action against licensee for violation of the real estate law.
    b. action for claiming commission on an open listing.
    c. listing agreement.
    d. agreement to purchase.

141. Priorities for real property taxes are:

    a. after a loan.
    b. before a loan.
    c. commensurate with loan.
    d. none of the above.

142. A contractor working on the foundation of a new dwelling was paid and dismissed by the owner, who did not like his work. The owner proceeded to hire other contractors to complete the work. A trust deed securing a construction loan had been recorded one week after the initial foundation man had been fired. One week after completing construction and receiving "certificate of occupancy," the first foundation man, claiming breach of contract and lack of agreed compensation, filed a mechanic's lien, which:

    a. would always take priority over trust deeds.
    b. was subordinate to the earlier recorded trust deed.
    c. takes priority over the trust deed because the work on the foundation commenced prior to recording the deed.
    d. none of the above.

143. One can differentiate between trust deeds by:

    a. information in the body of deed.
    b. the heading at the the top of deed.
    c. dates of the recording.
    d. none of the above.

144. The objective of the tax assessor is to:

    a. justify services rendered.
    b. provide stability in taxing.
    c. assure that similar properties receive similar taxation.
    d. none of the above.

145. Which of the following is NOT a lien?

    a. Attachment
    b. Judgment
    c. Mechanic's lien
    d. Estate at suffrage

146. In contracting, if a person who is NOT fully informed still signs the contract without understanding what he is signing, the contract would be:

   a. valid.
   b. voidable.
   c. void.
   d. illegal.

147. The destruction, material alteration of, or injury to the premises by a tenant is:

   a. bad.
   b. wear and tear.
   c. usury.
   d. waste.

148. The lowest part of the frame of a home, resting on the foundation and supporting the upright framing, is the:

   a. base.
   b. jamb.
   c. ridge board.
   d. sill.

149. Appurtenances attached to land or improvements, that usually CANNOT be removed, are called:

   a. emblements.
   b. chattels.
   c. binders.
   d. fixtures.

150. When an appraiser is determining the replacement cost of a new property, he would NOT use which of the following?

   a. Quality survey
   b. Observed conditions
   c. Comparative square foot
   d. Unit cost in place

EXAM 4

Practice Exam 4 Answers

1. **c.** Law of supply and demand: If there is high demand and low supply, then values will rise.

2. **c.** It is called "Motivation," and tells you how serious they are about selling.

3. **b.** Attachment is the process whereby property is seized and retained in custody of court as security for satisfaction of judgment plaintiff "hopes" to obtain in pending litigation. Execution is the final act. Hereditament is property that is capable of being inherited.

4. **d.** Public buildings do NOT have "income production" capacities.

5. **d.** A broker's license is required. The other answers are nonexistent. For selling real property securities, a broker must obtain an "endorsement" to complement his broker's license.

6. **d.** Definition refers to the use, which at the time of appraisal is most likely to produce the greatest net return to the land and/or buildings over a given period of time.

7. **a.** The DRE looks at this question as measured by "cost to cure." Economic obsolescence is the most expensive to cure—generally incurable.

8. **b.** Should be expressed, in writing.

9. **d.** All money for salespeople MUST come from/through their broker.

10. **c.**

11. **d.** Owners, taking back 2nds, 3rds, etc.

12. **d.** The lender or broker will have the appraisal made, if the seller has not already done so.

13. **d.** Sale of business opportunities fall under DRE jurisdiction.

14. **b.** Lessor owns the property, lessee holds leasehold estate.

15. **d.** There is generally no down payment required with a VA loan.

16. **b.** Breach of condition – possible loss of property; Breach of covenant – possible money damages.

17. **b.** Furring are strips of wood applied to walls; footing is the bottom of a foundation; facade is the front of a building.

18. **d.** Cannot function in any way as to use his broker license while operating under other broker's license as salesperson, other than acting as a salesperson.

19. **d.**

20. *c.*   For the "willing" buyer, write an offer and start the negotiating process. Be realistic, but don't you decide what the principals will do.

21. *d.*   All are influences affecting value. The four forces are: (1) Political or governmental regulations; (2) Economic adjustments; (3) Social ideals and standards; (4) Physical characteristics.

22. *c.*   A duty of the listing broker is to assist the seller in evaluating all offers to purchase.

23. *c.*

24. *b.*   Functional utility is the "usefulness, attractiveness, and utility" of a property.

25. *d.*   All income is used for qualifying. This includes wages and any other form of income available—interest, dividends, trust payments, etc. Wive's incomes are no longer handled differently than husbands'.

26. *d.*   Ordinary real estate loans are NOT usually real property securities as defined by law.

27. *d.*

28. *b.*   First installment of county property taxes becomes due on November 1.

29. *c.*   The maker of a check represents there is money in bank to cover; maker of a note makes no such representation and failure to pay (redeem) is not a crime.

30. *d.*   Borrower applies monthly amounts of insurance premiums and taxes, which are available as necessary for the lender to pay these obligations.

31. *c.*   A partnership does NOT protect principals' assets against creditor. For the limited partnership, only the general partner's assets would be vulnerable.

32. *d.*   It is mandatory that funds be available and the commissions formed.

33. *d.*   Because a, b, and c are all grounds for disciplinary action.

34. *d.*

35. *c.*   Remember: **D-U-S-T**.

36. *c.*   Otherwise referred to as a "feasibility" study, which will help determine if this or other alternatives should be pursued.

37. *d.*   Upon death, the listing contract (for personal service) would terminate. Had the father been incorporated, the renegotiation would not be necessary, as the corporation does not die.

38. *b.*   Life insurance companies will generally give the longer term, sometimes 30 years.

EXAM 4

39. **c.** The parcels are 5 acres each, and join to form a square parcel, with a total of ten acres. Therefore, 10 acres = 43,560 sq. ft x (10) = 435,600 sq. ft. By taking the square root of the area, a side length = 660 ft.

Alternative

Comparing sides of the 10-acre parcel and the section, the parcel side represents 1/8 of the length of the section side (there could be eight such parcels along the section side). Therefore, a section side = 1 mile = 5,280' and the side of the parcel = 5,280' ÷ 9 = 660'. With four sides, the wire needed = 4 x 660' = 2,640'.

40. **c.** Pledge – depositing of personal property (note and T.D.) by a borrower with a creditor (lender) as security for a debt (loan).

41. **a.** For junior trust deed, under $10,000 for 2 to 3 years = 10% $4,500 x 10% (.10) = $450.

42. **d.** Adequate description of the subject property would be sufficient. The title company will require "legal" to insure the sale.

43. **a.** Must obtain a Real Property Security Dealer's Endorsement, which requires him to provide a bond ($5,000).

44. **d.** The "A.B.C." controls issuing liquor licenses. When a married person applies, both husband and wife must apply together.

45. **b.** IRS does allow capital losses deductions for land held for investment. NOTE: Land does not wear out; therefore, there is no depreciation.

46. **d.** Remember, the person must have authorization from the broker to withdraw from the account.

47. **c.** Tax is imposed upon retailers for sales of tangible personal property at retail. Items typically exempt are: food, drugs, certain necessities, and property subject to excise tax—liquor and gasoline.

48. **d.** Real estate contracts must be in writing, but NOT all other contracts must be in writing.

49. **c.** Joists are structural parts supporting floor or ceiling loads.

50. **c.**

51. **d.** Gives appraiser opportunity to support his observations and opinions.

52. **a.** A signed agreement whereby the lease amount is specifically set (for a short period of time) would probably NOT include an escalator clause.

53. **d.** Fines up to $5,000; imprisonment up to 5 yrs., or both.

54. **b.** An increase of one point (1%) in the "cap rate" would result in a reduction in value of the building of $50,000. Value = Income divided by Cap Rate = $55,000 ÷ 11% (.11) = $500,000.

55. *b.*   The original price now will be equal to only 91% (100% - 9%) at the time of sale. To determine the new required sale price:
Value divided by its percentage value = $150,000 ÷ 91% (.91).
New sale price must be = $164,835.16.
Therefore, appreciation was $164,835 - 150,000 = $14,835.

56. *a.*   No matter when, property taxes and assessments take priority over all other liens.

57. *d.*   The property, upon death, automatically passed to Mr. "Z" as surviving spouse. The will was invalid, as to passing the title. Mr. "Z" now holds title to property in severalty.

58. *c.*   The "financing statement" (UCC-1) filed with the secretary of state is used to give public notice of the transaction and to "perfect" (complete) the security interest.

59. *d.*   All other answers do constitute "constructive eviction" by the landlord, which would allow the tenant to abandon the property and refuse to pay further rent, and doing so without incurring liability for breach of lease agreement.

60. *d.*   Stock in trade CANNOT be used to secure a loan, for when the merchandise is sold, there is no longer any security.

61. *a.*   Recapture relates to depreciation taken; others relate to the physical deterioration of property.

62. *b.*   Joint tenancy carries "right of survivorship" – NO wills; singles CANNOT hold title as community property; severalty means "one" owner, which is NOT the case in this situation.

63. *c.*   Includes the outside surfaces of the paint on exterior walls, inside the unit, and to the outside surfaces of glass windows and doors. Anything beyond these would be extending into the common areas, owned in common with all others.

64. *a.*   The previous owners did NOT pay off the bond but allowed the buyer to assume the obligation and pay $2,000 less in cash.

65. *c.*   If the broker gives deposit back prior to buyer's check clearing, he may be giving away a free $5,000 to the "buyer."

66. *b.*   Sale price: 12% = 225,00 - 27,000 = $198,000
Monthly interest = 198,000 x 12% ÷ 12 = 198,000 x (.01) = $1,980
Monthly principal (per agreement) = 520
Monthly taxes = 2,700 ÷ 12 = 225
Monthly insurance = 804 ÷ 12 = 67
Total Payment (P + I + Tax + Insurance) Monthly = $2,792

67. *d.*   Can defer if purchased within (before or after) 24 months of sale.

68. *d.*   Title insurance has been furnished, and money necessary to pay seller's equity, less costs and expenses, are in the hands of the broker or escrow holder. Transfer of title and money are thought of as simultaneous acts.

EXAM 4

69. **d.**   A lien is a charge against property, whereby the property is made security for payment of the debt, i.e., attachment.

70. **c.**   Gross Rent Multiplier is a rough, quick way of converting gross rent into market value.

71. **d.**   They are jointly (collectively) and severally (individually) responsible.

72. **c.**   For straight-line, the value is divided by the number of years over which depreciation is run—the same amount for each year. For "accelerated" methods, allow greater amounts of depreciation for the earlier years, and less for the later years.

73. **d.**   With more streets, there's more cost and less land for homes.

74. **d.**

75. **b.**   Until proved either valid or void, it is voidable.

76. **b.**   Accession – addition to property through efforts of man or by natural forces. Accretion – Accession to property through natural forces, for example, alluvium. Alluvium – Gradual increase of the earth on ocean front or bank of stream resulting from action of water.

77. **a.**   The State of California is the beneficiary.

78. **c.**   When borrowers with lower incomes and weaker credit ratings are allowed to borrow, the lender must cover the increased "risk." Thus, the overall increase in costs of borrowing.

79. **b.**   A bill of sale is used to convey title to personal property, NOT real property.

80. **d.**   Bequeath – to give, hand down, leave by will; Bequest – that which is given by terms of will; Devise – gift by will.

81. **a.**   By delivery, or placing it in the mail within 3 days.

82. **b.**   Following recordation of a notice of completion, a general contractor has 60 days to file; a subcontractor has 30 days. "b" has exceeded allowed time and therefore is ineligible to file. "c" must hurry, for he has only one day left.

83. **d.**   Performance comes after the contract is formed.

84. **d.**   Zoning falls under "Police Power."

85. **d.**   California Code passed in 1965.

86. **c.**

87. **c.**   Typically, industrial properties grow obsolete more rapidly than the other properties mentioned above. Most are a special design, not easily converted for another use. Frequently, once they become vacant, they tend to stay vacant longer than any other type of real estate.

88. *d.*   All require "full disclosure" by the broker to all parties.

89. *b.*   "Metes" means measurements; "Bounds" means boundaries.

90. *a.*   A mistake is NO justification for invalidating an otherwise good, valid contract agreement.

91. *c.*   Example: (1) contracts for the sale of real property; (2) contracts NOT to be performed within one year.

92. *c.*   Income (A): $500 x 12 = $6,000 per month
Income (B): $550 x 12 - 10% = $6,600 - 660 = $5,940

93. *d.*   A broker, acting for one of his clients in an office transaction in the capacity of escrow, would fall outside the jurisdiction of the Corporations Commissioner. He then would be operating under his broker's license and under the Real Estate Commissioner's authority.

94. *d.*   Law also goes on to say that any loan created that is to be sold to "FNMA," "GNMA," "FHLMC," or any loan made by an institution regulated by the Federal Home Loan Bank Board or any other Federal Agency (i.e., FHA, VA) is included. There are NOT many loans that are not covered.

95. *c.*   VA guaranteed loans must be for primary residence only. The buyer signs a statement declaring that he is buying a home into which he will move and reside as a primary residence.

96. *a.*   Brokers may provide the escrow service in transactions where they represent either the buyer or seller. They must be an agent representing one or the other.

97. *c.*   Exclusive agency gives seller the right to sell without owing a commission.

98. *d.*   This could be interpreted to be "block-busting." The broker has violated the law. If the salespeople follow his instructions, they have also violated the law.

99. *c.*   A "note" can be assigned; a trust deed (or deed of trust) can be foreclosed; any document can be executed with an "X" mark, with proper witnesses. Once a deed has been delivered, it has done its job (transfer of title or interest) and there is nothing remaining to be assigned.

100. *a.*   The side of a section = 1 mile = 5,280 ft.
The side of a square acre = 208.71 ft. = 209 ft.
Therefore, the number of square acres on the section side = 5,280 ÷ 209 = 25.26 = 25 parcels.

101. *d.*   An acre "has no shape"; it is a measurement of area. It can take any shape, but does NOT define a shape.

EXAM 4

102. **a.**
Base bid (accepted sealed bid)	= $150,000
Plus 10% (.10) x $10,000	= $1,000
Plus 5% (.05) x 140,000	= $7,000
Minimum opening "overbid"	= $158,000

103. **c.**   Gross rent multiplier = sale price divided by gross monthly rent
= $125,000 ÷ $750 = 166.67.

104. **c.**   FHA does NOT loan money, it just insures loans set up by approved lenders when the loan packaging conforms to FHA standards.

105. **c.**   If the subject matter of an agreement ceases to exist, the contract would therefore be impossible to complete, and thus void.

106. **b.**   Almost without exception, things payable are liabilities.

107. **b.**
Gross scheduled income = 300 x 10 x 12	= $36,000
Less vacancy factor: Minus 10%	= - $3,600
Effective gross income	= $32,400
Less expenses	= - $6,760
Net operating income (NOI)	= $25,640

Indicated value (income approach):
Income divided by "cap rate" = $25,640 ÷ (.08) = $320,500

108. **b.**   Taxes are NOT part of financing costs. All others are.

109. **d.**   Charge – (take away from) seller's account; Credit – (apply to) buyer's account.

110. **a.**   Federal law violations must be filed within 180 days.

111. **a.**   Taxes are considered progressive: the more you make, the more you pay.

112. **a.**   Administrator – male; Administratrix – female. If named in a will, Executor or Executrix.

113. **d.**   People for ages have established value by "comparing."

114. **a.**   The estate lives as long as "B" lives. Therefore, it would pass to heirs of "A." Upon "B's" death, the estate (a life estate) would either: (1) revert back to grantor (estate in reversion), or (2) pass to grantor's designee (estate in remainder).

115. **d.**   Seller may reject offer, and if parties work effectively, the negotiations may continue through counter offers. Buyer cannot reject the offer. If the buyer revokes the offer (rescinds), it is very hard to get the negotiations going again.

116. **d.**   Until title transfers, sellers/owners are in control. It is not generally nor practically a good idea to allow early "move-in"; it usually invites trouble.

117. **d.**   Lenders love nice "cream puff" properties in the middle of nice conforming neighborhoods, as compared to other properties, which have various negatives either with or near the property.

118. *c.* The deed is valid but the party who receives title with a grant deed and who does NOT record the deed runs the risk of losing his interest to a subsequent recorded interest. It is considered a valid transfer,, but the purchaser could lose any interest to a later buyer if buyer had no knowledge of the previous transaction.

119. *c.* The statement of the question is a definition of ownership.

120. *d.* To execute a deed is to "sign, seal, and deliver"; to execute a contract is to perform the contract.

121. *c.* Deals with the "**T-TIP**" club, required to have a "joint tenancy" ownership, which means right of survivors.

122. *b.* When material fact is purposely left out of contract, the law says it is intention to defraud. Until proven, contract is voidable.

123. *c.* Leasehold interest is a "personal property" interest in real estate.

124. *b.* Loan amount = Interest payment divided by Rate
= $50,050 ÷ (.11) = $455,000; Loan value = 65% of property value
= 100% - 35%
Therefore, Loan value ÷ (65%) = Property value
= 455,000 ÷ (.65) = $700,000

125. *d.* This is NOT uncommon, but must be brought to the attention of the seller. If nothing is done to repair this, it should be brought to the attention of prospective buyers, who will not then be able to claim not being informed.

126. *a.* Net Income = $50,000 - $10,000 = $40,000 per year; Property Value = Net Income divided by "cap rate" = $40,000 ÷ 10% (.10)= $400,000
Therefore, Total Value - Building Value = Land Value
= $400,000 - $300,000 = $100,000

127. *b.* A broker who belongs to the NAR may call himself a Realtor®. The word "Realtor®" is NOT synonymous with "real estate agent."

128. *a.* Key words that describe cash flow are: (1) income, (2) projected, and (3) future. Capitalization is the net income technique of appraising.

129. *a.* Deed restrictions are primarily applied on and for real property. You can lease personal property, and one might have to execute a security agreement and record a financing statement with the Secretary of State or County Recorder.

130. *b.* The power to make laws is reserved for the legislative branch of government, as compared to the judicial or executive branches. The Real Estate Commissioner has the power to make regulations in accordance with the laws enacted, and enforces the laws and regulations.

EXAM 4

131. *d.* (Negative question) Does NOT have to prove he was acquitted of alleged crime. "B" relates to "any" charge. It is highly unlikely the Commissioner would bring charges outside of his authority, but possible. The "best" answer is "D".

132. *c.* City, acting as a legal person, would hold title to such properties as would any other individual.

133. *c.* The law says that if both parties are mistaken as to material fact in a contract, there can be NO mutual consent, and therefore the contract is "no good" or "void."

134. *b.* Old tenant-lessee holds title to the growing crops, even after his tenancy has terminated.

135. *a.* Depreciation does NOT contribute to the production of income but would reduce it. The four elements are: Labor, Capital, Land, and Coordination.

136. *a.* Full disclosure required by the code of ethics of the American Institute of Real Estate Appraisers.

137. *b.* Except for the general partner, liabilities are limited as to creditors attacking personal property and assets outside the "relationship." Limited partners are not liable beyond their investment in the partnership. Corporations have a "veil" which does the same thing, limiting creditors to corporate assets only. A surviving joint tenant holds property free from debts of deceased tenant and from liens against the tenant's interest.

138. *a.*

139. *d.* Notice is sent to the beneficiary of junior trust deeds, informing him of pending foreclosure on the more senior note and trust deed.

140. *b.* Deals with "...who first produces a buyer, ready, willing, and able." That person may be eligible for a commission.

141. *b.* Taxes take priority over liens and encumbrances, no matter when recorded.

142. *c.* "Scheme of improvements" begins upon first work on property, which beat the deed recording by more than one week, establishing priority.

143. *c.* Recording sets priorities.

144. *c.*

145. *d.* Estate at sufferance is a type of leasehold, and is NO lien.

146. *a.* Ignorance on the signer's part is NO excuse in the eyes of the law.

147. *d.*

148. *d.* Also in the element forming the lower side of a door opening.

149. *d.*   Personal property which was turned into real property.

150. *b.*   Probably looks great with NO wear and tear, yet, it's new.

EXAM 4

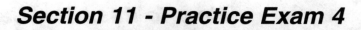

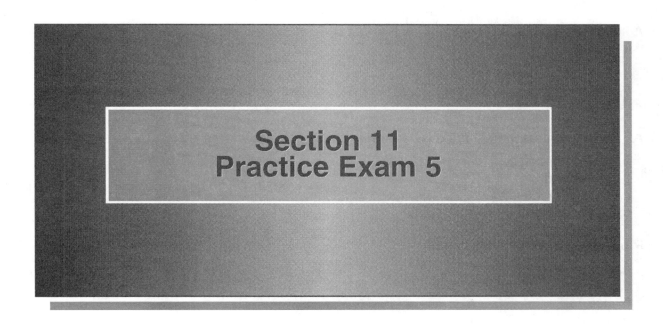

Section 11
Practice Exam 5

NOTE: For better self-testing, the answers to this exam have been moved to the end of the exam.

1. Seller "ABLE" recently sold a property for $141,450, which was 15% more than he paid for it. He held the property for two years, during which time his interest expenses were 10% of his purchase price (5% per year). Taxes were $80 per $1,000 of assessed valuation, and the property was assessed at 25% of the original purchase price. Seller's ownership resulted in a net:

    a. $11,070 loss.
    b. $3,690 gain.
    c. $1,230 gain
    d. none of the above.

2. When using the cost approach to determine the value of land and improvements of a property, an appraiser would use:

    a. one approach to arrive at a value for both.
    b. one approach to arrive at a value for each.
    c. separate approaches to arrive at a value for each.
    d. none of the above.

3. Which of the following is nearest to a synonym of "metes and bounds"?

    a. Angles and degrees
    b. Measures and perimeters
    c. Degree of perimeters
    d. Angles and measures

4. A subordination clause written into a 1st trust deed would benefit the:

    a. trustee.
    b. trustor.
    c. beneficiary.
    d. lender.

5. An appurtenant easement need NOT be mentioned in a deed since it:

    a. is hypothecated.
    b. is pledged.
    c. goes with the land.
    d. all of the above.

6. Productivity is a direct function of:

    a. demand.
    b. supply.
    c. use.
    d. value.

7. A "walkup" in real estate terms refers to:

    a. manufacturing properties.
    b. drive-in restaurants.
    c. manufactured home parks.
    d. apartments.

8. Under real estate law, a manufactured home park is:

    a. an area or tract of land where 5 or more manufactured home lots are rented/leased for human habitation.
    b. an area or tract of land where 2 or more manufactured home lots are rented/leased to accommodate manufactured homes used for human habitation.
    c. an area or tract of land where 1 or more manufactured home lots are owned outright by a manufactured home owner.
    d. none of the above.

9. On a property, a pump and well would be considered:

    a. an improvement.
    b. taxable as capital gains.
    c. both a and b.
    d. none of the above.

10. If a broker procures a loan for a principal for $89,000, she would provide which of the following documents?

    a. Real Property Security Statement
    b. Broker's Loan Statement
    c. Both a and b
    d. Neither a nor b

11. Which of the following is an encumbrance?

    a. Freehold estate
    b. Homestead
    c. Lease agreement
    d. Recorded subdivision map

12. A broker was hired by a seller to sell her land for a prescribed commission. However, the broker incurred more expenses while trying to sell the land than he anticipated. If the broker asked the seller to increase the commission at the time of the sale, and the seller agreed to do so, this would be:

    a. against the law.
    b. illegal.
    c. legal.
    d. none of the above.

13. Base lines run:

    a. north and south.
    b. east and west.
    c. north and east.
    d. none of the above.

14. After a broker shows a client's property to a prospective buyer, the broker should:

    a. notify the office staff of the showing by memo.
    b. confirm showing with the buyer by written memo.
    c. notify the seller in writing as to the prospect's identify.
    d. wait until the prospect contacts the owner.

15. Businesses in California may take the form of an individual proprietorship, partnership, or corporation. Each form has its advantages. One advantage of operating as a general partnership is that:

    a. each partner has the use of assets of the partnership.
    b. management of the business can be left to the other partner with little concern.
    c. personal assets of a partner cannot be touched by creditors of the business.
    d. there is less responsibility and more time can be spent away from the business.

16. The trust deed (and note) that normally takes priority is the one that is:

    a. for the greatest amount.
    b. a construction loan.
    c. executed/delivered first.
    d. recorded first.

17. If a home were properly insured with fire insurance to indemnify the owner, he could expect to:

    a. always gain.
    b. gain, but never lose.
    c. lose, but definitely not gain.
    d. neither gain nor lose.

EXAM 5

18. An appraiser observes wide cracks in the corner of a basement, spreading up two walls. This was most likely caused by:

    a. weak joists.
    b. deterioration due to dampness.
    c. house settling.
    d. none of the above.

19. A house sold for $120,000 on which a seller was to pay 6% brokerage fee. Other costs were 1% prepayment penalty on existing $90,000 first loan balance, escrow fees of $500, title insurance premium of $400, and 3 points (%) loan discount fee on a new loan of $110,000 (VA). The seller's costs would be what percent of his equity?

    a. 10.25%
    b. 17%
    c. 41%
    d. 13.7%

20. For a limited partnership, the limited partners would have which of the following as their liability?

    a. Amount of investment written into partnership agreement.
    b. 25% of his investment.
    c. Same as all other partners.
    d. No liability.

21. An incompatible positioning of a residence on a parcel of land would be an example of:

    a. economic obsolescence.
    b. functional obsolescence.
    c. physical obsolescence.
    d. wear and tear.

22. Buyers submitted an offer to purchase the home of Sellers. The purchase was made "subject to" the existing VA loan. In a subsequent foreclosure, should VA sustain losses, who would be liable for those losses?

    a. Buyers
    b. Sellers
    c. Both Buyers and Sellers
    d. Neither Buyers nor Sellers

23. Under an FHA program, monthly payments made (principal + interest) on a home loan must be:

    a. level payments.
    b. horizontal payments.
    c. varying payments.
    d. unamortized payments.

24. A broker suggested to his sales staff that they seek new listings in an area where minorities have recently begun to move into. He also suggested that they take listings only from white owners, since they would most likely be sellers due to the fact that the minorities are "moving in." Regarding two possible areas of concern, (1) instructions to his sales staff; and 2) his discrimination regarding their seeking of listings from whites, the broker is in violation of the Fair Housing Act (guilty of discrimination) as follows:

    a. regarding (1) and (2).
    b. regarding (1), not (2).
    c. regarding (2), not (1).
    d. no violation.

25. "A" has been given power of attorney for the purpose of selling "B's" house. Which of the following is NOT true?

    a. "A" cannot sell the property if "B" has recorded a homestead on it.
    b. Power of attorney must be recorded for "A" to sell the property.
    c. Power of attorney is terminated in the event "B" is declared incompetent and unable to enter into a legal contract.
    d. "A" may purchase the property, providing he/she pays a fair market value for the home.

26. A real estate licensee attempted to solicit a listing in a neighborhood by stating to owners that "non-whites" would be moving into the neighborhood, causing property values to decrease. This conduct would be considered all of the following, except:

    a. blockbusting.
    b. illegal conduct.
    c. panic selling.
    d. acceptable practice.

27. An agent obtains a listing to sell a registered franchise from the owner. The sale will include both building and land. Before he begins servicing the listing, the agent must:

    a. file an application and receive a permit from the DRE.
    b. file an application for exemption of registration of the offering with the corporations commissioner.
    c. obtain a "cooperative" sales agreement from a stock broker.
    d. none of the above.

28. A landlord is required to keep all but which one of the following in good order?

    a. Commercial rental property with certain commonly used areas for convenience of all tenants.
    b. High-rise apartment building with extensive lobby and hallways.
    c. Theater's lobby and restroom facilities.
    d. Private dwelling leased for occupancy by one family.

29. A "Notice of Completion" benefits:

    a. contractors.
    b. laborers and material suppliers.
    c. lenders.
    d. owners.

EXAM 5

30. In order to maintain a "release schedule," the beneficiary of a blanket loan usually charges a higher proportionate payment amount to release each lot:

    a. to have better security on remaining lots.
    b. to protect against the better lots selling first.
    c. to protect the investment as individual lots are sold.
    d. all of the above.

31. Which represents the largest area?

    a. 1/10 of a township
    b. 2 miles square
    c. 2 square miles
    d. 3 sections

32. A buyer purchases a residence from $45,000, later selling it for $50,500. Within one year, buyer purchases another home for $62,000. After living there for two years, buyer sold that home for $60,000 and moved into an apartment. What would be buyer's capital gain realized from the sale (NOT considering any expenses)?

    a. None
    b. $5,500 gain
    c. $3,500 gain
    d. $2,000 loss

33. An office building purchased for $200,000 with 25% down and 75% financed, had $1,500 per month payments with 12% annual interest. Ten years later, the property sold for $400,000. What is the owner's equity at the sale (includes original investment)?

    a. $100,000
    b. $150,000
    c. $200,000
    d. $250,000

34. A principal gives a broker $50,000 with which to purchase 2nd notes and trust deeds. He stipulates that he must receive a minimum of 18% on his investments, after broker's expenses. Broker states that if notes do not yield the investor his 18%, he will make up the difference. If the investor accepts this offer, the broker:

    a. must post a bond.
    b. broker's license is all that is required.
    c. broker is in violation of California law.
    d. none of the above.

35. All but one of the following constitutes completion for purposes of filing a mechanic's lien.

    a. Cessation of labor for 60 days.
    b. Acceptance and possession of structure by owner.
    c. Filing of notice by owner.
    d. Cessation of labor for one month on any form of home improvement.

36. Which of the following is NOT real property?

    a. Giant redwood tree growing in yard.
    b. Stock in mutual water company.
    c. Owner has removed fence, stacking the wood on the ground.
    d. None of above.

37. An appraiser's final step in estimating value is to correlate the three indications of value obtained through the cost, income, and market data approaches. The final estimate of value is obtained by:

    a. averaging the three values.
    b. assigning weights to the three individual values, and then averaging those values.
    c. both a and b.
    d. none of the above.

38. When an investor purchases income property, he should realize that there will be certain expenditures for upkeep, replacement, and management designed to produce greater income. When the point is reached, beyond which adding to improvements will not result in increasing returns, this is an example of the principle of:

    a. conformity.
    b. diminishing returns.
    c. supply and demand.
    d. substitution.

39. A broker has the listing on a seller's home (exclusive agency), and has expended much time, money, and effort in attempting to generate a sale. While the listing is still in force, the seller sells the property herself to a coworker. The broker would be entitled to:

    a. costs and expenses.
    b. 1/2 the normal commission agreed on.
    c. no commission.
    d. full commission per listing agreement.

40. In the condominium concept, one buys a common interest in the common areas and an exclusive interest in a particular unit. Which of the following is NOT correct about condominiums?

    a. Can be part of an office building.
    b. Can be only a "life estate" with right of survivorship.
    c. Owner has interest in real property.
    d. Can be liened generally or specifically.

41. Under a real property sales contract, buyer is considered to be a(n):

    a. lessee.
    b. tenant in common.
    c. equitable owner.
    d. vendor.

EXAM 5

42. By what method does a tenant rent out his apartment if he has a leasehold interest in the apartment?

   a. Assign
   b. Sublet
   c. Transfer
   d. Suffrage

43. A loan (trust deed) held by an individual is:

   a. a chattel real.
   b. real property.
   c. a real chattel.
   d. personal property.

44. An investor purchased an income property at $200,000, with a capitalization rate of 10%. If the next income increased by 10% (with NO additional expense), and the "cap" rate increases to 12%, the new value of the property would be:

   a. $220,000
   b. $265,000
   c. $299,000
   d. $183,333

45. The grantor is the:

   a. buyer.
   b. seller.
   c. renter.
   d. lender.

46. Rezoning ordinances, attempting to rid an area of nonconforming uses, may require all of the following conditions, except:

   a. allowing reasonable time within which abuses may be eliminated.
   b. prohibition of expansion.
   c. prohibition of rebuilding.
   d. retroactive zoning ordinances.

47. A landlord does NOT have to file a notice to vacate when tenancy is:

   a. an estate for years.
   b. estate for year-to-year.
   c. periodic.
   d. estate at suffrage.

48. A section of land is to be enclosed with a double strand of wire. If a rod equals one pound of wire, how many pounds of wire will be required?

   a. 640
   b. 1,280
   c. 1,920
   d. 2,560

49. Which of the following is considered a "debit" to the buyer?

    a. Accrued interest
    b. Purchase price
    c. Rentals payable in advance
    d. Selling expenses

50. Of the following statements concerning a life estate, which is NOT true?

    a. All conveyances for life estates must be in writing to be enforceable.
    b. It is a freehold estate.
    c. Person holding a life estate does not have fee title.
    d. It cannot extend beyond the life of the life tenant.

51. Which of the following relates to "economic obsolescence"?

    a. Legislative acts
    b. Massive cornices
    c. Outdated fixtures
    d. Worn-out stairs

52. In a single-family dwelling, the extended (spread out) part of the bottom of the exterior of the foundation is called the:

    a. base.
    b. footing.
    c. foundation.
    d. pier.

53. A valid lease need NOT contain:

    a. amount of payment.
    b. description of property.
    c. names of parties to lease and terms of lease.
    d. stipulated transfer fee.

54. When a broker sells six notes and trust deeds taken back by a developer of a new subdivision, he must give to each prospective purchaser a:

    a. final public report.
    b. loan disclosure statements.
    c. notice of intended sale.
    d. real property security statement.

55. Mr. "O" intentionally causes Mr. "G" to believe that a real estate broker is his agent. In fact, the broker is not Mr. "O's" agent. However, under the above conditions, the agency relationship is:

    a. actual.
    b. implied.
    c. nonexistent.
    d. ostensible.

56. A "quitclaim" deed implies that the:

    a. grantor has not previously transferred the property to another.
    b. grantor has not created an encumbrance against the property that has not been revealed.
    c. grantor actually owns the property.
    d. none of above.

57. Cost estimating methods currently used by builders, architects, and appraisers are:

    a. capitalization of residual income.
    b. capitalized cost of replacement.
    c. quantity survey, unit in place, comparative square, or cubic foot.
    d. unit, unit in place, quantity survey.

58. A broker had signed an agreement to locate property for his principal. Having found a property which suited his principal, which could be purchased for less than he was willing to pay, the broker bought the property himself. Later the broker sold the property to his principal at the higher price, keeping the difference for himself. This is considered:

    a. commingling.
    b. conversion.
    c. divided agency.
    d. secret profit.

59. On which of the following types of business collateral would one file with the secretary of state (Sacramento) to perfect a security transaction?

    a. Consumer goods
    b. Growing crops
    c. Trade fixtures
    d. Uncut timber

60. A 60-year-old man has been living in a home he bought 9 years ago, for which he paid $90,000. He recently sold the home for $120,000, incurring $9,600 selling expenses and brokerage fees. What is the amount of capital gains on which he will have to pay income taxes?

    a. $20,400
    b. $30,000
    c. None
    d. None of the above

61. An investor put $10,000 down on a property purchased for $100,000. He received a 9% gross return on the purchase price, and had a 9% interest expense on the loan amount as his only expense. What would the percentage return on his investment be?

    a. 0%
    b. 11%
    c. 9%
    d. None of the above

62. Which of the following appraisal methods requires a computation for "accrued depreciation"?

 a. Cost
 b. Income
 c. Market data
 d. All of above

63. A power-of-attorney is terminated by:

 a. death of principal.
 b. expressed revocation of principal.
 c. incapacity of principal to contract.
 d. any of the above.

64. Mr. and Mrs "H" own a house worth $200,000, with an outstanding 1st loan of $110,000. Without Mrs. "H's" knowledge, Mr. "H" filed a homestead on the property, for their joint benefit. Subsequently, Mr. "H's" creditors obtained a judgment against him. Which of the following is true? The homestead is:

 a. ineffective, due to the $75,000 limit.
 b. invalid, since only Mr. "H" signed and filed.
 c. effective, due to filing prior to date of judgment.
 d. none of the above.

65. Regarding condominium ownership, which answer is most correct? Owner has:

 a. an undivided interest in common with others in common areas.
 b an equity interest in real property.
 c. exclusive ownership of respective unit, which is separate and distinct from that of all other owners.
 d. all of the above.

66. A broker's loan statement is now called a:

 a. broker's disclosure statement.
 b. mortgage loan disclosure statement.
 c. mortgage statement.
 d. none of the above.

67. The lower the loan-to-value ration, the greater the:

 a. interest.
 b. down payment.
 c. loan.
 d. term.

68. Which of the following would NOT be considered a "deferred payment" form of contract?

 a. Conditional sales contract
 b. FHA purchase contract
 c. Installment sale contract
 d. Land contract

EXAM 5

69. A property sells for $121,000. The purchaser gives $10,000 down payment, agrees to place an additional $5,000 down, and take over an existing VA first loan of $100,000, with the remainder to be in the form of a 2nd note and trust deed. For these conditions, how much would the documentary tax stamps be?

    a. $1.10
    b. $5.50
    c. $133.10
    d. $23.10

70. Which of the following could be used with a purchaser without the immediate involvement of a title change?

    a. Grant deed
    b. Land contract
    c. Quit claim deed
    d. Warranty deed

71. When all expenses, including taxes and insurance, are paid by the lessee along with a new amount of "rent" as agreed upon to the landlord, this is referred to as a:

    a. gross lease.
    b. net lease.
    c. percentage lease.
    d. sandwich lease.

72. A lender with vast funds for investment, who prefers larger loans without collection responsibilities, would most likely be a:

    a. commercial bank.
    b. insurance company.
    c. private lender.
    d. savings bank.

73. Capitalization is a process by which an appraiser:

    a. converts income into value.
    b. determines depreciation.
    c. establishes cost.
    d. finds gross income.

74. A fire station building and a small appliance sales and repair store were recently leased on long-term leases at the same lease payment. Between the two, the fire station building would probably have a stable capitalization rate, which would be:

    a. higher.
    b. lower.
    c. same as.
    d. varying; sometimes higher, sometimes lower than the other property.

75. Under a real property sales contract, Buyer "A" makes a $2,000 down payment to Seller "B" on a property he had been renting. The agreement is filed with the county recorder. Subsequently, "A" moves to Florida, without making any further payments, and with no notice of his intentions being made to "B." Which of the following would be true?

    a. Seller could resell the property and obtain a deficiency judgment against "A."
    b. New buyer should not be concerned about the previous sales to "A."
    c. "A's" activity has no effect upon the marketability of the property.
    d. There would be a cloud on the title to the property.

76. Past expenditures for residential improvements are called:

    a. costs.
    b. investments.
    c. price.
    d. value.

77. If land was selling for $10,000 per acre, what would the following parcel sell for? The SE¼ of the SE¼ of the SE¼ of Sec. 4 and the S½ of the SW¼ of the SW¼ of Sec. 3 and the N½ of the NE¼ of the NE¼ of the NE¼ of Sec. 9 and the N½ of the N½ of the NW¼ of the NW¼ of Sec. 10.

    a. $400,000
    b. $425,000
    c. $450,000
    d. $500,000

78. The best hedge against inflation would be:

    a. equity assets.
    b. government bonds.
    c. mortgages/loans.
    d. savings accounts.

79. The recording of which of the following creates a lien?

    a. Attachment
    b. Easement
    c. Notice of nonresponsibility
    d. Restriction

80. An appraiser, engaged to appraise a single-family residence, took away an amount of value because of "functional obsolescence." To which of the following was he referring?

    a. Dry rot
    b. Poor neighborhood
    c. Single car garage
    d. Zoning

EXAM 5

81. Seller has paid the 1st half of the annual tax bill of $1,200. Buyer agrees to assume existing fire insurance policy, originally dated Oct. 1, 1986, with a three year premium of $900. Escrow to close on Mar. 1, 1988. What would be the net buyer proration for closing?

    a. $200 credit
    b. $275 debit
    c. $675 credit
    d. $475 debit

82. Which of the following lenders would NOT be approved (respectively) by VA or FHA?

    a. Federal bank
    b. Institutional lender
    c. Insurance company
    d. Private lender

83. The ratio of "physical deterioration" of a single-family residence, compared to its original replacement cost, would be greater in the initial 10 years for which of the following?

    a. Lower quality home
    b. Fair quality home
    c. Good quality home
    d. Excellent quality home

84. A developer of a subdivision included a clause in each purchase agreement prohibiting signs offering individual properties for sale, until he had sold all the subdivision. Until developer completes sales of all parcels, which of the following is true?

    a. Buyers may put up any size sign to attract prospective buyers for resale.
    b. Buyers may put up reasonable size signs to attract prospective buyers for resale, for the original clause prohibiting signs would be unfair restraint and in violation of fair trade laws.
    c. Buyers cannot put up any signs, as it would be against the law.
    d. None of the above.

85. If NOT specified in escrow, what is the number of days normally allowed to close an escrow?

    a. 30 days
    b. 45 days
    c. 60 days
    d. A reasonable time

86. Savings Banks are regulated by the:

    a. Federal Deposit Insurance Corporation (FDIC).
    b. Federal National Mortgage Association (FNMA).
    c. Government National Mortgage Association (GNMA).
    d. local county authorities.

87. A nonresident licensee is subpoenaed by processing through the:

    a. DRE.
    b. state attorney general.
    c. California secretary of state.
    d. county attorney.

88. In which of the following would an appraisal be required by real estate law?

    a. Sale of subdivided land outside of state.
    b. Sale of subdivided land within state.
    c. Sale of land contract to new investor.
    d. Sale of trust deed to new investor.

89. Locating a building in "incompatible" neighborhood surroundings would be an example of:

    a. economical obsolescence.
    b. functional obsolescence.
    c. poor design characteristics.
    d. physical wear and tear.

90. Regarding "adverse possession," which of the following is true?

    a. Must pay taxes before delinquent.
    b. Must live on property for 5 years.
    c. Possession must be hostile to true owner.
    d. All of the above.

91. A building has inside dimensions of 25' by 50'. Outside walls are 6" thick. What is the total land area covered by building in square feet?

    a. 1,250
    b. 1,288
    c. 1,176
    d. 1,326

92. An appraiser has recommended that a refined older home located on a well landscaped corner be "razed." This would be for which of the following reasons?

    a. Contribution
    b. Highest and best use of land
    c. Regression
    d. Substitution

93. Which of the following enforces the Truth in Lending Law?

    a. Corporations Commissioner
    b. Fair Employment Practices Commission
    c. Federal Trade Commission
    d. Real Estate Commissioner

94. An investor purchased a parcel of land that was 200 ft. deep for $200,000. (This equated to $8 per sq. ft.) The price per front foot would be:

    a. $8.00.
    b. $1,000.
    c. $1,600.
    d. None of above.

EXAM 5

95. A man owns 3/4 acre parcel "A," which is rectangular shape and 110' deep. He purchased parcel "B," an adjoining parcel of the same depth, but which is 2/3 of the area of "A," for $14,000. He then subdivided the total lot (A+B) into lots 82.5' wide and sold each for $10,000, realizing a 50% return on his total combined purchase price of (A+B). What was the original cost of the 3/4 acre parcel "A"?

    a. $50,000
    b. $60,000
    c. $14,000
    d. $26,000

96. A home being sold has a $2,000 (uncallable) assessment bond against it. Similar homes in the area are selling for $75,000. If the buyer is to assume the bond payoff responsibility, what can the sellers expect to get for their home?

    a. $75,000
    b. $77,000
    c. $76,000
    d. $73,000

97. A covenant given by a lessor to lessee in a lease agreement, either stated or implied, would be:

    a compliance.
    b. suitability.
    c. quiet enjoyment.
    d. none of the above.

98. When local building codes are a matter of law, a contractor would have to comply with:

    a. local code.
    b. state code.
    c. more stringent of a or b.
    d. neither a nor b.

99. The Real Estate Commissioner has the primary authority over subdivision matters involving which of the following?

    a. Financial arrangements to insure completion of community facilities.
    b. Design and improvement of drainage.
    c. Street alignment.
    d. All of the above.

100. When using the cost method, an appraiser may use the unit cost per square foot or per cubic foot in computations. On a unit cost basis, the cost of small house vs. large house would be:

    a. small house costs more.
    b. cost is same for both.
    c. large house costs more.
    d. small house costs less.

101. If a lender desires to protect against subsequent mechanic's liens, it must post a bond with the county recorder's office for:

    a. 50% of loan.
    b. 60% of loan.
    c. 75% of loan.
    d. $5,000.

102. In accordance with the Federal Civil Rights Act of 1968, which of the following comes within the scope of the federal jurisdiction?

    a. Cal-Vet loans
    b. Conventional loans
    c. FHA and VA loans
    d. All of the above

103. A neighborhood includes a more or less unified area, with somewhat definite boundaries and a very homogeneous population in which the inhabitants have a more than casual community of interests. This is called:

    a. neighborhood brightness.
    b. social disformity.
    c. social uniformity.
    d. none of the above.

104. After closing a transaction which involves a new trust deed, the broker must cause that deed to be recorded within what time period?

    a. 30 days
    b. 7 days
    c. Reasonable time
    d. No time limit is specified

105. A broker, trying to secure listings for his office, has been advising homeowners that members of minority groups are moving into their neighborhood and it might be wise to sell before values drop. Broker is in violation of:

    a. federal fair housing law.
    b. California real estate law, and is subject to disciplinary action by the commissioner.
    c. both a and b.
    d. neither a nor b.

106. According to the Truth in Lending Law, which of the following is NOT to be included in the finance charges?

    a. Appraisal fees
    b. Loan payments
    c. Interest payments
    d. Finder's fees

EXAM 5

107. (Statement #1) The value of a property tends to coincide with the value indicated by actions of informed buyers in the market place of comparable properties. (Statement #2) The cost of producing (new construction) an equally desirable substitute property usually sets the upper limit of value. (Statement #3) The compensation to which owner is entitled when deprived of the use of his property is based on that value "indicated by the actions of informed buyers in the market for comparable properties."

The above 3 statements are versions of which one of the following principles?

    a. Change
    b. Highest and best use
    c. Substitution
    d. Supply and demand

108. A disadvantage of real property ownership is the lack of "liquidity" of investment. One approach to solve this disadvantage is through:

    a. Amortization
    b. Hypothecation
    c. Leverage
    d. Syndication

109. A net lease provides:

    a. net income to the lessor.
    b. lessor with participation in the profits of lessee.
    c. that the lessor is responsible for paying taxes and insurance.
    d. security for lessor with regard to improvements made by lessee.

110. A father left his son, Tom, 2/3 interest in a property, and Tom's wife 1/3 interest. They hold the property jointly in which of the following ways?

    a. Community property
    b. Joint tenancy
    c. Partnership
    d. Tenants in common

111. A lease based on gross income of lessee is a:

    a. gross lease.
    b. ground lease.
    c. net lease.
    d. percentage lease.

112. The terms depression, recession, and recovery are associated with what cycle?

    a. Money market
    b. Capital market
    c. Business
    d. Real estate

113. A commercial acre is defined as an:

    a. acre of land in an industrial development.
    b. acre of land in a commercial shopping center.
    c. acre of land in a new subdivision.
    d. acre of land less that needed for streets and alleys.

114. Of the following, which would be considered a federal basis for prohibiting discrimination?

    a. *Jones v. Mayer* case of 1968
    b. Title VIII of Civil Rights Act of 1968
    c. 13th and 14th Amendments of U.S. Constitution
    d. All of above

115. A homeowner purchased a property and moved into the residence on January 2nd. The homeowner's exemption was filed for and granted. If the purchase price was $107,000 and the taxes are 1.25% (1% tax + 1/4%), what would be the homeowner's amount of tax for the first installment due in November?

    a. $1,250
    b. $625
    c. $668.75
    d. $1,337.50

116. Which of the following would be most like having an "annuity"?

    a. Farm property in path of progress.
    b. Well located new apartment building.
    c. Lease to an inexperienced individual running a hardware store.
    d. Well secured long-term ground lease.

117. What two factors should a licensee know best about the Truth-in-Lending law?

    a. Commission schedule.
    b. Finance charges and annual percentage rate.
    c. Length of loan.
    d. When law became effective.

118. When a lender advances funds into escrow for a VA or FHA loan, the discount fee (points) is typically charged are equivalent to:

    a. discount to buyer.
    b. prepaid taxes.
    c. prepayment penalty.
    d. prepaid interest.

119. When a subdivider fails to comply with the Subdivision Map Act, the Real Estate Commissioner may:

    a. demand further work stopped.
    b. fine the subdivider $5,000.
    c. fine the subdivider $500 plus six months in jail.
    d. do nothing, as he has no jurisdiction.

120. The "Subdivided Lands Law," which is statewide in its operation and is directly administered and enforced by the Real Estate Commissioner, is designed to protect the purchasing public from fraud, misrepresentation, and deceit in the sale of subdivisions. This is accomplished by:

    a. disclosure in a public report of pertinent facts about the property and terms of its offering.
    b. making the issuance of the public report the authorization for subdivider to make the offering for sale or lease.
    c. impose stiff punishment for willful violators who fail to comply—$5,000 fine, one year in prison, or both.
    d. all of the above.

121. If real property is sold on credit and the seller retains legal title, the instrument used would be:

    a. bailment.
    b. mortgage.
    c. real property sales contract.
    d. security agreement.

122. An investor purchased two lots for $21,000 each, divided them into three lots and sold each for $16,800. His return on his investment was:

    a. 16.2%
    b. 12%
    c. 14%
    d. 20%

123. Trust deeds and mortgages differ in all the following ways, except:

    a. parties.
    b. security for loan.
    c. statue of limitations.
    d. title.

124. A two story commercial building measures 50' x 100'. The first floor height is 14 ft.; the second floor is 12 ft. Replacement costs for the first and second floors (per cubic ft.) are $0.75 and $0.60. Based on the above, the replacement cost of the building would be:

    a. $52,000.
    b. $36,000.
    c. $16,500.
    d. $88,500.

125. An investor paid $450,000 for income units. The tax bill showed assessments as follows: Land Value = $87,500; Improvement Value = $262,500. Using the assessor's ratio, the allowable value of the improvements for depreciation would be:

    a. $87,500
    b. $262,500
    c. $337,500
    d. $350,000

126. Real estate professionals would know that the expression "Inwood and Hoskold" would relate to:

    a. architects.
    b. estimating values.
    c. land developers.
    d. types of construction.

127. California "DRE" may suspend or revoke a broker's (or agent's) license for all of the following, except:

    a. licensee fails to exercise reasonable supervision over employees (agents).
    b. licensee is convicted of a felony (not real estate related).
    c. licensee acted unethically.
    d. two reliable witnesses verify that the licensee has been declared legally incapable.

128. Relative to taking a listing, the principal (seller) insists upon restricting a listing agreement due to race and/or color. In such a case, the licensee should:

    a. take the listing, for he cannot be held responsible for the acts of the seller.
    b. accept the listing and then report the seller to the Fair Employment Practices Commission.
    c. refuse to take the listing.
    d. none of the above.

129. The "clause" in a note and trust deed which requires (allows) the balance of the debt to become due and payable immediately upon the happening of a specified event is known as a(n):

    a. acceleration clause.
    b. alienation clause.
    c. release clause.
    d. subordination clause.

130. California law requires, for specific conditions, that an appraisal be conducted on a property prior to concluding the sale of a trust deed and note on subject property to a new buyer. In which of the following would this be required?

    a. When transaction involves mortgage loan broker.
    b. When trust deed is secured by subdivided land.
    c. In a real property security transaction.
    d. None of above.

131. For a deed to become "effective," it must be:

    a. recorded.
    b. signed and delivered.
    c. verified.
    d. none of above.

132. An investor bought a 5-unit building for $156,000. The average unit rent is $500 per month, with no vacancies. Profit realized is 53.3% of gross annual rental income. What is the yield, based on original cost (purchase price)?

    a. 7.5%
    b. 9.5%
    c. 10.25%
    d. 14%

133. It is generally agreed that when the depth of a lot increases beyond that of other lots in the area, the following is true.

    a. Value per square foot and front foot decreases.
    b. Value of overall lot decreases.
    c. Value per front foot increases.
    d. Both a and b.

134. A "bearing" wall is:

    a. a wall having no bearing on the strength of the structure.
    b. at right angles to exterior walls.
    c. a hallway wall.
    d. a wall or partition supporting a vertical load in addition to its own weight.

135. A sale is to be conducted and requirements of "bulk sales law" are to be met. The sale cannot be held until how many days have passed since the publication of the "notice of intention to sell a business"?

    a. 5
    b. 12
    c. 30
    d. 60

136. The replacement cost approach is more difficult to apply to older properties than newer ones because:

    a. zoning and building codes are subject to change.
    b. land prices are more difficult to determine for older properties.
    c. depreciation schedules are difficult to determine on older properties.
    d. historic costs are difficult to obtain.

137. A lot in the northeast section of township "X" on the northeast corner of Avenue "B," numbered 18500 and measuring 65' x 135' deep, is a:

    a. physical description.
    b. government description.
    c. legal description.
    d. assessor's description.

138. All of the following are used to calculate depreciation, except:

    a. straight-line.
    b. 200% declining balance.
    c. sum of the digits.
    d. obsolescence.

139. On July 1st, an investor purchased 10 acres of raw land for $50,000, cash. On Nov. 1st, he paid a full year's taxes on the property, amounting to $450. Assuming no growth in value (appreciation), and that the credit union would be paying their current 9% interest on deposits for the next year, how much will it cost the buyer to "own" the land for one year instead of leaving his money in the credit union?

    a. $4,500
    b. $4,741
    c. $4,977
    d. $4,527

140. A property is encumbered by two notes and trust deeds. Trustor fails to make payments on first loan, but continues to pay the second note holder. Trustee for first loan files "notice of default" (foreclosure). The beneficiary of the 2nd loan should:

    a. refinance the first loan and foreclose on their 2nd loan and trust deed.
    b. reinstate the first loan, but take no further action.
    c. file a "notice of default" on their 2nd, but do nothing about the first loan.
    d. reinstate first loan, keeping it current, and foreclose on their 2nd trust deed.

141. A lease agreement with a clause prohibiting the lessee from "subleasing" without the lessor's approval was violated when the lessee leased to another party without the lessor's knowledge. The lease is NOT:

    a. affected until the lessor hears about it.
    b. unenforceable.
    c void.
    d. voidable.

142. Which of the following codes gives authority to the Housing and Community Development Agency to develop rules and standards for manufactured homes pertaining to plumbing, accessories, fire prevention, waste discharge, and alterations or conversions?

    a. Business and Professions Code
    b. Health and Safety Code
    c. Real Investment Code
    d. Vehicle Code

143. A buyer and seller had agreed to a condition of sale and had opened escrow. Subsequently, the seller learns of a pending freeway that will increase the value of his property and immediately cancels his sale. The buyer still desires to buy. The buyer's strongest course of action would be:

    a. acceptance of settlement.
    b. file "lis pendens" action to force the sale.
    c. file suit for damages.
    d. unilateral recession.

144. In negotiating a contract, how would an attorney-in-fact sign a contract for the principal?

    a. His signature, plus "attorney-in-fact" after his name.
    b. Principal's name signed, with "attorney-in-fact" signing underneath.
    c. Sign the Principal's name.
    d. Sign the attorney-in-fact's name only.

145. Upon the death of a partner:

    a. the deceased partner's heirs hold title to the partnership property.
    b. the surviving partners have title to the partnership property for the purpose of winding up the partnership affairs, and accounting to the estate of the deceased partner.
    c. the interest of the deceased partner is extinguished.
    d. the heirs of the deceased partner become tenants in common.

146. If a seller, under a real property sales contract, notices that the vendee (buyer) has ordered work on the property he is selling, and he wishes to protect himself against a possible mechanic's lien being filed against the property, the seller must:

    a. declare a breach of contract with the buyer.
    b. serve the buyer with a Notice of Nonresponsibility.
    c. file suit against the contractor for acting without his authorization.
    d. record and post a Notice of Nonresponsibility.

147. Concerning real estate syndicates, which of the following statements it NOT correct?

    a. Selling agents must have real estate or securities license.
    b. No permit needed for "private offering."
    c. Permit must be obtained before offering can be made to the public.
    d. All offerings are controlled by the Real Estate Commissioner.

148. The sale of a "business opportunity" usually does NOT include which of the following?

    a. Fixtures and goodwill
    b. Personal property
    c. Real property
    d. Stock-in-trade

149. The maximum VA loan that a veteran can obtain, considering current practices, with a "zero" down payment, is which of the following?

    a. The "C.R.V." (VA appraisal)
    b. Sale price
    c. Four times the veteran's entitlement
    d. None of the above

150. A broker who sells final results rather than time is known as a(n):

    a. employee.
    b. independent contractor.
    c. associate agent.
    d. subagent.

Practice Exam 5 Answers

1.   c. $141,450 ÷ 115% (1.15) = $123,000
Assessed Value = 25% x Purchase Price = (.25) x $123,000 = $30,750
Taxes = $80 x $30,750 ÷ 1000 = $80 x 30.75 = $2,460 x 2 yrs = $4,920
Interest Expense = 10% (.10) x $123,000 = $12,300
Gross Expenses = $4,920 + $12,300 = $17,220
Sale Price - Purchase Price = $141,450 - 123,000 = $18,450
Net Profit = $18,450 - 17,220 = $1,230 Gain

2.   c.   Value of land - comparison approach; Value of improvements based on today's building costs.

3.   d.   "Metes" means distance or angles; "Bounds" means boundaries or measures.

4.   b.   Allows the borrower to more easily obtain additional funds (i.e., for construction loan) with the new funds being secured by a new first trust deed, which moved ahead of the original first deed, which has now subordinated to the subsequent loan.

5.   c.   Automatically goes with the land.

6.   c.   The more a commodity/product is "used," the more will be produced.

7.   d.   Multilevel tenement apartments, without elevators.

8.   b.

9.   a.

10.   b.   A Broker's Loan Statement is required anytime a broker procures a loan.

11.   c.   Anything which affects or limits fee simple title to real property is a burden.

12.   c.   A contract to be performed may be altered with consent of all parties involved.

13.   b.   Base lines run east and west; meridian lines run north and south.

14.   c.   The broker who is the procuring cause of the sale is the one entitled to the commission. To protect himself, the broker must inform the seller, in writing, of the prospects to whom he has shown the property, no later than at the end of the listing period.

15.   a.   All partners must also agree to a sale or transfer of the property.

16.   d.   First to record is first in rights. If a trust deed is without a subordination clause relinquishing priority, and is recorded first, it will take priority over subsequently recorded instruments.

17.   d.   "Indemnify" means to "make compensation for incurred lose/damage."

EXAM 5

18. c.

19. c. Total costs: Broker's fee................... $7,200
Prepayment penalty....................... $900
Escrow and title fees..................... $900
Discount fee on new loan.............. $3,300
Total Costs $12,300

Equity = Sale Price - Old Loan Balance
= $120,000 - 90,000 = $30,000
Percentage = $12,300 ÷ $30,000 x (100) = 41%

20. a. However, the "general partner" has NO such limit to his liability.

21. b. Because the home is not correctly situated on the lot it occupies, it does not function as well as it could, suffering a lost in value.

22. b. Veteran is liable to VA, unless he or she had obtained a prior release.

23. a. Level payments means the same amount (P+I) throughout the entire repayment of the loan.

24. a. It is a violation to discriminate in any manner concerning race, color, religion, national origin, sex, or marital status.

25. d. An attorney-in-fact CANNOT deed or convey the property to self. If he desires to purchase it, he/she must "give up" the power of attorney.

26. d. The answer was for that which was NOT acceptable, or wrong.

27. d. Those allowed to sell a nonexempt franchise are: (1) Real estate brokers; (2) Broker dealers or agents under the "securities law" licensed by the corporations commissioner; and (3) Person identified in application registered with the corporations commissioner for an offering of a California franchise.

28. c. Landlord may be liable where injury results from defective conditions of parts of premises over which landlord retains control. Landlord has a statutory duty to maintain dwelling house "fit for human occupation" by repairing conditions which render premises unlivable (except such that are caused by tenant's negligence). Generally, landlord is not liable where entire building is leased. Injuries to tenants (or invitees) resulting from defective conditions of areas such as lobby or restrooms are responsibility of the tenant.

29. d. With the filing of said "notice," owner shortens the time for mechanics' liens to be filed.

30. d. Having more paid off (than proportionate) to release each lot sold will result in the entire loan being cleared before all the property is reconveyed.

31. b. 2 mi. sq. = 2 mi. x 2 mi. = 4 sq. mi.
1/10 of section = (.10) x 36 sq. mi. = 3.6 sq. mi.
3 sections = 3 x (1 sq. mi.) = 3 sq. mi.
2 sq. mi. = 2 sq. mi.

32. c. *No. 1: $50,500 - $45,000 = $5,500 (gain – deferred)*
        No. 2: $60,000 - $62,000 = 2,000 (loss)
        Net gain (taxable) = $3,500

33. d. *Since monthly payment included "interest only," there was NO principal reduction. Therefore, $400,000 - 150,000 = $250,000 equity.*

34. a. *Since broker "guarantees" yield, he is selling real property securities and would need to post a $5,000 bond.*

35. d. *Cessation for 30 days must accompany an owner's filing of the "notice of cessation."*

36. c. *Wood stacked on ground is personal property; the redwood tree is growing in the ground, and stock in the mutual water company is appurtenant to the real property.*

37. d. *There is no "averaging" used in correlating value estimates by appraisers. The final step is to estimate value through correlation by placing more emphasis on the approach that appears to be most accurate.*

38. b.

39. c. *In an "exclusive agency agreement," the seller reserved right to sell herself without paying any commission to the broker.*

40. b. *Key word – "only"*

41. c. *No title passes, but buyer is equitable owner of the property. Should record a "memorandum of agreement" or land contract to give constructive notice.*

42. b. *A "sublease" is a lease given by a tenant.*

43. d. *A loan or trust deed is a lien; chattel real or real chattel are technical names for leasehold estates.*

44. d. *$200,000 x 10% (.10) = $20,000 net income*
        $20,000 + 10% = 20,000 + 2,000 = $22,000 new net income
        Value = Income divided by "cap" = $22,000 ÷ (.12) = $183,333

45. b. *The grantor is the one who signs the deed.*

46. d. *Other answers are used frequently to gradually decrease nonconforming areas.*

47. a. *An estate for years ends at previously agreed upon termination date.*

48. d. *1 mile = 320 rods; 1 section is 4 miles around*
        Therefore 1 sec. = (4 mi.) x (320 rods) = 4 x 320 = 1280 rods per strand
        For 2 strands, 2 x 1280 rods = 2560 rods = 2,560 pounds

49. b. *Debit is a charge: the buyer is charged the purchase price.*

EXAM 5

50. *d.*   Can be based on life of someone other than the life tenant.

51. *a.*   All others relate to "functional obsolescence."

52. *b.*   Base of foundation wall, pier, or column.

53. *d.*   There is NO transfer fee involved with leasing.

54. *d.*   Selling a real property security requires a real property securities dealer endorsement dealer.

55. *d.*   Ostensible agency is often referred to as a "presumptive" agency, where one party intentionally induces another to believe that another is his agent, though in fact he has not employed that person as an agent.

56. *d.*   Grant deed has warranties, NOT the "quitclaim" deed. It implies nothing, not even that the party giving the deed does in fact own an interest in the subject property.

57. *c.*

58. *d.*   The broker is required to obtain the property for the principal at the lower price, saving the principal the difference.

59. *c.*   Others (personal property) are recorded with local county recorder.

60. *c.*   Persons 55 years old or older who have owned and resided in the property being sold for 3 of the 5 years can have a once-in-a-lifetime exclusion of $125,000 in gain (1/2 for individual). Therefore, no tax liability.

61. *c.*   Gross income = $100,000 x (9%) = 100,000 x (.09) = $9,000
Interest expense = $90,000 x (9%) = 90,000 x (.09) = $8,100
Net return = $9,000 - 8,100 = $900
Percent return on investment = $900 ÷ 10,000 x (100) = 9 (9%)

62. *a.*   It is an estimate of the accumulated depreciation, which has already taken place in the property improvements, with allowance for condition based upon the "effective age of improvements."

63. *d.*   Instrument of revocation must be recorded in same office as the power of attorney. For dealing with real property, power of attorney must be acknowledged and recorded in county recorder's office.

64. *a.*   The equity is $90,000. The homestead protects up to $75,000. Therefore, the homestead will not protect against the sale.

65. *d.*

66. *b.*

67. *c.*   If the down payment is smaller, the loan must be larger.

68. **b.** The forms of a, c, and d are where the balance of principal to sellers will be deferred until a later time. The FHA agreement requires that all sums are due and payable to sellers at end of escrow.

69. **d.** Do NOT pay on old existing loan being taken over. Therefore, ($121,000 - 100,000) ÷ 1,000 x ($1.10) = 21.0 x $1.10 = $23.10.

70. **b.** The land contract does not pass title until some later time, whereby the buyer (vendee) has performed certain requirements (i.e., accumulate a minimum amount of equity for down payment); title in the meantime remains with the seller (vendor).

71. **b.** Net lease. Lessor receives a net amount for lease payment, lessee pays for expenses; property taxes, fire insurance, and operating expenses.

72. **b.**

73. **a.** When he ascertains the true net income for investment, an appraiser uses the "capitalization approach" to estimate value.

74. **b.** Since the lessee of the fire station building would be the government, classified as a more stable tenant, the owner would probably be willing to accept a lower return on investment.

75. **d.** Seller "B" would need a quitclaim deed from "A," or would need to seek a "quiet title action" in court to clear the cloud on his title so he could sell the property to another.

76. **a.** They have nothing to do with establishing value.

77. **c.** Sec. 4: SE¼ of SE¼ of SE¼ = 1/4 x 1/4 x 1/4 x 640 acres = 10
Sec. 3: S½ of SW¼ of SW¼ = 1/2 x 1/4 x 1/4 x 640 acres = 20
Sec. 9: N½ of NE¼ of NE¼ of NE¼ = 1/2 x 1/4 x 1/4 x 1/4 x 640 acres = 5
Sec. 10: N½ of N½ of NW¼ of NW¼ = 1/2 x 1/2 x 1/4 x 1/4 x 640 acres = 10
Total Acreage = 45 acres
Price (total) = $10,000 x 45 acres = $450,000

78. **a.** A fine example of an "equity asset" is a single-family residence, which during an inflationary market condition, has a value that tends to follow the inflationary trends.

79. **a.** Attachment is an "involuntary lien."

80. **c.** In todays world, this feature would be considered "outdated," or in other words, functionally obsolete.

81. **b.** Taxes: $1,200 ÷ 12 = $100 per month. Seller owes buyer for 2 months
= $100 x (2) = $200 credit buyer
Insurance: $900 ÷ 36 = $25 per month. Buyer owes seller for 19 months
unused premiums = $25 x (19) = $475 debit buyer
Net = debit buyer ($475 - 200) = $275 debit buyer

82. **d.** VA and FHA do NOT guarantee or insure loans made by private lenders.

83. **a.** Home built with poor quality materials and labor (workmanship) should require more maintenance and will deteriorate more rapidly.

84. **b.**

85. **d.** There is NO standard time. Make certain that there is sufficient time allowed to accomplish the work to be done.

86. **a.**

87. **c.** The secretary of state is designated by California law to process violations of nonresident licensees.

88. **a.** To protect California buyers of land subdivided outside of the state, an appraisal is required.

89. **a.** Results would be an adverse influence on production of income (commercial building), or use and enjoyment (residential building).

90. **c.** Need NOT always live on property nor pay taxes prior to their being late.

91. **d.** The 6" walls add one foot to each dimension of the building. Therefore, area covered = 51' x 26' = 1,326 sq. ft.

92. **b.** Probably the economic value of the building has deteriorated to where no amount of repair can justify keeping the building, and the highest and best use cannot be served. Therefore, tear it down and build a new building.

93. **c.** The Federal Trade Commission (FTC) enforces the Truth in Lending Law.

94. **c.** $200,000 ÷ $8.00 = 25,000 sq. ft. (total area)
Width = Area divided by length = 25,000 ÷ 200 = 125 ft. wide
Cost per ft. = $200,000 ÷ 125 ft. wide = $1,600

95. **d.** Areas: "A" = 3/4 acre; therefore, "B" = (2/3) x (3/4) = 1/2 acre
Total area = 3/4 + 1/2 = 5/4 = 1.25 acres = (1.25) x (43,560) = 54,450 sq. ft.
Front Ft. = 54,450 divided by width = 54,450 ÷ 110 = 495 ft.
No. of New Lots = 495 ÷ 82.5 = 6 lots
Gross new sale price = ($10,000) x (6) = $60,000
Cost (A+B) = $60,000 ÷ 150% (1.50) = $40,000

Cost of Parcel "A" = Cost (A+B) - Cost "B" = $40,000 - $14,000 = **$26,000**

96. **e.** Buyer would expect the price to be adjusted down to compensate for their paying off the bond assessment.

97. **c.** It is a right of the lessee to enjoy the possession of the property without disturbing other tenants or being disturbed.

98. **c.**

99. *a.* DRE has authority to see that the developer/subdivider posts bonds as required (completion bonds) to insure performance of completion of community facilities.

100. *a.* Bathroom and kitchen facilities are the most expensive areas to build, and if those costs are spread over a smaller home (per sq. ft.), the costs of the home would be higher than for a larger home.

101. *c.* No less than 75% is required. The purpose of the bond is to assure payment of any judgment in suits which may be brought to foreclose on mechanic's liens on the property.

102. *d.* Covers "all" loan situations.

103. *c.*

104. *b.*

105. *c.*

106. *a.* Appraisal fees are excluded, as are: credit reports, notary, impounds, document preparation costs, title insurance, and property insurance.

107. *d.*

108. *d.* Allows investor to withdraw at any time, without having to sell the syndicated property.

109. *a.* Lessor receives specified payment amount each period. Lessee pays all variable items, i.e., taxes, insurance, other expenses.

110. *d.* Unequal holdings could NOT be joint tenancy.

111. *d.* Lease payment determined as a percentage of gross volume of business (income) together with a provision for a minimum amount payment.

112. *c.*

113. *d.*

114. *d.* All are basis for prohibiting discrimination.

115. *b.* ($107,000 - 7,000) x (1.25%) = 100,000 x (.0125) = $1,250 ÷ 2 = $625

116. *d.* Like monthly money in the bank.

117. *b.* The two most important items found on the statement.

118. *d.* Offsets typically lower interest rates than for conventional financing involvement.

119. *a.* State law, but locally enforced, requires city and county to adopt ordinances to regulate the provisions of the act. Commissioner can stop further work if he/she believes that action is necessary.

EXAM 5

120. **d.** All are means of preventing dishonest dealing with regards to subdivisions.

121. **c.** Same as "land contract."

122. **d.** Original purchase (total) = $21,000 x 2 = $42,000
Final Sale Price (3 lots) = $16,800 x 3 = $50,400
Gross profit = $50,400 - 42,000 = $8,400
Percentage return = $8,400 ÷ $42,000 x (100) = 20%

123. **b.** Whether mortgage or trust deed is used, the property is security.

124. **d.** (1st Floor) 50' x 100' x 14' x ($0.75) = $52,500 (2nd Floor) 50' x 100' x 12' x ($0.60) = 36,000
Total Cost of Building = $88,500

125. **c.** Assessments = $87,500 + 262,500 = $350,000 "Improvement" ratio to total = 262,500 ÷ 350,000 x (100) = 75%
Therefore: Cost ratio = $450,000 x 75% (.75) = $337,500 Value for depreciation.

126. **b.** Two men who created an appraiser's handbook for establishing value.

127. **c.** Ethics violations are covered by the civil code.

128. **c.** NOT allowed in any way to join in promoting discrimination.

129. **a.** Alienation clause is a form of acceleration clause whereby upon the "sale" of the property, the loan would become due and payable.

130. **c.** Each parcel relating to a transaction MUST have an appraisal.

131. **b.** Deed does NOT have to be verified or recorded to be valid. It must be delivered to become valid.

132. **c.** $500 x 5 units x 12 months = $30,000
Gross Annual Income Profit = 53.3% (.533) x $30,000 = $15,990
Yield = $15,990 ÷ $156,000 x (100) = 10.25%

133. **c.** In general, the more frontage on the street, the higher the value of the land.

134. **d.**

135. **b.** Law requires the purchaser to: (1) record with county recorder's office; and (2) publish notice in local newspaper (general circulation) at least 12 working days prior to transfer, and notify (by registered mail) tax collector at least 12 working days prior to the transfer.

136. **c.** There are often wide variations between appraisers as to the "effective age" of older property.

137. **a.**

138. *d.*   *Obsolescence is NOT a "method" for computing depreciation, but is a "type" of depreciation.*

139. *c.*
Taxes Paid...	*$450*
Loss of interest on $50,000 = 50,000 x (.09) =	*4,500*
Loss of interest on tax money = $450 x (.09) x 2/3 =	*27**
Total cost of owning property =	*$4,977*

(*) Time was for only 8 months = 2/3 year

140. *d.*   *Must keep the first current, or it will foreclose and wipe them out.*

141. *d.*   *Lease is voidable at the will of the lessor, but NOT by the lessee, even though the terms have been violated.*

142. *b.*

143. *b.*   *Would put on record for the world to see that the buyer has a claim against the seller's property, and may force the sale.*

144. *b.*   *Per Civil Code, "When an attorney in fact executes an instrument transferring real property, he must subscribe the name of the principal to it, and his own name as attorney in fact."*

145. *b.*

146. *d.*

147. *d.*   *Offerings are controlled by the Corporation Commissioner.*

148. *c.*   *Frequently, if real property is involved, it is in the form of a leasehold interest, which again is personal property. If real property is available for purchase, it is usually handled in a separate and concurrent transaction, using different escrows.*

149. *c.*   *The current policy allows for four times the veteran's entitlement.*

150. *b.*   *Independent contractor's sell results; employees are under the control of the employer; subagents get their authority from the agent.*

EXAM 5

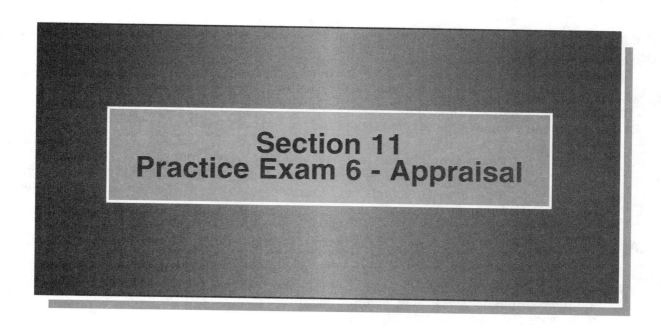

1. A $2,000 down payment was made on a property, which was purchased for $20,000. The gross return on the purchase price was 9%. The only expense in the transaction was a 7% interest charge. The percentage return on this investment would be:

    a. 11%
    b. 13%
    c. 27%
    d. 8%

      ANSWER: c.   *$20,000 x . 09 = $1,800 Gross return*
                      $18,000 x .07 = $1.26 Interest expense =
                      Gross return - interest = net return = $1,800 - $1,260 = $540 net return.

                      Net return divided by Investment = % return on investment
                      $540 ÷ $2,000 = 27%.

2. If a $52,500 loan was made on a property which was equivalent to 70% of the appraised value. What was the amount of the appraised value?

    a. $90,000
    b. $80,000
    c. $50,000
    d. $75,000

      ANSWER: d.   *$52,500 ÷ .70 = $75,000 appraised value.*

3. If the rent of commercial property increased well above the maintenance or servicing costs, the resulting situation would:

    a. not affect the vacancy rate.
    b. increase the effective gross income.
    c. increase the demand for space.
    d. increase the vacancy rate, and tenants would tend to conserve on space.

> **ANSWER: d.** *When rent controls are not a factor, rental prices can become highly competitive. When established rent is too far above housing and servicing requirements, tenants tend to conserve on space, and the vacancy rate will increase.*

4. A net lease may be said to have which of the following characteristics?

    a. It is a percentage of the profits.
    b. It does not benefit the lessor.
    c. It produces a net income for the lessor.
    d. The lessor pays for all variable expenses.

> **ANSWER: c.** *A net lease provides a lessor with a fixed income, which is founded on an agreement requiring the lessee to pay all variable costs, such as insurance and property taxes.*

5. The prospective purchaser of real property would be most concerned with the:

    a. economic life remaining in the improvements.
    b. physical life remaining in the improvements.
    c. chronological age of the improvements.
    d. effective age of the improvements.

> **ANSWER: a.** *Effective age indicates existing conditions, as related to past maintenance. Chronological age is related to past events affecting a property. Of course, remaining physical age is important to the purchaser, but she is more concerned with the estimated period over which she may utilize the property for profit.*

6. A new, large-scale shopping center requires a loan for financing purposes. The lender would place major emphasis on which of the following features?

    a. Long-term leases
    b. Short-term leases
    c. Anchor tenant (A+ credit/large company)
    d. The experience and background of the developer

> **ANSWER: c.** *A large company, having an excellent credit rating and offering very good potential for payoff of the loan, would be called an "Anchor Tenant."*

7. Real estate appraisers may use the 4-3-2-1 Rule as a useful tool in their work. It applies to the:

    a. lot and improvements.
    b. tract evaluation.
    c. house, lot, and garage
    d. method for appraising lots of differing depths.

    ANSWER: d. *The 4-3-2-1 Rule is used to measure the value of adjacent lots, which have different depths. Lot value is considered to be 40% in the first quarter (front of lot), 30% in the second quarter, 20% in the third quarter, and 10% in the last quarter of depth.*

8. The least protection against blighting in any given area is provided by which of the following?

    a. Zoning ordinances.
    b. Artificial and natural barriers.
    c. A neighborhood not fully developed.
    d. Residents aware of the hazards of blighting.

    ANSWER: c. *A partially developed neighborhood receives little protection from blighting influences. Unfavorable elements, such as poor upkeep and divergent uses of property, are difficult to restrict or control.*

9. When comparing a rental situation with the ownership of a home, which of the following does NOT represent a cost of home ownership?

    a. Repayment or amortization of a loan.
    b. Depreciation of the investment in a home.
    c Property taxes and bond assessments.
    d. An equity investment, which does not produce an income.

    ANSWER: a. *When an owner amortizes, or pays back, the principal on a loan by means of regular installments, it is not an expense because his equity is increased. In effect, he puts money out in one direction, but receives it back from another direction.*

10. To a land developer, suburban land is preferable to urban land for development purposes. Which of the following reasons is applicable?

    a. Development costs are lower.
    b. Suburban land has the potential for containing a complete community.
    c. The value of adjoining land is increased.
    d. Low-cost housing for single persons can be provided.

    ANSWER: b. *When working with suburban land, the developer, in conformance with zoning ordinances, has the freedom to select suitable areas for school, commercial properties, and residences. In urban areas, where growth patterns and zoning requirements are usually well established, the developer has much less freedom of choice.*

EXAM 6 APPRAISAL

11. An appraiser would NOT be in violation of the USPAP if he:

    a. pays people to refer clients to him.
    b. accepts an appraisal assignment, knowing that he is not fully qualified to handle the assignment.
    c accepts an appraisal fee based upon a percentage of the value estimate.
    d. accepts an appraisal fee for service on a property in which he has an interest, a fact which has been disclosed to his client in writing.

    > *ANSWER: d.* *It is permissible to collect a fee for service on a property in which the appraiser has an interest, providing the fact has been disclosed properly to the client.*

12. Which of the following may value real estate for a federally related loan transaction?

    a. Real Estate Brokers
    b. Certified Public Accountants
    c. Licensed or Certified Real Estate Appraisers
    d. Chartered Evaluators

    > *ANSWER: c.* *Brokers may value real estate for non-loan purposes, CPAs value business interests, Chartered Evaluators are British Appraisers.*

13. The U.S. Bureau of Labor Statistics publishes a cost of living index. If a lease contains an escalator clause, which requires periodic adjustments in relation to changes in the index, the lease is called a(n):

    a. fixed lease.
    b. standard lease.
    c. index lease.
    d. federal lease.

    > *ANSWER: c.* *If rentals are adjusted in relation to the movements of a recognized national index, such as the cost of living index, the controlling lease is called an Index Lease.*

14. Appraisers, builders, and architects use which of the following methods for estimating costs?

    a. Comparative square foot, unit in place
    b. Comparative square or cubic foot, unit in place, quantity survey
    c. Residual income, resulting from capitalization calculations
    d. Replacement costs, resulting from capitalization calculations

    > *ANSWER: b.* *There are three accepted methods for cost estimation.*
    >
    > *1. comparative square foot or cubic foot, also called the Unit Method*
    > *2. Unit cost in place*
    > *3. Quantity survey*

15. The price of real property _____ as the value of the dollar decreases. The price of real property _____ as the value of the dollar increases.

    a. increases, decreases
    b. increases, increases
    c. decreases, increases
    d. decreases, decreases

    ANSWER: a.   *When the value of the dollar decreases, it loses a portion of its purchasing power. This means that more dollars are required to purchase a given piece of property. In order to accomplish this, the price of the property must be increased. Conversely, when the value of the dollar increases, it gains purchasing power. This indicates that fewer dollars are necessary for the purchase of a given piece of property, and thus, a decrease in price is required to adjust for the change.*

16. When a building is positioned on a lot in such a way that it reflects consideration of noise, sun, wind, privacy, and other factors, the act of positioning is called:

    a. land use conformity.
    b. orographic arrangement.
    c. profile elevation.
    d. orientation.

    ANSWER: d.   *The phrasing of the question is a good definition of orientation.*

17. The four essential elements of value are:

    a. Cost, Demand, Utility, Scarcity
    b. Cost, Demand, Capitalization, Scarcity
    c. Demand, Improvements, Selling Price, Time on Market
    d. Demand, Utility, Scarcity, Transferability

    ANSWER: d.   *"DUST"*

    Cost, selling price, and time on market have nothing to do with value. Capitalization is a mathematical tool.

18. Amenity type properties are appraised most often by which of the following methods?

    a. Income method
    b. Market data method
    c. Cost method
    d. Risk-rating method

    ANSWER: b.   *Amenity type properties are single family residences, and the market data method is most often used for these.*

**EXAM 6
APPRAISAL**

19. An appraisal is an:

 a. estimate of value.
 b. opinion of value.
 c. opinion of listing price.
 d. opinion of selling price.

 ANSWER: b. *Appraisers are licensed and certified to provide a professional opinion of value. Anyone may estimate. Answers "c" and "d" are professional services provided by licensed real estate agents and brokers engaged in the sale of real estate.*

20. If a structure is repaired without changing the interior or exterior design, this process is called:

 a. modernization.
 b. reclamation.
 c. remodeling.
 d. rehabilitation.

 ANSWER: d. *When a property is restored to satisfactory condition without changing style, form, or plan, this is known as rehabilitation.*

21. An appraiser should have knowledge of economic trends, which affect property values. For example, in an area which has heavy bonded indebtedness and high property taxes, he would probably conclude that:

 a. large investors would be attracted to the area.
 b. new construction and general industry would tend to leave the area.
 c. there would have to be better schools and services in the area.
 d. there would be a good market for street bonds.

 ANSWER: b. *Under these conditions, new business ventures would be discouraged by the upward tax trend, and would be inclined to seek other locations. Assessment bonds would be difficult to market. High taxes do not necessarily imply better schools.*

22. A buyer with a low income considers many factors in choosing a home, the most important of which would be:

 a. the surrounding neighborhood.
 b. his income.
 c. the type and size of home.
 d. location.

 ANSWER: d. *The location of the home in relation to his workplace would be a major consideration, since it would have an important impact on his commuting problems and costs.*

23. To be effective, good property management should begin:

    a. upon completion of construction.
    b. when expenditures have been made for property improvement.
    c. after the property has been acquired.
    d. before the property has been acquired.

        ANSWER: d.   *Good management should have an opportunity to participate in the decision leading up to the acquisition of the property.*

24. An appraiser, when using the reproduction cost method on property which has been improved with fences, shrubs, trees, lawns, and sidewalks, should always:

    a. evaluate each of these items separately.
    b. regard these items as part of the improvements.
    c. treat these items as a part of the land.
    d. consider them as having no influence on the appraisal.

        ANSWER: a.   *A good comparative value can only be determined by treating each one of these items separately, thus enabling the appraiser to make a direct dollar adjustment for each item.*

25. As compared with other commodities, capital turnover in real estate investments is:

    a. slower.
    b. slightly above the average.
    c. faster.
    d. about equal.

        ANSWER: a.   *Because of the large amounts of money involved, together with the fixed nature of real property, the turnover of capital is slower as compared with other commodities.*

26. The sale and leaseback of a property is a situation in which the buyer would have the least concern with the:

    a. lessee's credit rating.
    b. structural soundness of the building.
    c. book value of the property, less depreciation.
    d. location of the property.

        ANSWER: c.   *The seller, not the buyer, is affected by book value minus the depreciation charge. The other statements in the question would be of considerable concern to the buyer.*

EXAM 6
APPRAISAL

27. Owner-occupied homes in a residential area have an immediate effect on the local economy in which of the following ways?

  a. Property values would be maintained at a maximum.
  b. This situation would induce property speculation.
  c. Rental incomes would be at a maximum.
  d. There would be a lower occupancy turnover.

  ANSWER: d. *Owner-occupied homes lend economic stability to a neighborhood and lessen the possibility of turnover. Property values are maintained at maximum figures over a long term, rental income is nonexistent, and property speculation is not attractive to investors.*

28. The Gross Multiplier is an arbitrary number employed by appraisers in the evaluation of certain types of income property. It is calculated in which of the following ways?

  a. The confirmed sale price of the property is divided by the gross monthly rental.
  b. The gross monthly rental is divided by the appraised value of the property.
  c. The market value of the property is multiplied by the capitalization rate.
  d. The gross monthly rental is multiplied by the capitalization rate.

  ANSWER: a. *The Gross Multiplier is a number used by appraisers to estimate the value of certain types of income property. When the gross monthly rental is multiplied by this number, the result is the actual sales price of the property.*

29. When lessees pay one month's rent in advance of the lease period, accounting procedures regard this as:

  a. deferred expense for the lessor.
  b. deferred income for the lessor.
  c. accrued income for the lessee.
  d. accrued expense for the lessor.

  ANSWER: b. *This is deferred income for the lessor because it is income earned, but not yet received. For income tax purposes, it is reported as income for the year in which it is received. Deferred expense indicates expense paid in advance, but not used. Accrued expense indicates expense owing, but not yet paid.*

30. Unearned increment is considered in the appraisal of income producing property. Select the best example of unearned increment from the following.

  a. Unanticipated value increase due to circumstantial changes.
  b. Mortgage interest.
  c. Land depreciation.
  d. Property maintenance.

  ANSWER: a. *If the value of a property increases through no efforts, thinking, or planning on the part of the owner, such an increase is called Unearned Increment.*

31. Depth tables are used by appraisers as a tool to:

    a. show the depth of water in arid areas.
    b. determine the value of commercial properties on which the lots vary in depth.
    c. facilitate the calculation of interest payments on declining balances.
    d. determine the relationship between beach properties and high-tide elevations.

    > *ANSWER: b.   If lots have the same front footage, a shallow lot is less valuable than a deep lot. When evaluating commercial properties, appraisers use Depth Tables to estimate the relative value of lots which vary from a normal depth.*

32. If the purchasing power of the dollar decreases, the price of property_____. If the purchasing power of the dollar increases, the price of property_____. In both cases, the value of the property_____.

    a. increases, decreases, increases
    b. decreases, increases, increases
    c. decreases, decreases, increases
    d. increases, decreases, could remain the same

    > *ANSWER: d.   When the purchasing power of the dollar decreases, prices increase. When the purchasing power of the dollar increases, prices decrease. When measuring the value of a commodity as a reflection of such changes in the purchasing power of the dollar, it can be said that, for example, the value of a home, which sold for $39,000 in 1958, could have the same value in 1995 at a selling price of $120, 000.*

33. If a lessor wanted a long-term, uncomplicated income from a sale-leaseback arrangement, the type of lease best fitting this requirement would be a:

    a. step up.
    b. percentage.
    c. net.
    d. none of the foregoing.

    > *ANSWER: c.   The lessor receives a net amount as rental, whereas the lessee, or tenant, pays for taxes and insurance and handles all maintenance problems. This is a simplified arrangement for the lessor.*

34. If other factors are equal, and if the areas of living space are comparable, how are the costs of a two-story house and a one-story house related?

    a. There is no cost relationship between the two types of houses.
    b. The cost factors are equal.
    c. It is more costly to build a two-story house.
    d. It is less costly to build a two-story house.

    > *ANSWER: d.   For a given square footage of living space, a two-story house is less costly than a single story house because certain basic factors are reduced by 50%; for example, heating ducts, roof area, lateral plumbing lines, and foundations.*

EXAM 6
APPRAISAL

35. Which of the following approaches would an appraiser use in determining today's value of a single-family residence, which was built about 1930?

   a. He would refer to a cost index and adjust for changes over the years.
   b. Draw a conclusion from comparable sales figures in 1930.
   c. He would use today's reproduction costs and adjust for depreciation accordingly.
   d. He would use 1930 construction costs as a starting point for his calculations.

   ANSWER: c.   The simplest and most feasible approach would be to use today's reproduction costs and to make allowances for any recognizable depreciation in determining the value of the property.

36. If an appraiser observes wide cracks in the walls of a basement, he will attribute the probable cause to:

   a. normal curing of the concrete.
   b. settling of the house.
   c. weakening joists.
   d. deterioration due to moisture.

   ANSWER: b.   Settling of the house on its foundations would cause such wide cracks. The other answers would not have this effect.

37. An investor constructs an office building and soon discovers that he can only rent a small percentage of the office space. Also, the electrical, plumbing, cooling, and heating systems are found to be oversize. This is an example of what kind of obsolescence?

   a. Incurable locational
   b. Curable functional
   c. Curable economic
   d. Incurable functional

   ANSWER: d.   If such an office building has excessive capacity and more-than-adequate facilities, it will suffer a loss of value due to functional obsolescence, which is incurable. Economic obsolescence creates a loss of value due to causes outside the building.

38. No provision is made for which of the following elements in the calculation of a capitalization rate during an appraisal of income property?

   a. Income taxes and mortgage payments
   b. Return on Investment
   c. Return of Investment
   d. Depreciation on the improvements

   ANSWER: a.   Capitalization rates include only return of investment and return on investment. Depreciation is associated with return of investment. Taxes are not a factor in computing capitalization rates.

39. Which of the following is NOT an example of functional obsolescence?

    a. Excessive strength in the foundation members and exterior walls.
    b. Excessive number of partitions in an office building.
    c. Proximity to a chemical plant, which gives off noxious fumes.
    d. Archaic architectural design.

        ANSWER: c.   *Proximity to a chemical plant is a form of economic obsolescence, since the cause lies outside the property. The other answers represent functional obsolescence, since they are within, or are inherent to, the property.*

40. If each of the following properties was purchased for $150,000, which would make provision for the most dollars of allowable depreciation?

    a. A farm
    b. An apartment building
    c. A commercial property
    d. An industrial property

        ANSWER: b.   *In this example, the apartment building would probably use the least amount of the cost basis for land value. This indicates that the largest portion of the $150,000 would be depreciated.*

41. Which of the following would be an example of economic obsolescence?

    a. Exorbitant tax rates for civic improvements.
    b. Old fashioned design features.
    c. Deferred maintenance.
    d. Only one bathroom in a two-story residence.

        ANSWER: a.   *Economic obsolescence is caused by extraneous factors. A high tax rate would be such a factor. The other factors are contained within the property.*

42. When an appraiser evaluates real property, his concept of annual, or periodic, depreciation applies to which of the following?

    a. Actual life
    b. Economic life
    c. Physical life
    d. Theoretical life

        ANSWER: b.   *Ordinarily, a loss in value is considered on an annual basis. Economic life treats such loss, whether accrued or future, at a periodic rate.*

43. By definition, economic obsolescence would NOT apply to which of the following?

    a. Location of a government building adjacent to the property.
    b. Neighborhood reconstruction projects.
    c. Antique fixtures in a building.
    d. Regulatory changes.

        ANSWER: c.   *The antique fixtures would represent functional obsolescence, not economic obsolescence.*

**EXAM 6
APPRAISAL**

44. Economic obsolescence would be created by which of the following?

    a. Old fashioned ceiling heights.
    b. Poor architectural arrangement of floor space.
    c. Inadequate parking facilities.
    d. An excessive number of similar properties available in the area.

    ANSWER: d.   *Economic obsolescence is created by causes lying beyond, or outside, the property. An oversupply of similar, or competitive, units in the same area fits this parameter. The other answers to the question represent deficiencies in the property itself.*

45. Depreciation is a factor least affected by which of the following statements?

    a. A change in value resulting from inflation or other positive economic forces.
    b. Obsolescence resulting from adverse external changes in the neighborhood.
    c. Value deterioration due to action of natural elements.
    d. Obsolescence due to faulty design or inferior quality of construction.

    ANSWER: a.   *"a" represents an unearned increment, or increase in value, due to external causes. It is NOT a depreciating factor, whereas the other answers to the question are all depreciating elements.*

46. An investigation of a certain building reveals that there is a serious deterioration of the foundation and supporting beams in the basement. An appraiser would classify this type of defect as:

    a. curable physical deterioration.
    b. incurable physical deterioration.
    c. curable functional obsolescence.
    d. incurable functional obsolescence.

    ANSWER: b.   *In this context, this type of physical deterioration is classified as incurable because it is not economically profitable to replace, or to cure, the conditions as of the date of the appraisal.*

47. A change in the flight patterns of an airport creates excessive noise over an apartment building. This results in increased vacancies and loss of property value. This loss of value would be called:

    a. functional obsolescence.
    b. ecological obsolescence.
    c. physical deterioration.
    d. economic obsolescence.

    ANSWER: d.   *Economic obsolescence results from adverse factors beyond the confines of the property.*

48. Accrued depreciation may be estimated by five general methods. Which of the following would be considered as indirect methods?

   a. Capitalized income and market methods
   b. Breakdown and engineering methods
   c. Capitalized and engineering methods
   d. Market and breakdown methods

   ANSWER: a.   The capitalized income and market methods are considered to be indirect methods. Straight-line, engineering, and breakdown methods are classified as direct methods.

49. Some forms of depreciation are curable, some are not. Which of the following forms is NOT curable?

   a. Physical depreciation
   b. Physical wear and tear
   c. Economic obsolescence
   d. Functional obsolescence

   ANSWER: c.   Economic depreciation, or obsolescence, takes place beyond the confines of the property. Thus, the property owner cannot exert control over such features as economic recession, aircraft noise, adverse zoning, or the departure of major industries from the area. These situations can only be regarded as incurable.

50. Which one of the following illustrates the most common type of depreciation?

   a. Faulty plumbing
   b. An increase of amenities
   c. Outmoded appliances and poor architectural design
   d. Deferred maintenance

   ANSWER: d.   Deferred maintenance is maintenance which has been postponed to some later date. This is a common practice, and it tends to deteriorate the physical condition of a structure.

51. If a buyer plans to purchase an older building, he would give most careful consideration to the:

   a. economic life remaining.
   b. actual life.
   c. economic life.
   d. effective life.

   ANSWER: a.   The buyer would be most concerned with the future potentials of the property; the economic life still remaining.

EXAM 6
APPRAISAL

52. All of the following would cause economic obsolescence, except:

    a. improperly placed improvements.
    b. old fashioned kitchens.
    c. unfavorable zoning changes.
    d. industries moving out of the neighborhood.

    ANSWER: b. Old fashioned kitchens represent a form of functional obsolescence. The other three items are caused by factors outside the property. Therefore, they are forms of economic obsolescence.

53. If an appraiser wishes to measure the extent of accrued depreciation, he would rely upon which one of the following methods of calculation?

    a. Cubic foot
    b. Square foot
    c. Front foot
    d. Straight-line method

    ANSWER: d. Appraisers do NOT use footage as methods of calculating depreciation; therefore, they would select the straight-line method.

54. In the determination for replacement costs of a new property, an appraiser would use all of the following methods, except:

    a. comparative square foot.
    b. observed condition of the property.
    c. quantity survey.
    d. unit cost-in-place.

    ANSWER: b. Observed condition is a method for estimating accrued depreciation, and it is NOT used to determine replacement costs.

55. In the course of evaluating apartment property net income, an appraiser would regard an annual payment for a street paving assessment as a(n):

    a. fixed expenditure.
    b. operating expense.
    c. expense related to income.
    d. capital outlay.

    ANSWER: d. Assessments for street improvements are considered to be capital expenses, which increase land values. They are NOT regarded as expenses deductible from income.

56. The income approach to valuation requires the measurement of, and the provision for, future depreciation. For this purpose, an appraiser would use all of the following methods, except:

    a. sinking fund rate.
    b. cost of reproduction.
    c. straight-line.
    d. a capitalization rate, which includes a risk rating.

    ANSWER: b. *The cost of reproduction method treats more of past loss in value rather than of expected loss of value in the future. The answers, "a," "c," and "d" are methods developed to analyze the problems of future depreciation.*

57. An appraiser would have to be able to identify land values separately in which one of the following appraisal techniques?

    a. Market data approach
    b. Income approach
    c. Cost approach
    d. All of the foregoing

    ANSWER: c. *The cost approach requires the appraiser to identify land values separately from the reproduction cost of the improvements located on the land. In the other appraisal methods, the appraiser develops the entire property as one total value, then separates land value from improvement value.*

58. The most important economic characteristic of property is:

    a. lot size.
    b. lot shape.
    c. location.
    d. capital improvements.

    ANSWER: c. *Location! Location! Location! Forget everything else!*

59. In the construction of a building, there are several indirect costs involved, one of which is:

    a. building permit fees.
    b. material costs.
    c. labor costs.
    d. subcontracts.

    ANSWER: a. *"b," "c," and "d" are direct costs. A listing of indirect costs would show such items as permits, surveys, consulting fees, architects, engineers, legal, taxes financing charges, and administrative and overhead costs.*

**EXAM 6
APPRAISAL**

60. Sites for industrial buildings are usually gauged by the:

   a. cubic foot.
   b. front foot.
   c. acre.
   d. square foot.

   > ANSWER: d.   *Industrial building sites are usually valued according to square footage. Acre is a unit of measure seldom used.*

61. The income approach to appraisal requires the selection of an accurate capitalization rate because:

   a. the appraised value of property increases if the capitalization rate is decreased.
   b. the appraised value of property increases if the capitalization rate is increased.
   c. a provision for return on the investment is a limitation on the calculation of a capitalization rate.
   d. a property, which has a reliable tenant, would justify a higher capitalization rate than one with a tenant who has a poor financial background.

   > ANSWER: a.   *Appraisal value increases when the capitalization rate is decreased. The capitalization rate represents the integration of the rate of income, expressed as interest, and the rate of recapture, expressed as depreciation.*

62. "Just compensation" is a term used in condemnation proceedings. In determining the fair market value of a property, the court would use any of the following, except the:

   a. comparative income data approach.
   b. cost approach.
   c. income approach.
   d. market data approach.

   > ANSWER: b.   *The court seldom uses the cost approach, unless the property is unique in some way and has very little turnover.*

63. If an appraiser used all three methods in evaluating a residential property, he would combine the results in what way?

   a. He would give reasonable weight to each estimate and divide by 3.
   b. He would add the three estimates and divide by 3.
   c. Both a and b.
   d. Neither a nor b.

   > ANSWER: d.   *The appraiser's resultant estimate would be founded on judgment and professional experience rather than on some arithmetical process.*

64. The cost of replacement method is least effective in evaluating which of the following properties?

    a. A new single family residence.
    b. A new school building.
    c. An older single family residence.
    d. All of the foregoing.

      ANSWER: c.   *Depreciation is difficult to estimate on older properties, with the result that the reproduction cost method might have rather wide variations. It is not necessary to estimate depreciation on new properties.*

65. When lot size increases in depth, the value of:

    a. square footage increases.
    b. front footage increases.
    c. front footage decreases.
    d. square footage and front footage, as a unit, decreases.

      ANSWER: b.   *When the depth of a lot increases, the front foot value will increase. Also, increasing the depth will increase the square footage, but, usually, the square foot value will be reduced.*

66. Value is the present worth of future benefits, arising out of ownership, to typical users and investors, is one definition of value. To which one of the following appraisal techniques does it relate?

    a. Comparison
    b. Reproduction cost
    c. Income
    d Market data

      ANSWER: c.   *The income approach depends largely upon the anticipation of future performance. Today's dollars are used as a measure of future benefits.*

67. Provision for the recapture of capital improvements is made in which of the following during an income evaluation approach to appraisal?

    a. Cost of replacement new today.
    b. Cost of replacement new at installation date.
    c. Depreciation accrual.
    d. Condition of improvements, as observed.

      ANSWER: c.   *Funds are set aside on an annual basis for any depreciation which may be allowable.*

EXAM 6 APPRAISAL

68. Quality of income is an important factor in making an appraisal. It is best expressed in which of the following statements?

a. In establishing a proper relationship between risk involved and income produced, it is necessary to develop an accurate capitalization rate.
b. In the amount of income produced by the real property.
c. In making a reasonable allowance for recapture of investment in improvements and in other depreciable items.
d. In making a proper determination of the anticipated period of time during which the improvements would produce income.

ANSWER: a.   The capitalization of net income from real estate investments is at a rate which is a function of the risk involved. The quality factor of net income is interpreted in terms of risk.

69. If an appraiser were called upon to evaluate a public building, which had unique and distinctive architecture, he would employ which of the following methods of valuation?

a. Replacement
b. Comparison
c. Capitalization
d. None of the foregoing.

ANSWER: a.   Since there is no income for capitalization and no means for comparing sales, replacement cost is the only approach available.

70. It is preferable to use the replacement cost method of appraisal on new buildings, as opposed to old buildings, because:

a. it is easier to estimate depreciation.
b. values of land change.
c. it is difficult to estimate historical values.
d. local codes are changed from time to time.

ANSWER: a.   As the age of the improvements on a property increases, it becomes more difficult to forecast the allowable depreciation.

71. A lending institution hires an appraiser to evaluate a property for loan purposes. Select one of the following factors which would have the greatest influence on her appraisal.

a. The type of neighborhood surrounding the property.
b. The size of the loan.
c. The credit rating of the loan applicant.
d. None of the foregoing.

ANSWER: a.   The appraiser would have a basic interest in the kind of neighborhood and its resulting effect on market value. The other items in the question would be a matter of concern only to the lender.

72. One particular appraisal method would be more costly, detailed, and difficult than others. Which would it be?

    a. Unit of cubic foot method
    b. Unit of square foot method
    c. Unit cost in place
    d. Quantity survey

        ANSWER: d.   *The quantity survey is used by contractors in calculating the cost of construction of improvements. It is rarely used by appraisers because costly details are not necessary for most of their evaluations.*

73. Net income is determined by an appraiser using which one of the following?

    a. Real property taxes
    b. Capital additions
    c. Depreciation reserves
    d. Mortgage amortization and interest

        ANSWER: a.   *Real property taxes are considered as a fixed expense. Appraisers use them as deductions in computing net income. The other items are NOT in this category.*

74. In determining the value of a property, an appraiser would use the:

    a. cost approach.
    b. market approach.
    c. income approach.
    d. any or all of the above.

        ANSWER: d.   *Appraisers use all three approaches to determine value.*

75. Appraisal fees:

    a. may vary.
    b. are always a fixed amount.
    c. are based on a percentage of the appraised value.
    d. are set by the loan broker.

        ANSWER: a.   *An appraiser's fee is set by the difficulty of the work and by the level of expertise required to complete the work. Percentage fees are illegal.*

76. The term "highest and best use," as the fundamental concept of value, is best defined as:

    a. that which produces the greatest net return on the investment over a given period of time.
    b. that which produces the highest gross income.
    c. that which complies with all laws and restrictions.
    d. that which makes the highest general contribution to the community.

        ANSWER: a.   *Appraisers always consider the highest net income as the basis for the highest value.*

EXAM 6 APPRAISAL

77. The cost of an improved parcel of real property would probably be equal to its value in which of the following instances?

   a. Highest and best use of the parcel.
   b. The parcel as a new piece of property.
   c. When a and b are both present.
   d. None of the foregoing.

   ANSWER: c.   *A new piece of property would offer the best possibility of equality for cost and value. Determination of the highest and best use of a parcel would probably justify the cost of additional improvements, with the expectation of creating a profit.*

78. All of the following are methods for estimating accrued depreciation, except the:

   a. engineering method.
   b. market analysis method.
   c. economic method.
   d. cost of reproduction method.

   ANSWER: c.   *There are five recognized methods for measuring past, or accrued, depreciation:*

   1. The breakdown method
   2. The engineering method
   3. The straight-line method
   4. The market method
   5. The capitalized income method

   The economic method is NOT included in this category.

79. All of the following are methods for appraising unimproved real property, except the:

   a. development method.
   b. abstractive method.
   c. market data method.
   d. reproduction method.

   ANSWER: d.   *There is NO structure to reproduce on unimproved property. Therefore, the reproduction method is not applicable.*

80. There are three methods normally used in the evaluation of real property. However, one of these might prove more effective and accurate than the others, depending on the type of property being appraised. For example, the comparison approach would be the most desirable choice in the appraisal of:

   a. so-called amenity properties.
   b. service properties.
   c. industrial properties.
   d. apartment properties.

   ANSWER: a.   *Because of the appeal of amenities and of the effect of emotional factors related to single-family residences, the best basis for the analysis of current market value is by means of comparison.*

81. Two buildings, comparable in all respects, are leased to two different tenants, one the owner of a retail store, the other an agency of the federal government. How would the capitalization rates compare between the two buildings?

    a. The capitalization rate on the federal building would be higher.
    b. The capitalization rate on the federal building would be lower.
    c. The capitalization rate would be the same for each.
    d. The capitalization rate would be lower on the retail store.

> **ANSWER: b.** *A lease to a federal agency offers greater security to a lessor than does a lease on a retail store. This probably means that the lessor would accept a lower rental and lower income on the federal agency building. In turn, this indicates that the capitalization rate for the federal building would be lower and that it would be higher for the retail store. Since both buildings have equal size and value, these conclusions could be verified by the following computations:*
>
> *Assume the cost of both buildings at $200,000: the annual rental from the retail store at $12,000: from the federal building at $10,000: then: $12,000 ÷ $200,000 = .06, or 6% cap rate for the retail store. $10,000 ÷ $200,000 = .05, or 5% cap rate for the federal building.*

82. When real property is leased to various tenants, appraisers find it helpful to use a gross multiplier, which is founded upon:

    a. gross income as a function of capitalized value.
    b. rental value versus the selling price of the property.
    c. gross income versus estimated gross income.
    d. gross income as related to future net income.

> **ANSWER: b.** *Use of the gross multiplier implies a definite relationship between gross income and market value.*

83. The highest annual operating expense of an apartment normally would be assigned to:

    a. utilities.
    b. general maintenance.
    c. management fees.
    d. property taxes.

> **ANSWER: d.** *Property taxes in recent years have showed steady increases, and are becoming a greater factor in overall operating expenses.*

84. When computing the net income of an office building, an appraiser would consider, as a management expense, which of the following?

    a. Salary paid to a manager.
    b. The owner acting as his own manager.
    c. A tenant performing as manager in lieu of rental.
    d. All of the foregoing.

> **ANSWER: d.** *Calculation of net income for properties requires an assessment of management fees, regardless of the manner in which the service is performed.*

85. As part of his determination of value by means of the cost approach, an appraiser would employ the market data approach to determine the:

   a. value of the land.
   b. value of the improvements on the land.
   c. integration of property values.
   d. comparable values of adjoining properties.

> **ANSWER: a.** *The market data approach is used by an appraiser to compare the selling prices of similar land sites in the area. When values, so found, are added to the costs of improvements, this procedure is called the cost approach, and the result is a total value estimate of both land and improvements.*

86. The three types of depreciation are:

   a. physical, actual accrued.
   b. physical, effective, accrued.
   c. actual, economic, functional.
   d. physical, economic, functional.

> **ANSWER: d.** *Accrued is a measure of all forms of depreciation, effective refers to age of structure. There is NO such thing as "actual."*

87. There are different types of rent, one of which relies upon a comparison of the income from similar space in the market place. This type of rent is called:

   a. economic.
   b. development.
   c. maximized.
   d. contract.

> **ANSWER: a.** *Income derived from space available in the open market is called economic rent.*

88. Economic obsolescence in commercial income property would be evaluated by which of the following?

   a. The property requires the installation of fire escapes.
   b. Rentals in the building are fairly distributed.
   c. The building is in excellent operating condition.
   d. The tenants in the area are prospering.

> **ANSWER: d.** *The fact that tenants in the surrounding area are prospering represents an economic condition outside the property and is a degree of economic obsolescence. "a," "b," and "c" are concerned with factors within the property itself.*

89. In the determination of net income for an apartment building, an appraiser would only consider which of the following expenses?

  a. Mortgage amortization
  b. Depreciation of the building
  c. Capital investment increases
  d. Real property taxes

> ANSWER: d.   Real property taxes, potential gross income, effective gross income, expenses, and net income before recapture are all items of concern to an appraiser. The following elements are NOT included in the appraisal process:
>
> 1. Building depreciation reserve
> 2. Mortgage amortization and interest
> 3. Income tax
> 4. Special corporation costs
> 5. Additions to capital

90. The first phase of an appraisal of unimproved land is an evaluation of which of the following factors?

  a. Residual value
  b. Replacement costs
  c. Comparative value
  d. Highest and best use

> ANSWER: d.   The first objective of an appraisal of unimproved land is to determine the use which produces the greatest net return, or the highest and best use, since the value of the land is directly related to its use. This would be accomplished by comparing it with similar properties in the same zoning classification.

91. The best protection against the inroads of inflation would be:

  a. equity assets.
  b. trust deeds.
  c. savings accounts.
  d. government bonds.

> ANSWER: a.   Equity assets imply ownership in property, which tends to increase in value, paralleling price increases due to inflationary influences. They are a "hedge" against inflation. "b," "c," and "d" represent assets having a fixed return. As such. They tend to lose value during a period of inflation.

92. An improvement assessment of $4,000 has been levied against a residential property, which has been valued at $50,000. The status of the appraised value is now:

  a. $48,000.
  b. $54,000.
  c. reduced by $4,000.
  d. $50,000.

> ANSWER: d.   The assessment has NO effect on the value of the property, and the appraisal will remain at $50,000.

**EXAM 6
APPRAISAL**

93. What principle underlies the sequence of: Integration, Equilibrium, and Disintegration?

    a. Supply and demand
    b. Competition
    c. Progression to regression
    d. Change

> **ANSWER: d.** *Evidence of change is given by the fact that neighborhoods tend to pass through a three-stage age cycle, namely:*
>
> *1. Integration - a period of development;*
> *2. Equilibrium - a static period; and*
> *3. Disintegration - a period of decline or decay.*

94. In a situation where the cost of property is greater than its actual worth, it would be reasonable to assign the cause to:

    a. increased interest rates.
    b. unearned increments.
    c. over improvement.
    d. inflation.

> **ANSWER: c.** *When improvements to land are more costly than necessary, this condition is known as "over improvement." For example, if a $100,000 residence were to be built in a $75,000 neighborhood, the result would be a loss in value, probably on the order of several thousands of dollars.*

95. On an operating income statement a fixed cost would be:

    a. property taxes.
    b. employee salaries.
    c. mortgage payments.
    d. money set aside to buy a new AC system.

> **ANSWER: a.** *Property taxes and insurance are considered "fixed" because they only change by set rates over time. Employee salaries are an example of variable expense. Mortgage payments add to the owner's equity and are not an expense. Money set aside to repair/replace major building components are Replacement Reserves.*

96. The basic principle of the appraisal process states simply that value will tend to be set by the price a buyer will have to pay for an equivalent, or similar, substitute. The value of a property to its owner cannot ordinarily exceed the value in the market to people generally, when it can be replaced without undue expense or serious delay. This refers to the principle of:

    a. conformity.
    b. supply and demand.
    c. highest and best use.
    d. substitution.

> **ANSWER: d.** *The question is a statement of the principle of substitution as applied to the three appraisal methods of Comparison, Income, and Cost.*

97. Productivity has a direct relation to:

   a. value.
   b. use.
   c. demand.
   d. supply.

   ANSWER: b.   Productivity is related to the "highest and best use" of land or improvements. It is that use which, at the time of an appraisal, is most likely to produce the greatest net return to the land and building over a given period of time.

98. The value of commercial property would not be affected by which of the following factors?

   a. Zoning
   b. Property income
   c. Original cost of the property
   d. Purpose of the appraisal

   ANSWER: c.   Current market value of property is NOT affected by the original cost.

99. The definition of a residential neighborhood is:

   a. an area outlined by traffic patterns.
   b. a geographic location.
   c. a community of individuals with similar social and economic status.
   d. a community.

   ANSWER: c.   The answer to the question is a good definition of "neighborhood."

100. If demand is equal in all respects:

   a. prices increase as the availability of property decreases.
   b. prices increase as the availability of property increases.
   c. prices decrease as the availability of property decreases.
   d. none of the foregoing.

   ANSWER: a.   This question relates to scarcity of property. Scarcity is one of the elements of value. If the number of properties available is an area decreases, this relative scarcity will create price increases.

EXAM 6
APPRAISAL

NCS Trans-Optic 08-15193:321

DE 1

1. WRITE YOUR IDENTIFICATION NUMBER IN THE SPACES PROVIDED BELOW.

2. BELOW EACH DIGIT OF YOUR IDENTIFICATION NUMBER BLACKEN THE CIRCLE THAT CORRESPONDS TO THE DIGIT IN THAT COLUMN.

IDENTIFICATION NUMBER

DEPT. OF REAL ESTATE - ANSWER SHEET

RE FORM-420 (12/81)   **PRINT CLEARLY**

1. EXAMINEE NAME (LAST, FIRST, & MIDDLE)

2. EXAMINEE SIGNATURE ▶

3. TITLE   ☐ BROKER   ☐ SALESPERSON

4. SESSION   ☐ AM   ☐ PM

5. EXAMINATION DATE

6. BIRTHDATE

7. EXAMINATION LOCATION   ☐ LA   ☐ SAC   ☐ SF   ☐ SD   ☐ SA   ☐ FR   ☐ _____

8. EXAMINATION CODE NUMBER

9. BOOK NUMBER

1

PROPER MARK ●   IMPROPER MARKS ⊙ ◑ ⊘ ⊗

IMPORTANT: ERASE CLEANLY ANY ANSWER YOU WISH TO CHANGE.
SEE IMPORTANT MARKING INSTRUCTIONS ON SIDE 2.

ENTER FIRST 3 LETTERS OF LAST NAME

SAMPLE

436

SIDE 2

DEPT. OF REAL ESTATE—ANSWER SHEET

IMPORTANT DIRECTIONS FOR MARKING ANSWERS

PRACTICE

- Use only the black lead pencil provided.
- Do NOT use ink or ballpoint pens.
- Make heavy black marks that fill the circle completely.
- Erase cleanly any answer you wish to change.
- Make no stray marks on the answer sheet.
- NOTE: IMPROPER MARKS MAY SIGNIFICANTLY DELAY THE RELEASE OF YOUR RESULTS.

EXAMPLES

RIGHT
1 ● ○ ○ ○

WRONG
2 ○ ◉ ○ ○

WRONG
3 ○ ○ ⊗ ○

WRONG
4 ○ ○ ○ ◉

WRONG
5 ○ ○ ○ ◉

DO NOT WRITE IN THIS SPACE

SAMPLE

DO NOT WRITE IN THIS SPACE

Order Department

SOMETIMES OUR TEXTBOOKS ARE HARD TO FIND!

If your bookstore does not carry our textbooks, send us a check or money order and we'll mail them to you with our 30-day money back guarantee.

Other great books from Educational Textbook Company:

California Real Estate Principles, 9th ed., by Huber ························$50.00 _____
How To Pass The Real Estate Exam (850 Exam Questions), by Huber·········$50.00 _____
California Real Estate Law, by Huber & Pivar ·····························$50.00 _____
Financing California Real Estate, by Huber ·······························$50.00 _____
Real Estate Economics, by Huber & Pivar·································$50.00 _____
Real Estate Appraisal, by Huber & Pivar ································$50.00 _____
Mortgage Loan Brokering, by Huber & Pivar·····························$50.00 _____
Property Management, by Huber & Pivar··································$50.00 _____
Escrow I: An Introduction, by Huber·····································$50.00 _____
California Real Estate Practice, by Huber & Bond ·····················$50.00 _____
California Business Law, by Huber, Owens, & Tyler·····················$65.00 _____
Six-Hour Survey, Continuing Education, by Huber ·····················$15.00 _____

Subtotal _____
Add shipping and handling @ $5.00 per book _____
Add California sales tax @ 8.25% _____
TOTAL _____

Allow 2-3 weeks for delivery

Name: _____
Address: _____
City, State, Zip: _____
Phone: _____

Check or money order: Educational Textbook Company, P.O. Box 3597, Covina, CA 91722

For cheaper prices and faster results, order by credit card direct from
Glendale Community College:
1-818-240-1000 ext. 3024